ONE CAREFUL OWNER

JANE HARVEY-BERRICK

HARVEY
BERRICK
PUBLISHING

One Careful Owner

Copyright © 2017 Jane Harvey-Berrick

Cover design by Hang Le www.byhangle.com
Cover photograph by Michael Anthony Downs www.michaelanthonydowns.com
Models: Tyler Gattuso and Tanner

DEDICATION

To Pip. One of the little-bigheart tribe

CONTENTS

PROLOGUE

Snow was falling in thick, soft blankets, coating the roads, the buildings, the few cars that passed down the street.

Shuddering from the cold, he stared up at the sky, but dark clouds hung heavy and low, obscuring the stars.

The wind lifted his tie, slapping it against his damp cheeks, the icy blast a reminder to keep walking.

Hands shoved deep into his pockets, he trudged along the sidewalk as his body slowly numbed.

He walked or ran most days, but the sub-zero temperatures and the storm closing in meant he'd taken the car today. He didn't remember that until he was halfway home.

He'd left his jacket, too, and now his thin white shirt was transparent, sticking to his back and chest, no protection against the snow swirling around him.

He thought about calling Charlotte to come for him, but then she'd ask why he wasn't driving, why he was walking the snow-slick streets, and he couldn't tell her. He couldn't.

He'd forgotten his car, he'd forgotten everything because Carl had been killed. His brother was dead.

No, he wouldn't tell her, not over the phone. He couldn't. Because then it would be real.

So he plodded through the snow, his office shoes soaked and the cuffs of his suit pants dark with slush.

Snowflakes caught on his eyelashes and shoulders, whitening his hair. He was slowly freezing and yet his lungs burned with every breath.

As he neared the house, dazed and reluctant, his steps grew slower. And then he stopped, staring across at the ultra-modern white box with a sleek aluminum front door.

Feeling both relief and horror, he dragged his feet up the last three steps to his home.

And nearly tripped over Stan.

His tail acting as a muffler for his nose, Stan was shivering, tied to the top step, curled into a tight ball.

His eyes opened as the man bent down to stroke him, sinking his frozen fingers into the thick fur and immediately feeling its warmth.

"What are you doing out here, buddy?"

Stan whined softly then stood up slowly, his movements awkward, and he pressed his heavy head against the man's legs.

A hot jet of anger cut through the ice in his heart.

What kind of person put a dog out in this weather? He knew Charlotte didn't like Stan, but this was going too far.

His hands were shaking with cold, his fingers had long ago become numb. It took three attempts to fit the key in the lock and open the front door.

He shuffled inside, feeling his skin prickle, the warmth trying to reach the coldness that was part of him. Stan hobbled behind, an uneven gait, his legs stiff, and the man listened to the familiar click of his nails as Stan crossed the wooden floor.

Charlotte wasn't in the living room and he wondered if she'd gone to bed, even though it was still early. Stan followed him to the bottom of the stairs, whining softly when the man climbed them slowly. Stan knew that he wasn't allowed upstairs.

Perhaps the man should have called out, but he didn't know what to say, so he walked into the bedroom.

Reflected in the enormous mirror that Charlotte had hung above her dresser, he saw his wife.

With another man.

Fucking her from behind. Balls deep.

And not just any man. His best friend and partner.

"W-what...?"

He stuttered for the first time since he was 14 as fury, shock and rage burned his voice to ashes.

"W-what...?"

He couldn't get the words out, but blind hatred turned his vision red, and that was enough.

"Alex!" Charlotte screamed and tried to cover herself with the sheet, leaving Warren to face him.

He raised his hands in surrender, and Alex saw fear and guilt in his friend's eyes.

His friend. His best friend. His Best Man. But now he didn't have any words for him. He didn't have any words at all.

So he punched his friend in the face with his numb hand, and didn't feel anything when the knuckle broke.

Not a thing.

Nothing.

Chapter One

BEGINNINGS

Eighteen months later...

Dawn

Tanner's hooves kicked up small spirals of dirt as he ambled through the forest, picking his own path. It was peaceful and a deep sense of calm spread through me. It had been too long since I'd come out for an early morning ride. I rarely had the chance anymore—life always seemed to get so busy.

Even though it wasn't more than half-an-hour after sunrise, humidity was beginning to climb. I felt sweat trickle down my back and armpits, but I didn't care. It was too beautiful out here to worry about anything.

The lake's surface was quiet, stretching glassily toward the horizon, and I watched the tiny ripples reach the muddy bank as lazy clouds drifted across the sky.

As I rode into the small clearing, the quality of the light changed from the deep green of the forest to the soft glow of the rising sun.

I breathed deeply, enjoying the muted sounds and sense of being utterly alone. It was a rare moment to be carefree.

But as Tanner neared the lake, I spotted a bundle of old rags on the ground. God, I hated that! How could people toss their trash somewhere so beautiful? Sadly, I was used to seeing discarded bottles, cans and sandwich wrappers on the trails.

I was going to pick them up and dump them in the garbage at home, so I dismounted and poked my riding crop through them. But they weren't rags exactly—instead, I found a tattered pair of jeans, a faded t-shirt and a washed-out plaid shirt.

That was odd. Who would have left them here? Someone camping maybe? I sighed wearily and picked up the clothes. I hated people littering in this beautiful forest.

Suddenly, Tanner shifted next to me and the hairs on the back of my neck prickled. I had the unpleasant sensation of being watched, and when I looked up, my breath stuttered in my throat.

A man was standing in the lake, waist-deep in the water, and he was glaring at me. Instinctively, I tightened my grip on Tanner's reins.

"Oh, crap! You startled me!"

He didn't reply, and his icy stare made me nervous.

He was a big man, tall and strong, with broad shoulders and clearly defined muscles. His unkempt beard was thick, and long tangled hair matted against his skull—he looked like one of the fabled Mountain Men.

He made no attempt to speak and his eyes narrowed as anger rolled from him in heavy waves.

I swallowed nervously and took a step back, but then my heel caught in a pile of leaves, and I dropped the clothes I'd been carrying.

He glared, his lips peeled back so he was baring his teeth.

It took everything in me to keep calm while I mounted. Tanner's large presence was a huge comfort. I borrowed him from my employer and he was usually a skittish horse, but right now he stood happily chomping on grass and ignoring the stand-off.

"I'm going now," I said weakly, trying to keep my voice from shaking. "Yes, I'm riding away."

The continued silence was unnerving, but at least he hadn't come any closer. I began to wonder if he understood English.

Close up, he seemed younger than I'd first thought. His hair was dark blonde, his beard a light brown tinged with red. I couldn't tell what color his eyes were from this distance. Maybe he was Eastern European?

Finally, the man spoke.

"M-m-mine."

I blinked, surprised.

"What?"

He screwed his eyes shut, took a slow breath and tried again.

"M-m-mine!"

I stared back, not having a clue what he was talking about, then my eyes dropped to the pile of clothes on the ground.

"Oh, these are yours?"

He scowled at me, folding his arms across his chest. His body language was screaming at me to leave, but otherwise he was silent, menacing, and that scared me more.

My eyes followed the movement of his arms as he clamped them across his body, the biceps bulging, an unspoken warning that this man was bigger and stronger than me, and that I was alone in the forest, miles from help.

At least he wasn't coming closer.

Then my eyes dipped to the waterline rippling at his waist.

"Oh!"

My eyes widened with the realization that he was completely naked. The water was clear enough that I'd seen everything. And I mean *everything*. As I glanced up, shocked, he met my gaze, raising an eyebrow suggestively, the implication that I'd been checking him out. I shot him a filthy look, jerking the reins to get Tanner moving.

"You're trespassing on private property," I snapped over my shoulder, just to show I wasn't really completely terrified. "You should leave."

His lips twisted in a sneer and he took half a pace toward me, his demeanor threatening.

Sensing his mounting fury, I rode away. I'd get the hell out of here and let Dan know that a crazy guy was camping illegally. I urged Tanner to go faster, only looking back once to make sure that the man wasn't following. But he was still standing in the lake, watching me.

My early morning ride left me completely shaken, and I hated feeling so vulnerable. So I was in a foul mood by the time I got to work at Petz Pets, and Ashley's shrill voice was like a jack hammer in my head.

I tried to ignore her endless description of a new pair of shoes that were to die for apparently, while I quietly phoned my friend Dan, who also happened to be Girard's police officer, telling him about the crazy guy at the lake. Then I had to listen to Ashley for half an hour, catching me up on all the gossip that I'd 'missed' over the weekend. Mostly it consisted of who'd slept with whom, who was having an affair, and how many Cosmopolitans she'd drunk.

I was trying not to listen, but it was impossible to ignore her piercing tone.

"Oh, that's so sad!" she said suddenly, her voice falling for a moment.

"What is?"

"Mrs. Humphries emailed to ask if we've seen Missy."

Missy—a two year-old black-and-white ball of fur with wicked long claws, as I knew from painful experience. She was also pregnant the last time I'd seen her and the kittens were due any day. Come to think of it, I'd expected to hear from Mrs. Humphries before now.

"When did she last see her?"

"Yesterday morning."

"She's probably making a safe place to have her kittens. Tell Mrs. Humphries to check all her neighbors' outbuildings and any other places that she thinks Missy might go to. She won't have gone far."

Ashley frowned.

"Mrs. Humphries is out by the State Game Lands. She doesn't have many neighbors."

I shivered, recalling the scary homeless man I'd encountered. I wondered if Dan would have a chance to check into it today.

Ashley typed something, muttering under her breath and chewing on the inside of her mouth.

"Oh, you're going to love this," she cackled as she worked her way through the overnight messages and today's calendar. "A new client has emailed to make an appointment. That's weird—people usually phone. Jeez, he's sent me his dog's entire life story! Whatever, but get this—he only wants a male veterinarian."

I glanced up, frowning. "Seriously?"

"Yep. I had to read his message twice to check I wasn't seeing things. And guess what? His address is *Tanglewood*. He must be the one who bought Old Joe's cabin—you know, the place Bob Delaney was going to buy and develop. What do you want me to do?"

I was surprised. I didn't know that Bob had wanted to buy the place, but it made sense since he owned the adjoining property along the lake. Sort of. Joe had never minded me riding over his land, but I knew for a fact that Bob wouldn't like it. Mostly because he hated me. And as for Stella's opinion of me … I didn't want to think about that.

I'd ridden past Old Joe's cabin many times. It was a dreary, depressing place, dank and dark and falling apart, deep in the woods. The kind of place you could imagine in a horror movie, except for its location by the lake, which was beautiful.

I gazed at Ashley, constantly amazed by the random information she had rattling around in her head. The FBI needed her on their team.

I redirected my thoughts back to the question. "Does Gary have any slots this afternoon?"

Gary was our chief veterinarian and also owned the business. He was good with prickly customers.

"Yes, three o'clock."

"Problem solved."

Ashley gave me an overly-dramatic look of astonishment.

"It doesn't bother you that the new client is a sexist asshole?"

Yes, the request was irritating, but Ashley was something of a drama queen and I wasn't going to give her the satisfaction of a reaction.

"Not my concern," I answered, giving a firm look that bounced right off her.

"I'd be pissed as all hell because he obviously doesn't think women can be vets," she said, not willing to let it drop.

I tuned her out after that, instead prepping the examination room and reading through my list of patients for the day.

Then our first customer arrived, a West Highland Terrier with eczema, and I didn't think about the new client again until after lunch when Gary got an emergency callout to a valuable stud animal with a suspected fractured tibia.

Ashley gave me a wide smile as Gary's Jeep disappeared in a cloud of dust and gravel.

"So ... since Gary has been called away ... are you going to see this new client? The sexist asshole?"

I sighed, but tried not to look too irritated as I glanced at the clock on the wall. It was just after 2.45PM so she might be able to catch the new client before he left his house.

"Call him and explain what's happened. If he wants to see me, that's fine, otherwise reschedule an appointment with Gary."

She picked up her phone and started to place the call, but stopped suddenly.

"Too late," she said, jerking her thumb at a battered pickup truck that had pulled into the parking lot.

I turned to look, but for a minute, there was no movement and I began to wonder if the new arrival would ever leave his truck. Finally, I saw the driver's door swing open and a man jumped out. For some reason, I'd expected an older guy to be the sexist new client, but judging from the way he moved, I was wrong.

In fact, I could see that he was tall and muscular and ... then I recognized him.

It was the man from the lake. The naked man who'd scared the crap out of me. I'd been thoroughly rattled seeing him this morning. Being alone with him had made me realize again how vulnerable I was riding by myself and I'd decided to rethink my regular route.

But now I was facing him for a second time. He still reminded me of a Mountain Man, and he appeared to be wearing the clothes that I'd thought were rags. His long, shaggy brown hair and thick beard hid most of his face. A shudder of apprehension ran through me.

He seemed just as ill at ease as he had been by the lake, his eyes darting around restlessly, but then he walked around to the passenger door and I lost sight of him.

When he reappeared, he was carrying a large dog, one that easily weighed 80 or 90 pounds. He must have been strong because he carried the weight easily. I recalled the thick slabs of muscle that sculpted his chest and arms when I'd seen him earlier.

Yes, there was no doubt that he was strong, but as he held his pet, his hands were gentle.

I watched his chin bob, and I realized that he was talking to his dog.

Carefully, he set the animal on the ground and fixed a leash around its neck.

The dog immediately sat down and refused to budge. His coat was thick and looked glossy and healthy, his muzzle starting to gray. I guessed he was part retriever, part mastiff—large and solid. And heavy.

Ashley giggled as the man tugged on the leash, but the dog still wouldn't move. The man stood still, looking at his pet, his hands on his hips, then he shook his head in defeat. Bending down, he scooped up the dog again and shouldered his way through the door into the office.

Now he was closer, I could study him in more detail.

His hair was a tangle of light brown with sun-blond lights, still uncombed, an off-putting mess of wild, crazy curls. His clothes were even worse now I could see him wearing them, unkempt and torn as if he'd given up, but they were clean. And when he stopped in front of Ashley, I caught the faint scent of soap and laundry detergent—no cologne. This man was a paradox.

Ashley smiled tightly from her position behind the reception desk.

"Mr. Winters and Stan, is that right?"

He nodded but didn't speak, still holding his dog in his arms. His face was grim, as if he'd never smiled, never thought of smiling.

So this was the man who'd bought Old Joe's place? I immediately felt guilty that I'd assumed he was trespassing and camping illegally. I didn't know that somebody had already moved into the property. Technically, *I'd* been the interloper this morning. I felt like such a judgmental bitch. But he'd really scared me, and I hadn't been thinking clearly.

"I'm so sorry," Ashley said with fake sweetness, "but Dr. Petz, our *male* veterinarian, had to go out on an emergency visit. Dr. Andrews over there is available."

He turned to stare at me and his body stiffened. I saw a flicker of recognition in his eyes before he dropped his gaze to the floor again. I thought for sure that he'd turn and walk out, but then he glanced at his dog and I saw the expression soften in his curious golden-brown eyes as he peered up at me and nodded slowly.

"Great!" said Ashley, her gaze glancing across to me. "I've got basic information from your email, but if you could just fill out this form and..."

"Maybe you'd like to bring Stan into the examination room, Mr. Winters," I interrupted quickly. "He looks rather heavy."

The man blinked twice, but carried the dog inside without commenting or even looking at Ashley.

"Rude!" Ashley said, not quietly enough, and although I agreed, I shot her a look and took the form from her.

She leaned toward me, her eyes wide as her shrill voice dropped to an urgent whisper.

"I'll keep my ears open, Dawn. He looks kind of weird. You know, serial killer weird."

I pressed my lips together and followed my new client.

The dog was sitting on the examination table, drooling heavily and panting. I could tell he was an older animal from the salt-and-pepper muzzle, and his breath was pretty bad. That usually indicated either a gastrointestinal problem or dental issues.

The man was standing in the furthest corner of the room with his hands in his pockets, his head hanging down, peering at me warily through the thick curtain of uncombed hair.

"So this is Stan," I said, stroking the dog's head. "A reluctant patient?"

His tail thumped twice.

"I guess you don't like going to the vet, huh, boy?" I looked up again at his silent owner. "Don't worry about it. We get a lot of animals like that on their first time here. He'll get used to us and we'll take good care of him."

He stared back at me, his face unreadable.

"And, um, I really must apologize for this morning," I said, still stroking Stan's head. "Old Joe didn't mind me riding across his land. When I saw you, I didn't know that ... well, I made assumptions. It won't happen again."

His head tilted to one side, but he didn't reply, and my cheeks flushed with annoyance and confusion.

"So, how can I help you today?" I asked briskly.

Stan stared at me docilely then yawned widely.

"Phew! That's some serious halitosis he's got there. What do you feed him?"

Mr. Winters blinked rapidly, crossed his arms across his chest the way he had this morning, then took several deep breaths. His eyes screwed shut and his whole face contorted. I was afraid he was having a seizure, but then his eyes opened wide and he coughed out a single word.

"B-b-acon."

"Bacon?"

He nodded, then took another breath.

"Eh ... eh ... eggs."

It took him three tries to aspirate the word, and a sudden ache twisted my heart.

My new client wasn't rude—he had a speech impediment. A severe one.

My heart softened as I stared at this rough-looking man. Then his gaze dropped to the floor, unable to meet my eyes.

But before he looked away, I saw pain and frustration as well as humiliation.

Was it always so hard for him, or was it me? Was *this* the reason he asked for a male veterinarian?

I couldn't imagine how hard it would be to go through life without that basic ability of human communication, of connection. I felt wretched that I'd judged him so harshly when we'd first met.

No wonder he'd done everything to avoid speaking either to me or Ashley.

No wonder he hid behind his long hair and straggly beard.

How lonely that must be.

"I'm guessing you're worried about Stan's drooling?" I asked gently.

There was no doubt that he loved his dog. I could see the concern in his eyes when he looked my way, see it in the gentle way he handled his pet.

Two intelligent eyes blinked up at me and he nodded.

"Is Stan okay with me touching his mouth?"

He nodded again.

"Okay, let's have a look at those teeth, Stan."

I saw the root of the problem right away: gum disease. His teeth were yellow and stained, and Stan also had a plaque issue. But the immediate problem was his inflamed gums. He must have been in a considerable amount of pain, but he didn't growl or pull away as I checked the rest of his mouth carefully.

"Oh dear, Stan, you should have brushed."

After giving him a full examination and taking his temperature, which was slightly elevated, I gave his owner the news.

"Several of those teeth will have to come out eventually, and the rest need to be cleaned to get rid of residual plaque. But right now, I want to treat his gingivitis—gum disease—it's an early stage of periodontal disease, although he's got quite a nasty infection. And I'd like to schedule a procedure to remove the plaque build-up. Do you have insurance?"

I was already planning the lowest premium our practice could charge, and wondering whether or not Gary would agree to fund the procedure through our charitable program, when Mr. Winters nodded again and pulled a card out of his wallet.

The wallet looked new and expensive. My eyes narrowed with suspicion, but then I saw that it was embossed in gold A.W., and his pet insurance card appeared valid.

I couldn't figure him out.

"Also I'll need you to fill out some forms. I noticed Stan's never been neutered?"

He grimaced and shook his head. I had to hold back a smile—many men reacted like that. Besides, Stan was too old for the procedure now.

I glanced at my new client thoughtfully.

"And Mr. Winters, bacon and eggs is not a healthy daily diet for Stan. He needs suitable food for a senior dog. How old did you say he is?"

I winced at the word 'say' but covered it up, turning to the wall-mounted computer screen to see what information Ashley had already entered.

"Ah, he's about nine or ten. A rescue dog. Where did you find him?"

I kicked myself for forgetting *again* that I needed to stick to questions that could be answered with a nod or a headshake. I moved on quickly.

"Well, he seems fine, given his age. But you really should improve his diet. I'll give him a shot now. It's a three-in-one: painkiller, anti-inflammatory and mild antibiotic. That will make him more comfortable until we can take care of those gums and teeth."

I stroked Stan's head and he nuzzled my hand.

For a second, I thought I saw the man smile, although it was hard to tell behind his bushy beard, but after I'd given Stan his shot, he simply nodded at me and lifted him down from the examination table.

"How'd that go?" Ashley asked brightly as we walked out with Stan.

"Fine," I said flatly, then scheduled the next appointment while Mr. Winters stood beside me, a silent, looming presence.

I couldn't get Mr. Winters out of my head. When I'd met him this morning by the lake, I was so certain that he was dangerous, but now I saw all his actions in a completely different light and I was ashamed of my assumptions and reactions.

Of course he'd been angry when we first met. I was trespassing on his land and had even told him off for being there. I'd misread his silence, too. And all the time, he'd been stuck standing naked in the water because I was ridiculing his clothes.

My skin felt hot at the memory. I was ashamed of myself, but I couldn't quite dispel a quiver of interest at the hardness of his body, the obvious masculine strength. It had been a while since I'd seen something that good in real life. Not since college, unless it was some actor on TV.

Everything about him was a contradiction. His expensive-looking wallet and premium pet insurance; his rusting truck and his ragged clothes—and the fact that he'd apparently paid cash for Old Joe's cabin—no mortgage required, or so Ashley told me.

She'd heard it from Jenny who worked for the town's only attorney Simeon Spender, the man who'd handled Old Joe's estate, so I guess it really was true.

No one knew what had brought him to Girard, Pennsylvania, population 3,065. On the few occasions he was seen in town, he hadn't spoken to anyone or even tried to. Of course, now I knew why, but the town had decided that he was 'strange', 'a recluse' or even 'creepy'.

I wondered if anyone else had sensed his loneliness and isolation behind that forbidding appearance. Did he hide because of his stutter, or was there something else?

I dreamed about him that night. Totally inappropriate dreams for a respectable single mother who rarely dated and whose eight year-old daughter was sleeping in the next room.

I woke up ratty, in a bad mood and stupidly aroused. Not a great combination. So, pushed the thoughts from my mind as I dropped Katie off at her friend's house, and then headed to work, thankful that I was only doing a half-day today. During school vacations, Gary let me work part-time as much as possible.

I arrived just as Ashley was parking her Honda, but she didn't get out of the car, instead she waved to catch my attention, pointed behind me, then ducked down, peering over her steering wheel.

I soon saw the reason. Mr. Winters' was climbing out of his rusting truck, a large cardboard box in his hands. He placed it by the office front door and then walked away.

I saw him glance in our direction, and I felt hugely embarrassed that he'd seen us cowering in the parking lot, but his long hair fell across his face, screening his expression, so I couldn't tell what he thought about our crazy behavior.

When he sped away in his battered pickup, I realized that I'd been holding my breath.

Ashley gave a theatrical shudder as she climbed out of her car.

"Ugh, that guy gives me the creeps. What do you think is in the box? Oh God, don't open it! It might be a head!"

I didn't bother to answer, instead cautiously lifting one of the flaps.

I jumped back with a squeal, and Ashley shrieked. A sudden flutter of wings had startled me.

Sitting in a nest of torn up rags was a Golden Eagle, very young, its flight feathers still fluffy, and its left wing obviously broken as it trailed next to him, the poor bird crying loudly.

I sent Ashley to find a pet carrier and took my latest customer inside.

Some people think it's not possible to mend a bird's broken wing, but if you're careful and patient, they can make a full recovery.

Golden Eagles were rare around here and protected, but there were a few. Mr. Winters must have found this one in the forest.

I suppose I wasn't surprised that he hadn't stayed to speak to us, but I was taken aback to find a note in neat handwriting offering to pay for the young eagle's treatment.

The bird didn't have any other injuries, so I cut a 12 inch strip of veterinarian bandaging tape, a special type that doesn't stick to fur or feathers. Then, as gently as possible, given the bird's distressed squawks, I folded the broken wing against his side in the most natural position I could manage, while avoiding his sharp beak. Then I strapped the wing to his body and asked Ashley to call the aviary veterinarian in Pittsburg.

In three or four weeks, the bird would be good as new. I hoped.

It was lucky that Mr. Winters had found him. He wouldn't have survived in the wild like that.

For such a big man, he was incredibly gentle.

And that intrigued me even more.

Chapter Two

RENDEZVOUS

Dawn

"Ashley, did you manage to get hold of Mr. Winters? He missed a scheduled appointment."

It had been several weeks since anyone had seen him, although there had been two more 'special deliveries' of injured animals—an opossum who'd died shortly after coming to us, from old age, I suspected; and a raccoon with a broken leg who was recovering happily at Cleveland Metroparks Zoo.

Ashley glanced up from the computer, wrinkling her nose at the mention of his name.

"Who? The creepy weirdo?"

"He's not creepy, he's just ... shy."

"Whatever. And no, he didn't return my messages. He's probably out there in the woods making himself a squirrel-skin coat and talking to the trees. You shouldn't go riding over there by yourself anymore. He's a freak."

"Ashley! He's just ... a little different. You can't go around saying things like that. He was super sweet with his dog. And he brought in that fledgling eagle and the raccoon with the broken leg."

She thought about that for a moment.

"You know what I think?"

I'm dreading the answer.

"I think he's got a thing for you."

"A 'thing'?"

"Yes, and he's hurting these animals so he's got an excuse to see you."

I was shocked.

"That's a horrible thing to say! If he wanted to see me, well, he would have come in for the scheduled appointment. I wish he would. In fact, he's gone out of his way to *avoid* seeing me. You can't go around saying he hurts animals!"

"Yeah, I guess. But you've got to admit he's not *normal*."

I sighed.

This conversation was going nowhere.

"Would you mind trying his number again?"

She rolled her eyes, but picked up the phone and dialed.

Stan

That was one of the longest weeks of my life—certainly one of the worst since I'd been in this country. I hate it when the boss is unhappy. He'd looked real sick. I thought he might die. And I didn't want to be alone again. I would have curled up beside him and been content to die right there with him.

But then he woke up, and I felt hope in my old heart. For the first time in a long while, his eyes were clear and he smelled like himself again, not filled with chemicals. But right now he smelled like my friend. I was very happy about that.

I felt better, as well. My teeth weren't nearly so sore, and I was even considering whether chewing bones might be on the menu again. It had been a while since I'd had a bone to gnaw on.

I sat outside, enjoying the sun on my fur, and the scent of the rich dirt. I licked my balls thoughtfully. I was very proud of my balls—they were large and shiny and swayed pendulously when I walked, a punctuation mark against my sandy fur.

I paused to stare up at the boss, my chocolate eyes sympathetic. Maybe if he could lick his own balls, he'd be happier.

Or maybe getting royally screwed by his cheating ex-wife and losing his business meant that nothing made you happy anymore. And he'd lost Carl. We both had.

My own contentment drooped at the memory. My friend. My first protector. I used to think all humans were cruel, monstrous, until I'd met Carl. He was gentle, kind to me.

And his brother was exactly the same.

The boss plopped down in the dirt next to me and I leaned against his sun-warmed back, soaking up the evening rays.

"I couldn't do this without you, Stan," he said softly, sinking his fingers into my fur. "You're the only person I can talk to. You're the only one I trust—every other sonofabitch isn't worth the air they breathe. You're the only one."

My heart ached for the boss.

He needed more in his life than a beaten up ole hound dog, but I was all he had.

When we'd left the mountains behind, we'd traveled east, watching the sky grow larger, the horizons wider.

Now we sat in silence as the sun slunk across the sky, the lake glinting in the distance.

There's nothing as satisfying as an afternoon nap.

It was two days later, and I'd fallen asleep in the shade of my favorite tree. It was old, rising silent and solemn, a large copper beech that cast a soft amber light throughout the cabin across and the wooden deck. I listened for the boss, but all I could hear was *thunk, thunk, thunk*, a rhythmical ringing as he chopped wood, somewhere in the distance.

I stood up, shaking out the kinks in my spine, and ambled off for a stroll through the woods to find him, feeling at peace now the boss was healthy again.

But then my nostrils quivered as I picked up a new scent. Sweet and cloying—the scent of death.

My hackles rose as I paused, checking the direction of the wind, listening for anything that didn't fit.

I stepped lightly, keeping all my senses on high alert. Creatures were born in the forest, lived their whole lives, then died here. But this didn't feel right and a low growl rolled out of my throat. Underneath the odor of rotten flesh, I could smell Man. Someone who wore cologne. The same scent that hung around our porch sometimes, but fainter now, almost hidden.

And then I found it: the body of a cat with a collar around her neck—dead some time and already decaying in the summer heat.

I barked for the boss. He had to see this. He should know that someone had been on his land again. Someone who liked to kill animals. I barked more urgently, and after a short pause he came jogging through the trees, an axe still grasped in one hand.

"Stan? What's up, buddy?"

I stared at the cat, and he wrinkled his nose.

"Ah, shit!"

And then he looked closer. A thick piece of wire was wrapped around the cat's neck. She'd had been caught in a snare. I didn't think her neck had been broken, so she'd probably choked to death. I didn't like cats—always showing off, always pretending they were too good to enjoy a human's company. No, I pretty much hated them, but even so, I wouldn't have wished this end on my worst enemy. It was a slow and miserable way to cross over the rainbow bridge. And alone. She'd been alone.

No one should die alone.

The boss frowned, his lips pressing together in a flat line that meant he was upset or angry.

Sighing, he laid the axe on the ground, carefully untangling the wire as he dismantled the trap. Then he took off the cat's collar, putting it in his pocket and grimacing over the stench from the animal's body.

"I should get a spade," he muttered to himself, but I knew he had no more interest in having to come back here than I did.

It didn't take long to scratch out a shallow grave using the axe. Then he picked up the cat's body, laying it gently in the depression. Finally, he sprinkled dirt on top and found a few flat stones to lay over it, but I knew that scavengers would be feasting tonight.

My ears pricked up as I heard a new sound, and I followed it to the source. Three tiny kittens mewled weakly, their cries tired and desperate, eyes still tightly shut. They were hungry, thirsty, and very scared. A fourth was already dead, it's tiny body too still.

The boss cursed when he saw them, gripping the axe so his knuckles turned white. Then he laid the axe on the bed of pine needles, peeled off his shirt and picked up the kittens, one at a time, carefully wrapping the faded plaid around them.

He shook his head, his eyes sad when they met mine.

"They're in pretty bad shape," he said, his voice raw. "Their mom has been dead a while. They must be hungry and thirsty. Shit, I'd better call that vet."

He cradled the kittens with one hand while he pulled out his phone. I sniffed them thoughtfully. The boss was right—they were weak and hungry. One of them was barely moving, too exhausted to cry.

There were times when I really hated humans.

The call connected and I heard the tinny voice at the other end.

"Petz Pets, how may I help you?"

"Ah ... Ah ... k-k-kit-t-t..."

"Hello?"

"K-k-k..."

"What? I can't hear you. This is a really bad line. Try calling back."

The boss slammed the phone against his forehead when the call was cut.

"Fuck," he swore softly.

He held the kittens against his chest and scooped up the axe with the other.

But then I heard the sound of footsteps coming toward us. There were too many for it to be the lone killer, and I could hear a child's bubbling laughter.

A little girl ran toward us, giggling at something. Then she saw the boss, standing there with an axe in his hand, sweat streaked, hair matted, clothes ragged—and she screamed.

Over and over again, she screamed, her small body stiff with terror, her eyes wide and fearful.

The shrill, piercing shriek made me wince, but the boss just stood there, frozen in shock.

A man and woman came crashing through the trees, calling the girl's name. They shuddered to a stop when they saw the boss.

"Please don't hurt her," whispered the woman, her hand over her mouth as her husband crept toward the sobbing girl.

Keeping his eyes on the boss, he reached out, grabbing the girl's hand and backing away slowly.

"It's cool, man! We're cool! Nothing to worry about! Don't do anything you're going to regret. We're going now. It's cool!"

He kept babbling as they edged away, and all the boss could do was stare, his mouth turning down when he realized that they were all terrified of him.

He looked at the axe hanging loosely in his hand, the kittens hidden in his shirt, and then he turned away, his shoulders stooped as he strode toward the house.

I followed behind him. Because that was all I could do: let him know that he'd never scared me, never hurt me, and never would.

My own heart ached for the loneliness I felt in his.

Dawn

I'd sent my last patient away half-an-hour ago with drops for a nasty flea infestation, and then spent the time spraying the office and examination rooms to make sure other patients didn't end up with fleas.

Ashley was annoyed at having to wait while I finished up, but not so annoyed that she offered to help. But since she was Gary's daughter-in-law's sister, I couldn't say anything. And she knew it.

I'd just changed out of my scrubs and into jeans, when Ashley called me to the front office, her voice shrill with excitement.

"Look!"

Pulling into the parking lot was Mr. Winters' rust-bucket truck, closely followed by a police cruiser, blue lights flashing.

"Oh my God! It's the crazy guy!" Ashley breathed, her hand gripping my arm as we both gawked out the window.

I saw Jon Eastman, Dan's deputy approach the driver's side of the truck. I couldn't see what was happening after that, but then he stepped back and rested his hand on his service revolver.

I jerked backward, but Ashley was still watching, her eyes bright with interest, her hand clutched to her chest.

"STEP OUT OF THE CAR AND PUT YOUR HANDS ON THE HOOD RIGHT NOW!"

I saw the truck door open and Mr. Winters climbed out, his movements deliberately slow. I couldn't tell if he was scared because his hair was hanging in his face, but his body moved stiffly.

He was holding a cardboard box, and he placed it carefully on the driver's seat before obeying Jon. Then he put his hands on the hood and leaned forward, spreading his legs.

Jon stepped closer, pushing Mr. Winters' feet further apart and then brought out the handcuffs.

I watched, horrified, as Mr. Winters tried to twist around, but Jon shoved his face against the truck's hood, and when he turned in my direction, I saw blood. I think his lip was split, but it was hard to tell.

I didn't know what was going on, but I could hear Stan's distressed barking, and I knew I had to do something to calm him in case he tried to attack Jon and ended up being shot.

I tore open the door while Ashley clung to me.

"What on earth is going on here?"

"Stand back, ladies," barked Jon. "He could be dangerous."

"What's he done?"

Jon ignored me, tightening his grip, intoning loudly, "You have the right to remain silent..."

The words spurred me into action. I knew that Mr. Winters didn't communicate well, even when he wasn't severely stressed.

"Jon, he has a serious speech impediment—in all probability he won't be able to do anything *except* remain silent!"

There was a short pause.

"You know this guy?"

"Yes. Well, he's one of my clients. His dog had toothache. He brought him in a few weeks ago."

Circling behind Jon, I walked over to the passenger side of the truck and laid a soothing hand on Stan. His growls lessened immediately, his gaze becoming pleading as I continued to stroke him.

"What's in there?" Jon asked looking at me and Stan, then jerking his chin at the cardboard box.

I tried not to roll my eyes. Jeez, did he think Stan was Lassie? One bark, one grunt and he'd know, *Gee, Jimmy's in the well, I'd better go rescue him.* Idiot.

I thought I could guess—probably another injured animal—but Mr. Winters looked so wild, I decided to let Jon look first, just to be on the safe side.

He peered in the truck, then cautiously opened the box. We could all hear distressed mewing, and I knew immediately that I'd guessed right.

"That sounds like ... oh, what's this?"

I stepped forward and gazed down at the box.

Three tiny kittens, just a day or so old. Two were crying weakly, but the third...

"Oh, poor little things! Did you find them? Where's their mother?"

Mr. Winters nodded wordlessly, then shrugged his shoulders. Of course he couldn't explain—not like this.

He met my eyes briefly, then looked down at the box again.

"This one didn't make it," I said softly.

He closed his eyes, his mouth grim, his expression full of compassion. And the thought filtered through my confusion, *He cares.*

But then his head drooped and he wouldn't look at any of us. In fact, he looked guilty, and a kernel of doubt bloomed.

Then a second police cruiser pulled up and Dan climbed out. Thank goodness!

"I've got him, Dan," Jon called excitedly. "He didn't put up much of a fight. I haven't had a chance to look for the axe."

What?

"He say anything?" Dan asked, glancing at me, taking in the whole scene.

"He has a severe speech impediment," I said impatiently. "I was just explaining to Jon that he's my client. He brought in his dog a few weeks ago— and that Golden Eagle I told you about. Oh, and a raccoon! In fact, he's saved quite a few wild animals since he's been here. He bought Old Joe's place."

"That so," Dan said thoughtfully.

Mr. Winters watched cautiously as Dan wandered around the truck to stroke Stan, examining everything with his usual careful consideration.

"Dan," I said urgently, "he was bringing me these kittens. They look in a bad way and one has already died—I have to get some IV fluids into them immediately. Why don't you all come inside? We're officially closed for the day now, and I can check on Stan, as well."

"Who's Stan?"

"Mr. Winters' dog," I said over my shoulder, as I carefully lifted the box out of the truck, trying not to jolt the two surviving kittens.

But not before I heard Dan questioning Jon.

"What happened to his lip?" he asked coolly.

The younger officer flushed.

"He was resisting arrest and..."

"Thought you said he didn't put up much of a fight?"

There was a heavy silence loaded with meaning.

"We'll talk inside," said the Sheriff, at last.

I frowned as Jon pushed Mr. Winters' shoulder to make him move, treating him as if he was deaf as well as mute. I was angry, but my focus was on the kittens. They were so tiny, I'd have to use my smallest gauge needles.

Stan whined, and Mr. Winters planted his feet in the dirt, unwilling to leave him in the truck by himself.

"Get moving!" Jon snapped, pushing him again.

Mr. Winters let out a growl of frustration that made Dan pause, his eyes flicking from him to Stan and back again.

"If I let your dog out of the truck, is he going to behave?"

I opened my mouth to answer that Stan was gentle, but in all truthfulness, I couldn't be sure when everything was so tense.

Mr. Winters nodded furiously, and after a dubious look, Dan opened the passenger door. Stan all but fell out of the truck, sprawling painfully in the dirt as his back legs gave way, and Mr. Winters scowled angrily.

But then Stan shook himself and limped over, rubbing his heavy head against his owner.

"Okay," said Dan, scratching his mustache, "let's get this circus inside and find out what the hell's going on."

I took the kittens right into the consultation room and started to work on them immediately. Satisfied that their IV fluids were flowing, I went and found them some suitable milk substitute to drink.

When I returned to the front office, Mr. Winters had been handcuffed to a chair, leaving his left hand free to stroke Stan, who was much calmer now.

Ashley was sitting in her usual seat, watching everything avidly and discreetly texting under her desk. Half of Girard would know about this within the next two minutes.

"Have you arrested him?" Dan asked, raising his eyebrows at Jon.

"I was just getting to that when you drove up, Dan. I only got half way through Miranda."

Dan winced and I knew what he was thinking—Mr. Winters had been wrongfully detained and could sue the police department. And now I could see him up close, he had a split lip and blood was trickling into his beard.

"Well, Mr. Winters," said Dan, turning to him. "Looks like we've all gotten ahead of ourselves," and he threw a look at Jon. "But we had a complaint about a man with an axe terrorizing a young family out by your property. You know anything about that?"

Mr. Winters stared at him, and I knew that there was no point in him trying to speak.

Then I saw him wiggling his left hand. Then he did it again, clearly trying to send Dan a message.

"I don't know what you're trying to tell me," Dan said, equally frustrated.

"T-t-t..." he stuttered uselessly. "T-t-t..."

"Shit," mumbled Dan, rubbing his hands over his face.

"Uh, maybe he's saying that he wants to type his answers," I suggested. "Is that right?"

Mr. Winters nodded in relief, grateful that someone understood.

"This should be good," Jon muttered. "The guy's a freakin' hobo."

"Knock it off," said Dan crisply.

He unlocked Mr. Winters' handcuffs and stood back cautiously.

Mr. Winters rubbed his wrists, whispering soothingly to Stan, then took a seat behind Ashley's computer. We all gathered behind him in a semi-circle, burning with curiosity to see what he'd write.

My mouth dropped open as his fingers flew across the keyboard, touch-typing with the speed of a trained secretary.

> I WAS CHOPPING LOGS FOR THE FIRE WHEN STAN
> BARKED. I COULD TELL HE WAS WORRIED SO I
> WENT TO LOOK. I FOUND A DEAD CAT. I HAVE
> THE COLLAR.

And then he pulled a pink leopard-skin collar out of his pocket and handed it to the Dan.

"Wait! Let me see that!" I took the collar and my lips turned down. " 'Missy'. Mrs. Humpries' cat."

Ashley's snort of disapproval brought ugly suspicions to the fore.

"How did Missy die?"

> SHE HAD BEEN CAUGHT IN A SNARE. I HAVE IT IN
> THE BACK OF MY TRUCK. I DON'T KNOW WHO
> SET IT ON MY LAND, BUT IT LOOKS FAIRLY NEW.
> THEN I FOUND THE KITTENS. I WAS HEADING
> TO MY TRUCK SO I COULD BRING THE KITTENS
> TO YOU WHEN A GIRL CAME RUNNING OUT OF
> THE FOREST.
> SHE SCREAMED WHEN SHE SAW ME AND HER
> PARENTS THOUGHT I WAS THREATENING HER. I
> DIDN'T DO ANYTHING!! THEY LEFT, AND I CAME
> HERE. THAT'S IT.

Then he turned to look at us. I wanted to believe him, but it seemed a huge coincidence that the increase in injured animals had begun after he'd arrived in Girard.

But ... he just didn't seem the type.

"Thank you," I said quietly. "If you'd waited any longer ... well, the surviving kittens are very weak, but I think ... you got to them just in time. Mrs. Humphries will be devastated about Missy, but at least you saved two of them."

He nodded, his eyes darting to Dan and Jon.

Dan pulled at his mustache thoughtfully.

"That fits with what Mr. and Mrs. Metzner told me. They admitted that they'd pretty much freaked when I got them to describe exactly what happened."

Then he turned to Mr. Winters.

"I can only apologize, Mr. Winters. It seems everyone over-reacted. There won't be any formal charges."

"Are you kidding me?" Jon said, his voice spiking with outrage.

"Yeah, he's got a freakin' axe in his truck!" added Ashley, annoyed at being left out.

"And I've got a chainsaw in mine, but it doesn't make me Leatherface."

Dan's voice was sardonic, and I would have laughed if it hadn't all been so horribly serious.

Then Mr. Winters started typing again.

CAN WE GO HOME?

Any thoughts of laughter drained away. He sat in the chair, his shoulders slumped, his left hand rhythmically stroking Stan's head. He was seeking comfort from the one creature who truly understood him. Tears stung my eyes.

We must have all seemed so callous to him, vindictive even, accusing him of trying to hurt a little girl when all he'd wanted to do was save those tiny kittens.

I decided there and then that I wouldn't make any more assumptions.

And I could see that the day had drained the fight out of Mr. Winters.

Dan read his message and nodded.

"Of course. You're free to go whenever you like."

He stood up immediately, and Stan clambered to his feet grumbling softly.

"Mr. Winters," I said quickly, trying to think of something to say that would show we weren't all against him, "we've been trying to reach you to schedule another appointment for Stan after you missed the last one."

I'd tried to keep my voice gentle so it didn't sound like I was judging him, but he closed his eyes and grimaced, and I wasn't sure what that meant. I reached out and touched his arm, pulling away when his intense stare snapped to my hand.

"We'll email you," I said gently. "But please don't put it off too much longer. And don't worry about the kittens—I'll take good care of them."

My little speech apparently left him unmoved, his face cold and hard.

He didn't trust anyone.

Life had taught him not to trust.

I didn't know if he'd ever learn to trust me.

He glanced down, reminding me again how tall he was, and when I met his gaze, his expression lingered briefly. Then he turned around and walked out.

Dan sighed heavily.

"Well, that was a shitfest. How are those kittens?"

I gave him a weary smile.

"I think they'll be okay now. He got to them just in time."

"Hmm, and how long did you say that cat was missing?"

"A couple of weeks. She probably went into the forest to give birth to her kittens. I'll have to let Mrs. Humphries know what happened. Should I tell her about him? About Mr. Winters?"

"I guess that would be okay. And, Dawn, let me know if he brings in anymore injured animals, especially if it looks like they've been caught in snares."

"You think he's doing it?"

I felt indignant on Mr. Winters' behalf, especially since he wasn't here to defend himself.

"I don't know," Dan said bluntly. Then he turned to his deputy. "Jon, you and me are going to do some training on correct police procedures."

Chapter Three

OBSESSION

Dawn

I'd promised Katie ice cream. To be honest, she didn't have to beg me too much, because I loved ice cream just as much as she did, although I drew the line at having it for breakfast.

So mid-morning, we rode out to the Dairy Oasis at Lake Erie Community Park. Unfortunately, the line was out the door.

"Let's go play on the swings and come back in ten minutes," I suggested.

Katie huffed and puffed, but eventually agreed, and ran off while I headed for my favorite bench in the shade.

It was already occupied, and as I approached, I recognized Mr. Winters' sweet old dog, Stan. But I didn't recognize the man he was with. Not at first.

As I drew closer, I almost stumbled over my own feet, because then I *did* recognize the man sitting with Stan, and it really was Mr. Winters.

I'd thought of him often since the incident with the Sheriff's Department, so seeing him now, it was as if I'd conjured him up. Although he didn't look like the man I'd last seen.

After the axe incident, Girard townsfolk were agog—well, the ones who were connected to the Ashley-grapevine. The woman could have gotten a job with the 'National Inquirer'.

Some of her friends wanted him run out of town because of Missy, believing that he'd killed her or hurt her. Saner heads, like Dan's, prevailed. Live and let live, was his philosophy. It was one of the reasons we were friends through all these years.

But I couldn't believe how different the talk-of-the-town looked now, which explained why I hadn't recognized him. He'd shaved off his long beard, leaving just a little scruff, and had buzzed his hair military short. The transformation was stunning. He looked like a movie star with his strong jawline and sharp cheekbones. 'Handsome' didn't even begin to describe him. And I couldn't stop looking at his lips, surprisingly full and sensual now that they were uncovered—all things I'd never seen before because of his horrible shaggy beard.

But his eyes—those mesmerizing golden-brown eyes. Only the chaos and pain that I saw in them was familiar.

He was staring up the sky, his forehead creased with deep emotion, and Stan was watching him worriedly, a half-chewed sandwich abandoned on the grass.

I seriously considered finding another bench and leaving him in peace, but he just looked so lost and alone. And I also wondered if his appearance was some sort of ... I don't know ... some sort of sign that he wasn't hiding anymore.

"You know, you really should have him on a leash, Mr. Winters."

It was supposed to be a joke, since Stan was the most amiable, well behaved dog I'd ever met, but pretty lame as a conversation starter.

Mr. Winters looked at me, confusion apparent in his expression, and then I think he recognized me, too, because he blinked several times, and if it had been any other man, I would have thought he was checking me out. But it occurred to me that I looked very different, as well. Instead of blue scrubs, I was wearing my favorite shorts and a tank top, and I'd swapped my glasses for contact lenses.

He swallowed several times as if he might say something, but then just nodded and dropped his gaze to his own abandoned sandwich.

I felt him flinch slightly as I sat down next to him. He seemed even more tense than usual, his jaw clenched.

Stan gave me an anxious look, so I began stroking his head, something that calmed us both. His eyes closed as he happily blissed out.

"Are you okay?" I asked quietly.

I could tell that Mr. Winters was surprised by my question, and honestly I was, as well, but he nodded jerkily.

He took several deep breaths, and I got the impression he was working himself up to speak, but again, no words came out.

I tried a different approach. I knew he cared about Stan...

"I'm sorry if I'm intruding, but you haven't replied to our emails about Stan's next appointment. His teeth really need looking at again."

He grimaced and shook his head.

"Well, please don't leave it too much longer. We want to try and keep as many of Stan's teeth as we can." I paused. "You know, I wouldn't have recognized you if I hadn't spotted Stan."

His blank, stony expression was back. *Oh God!* I shouldn't have said that. It sounded judgmental and I hadn't meant that *at all*.

"Pardon me for saying so, but you seem ... upset?"

He closed his eyes and took a deep breath.

"B-bad ... deh ... deh ... day."

Bad day. I wished I understood why he was having a bad day. The sun was shining, and a soft breeze was blowing off the lake; the park was beautiful and the tall trees offered shady, dappled light from the growing heat.

But the chaos inside a person can be overwhelming. There's no law saying it has to match the outside.

"Okay," I said simply.

I sat stroking Stan, staring toward the lake. But I noticed that his owner kept giving me these small glances out of the corner of his eye, and I couldn't tell if he wanted me to leave or if he was working himself up to speak. So I sat with him in silence, waiting.

Stan must have approved of my presence, because after thinking it through, he transferred his head from Mr. Winters' leg to mine.

"Hey, Stan," I said softly, stroking his ears.

He hummed happily, and Mr. Winters frowned in disapproval.

"What?" I asked, staring at him questioningly.

Finally, he met my eyes.

They were beautiful, a soft hazel color with golden flecks, and framed with long black lashes, but full of questions, full of uncertainty.

He looked away, glanced down at Stan and frowned. Then he shrugged and I gave a quiet laugh, understanding his chagrin at Stan's transfer of affections.

"Stan already knows I'm a dog person."

I paused again, studying him more closely. His jeans were new, cheap and unbranded, but looked amazing on his long legs. His t-shirt was old and faded, softened by hundreds of washes, and clung to his muscled body.

When I'd first seen Stan, I'd searched for the Mr. Winters who looked like the proverbial mountain man—instead I'd found a brooding hottie. It was so confusing and...

"Mommy! Mom!"

Katie's impatient voice pierced the air. Mr. Winters looked up, alarmed, as she waved frantically. He actually flinched at the noise.

"Oh, excuse me a moment," I said with a reassuring smile. "Duty calls."

I stood up and walked away, meeting Katie outside the shop.

"The line's gone, Mom. Who was that man? I like his dog. Are you having Rocky Road or triple chocolate chip?"

"He's a client and his dog is a real sweetie. Well, I'll have Rocky Road today, I think. What about you?"

She screwed up her face in concentration, and I had to hold in a smile. We both knew that she'd have Rocky Road because she always did.

"Um ... um ... Rocky Road, please!"

I couldn't help laughing this time.

"Okay, want to go and find us a bench to sit on?"

I watched her running off, and then to my shock, she ran right over to Mr.

Winters. That was *not* what I meant when I'd told her to find somewhere to sit.

I almost followed her out of the shop, my mommy-sensors kicking into overdrive, but the line behind me was growing again and Katie was still in my eye-line. So I ordered the ice creams, paid, and waited impatiently, casting anxious glances in Katie's direction, then finally hurrying after her.

She was flopped on the grass with her arms around Stan who looked as if he was in heaven as she hugged him and talked to him.

Mr. Winters' on the other hand seemed somewhat startled but ... he was smiling...

Dear God, the man was beautiful!

Katie was chattering away as usual, although I couldn't tell if she was talking to Stan or trying to talk to Mr. Winters. She didn't tend to discriminate with her rapid-fire words. Watching the three of them ... I didn't know how to feel about that. Katie was usually wary around men—she just didn't have many of them in her life. She saw her father once every six or seven weeks, whenever it was convenient, with his busy schedule or so he said, and she'd never really liked Uncle Bob. I hadn't either, so when my sister got divorced, that was another one off of the list, and Mom and Dad had retired to Florida.

"I'm sorry about that," I said as I approached carrying the two ice creams. "Now, Katie, what have I told you about how to approach dogs you don't know?"

Katie wrinkled her nose.

"But I just *know* he's a sweetie," she reasoned. "I can tell. And anyway, you told me he was."

Stan licked her nose and she giggled.

"This is my daughter, Katie," I said, introducing her formally, although it seemed as if she'd already made herself at home with them.

"He's been telling me all about Stan," Katie said seriously. "His brother found him. He ran away to join the circus. What's your name?"

My eyebrows shot up. He'd been *talking* to her?

"This is Mr. Winters," I said faintly, questions shooting through me as Katie rambled on.

"He likes the *Katy* books, too. He's going to read to me."

Now I really didn't know what to say, and Mr. Winters looked equally confused. Katie and Stan were the only ones who were completely at ease.

"I'm sure Mr. Winters is far too busy for anything like that," I said at last, passing one of the cones to Katie. "Come on, Katie-kay, let's go eat our ice creams and leave Mr. Winters in peace."

"Bye, Stan. Bye, Mr. Winters," yelled Katie as she ran off.

He looked up when Katie left, his eyes following her for a second before moving back to Stan. He seemed suddenly so lonely, as if he'd enjoyed a few moments of our company. I touched his arm briefly and his eyes shot to mine as his mouth dropped open in surprise.

"Feel better, Mr. Winters," I said quietly.

I walked away more than a little confused. Katie skipped ahead, oblivious to the bewilderment that churned inside me.

I wasn't lying when I said I would never have recognized him but for Stan. The transformation was stunning. He'd been hiding an amazing face under all that hair and beard—I don't think Ashley would be calling him a weirdo loner if she saw him now. If anything, she'd say he was ... hot.

He obviously wasn't used to his new look, because he kept shaking his head, as if expecting his hair to flop over his face, covering his eyes the way it used to, and I could see him fighting back his anxiety because there was nothing to hide behind.

He'd become something of a talking point since he came to Petz Pets and was very nearly arrested. Ashley made sure to spread that enticing piece of gossip. But the few sightings of him in Girard since, his silence and his appearance, it had gotten the rumor-mongers circulating quickly.

Luckily, Dan stomped on the most outrageous of them—*escaped convict, serial killer*—so in the end, *weirdo-loner* was the worst the gossips could come up with.

I hadn't mentioned my theory of a speech impediment again, which was just as well, considering Katie thought he'd agreed to read to her.

I caught up to my hyperactive daughter.

"Katie-kay, what exactly did Mr. Winters say to you?"

She rolled her eyes, something that was becoming too much of a habit and reminded me of Stella.

"I already told you, Mom." Then she heaved a sigh. "He said Stan was a stray and his brother chose Stan's name and he thinks he's nine years old but he's not sure. I made up the bit about him running away to join the circus, but the rest is true. And he knew the *Katy* books. I asked him to read them to me. Is he a friend of yours? I like him. He listened to me."

My daughter had an active imagination, but she wasn't a liar. If she said Mr. Winters talked to her, then he did. So that blew my theory out of the water.

But there was certainly something about him. I wouldn't say strange, exactly ... he just seemed so sad. And lonely. Very lonely.

I wonder what had happened to him.

He'd looked apologetic when I mentioned Stan's missed appointment, so I hoped he'd bring him in another time. Although Stan was definitely much happier than last time I'd seen him—even if his diet didn't appear to have improved.

But Mr. Winters' appearance! That was the biggest shock. I wonder what caused him to shave off his long hair and thick beard. An image flashed through my mind of Mr. Winters standing in front of a bathroom mirror. I imagined him showering, drying himself with a towel, wrapping it around those lean hips, then tipping his head back and exposing his neck as he shaved —naked, as he ran a razor across his cheek, revealing the skin beneath, soft, vulnerable. His body hard, his heart guarded.

Dear God. I'd finally found a man I was attracted to and he was a mute loner and probably wanted in several states. Stella would be so proud.

Stan

I was proud of the boss. He'd talked to that cute kid like a real human being. Okay, he hadn't done so great when her mom was around, but it was a start.

I also knew that the doc thought he was a cool dude, and the boss wasn't exactly immune to her either. Attraction, pheromones, whatever you want to call it, I can scent them. And seeing as my sense of smell is a thousand times better than a human's, I know what I'm talking about. Pee-sniffing isn't just me getting my rocks off: I can tell who's been around, their age and breed, and I can definitely tell if a hot bitch has been marking her way for me to follow.

Hey, if you've got it, flaunt it. Or, at my age, use it or lose it.

But whichever way I looked at it, the boss and the doc were definitely having some serious eye contact. And that could only be a good thing.

I hoped.

Unless she broke his heart like that other bitch. In which case, she could kiss my hairy ass.

Dawn

I was still thinking about meeting Mr. Winters in the park when we arrived at Nancy and Spen's house.

They were friends of my parents, and since Mom and Dad relocated to Orlando, they'd become surrogate grandparents to Katie.

"My favorite girls!" Nancy said with a smile as she opened the door. "Go on through to the backyard, Katie-kay—Spen's got the grill working and there's a hamburger with your name on it."

Then she turned to me and smiled.

"You're looking well, Dawn. You have a little color in your cheeks. How are you? That little girl running you ragged? My, she could talk the hind leg off of a three-legged donkey."

I gave Nancy a hug. She and Katie had a lot in common, and I loved them both.

"We're good. How are you and Spen?"

"Breathing and vertical, which isn't so bad at our age, sweetheart. Come on through."

I could smell the grilling burgers as I walked into the backyard and my mouth watered. Despite the ice cream I'd had just an hour ago, my stomach rumbled.

Katie was chattering away to Spen and helping make lunch.

"...and we met Mommy's new friend," she said as she squirted ketchup and mustard into the rolls. "And he's got a really nice dog named Stan."

Nancy raised her eyebrows. "New friend?" she asked enquiringly.

My cheeks bloomed red.

"Not like that," I said hastily. "A new client—I've been treating his dog."

"I liked him," Katie announced, oblivious to the silent conversation going on behind her. "He listened to me." Then she turned and pinned me with her gaze. "Do you think he's handsome, Mom?"

"What? No!" I sputtered. "Well, he's not *bad* looking."

I was lying. He was gorgeous. Gorgeous *now*, anyway.

Katie frowned, then turned back to the pile of rolls.

"*I* think Mr. Winters is handsome," she announced, as if wondering why everyone else hadn't noticed that the sky was blue. "He talks funny."

"Winters?" Spen said, his eyes crinkling in confusion. "The man who bought Old Joe's place?"

"The one and only," I laughed weakly.

"The one that Dan arrested?" Nancy asked.

"Nearly arrested. And it was Jon, not Dan. But yep, that's him."

"Well, that's odd," said Nancy. "I was under the impression that he was ... rather unprepossessing. Ashley said that..."

Spen shook his head. "I've told you before not to listen to town gossip. He seemed like a decent enough fellow to me. Quiet, a little withdrawn perhaps."

"But is he handsome?" pressed Nancy.

All eyes swung to me.

"Ah ... he looks different from when I first met him..."

"He can come to your party!" Katie added. "And Stan."

Every year Nancy and Spen liked to throw a party to celebrate the Fourth. This year was no exception.

"Katie, I don't know..."

"Pleeeease!" she begged, her little face wrinkling as she out-stared Spen and Nancy.

"Maybe we *should* invite him," Spen said thoughtfully. "He hasn't been given the warmest welcome in Girard. It would do him good to get to know a few people. Although he may not come..."

"Thank you! Thank you! Thank you!" Katie sang, throwing her arms around Spen's waist.

Nancy raised her eyebrows.

"Well, this young man seems to have made quite an impression on Katie," she said to me.

"You've no idea," I muttered, shaking my head.

Chapter Four

KINDNESS

Dawn

Ever since I could remember, the Fourth of July meant a party at Nancy and Spen's house. It used to be an enormous affair when I was a kid, with half the town turning up to eat Nancy's homemade pies and drink Spen's moonshine, although I wasn't supposed to know about that. These days, it was much smaller, but even so, when Katie and I arrived, rather late, there were already more than 20 cars and trucks parked outside their house.

I sighed at the same time Katie squealed with excitement. I wasn't a huge fan of crowds, and generally avoided parties. That makes me sound like a recluse, and I wasn't, but I had my reasons.

There were a lot of things I loved about living in a small town—the community spirit, with bake sales to raise money for the church roof, Girl Scout cookies, and fireworks at the high school football field. But there was one thing that I hated, one thing you can never get away from: gossip. And having been on the receiving end of gossip for most of my adult life, I loathed it. Hence my dislike of crowds.

Katie jumped out of the car and ran toward the house. I envied her—so ready to throw herself into life. She hadn't yet learned to be cautious because people could smile out of one side of their mouths and lie to you from the other.

I followed more slowly, carrying a cooler filled with different salads that I'd thrown together.

But before I made it inside, I stopped and did a double-take. Parked at the far end of the street was Mr. Winters' rust bucket of a truck. My mouth popped open.

Never in a million years ... I didn't think that he'd come. If anyone was more of a hermit than me, it was Girard's newest and most mysterious arrival. Katie had kept on asking me if he was coming and I'd told her no. But it looked as though I was wrong.

My gut tightened with nervous anticipation. The thought of seeing him again ... I was surprised by the sudden rush of blood and a faintly dizzy sensation that washed over me.

And then I wondered how he'd cope with a party when talking to people was such a torment for him. My God, that was brave.

Courage isn't always in the grand gestures, but for a man like him, it was simply walking out of his own front door. If he could face a party, then so could I.

I dumped the cooler in the kitchen and laid out the salads on the buffet table, smiling at the enormous spread Nancy had provided.

I was steeling myself to head out into the backyard when she came barreling in.

"Dawn, sweetie!" and she gave me a big hug. "Where's Katie?"

"Probably on her second hotdog by now," I laughed.

"Probably," she agreed with a smile. "By the way, your Mr. Winters is here —isn't that a surprise?"

"He's not *my* Mr. Winters," I said patiently.

She gave me a mischievous grin.

"Spen drove out to give him the invitation but when I asked if he was coming, Spen said 'Hard to tell', so we weren't really expecting him. It must have been the prospect of seeing you again."

I gave her a pained look. "Nancy, please don't..."

She squeezed my hand. "No, no matchmaking, I promise. By the way, did you know he works in construction?"

I shook my head. The truth was I knew next to nothing about him.

"Spen says he's doing a magnificent job of fixing up Old Joe's cabin, like something out of 'Better Homes & Gardens'."

She paused as if waiting for me to fill in the blanks, but I had nothing to say. She looked faintly disappointed, but smiled at me again.

"Well now, come on outside and pretend you enjoy parties."

As I glanced around, I saw all the usual faces: Gary and Sheila Petz, their son Lloyd with his wife Leanne, Nancy's brother Ludo who was a marvelous plumber and therefore one of the most important people in town, and a bunch of others who waved at me and hugged Katie as she did the rounds.

I couldn't see him, I mean Mr. Winters, or Stan, but I did see Dan and his wife Crystal.

"Hey, Dawn! Where's pint-size?"

"Somewhere causing trouble," I laughed. "Listen for the yells."

Dan groaned. "I'm off duty!"

I'd known Dan and Crystal since high school. I even went on a date with

Dan when I was seventeen. Just the one time though, because then he started seeing Crystal. It was a long time ago and we were all friends.

Crystal gave me a hug and passed over a fruit punch.

"I've met the mysterious Mr. Winters," she said, giving me a sly smile and dropping her voice to a whisper. "I can see why everyone is talking about him," and she batted her eyelashes, making me laugh. "All the other single women have tried talking to him, but no one's had any luck. Maybe you should try."

I tried to seem unaffected. "Did he bring Stan?"

"His assistance dog? Yes, I expect he takes him everywhere."

"Assistance dog? I thought Stan was just a pet," but even as I said the words, I wasn't sure they were true.

Crystal looked confused. "Well, that's what I assumed because, you know, because of his disability."

She whispered the word 'disability', as if it wasn't something that was polite to discuss.

Then I heard Katie calling his name, her piercing voice carrying above the myriad conversations.

"Mr. Winters! Mr. Winters! It's me, Katie. Where's Stan? Is he here?"

I turned and found her running up to the man everyone was talking about.

He was wearing jeans and a sharply pressed white shirt. He was clean shaven and looked more handsome than ever. I stared, maybe even gawked, and I heard Crystal's snicker behind me.

"Excuse me," I said. "I think he might need rescuing from my daughter."

"Sure," she laughed, "but who's going to rescue him from you?"

I shook my head, her words stinging in a way that she hadn't intended. I knew I wasn't a prize, and I knew what the local gossips still said about me.

Instead of worrying about old news, I followed the sound of Katie's voice.

When I caught up to her, she was kneeling on the grass, her thin arms wrapped around Stan's neck. He panted happily, his tail wagging slowly.

"Does he like hotdogs?" she asked.

I stood stock still, astonished when Mr. Winters answered normally, his stutter almost unnoticeable.

"He's on d-duty. No hotdogs."

She rubbed her nose with a dirty finger. "Is he very fierce?"

I watched, intrigued, as he bent down to stroke Stan.

"Between you and me, he's as fierce as a bunny rabbit, but d-don't tell anyone. It's our secret."

"Bunnies can be quite vicious," she said seriously. "They have really strong teeth, and they can kick, too."

"Sorry!" I laughed as I walked across the grass to join them. "Comes from being a vet's daughter."

"Okay, no hotdogs. Sorry, Stan," said Katie, looking disappointed as she skipped away to join some other kids who were playing Frisbee.

"How are you, Mr. Winters?"

He nodded. "A-Alex."

"Oh!" I said, my cheeks turning pink. I hadn't expected him to speak to me. And then I realized that I was staring at him, but still hadn't replied. "Please, call me Dawn."

To hide my embarrassment, I bent down to fuss Stan's ears. He leaned against my leg, his eyes closed and a blissful expression on his face.

I looked up to find Mr. Win— to find Alex watching me, and something that might have been a smile softening his expression.

"I hope you don't mind me saying, but I'm a little surprised to see you here," I said honestly. "Pleased, but surprised."

He glanced around ruefully and shrugged his shoulders.

I could only imagine how he felt being here surrounded by so many strangers. I smiled to myself—Spen could be amazingly persuasive when he wanted to. Dad said he'd been a heck of a trial lawyer back in the day.

Alex seemed tense, his shoulders stiff and his expression tight as his gaze met many inquiring eyes watching us.

"Too many people?" I suggested quietly.

He nodded and grimaced.

"Well, you certainly look better than last time I saw you. Sorry, I shouldn't have said..."

My words trailed off when I realized he probably didn't want to be reminded of that. He'd told me he was having a bad day...

"S-stan likes K-k-katie," he said softly, surprising me by initiating a new topic.

I chuckled quietly.

"I think it's mutual. She's been talking about him non-stop ever since we saw you. And it's not like she doesn't get to meet animals all the time."

He took a deep breath, his lips forming the word shapes before he managed to speak.

"H-how ... k-kittens?"

I smiled.

"They're doing great! Mrs. Humphries has taken them home now. She's so grateful. She wanted to thank you in person ... but she'll write you, I'm sure."

He nodded, listening carefully, and I was happy that we were having something like a conversation. I started to relax and enjoy myself, pretending I couldn't see the quizzical stares of Spen and Nancy's friends.

I'd planned to ask Alex a little about his work on the house, when my nemesis appeared.

Stella strode toward us, her calculating gaze flipping between me and Alex questioningly.

Ugh! Why did she have to be here? And why did she have to look so fantastic and totally put-together when I was wearing an old denim skirt and a tank top?

"Hello, Stella," I replied in a clipped tone.

The temperature plummeted several degrees on the Kelvin scale, and Alex looked at us curiously.

"Aren't you going to introduce me to your date?" Stella asked stiffly, her cool gaze drifting over Alex.

I had two choices: tell her off and risk making a scene, or...

"Alex, this is Stella," I said flatly. "And this is Stan."

Alex gave me a puzzled look, obviously wondering why I hadn't corrected Stella's assumption that he was my date. I couldn't explain that I was saving him a world of trouble.

"Charmed," purred Stella, checking him out and ignoring both me and Stan.

I rolled my eyes. Typical Stella. Put a good looking guy in front of her, and she turned into some sort of rampant man-eater. A sweet, shy guy like Alex wouldn't stand a chance.

"Where are you from, Alex, I know you're not a local?" she said, still ignoring me.

Alex frowned, his lips flattening.

"Ah ... ah..."

"Actually he's your new neighbor," I said, feeling I had to say something when Alex was clearly struggling, then kicked myself for being so dumb and telling her he practically lived next door to her, even though there was a good chance Stella already knew that or would have found out soon enough.

Stella's mouth widened into a grin.

"How marvelous! You must come over for coffee, neighbor."

And she shot me a triumphant look.

The awkward pause stretched out, and then I saw Katie running toward us, smiling happily.

"Hi, Aunty Stella!" she sang, flinging herself into Stella's arms and receiving a warm hug in return.

I'd say one thing for Stella, she'd never held Katie's birth against her. Only me.

Then Katie ran off again, leaving the three of us in painful silence.

I could see Alex's confusion as his eyes flicked from Stella's face to mine.

"Yes," I said, my voice uncomfortably brittle. "We're sisters."

"Unfortunately," added Stella, under her breath.

Then she threw me a dirty look, and placed her hand on Alex's arm, squeezing gently. She looked like she was sizing up a piece of prime beef at the market.

"Nice to see you, Alex," said Stella, throwing me a final vicious glare. "I look forward to our next meeting ... as we're such close neighbors. Drop by any time."

Then she turned and stalked away.

Alex raised his eyebrows, his eyes meeting mine in a question. I smiled thinly.

"I'm surprised you haven't heard the local gossip about us."

I was trying for casual, but I knew that it wasn't working.

Alex shook his head, staring after Stella, and I sighed.

"I love living in a small town, but sometimes it can get too much," I admitted as his gaze finally returned to me. "Everyone knowing your business for a couple of generations back. But me and Stel ... obviously ... we don't get along, but she's never dragged Katie into our issues. I'm grateful for that. But as for the rest..." I blew out a breath. "Don't ask."

He didn't, but his expressive eyes stared into mine, as if to say that he understood, that he wouldn't pry. He was probably the last person to listen to gossip, having been a target of it himself. Although I didn't know if he was aware of it. But even if he didn't before, he couldn't have missed the way people were staring and whispering now.

Then I heard Katie calling to me. I didn't know if I was relieved or disappointed.

"Well, see you later," I said awkwardly.

He nodded as I patted Stan, and walked away.

An hour later, I'd had enough. More than enough. I'd tried to ignore Stella's presence, but she'd been tossing back glass after glass of red wine and I didn't want Katie to see her like that.

Definitely time to leave. Katie wouldn't be happy at the thought of going now. Not at all. Unlike me, my daughter was a party animal—the more people around the merrier. And other than school, she hardly ever had that. Guilt slithered up my spine again.

Being a parent means you're an expert in guilt. There's never enough time to be everything you want to be for your child, to do everything you want to do, to give them the things they need or deserve. And being a de facto single parent, well, you could double and triple the guilt complex.

It took me a few minutes to find Katie. She wasn't by the buffet or playing with the other kids. She wasn't in the kitchen or talking to Nancy. And she wasn't in either of the house's bathrooms.

I made my way into the backyard again, then saw her out of the corner of my eye. She'd just plopped down in the shade of a large oak tree. And she was with Alex. Again.

It made me sad. She obviously craved his attention—maybe because she got so little from her father.

I tiptoed closer, intrigued.

"I'm hot," she said, sprawling out in the shade next to a sleeping Stan, her face flushed and glowing.

Alex smiled at her and offered his bottle of water.

"Thanks, Mr. Winters," she said, taking several large gulps, wiping her mouth with her hand and passing the bottle back.

"M-my name is Alex," he said, his voice soft and hesitant.

Katie frowned.

"Mom says I'm supposed to call old people Mr. or Mrs. or Dr. if they're like my mom."

I put my hand over my mouth, trying not to laugh. I knew I shouldn't be eavesdropping, but I was fascinated to see the way Katie interacted with him. She certainly hadn't been this interested in talking to the couple of guys I'd dated in the last eight years.

"I'm not that old," Alex replied, his tone halfway between amusement and indignation.

I wondered. My guess would be early thirties, although anything over 16 probably seemed ancient to an eight year-old.

"Okay," she nodded, her face breaking out in another smile. "Will you be my boyfriend?"

Oh no! Poor Alex! He looked shocked, and he shook his head, his eyes wide.

"I guess I am a bit too old for you after all, K-katie."

She thought about this for a moment.

"Well, will you be my mom's boyfriend? I know she really likes you, and she hardly ever likes anyone."

What?! I'd been about to go and save Alex, but now I stood frozen, mid-step.

"Did she say that?" he asked curiously.

"Nuh-uh," Katie replied, shaking her head, "but it's something a woman knows." She sounded eighteen instead of eight. Then she said, "Are you dating Aunty Stella?"

And again, What?

"N-no!"

"But you like my mom?"

He nodded, more cautious now.

"She's pretty, isn't she?"

"Uh..."

"I told her to wear makeup today in case you were here, but she'd only wear mascara, not lipstick. Do you like lipstick on girls?"

Alex looked as though he was beginning to sweat from the inquisition. I didn't know whether to intervene, listen to his answer, or run the heck away!

"S-sometimes. It depends."

"On what?"

"On the girl; on the c-color lipstick, I guess."

"Well, what color would you like on my mom?"

"Uh, w-well..."

Okay, that was waaaay more than enough. And when he saw me, the look on

Alex's face was priceless—the obvious relief in his expression seemed to say that the cavalry had arrived just in time.

Stan opened one eye to see who was coming, then closed it again with a heavy sigh.

"Katie! Are you bothering Mr. Winters?"

"His name's Alex, Mom. He said I could call him that. He thinks you're pretty. He says you should wear lipstick, just like I said. He was going to tell me what color you should wear."

Alex looked as embarrassed as I felt—which was *very*.

"Katie!" I said, a little breathlessly. "That's enough."

She rolled her eyes. "Fine, Mom. I'm just trying to help. You haven't had a boyfriend in for*ever*. And, he's not dating Aunty Stella because I asked him and he said no."

Then she stood up and walked away with a very adult expression on her face.

"God, sorry!" I stuttered. "Sometimes she's just so ... sorry."

I was surprised when Alex laughed, looking far more relaxed than I'd expected, given his recent interrogation.

"She's a great k-kid."

"Yes, she is."

I hesitated for a moment, wondering if I should go, especially now that Katie was no longer chaperoning us. But Alex was smiling at me, and it was a lovely smile. Seeing him this relaxed, I started to see possibilities that I had no business looking for.

"Do you mind if I sit here for a while?" I asked carefully. "Nancy and Spen are lovely, but..."

"Too m-many people?"

He echoed my words from earlier as I gave him a wry smile.

"Is that why you're hiding out down here?"

He nodded, that same small smile making him seem so much more approachable, friendly even.

I plopped down crisscross applesauce and sighed. "Thank you for not asking. About me and Stella. It's a long story."

He nodded understandingly, then shrugged. He really could communicate a lot with his shrugs.

"Well, thank you ... um ... I'm sort of surprised you're still here, too."

He frowned, as if it was a puzzle to him, as well.

I paused, wondering what to say next, then gestured to his bottle of water. "Aren't you having a drink? I think they've got light beer since you're driving."

He frowned again and shook his head.

This time, we lapsed into complete silence, but it was a surprisingly companionable peace. I didn't feel the need to talk for the sake of it—maybe because I knew that he didn't want or need that either. And unlike most of the first dates I'd been on, it didn't seem likely that he'd talk endlessly about himself. Well, obviously not. He was easy company.

He leaned back against the tree, his eyes closing with a contented sigh that curved his full lips upwards.

I liked that he felt comfortable enough to do that, and it gave me the opportunity to study him close up. I was intrigued by the tiny flaws in his perfect face: a small scar on his chin, a mark on his ear where I guessed he'd once worn an earring, three freckles beneath his right eye.

Then my eyes dropped down to his hands, folded easily in his lap, and I saw that he had a tattoo on the inside of his left wrist, the cursive script running up toward his elbow.

"What does your tattoo say?" I asked, curiously. "Is it Latin?"

His eyes opened and he blinked at me. Then he frowned, his relaxed expression disappearing. It was like seeing storm clouds roll across the sun, blotting out the light, and for a moment I thought he wasn't going to answer.

"I-italian," he said at last.

Surprising myself, I lifted his hand, bringing the small script closer to me as I peered down.

"*Siamo tutti creature di Dio*," I read carefully. "What does it mean?"

He shifted uncomfortably as I held his hand. His palm was warm and dry, but I could feel calluses, too. Spen had mentioned that he was fixing up Old Joe's cabin.

I replaced his hand carefully in his lap, and his fingers twitched restlessly as he shifted away from me minutely. I waited patiently, hoping that he trusted me enough to share this little nugget, and to know that I wouldn't be gossiping about him tomorrow.

He took a deep breath. I recognized it now as his way of coping, of planning what he was going to say, giving the words a better chance of being born. I wondered if he'd learned how to do that himself, or whether a speech therapist had taught him.

"*W-we are all c-creatures of one f-f-f-family*."

His stutter was worse, which meant he was anxious now. I frowned, puzzled as I digested his words, and then I had a lightbulb moment.

"Oh! I know this! St. Francis? Isn't that one of his sayings? I always liked that one. It makes sense that you of all people would have this," and I glanced down at Stan, snoring softly in the shade. "I guess Stan is your family, isn't that right, boy?"

Stan opened one eye lazily when he heard his name, then dropped his head back to the grass with a soft thud, making me chuckle quietly.

"Francis of Assisi was the patron saint of animals, wasn't he?"

It wasn't really a question, but Alex seemed even more uncomfortable with the subject for some reason. I was about to change it, when I heard a familiar and unwelcome sound.

I sat up straighter, looking in the direction of the buffet tables.

"Oh no! Bob's here—Stella's ex-husband. She's been drinking and, oh, I don't like the look of this. I'll talk to him. Will you take care of Stella?"

"Uh…"

I didn't give him time to answer as I stood quickly and held out my hand to help him up. Hesitating slightly, he took it, rising in one smooth movement that brought him close to me.

My pulse leapt, and realizing that I was still gripping his hand, dropped it quickly. He was staring at me when raised voices drew my attention back to the other drama going on by the barbeque pit. It looked as if Stella was about to skewer her ex.

"…and all that time you were screwing that little bitch in *our* bed!"

"Shut your mouth, Stel, you're a drunk."

"And you're a lousy fuck, Bob. She's welcome to you! But I'm keeping the house!"

Several of the moms were holding their hands over their kids' ears, or trying to pull them out of ear-shot—which would have to be somewhere in the next state.

We walked over quickly, aware of the embarrassed glances from other party-goers as they pretended to ignore Stella and Bob's sideshow.

Stan trotted at our heels, but as soon as we got close to them, he growled, his hackles raised and his lips pulled back.

Alex's head whipped in Bob's direction, and his eyes narrowed. I had no idea what that was about and I didn't have time to ask.

Instead, I took Bob's elbow, trying to get his attention discreetly, and another woman laid a cautious hand on Stella's arm to slow the flurry of ugly words she was spouting.

"Alex!" shrieked Stella, suddenly flinging her arms around his neck as he approached. "He's just insulted me!"

He froze, shock registering on his face as everyone stared. Even Stan looked surprised.

Then she grabbed his face and kissed him hard, before whipping around and snarling at Bob, "At least I know what it's like to have a *real* man now."

She laid a proprietary hand on Alex's stomach, and I could see several of Spen's guests eyeing them speculatively.

"Is that right?" sneered Bob, as I failed to tug him away. "You've had so many men you can't keep track."

"Oh no," I muttered

"You bastard!" Stella screamed, and tried to launch herself at him.

Alex moved faster, catching her by the waist and pulling her back, dodging her flailing hands as Stan began to bark loudly.

"Stella!" I cried out, worried and appalled. Then I turned to Alex, speaking urgently, "Can you get her out of here? Please!"

He nodded and gripped Stella's wrists firmly, dragging her behind him even as she tried to wrench her hands free and throw herself at Bob's girlfriend, who was cowering behind a sun umbrella. She continued to fight Alex the whole way, and Stan was still barking his head off.

"Stupid bitch never could hold her alcohol," Bob laughed.

"There are children here, Bob!" I snapped. "Have a little dignity."

"Tell that to your drunk of a sister!"

"You're Nancy and Spen's guest," I reminded him more quietly.

He turned his back on me without a word, but at least he'd shut the hell up. He strode across to his shocked girlfriend, smiling smugly at the uneasy guests.

I shook my head and hurried after Stella. I'd never seen her so out of control. Bob didn't bring out the best in her, and things had been a thousand times worse since the divorce, but this...

She was still fighting Alex, and he was manhandling her all the way to his truck, his face stern and determined. I flinched when she tried to knee him in the groin, but he twisted away just in time, catching the blow on his hip. He grimaced and Stan barked even louder. Several of the guests backed away from him.

Nancy came hurrying towards us as Alex hauled Stella through the house and out into the front yard.

"Oh, dear! Oh, Stella!" and she pulled her into a hug.

To my surprise, Stella collapsed into her arms and started sobbing. I was relieved someone else had taken over for that.

I didn't get along with my sister, but I hated seeing her like this ... and I knew how it felt to have someone cheat on you. A new compassion for her obvious misery made me soften toward her.

I hung back as Nancy took charge.

"Will you take her home, Alex?" Nancy asked worriedly.

As Stella clung to Nancy, he nodded reluctantly and glanced across at me.

I wanted to read something important into that look, but his face was hard and closed, and I had no way of knowing what he was thinking.

He looked away, and much to Stan's annoyance, hefted him into the back seat of the truck. Then he helped Stella into the passenger seat, and turned to Nancy.

"W-where?" he asked, pointing to Stella.

Nancy gave him an odd look, which made me think that she'd believed Stella's outburst but was now confused because he didn't know where Stella lived. She frowned, shaking her head, and then gave him the directions.

I ducked back inside the house, so I didn't know if Alex saw me, but Stella did, her eyes glinting with malice as she stared coldly.

I watched as they drove away, together, until the truck turned a corner and they were out of sight.

I couldn't help wondering how much of this was planned and how much was just opportunistic. Either way, Stella had left with Alex, and her eyes told me that she'd won this round.

It exhausted me just thinking about it—it had been a long time since I'd considered this a game. She was my *sister*. We should be supporting each other. But that was years in the past.

Seeing her with Alex bothered me more than I liked. And I hated she'd used him the way she had, so publicly. I'd seen the shock and confusion on his face when she'd thrown herself at him. I could only assume that she wanted to convince Bob and all our friends that they were together, effectively cutting me out of the picture.

Good old Stella—killing two birds with one stone.

Not many men said no to Stella—and I had no reason to think that Alex would be one of the few. Our connection had felt real, but maybe that was just in my head. In any case, it had been brief.

I sighed. My older sister had always been the glamorous one, the popular one. I was quieter, more academic. And the only time a man had chosen me over her, well, that was almost a complete disaster. Except I had Katie. And I wouldn't be without her for the whole world.

"Are you okay, Dawn?"

Nancy's words were kind and I felt tears spring to my eyes.

"I'm fine," I lied, offering her a watery smile.

"He seems like a nice young man," she said tentatively. "A little on the quiet side." And she paused. "Too quiet for Stella, I'd say."

Then she patted my arm and walked away.

Chapter Five

EMPATHY

Dawn

I didn't mind pulling the night shift. I only did it once or twice a month. Katie enjoyed it because she got to stay with her friend Holly, and I enjoyed it because it gave me a chance to get up early and take Tanner for a ride—if it hadn't been too busy the night before.

We shared the night shifts with a larger veterinary practice in Erie, but tonight was my turn. I was enjoying the rare solitude, peace and quiet of being at home by myself.

I only lived 15 minutes from the office, and had the emergency calls switched to my cell phone. It cut down on costs not having a service to answer calls over the weekend. Fortunately, nobody abused the emergency call number. Well, it happened occasionally, but it was rare, and Gary would have a quiet word where necessary.

I missed my daughter, but I allowed myself to cherish these moments. What I didn't enjoy as much was being woken in the middle of the night. But that was part and parcel of a vet's on-call life.

My phone rang, waking me from a deep sleep, and I fumbled for the light switch, squinting at the clock. Nearly 2AM.

I answered on the third ring, hoping I sounded alert. "Petz Pets Emergency Line?"

"D-Dawn!"

The stutter gave him away, but I would have recognized his voice anywhere.

"Alex?"

"Y-yeah!"

"What's wrong?" I asked, definitely more alert now. "Are you okay?"

"S-s-s ... v-v-v ... Fuck!"

He screamed with frustration as he failed to get the words out, and I had to hold the phone away from my ear.

"Alex," I said, speaking as soothingly as I could, given that his voice and the sudden wakening had my heart was slamming against my ribs, "take a deep breath. Try to stay calm. Is it Stan?"

He grunted something unintelligible, then muttered, "Y-yeah!"

"Okay, come to the office. I'll be there in 20 minutes."

I hung up and yanked my jeans on, shoving my phone into my back pocket. I'd slept in my bra and t-shirt so all I needed was shoes and a coat and I was good to go.

As usual, I'd left a thermos of coffee by the front door, ready for the night shift, and I grabbed it as I ran to my car.

Fifteen minutes later, I was at the office. I flipped on all the lights and threw a plastic apron over my clothes as I prepped the examination room.

Time ticked by in silence, and I became increasingly anxious. Alex lived nearer to the office than I did, so where the hell was he? Had something happened? Had there been an accident? Maybe Stan? I wanted to call him back, but was reluctant to do that when he'd be driving and was obviously upset.

But then I saw headlights bleaching the road outside the office, and his truck screeched into the parking lot, tires churning on the gravel.

I opened the door as Alex leapt from the truck, then staggered inside with Stan ... no, it wasn't Stan.

Alex was carrying a dog that I'd never seen before, unmoving and covered with blood that glistened on his dark fur.

My heart sank, this dog was already dead, but Alex didn't know it.

He looked terrible, his face pale, his eyes wide and worried, blood on his face and smeared across his clothes. He'd been in a fight, that was obvious, but there was an eerie wildness in his eyes that had me stepping back.

"Put him on the table," I ordered.

Under the stark whiteness of the operating table, the dog looked even worse, his fur matted everywhere with dried blood, one ear hanging off and his cheek and throat torn. But his eyes were fixed and dilated, and his tongue lolled from his mouth.

I hated this. I hated seeing an animal so mutilated, but I had to do my job. I pulled out a stethoscope and listened intently. Nothing. I listened again, confirming what I already knew. This dog had been dead for a while. Now my job was to take care of the owner ... well, the person who'd brought in this poor creature.

I stood up slowly and sighed.

"I'm sorry, Alex. He's gone."

His eyes screwed shut and then he slammed his hand on the table, making me jump.

I felt very alone in this office by myself in the middle of the night. Fear seeped into me, and I touched my back pocket, reassured that I had my phone nearby.

The tide of Alex's anger seemed to turn, and he slumped into a chair, defeated, and pressed his fists against his eyes, cursing softly.

At that moment, he seemed more alone, more broken than I'd ever seen him. I needed to ... I don't know ... connect, reassure, something that showed him he wasn't alone.

And I wanted to know who'd hit him. He blinked when I touched his chin, turning his head this way and that, examining him closely.

His cheek was bruised, and his eyes were puffy, turning purple, his lips mashed and bloody. Then I lifted his hands and touched the split knuckles with the tip of my finger.

"What happened?"

He shook his head, edging away from me, subtly removing his hands from my grip.

"Well, can you tell me where you found this dog? He's obviously been in a fight and not an accident on the road."

He nodded sadly.

"And so have you," I added, my lips pulling together.

The expression on his face was heartbreaking. I saw hurt and regret, pain and sorrow, frustration and so much more.

He shook his head again, unable to express a single word, and he stood up to leave.

"Alex," I said gently, "let me help you."

He took a deep breath, his hands forming fists as he squeezed his eyes shut.

"D-dog f-f- ... d-dog fight!" he spat out.

"Yes, I got that," I said, trying to be patient as my own frustration mounted. "Was it ... was it an illegal dog fight? I mean, an *organized* dog fight?"

He nodded warily.

"Were you ... there?"

Obviously. He nodded impatiently.

Did that mean he'd been part of the fight? The thought sickened me. I just couldn't see this gentle man, this sweet guy involved in anything so barbaric. But the bloody remains of the dog and the fact that Alex had been in a fight, too, made me doubt everything.

"Can you tell me what happened?"

He scowled and took a step away from me.

"Alex?"

Disappointment and anger flashed in his eyes, before he turned and walked out of my office, covered head to toe in the dead dog's blood, sweat and saliva.

I knew what I had to do, but I didn't want to.

I just wished he could have talked to me. I wished he could explain. But strong emotion had robbed him of every sound, and instead I was left with silence.

Somehow Alex was involved in illegal dog fights.

I picked up the phone and dialed the police station.

I hadn't slept even though I'd gone home and back to bed.

I shuddered, thinking of the multiple bite wounds on the dog Alex had brought in. I'd seen dog-fighting videos as part of my training, and they were horrific. It was literally a fight to the death. Some owners cut off the animal's ears and tail to offer fewer targets for an attacking dog. They were trained to kill. It made the animals almost impossible to re-home on the rare occasions that they were rescued. I didn't understand how humans could be so cruel.

How on earth did someone like Alex Winters get involved in that? He seemed so gentle. But when I thought about it, Stan had multiple scars on his body that could have come from fighting.

I'd left the dog's body in the small mortuary we had at the office. Dan was coming by later in the morning to see it. I knew that dog fighting went on, but it was something that mostly seemed to happen in the cities. I was horrified to think that it could be happening here in Girard.

I showered and dressed slowly, as if I'd aged decades overnight.

Ashley was already in the office when I arrived, her indifference and curiosity putting me on edge.

"Where did you get the stiff?"

"Ashley!"

"What?"

"Never mind. It's a dog that was involved in a fight. I wasn't able to save him."

"Yeah? Because I didn't think we put the live ones on the slab," and she rolled her eyes at me and sashayed over to the coffee machine.

Honestly, she had the sensitivity of a rock.

Dan and Gary arrived at the same time, and I took them to see the body.

"Man, that's bad," Dan said, shaking his head. "And you say Alex Winters brought him in?"

"Yes."

"Did he say where he found the dog? Anything?"

"No, but you know what he's like—he can't speak when he's upset. And he was definitely upset last night." I hesitated, then plowed on. "And I think he'd been fighting, too. He had a split lip, and maybe a black eye. Oh, and his knuckles were all bloody."

"I'll go talk to him," said Dan thoughtfully. "He might be more relaxed in his own home."

"Do you think it's starting again?" asked Gary, as I glanced up at him in surprise. "The illegal dog fights?" Then he looked at me. "The last serious ones were before you started working here."

Dan sighed. "I don't think they ever went away. After that big ring was busted in Philly some years back, it just pushed it further underground and out of the cities. I've been hearing a few things lately..."

I shook my head. "There's no way that dog could have survived a drive from Philadelphia in his condition. I doubt it would have survived the two-hour ride from Pittsburgh."

"Well, we won't know anything for sure. I'll go speak to Alex."

We were all quiet, silenced by the violence and cruelty inflicted on this poor creature.

"The mystery man has made another appointment," Ashley said, pulling a face.

Three weeks has passed since I'd last seen Alex. Three weeks since he'd phoned me in the middle of the night. Three weeks since I'd seen him mute with pain and anger.

Dan hadn't gotten back to me, so I had no idea how the interview with Alex had gone either. But the rumor-mill didn't need facts to fuel it. Apparently, the latest about Alex included the suggestion that he'd moved from California to be near Stella, or that he was a movie star recently out of rehab and now in hiding, although no one could remember the name of his supposed movies. Someone had suggested he was Chris Hemsworth, but I think Mrs. Jenners was near-sighted.

I pressed my lips together to keep from snapping at Ashley. At least she wasn't calling him 'weirdo' anymore. She'd glimpsed him shopping for groceries, raved about his new haircut and beardless state, and ever since her gossip radar had been re-tuned in his direction. But I hadn't told her about his role in the dog fighting incident—whatever that was.

"Do you want to take the appointment or should I schedule it with Gary?" Ashley asked, her eyes wide and innocent. "I don't want things to be awkward since he and Stella ... well, *you* know."

I didn't know—and that was the problem. Ashley rattled on, insinuating that Alex and Stella were dating. Or hooking up. That seemed more like Stella's style. I had no idea if Alex had a 'style'. No one had seen them around town together, but since her house was next to his and he'd taken her home from the party...

And the dog fighting—I didn't want to believe he was involved. At least, not involved in setting them up or watching them or ... so why the hell had he been there?

I rubbed my forehead and gave myself a mental shake. I could be professional about this appointment. Although it would be easier if I didn't like him so much.

"No, that's fine, Ashley. I'm quite happy to see Stan and Mr. Winters."

Yes, I'd use last names—that kept things impersonal.

Ashley raised her eyebrows theatrically and turned back to her computer screen with a long-suffering sigh.

But when 11 o'clock rolled around, my stomach was churning and my hands felt clammy. I didn't know what I expected, but I was anxious to see him. And that was not good. Not when he was involved in something illegal; not when he and Stella...

"Good morning, Mr. Winters," Ashley said sweetly as the door to the office opened. "Please take a seat. Dr. Andrews will be with you shortly."

I didn't hear him reply, but I did hear Stan's nails clicking on the linoleum. At least he hadn't had to be carried in this time. I smiled to myself.

I was just about to tell them to come through, when I heard Ashley speaking again—and this time she was definitely flirting with him.

"I'm sure everyone's already told you, but you sure look different than when you first came here. Really good."

Silence.

"Although I think a little scruff suits you, too."

Silence.

"You are such a sweetie, Stanley," Ashley giggled.

"It's just Stan," I said, automatically correcting her as I walked into reception.

I caught her rolling her eyes before she patted Stan's head and handed Alex a leaflet.

"Dr. Andrews wanted you to have this brochure. It has information on healthy diets for senior dogs and such." She threw him a meaningful look. "It has *all* the information you need."

He murmured something as she sashayed back to her desk. What was that about a brochure? I hadn't mentioned anything to her.

"Hi, Stan," I said, stroking his head. "Glad to see you don't have to be carried this time."

I glanced up at Alex, and caught the ghost of a smile.

The bruising around his face had faded, although there was a new wariness in his eyes when he looked at me.

"Come on in."

Stan rose slowly to his feet and padded behind me as Alex followed soundlessly, and when we got to the examination table, he lifted Stan up.

I wanted to ask him how he was today, but I didn't. Stan was my patient, not Alex. He wasn't anything to me.

Instead, I concentrated on my job. I checked Stan's teeth and gums again as Alex watched me in silence.

"I'll schedule him for a procedure this afternoon. I'm going to scale and polish his teeth, but three of them have to come out, maybe four. You'll need to leave him with us for a few hours."

I looked up and saw the stricken expression on his face.

"He'll be fine," I said soothingly. "It's a routine operation."

"I w-want to s-s-stay."

"He'll be out for most of the time; we'll take good care of him, I promise you."

"No," he said emphatically, shaking his head. "St-st-staying!"

I stroked Stan reassuringly as his worried gaze flipped between us.

"That's fine," I relented. "Come back at 2PM. But no food or water for him. Okay?"

He nodded, obviously upset, and lifted Stan down.

I watched him walk out of the door, his head hanging as he murmured softly to Stan.

"The strong, silent type," Ashley winked at me. "And he cleans up real nice."

I couldn't argue with that.

But I wondered what she'd be saying if she'd seen him wild-eyed and covered in blood.

The fact that she hadn't seen him like that became patently obvious a few moments later when I picked up the forgotten healthcare pamphlet that she'd given him, 'Your Senior Dog'. There was a scrawled phone number and a short message:

Call me. Promise we'll have fun!
Ashley x

I withheld a sigh, wishing I could be like that, so straightforward, everything so easy. But life had made me cautious, and being a mother had made me fierce when it came to protecting Katie. Only carefully selected men made it to a first date, let alone anything more.

Ashley was six years younger than me, pretty and bubbly, and with few responsibilities.

Sometimes, I felt weighed down by mine—it would be nice to have someone to share them with.

Three hours later, Alex was back, and this time Stan was being carried, panting heavily and a mournful look on his expressive face.

My eyes darted between Ashley and Alex, but I couldn't discern any particular interest on his side. Or maybe that was wishful thinking.

Alex was concerned about Stan. I could tell that from the deep frown drawing his brows together and his lips pressed flat. But I couldn't help noticing the flex of his biceps as he hefted Stan's 80 pounds. I shouldn't have noticed and I shouldn't have cared, but I did.

I gave him a tight smile as he heaved Stan into our operating room.

"Just put him over there, please," I said, proud that my voice was calm and professional. "And don't touch anything—we've sterilized."

He nodded and laid Stan down carefully. Stan looked miserable, a stream of drool hanging from the corner of his mouth, and I stroked his soft fur reassuringly.

"We'll look after you, Stan. You'll just have to take it easy for a few days. Think of it as a vacation."

When I glanced up, Alex was staring at me intently. It was almost intimidating.

"Oh, you forgot your healthcare leaflet," I said a little stiffly.

He cocked his head to one side, still staring, still making me nervous.

"Your healthcare leaflet," I repeated, pushing Ashley's pamphlet into his hand.

He gazed at me uncomprehendingly, and my cheeks begin to color.

"Oh," I said softly. "I see."

He hadn't read the leaflet or seen Ashley's message, and now I'd handed her phone number right to him. Fate was definitely laughing at me.

A few minutes later, we were ready to start.

Alex leaned down next to Stan, pulling his ears gently and stroking his silky head, speaking quietly as I stood at a short distance, talking with Gary.

"Don't worry, buddy. They'll take good care of you. It's just a few teeth—nothing to worry about."

He didn't stutter once. Not when he talked to Stan. And if nothing else had made me realize how important Stan was to Alex before, now I truly understood.

Alex looked so guilty, lying to his dog, and I knew that Stan sensed it. His chocolate eyes stared up at his owner and he whined unhappily.

"Come on, Stan, it won't be that bad."

"We have to start now, Mr. Winters," I said quietly, interrupting whatever else he would have said to Stan.

I'd already given him much greater freedom to be in here that I gave to other clients, so I felt no compunction about kicking him out into the waiting room as I shaved Stan's paw so we could put in a needle for the anesthetic.

His eyes grew sleepy and finally closed, and we were able to proceed. Gary was monitoring the anesthetic, and I was doing the extractions.

As I worked, I studied Stan closely. He had a number of scars across his body, evidence of fighting, and Gary's eyes met mine over our surgical masks. We were both thinking the same thing—that Stan had been a fighting dog, which meant that Alex was more deeply involved in this dog fight ring than I wanted to believe.

"He said his brother rescued him two years ago," I said to Gary.

"Hmm," was his loaded reply, and I went back to working in silence.

Finally, the procedure was completed. Stan was going to feel very sore, but I knew this would help to keep him healthy for a while longer.

I snapped off my surgical gloves and apron, tossing them in the trash, then went to find Alex.

But reception was empty and I glanced at Ashley.

"He went outside," she said grumpily. "He's a real a-hole."

"Why's that?" I asked, surprised at her sudden U-turn.

She sighed theatrically and started typing at her computer.

Did that mean he'd turned her down?

As soon as I walked outside, a wall of heat pummeled me, the sky an unforgiving brilliant blue. Summer had cracked and scorched the dry dirt with the brutality of a furnace. The temperature was hitting the high nineties, and only the breeze coming off the lake made it even slightly bearable.

Alex wasn't in his truck or the parking lot. Instead, I found him on the opposite side of the road from the office, sitting in the shade of a sprawling white oak, his eyes closed.

He was shirtless, too, and I let my thirsty eyes drink in his beautiful body, his firm chest rising and falling rhythmically, his strong forearms resting in his lap, his long legs stretched out in front of him.

He hadn't shaved for a few days, and light brown scruff darkened his jaw, softening those hard edges. His lashes were long and thick, shading his eyes, making them seem bruised with shadows.

As I drew nearer, his eyes opened.

There was no slow rise to wakefulness, no confusion about where he was. He went from deep sleep to awareness with the flicker of his eyelids. It was disconcerting.

"The operation went well," I said, speaking quickly. "I had to remove four teeth in the end, so he'll need to be on soft food for a week. That will give his gums a chance to heal. Maybe some plain scrambled eggs tonight, and then something easy on his stomach—boiled rice and shredded chicken."

I saw relief rush through him and he stood up gracefully, grasping my hands.

"Th-thank you!"

His palms were warm and slightly rough. I smiled awkwardly, aware that I was blushing as I politely tugged my hands free. His touch felt too personal, too intimate, and it was uncomfortable because I knew it was only me feeling this way.

"He'll be waking up soon. Do you want to wait with him?"

He nodded, unable to speak anymore as I watched his raw emotions expressed on his too handsome face.

"He's going to be a bit groggy for a while; as an older dog, he might find it hard to throw off the effects of the anesthetic, and it might make him a little nauseous for a couple of days. Just let him rest and make sure he drinks plenty of water. I have a packet of antibiotics for you to give to him, three times a day with food."

Immediately, he turned and started to walk toward the clinic.

"Uh, Alex, you might want to put your shirt back on, or I'll have to resuscitate Ashley." Then I muttered under my breath, "Or peel her off of you."

I hadn't meant for him to hear that, but he turned and looked at me, surprise, confusion and a little irritation stamped on his face.

Without a word, he scooped up his t-shirt and yanked it down, not even bothering to shake off the grass and leaves clinging to it.

I led him into the recovery area, a small white room with several cages of different sizes. We'd put Stan in a large one at floor-level, an old quilt beneath him.

Gary was there, checking Stan's breathing as he worked off the effects of the anesthetic.

"You remember Gary? He's our Chief Veterinarian and the owner of the practice," I said, uncertain whether Alex would remember him from Spen's Fourth of July party.

Gary stood up and the two men shook hands.

"Well, Mr. Winters, Stan came through with flying colors. I'm sure Dawn will explain anything you need to know."

Alex mumbled his thanks, then sat on the floor next to Stan's cage and stroked his ears.

I was pleased to see that Stan's breathing was even and he blinked up blearily, sighing heavily.

Alex seemed overwhelmed, almost afraid to believe that Stan would make a full recovery. His large hands were so gentle when he touched his pet. It was difficult to imagine that he would use them to hit someone. But he had, and I remembered the rage I'd seen in his face. Now he was blinking hard, and I suspected that he was fighting back strong emotion.

I touched his shoulder briefly, wanting to reassure him. His skin was sun-warmed under his t-shirt, and I withdrew my hand quickly.

"Alex, he's fine, I promise. I wouldn't let anything happen to Stan."

He gave me a shaky smile that almost broke my heart, so I simply patted his arm, retreating into my professional demeanor.

As I walked away, I saw him wiping his eyes while Stan snuffled at his pocket.

"We'll be going home soon, buddy, okay? But don't scare me like that again, you hear me?"

His voice was clear and soft, without a suggestion of a stutter.

Stan gave up on finding any treats and settled for licking Alex's hand and sprawling more comfortably on his borrowed quilt.

After an hour, where Alex refused to leave Stan's side, I decided that he was well enough to be taken home.

"Scrambled eggs tonight," I reminded him as he nodded solemnly, "then something soft and easy to digest for a few days after that. He'll be a bit wobbly—older dogs find it harder to work off the effects of even minor operations, but he's going to be just fine."

I watched them leave together, Stan weaving slightly as he plodded across the parking lot, Alex watching him carefully. Then he lifted Stan into his truck and drove away slowly.

"Do you think he's gay?" Ashley asked thoughtfully.

I was startled by the suggestion. Nothing about Alex had set off my gaydar, but I could be wrong.

"I don't know," I said shrugging.

"I think he is," Ashley sighed. "What a waste. Maybe I should introduce him to my cousin in Cleveland. What do you think?"

I'd met her cousin Max. He was loud and flirty and a ton of fun. But he was also the sort of guy who'd pitch a fit at getting dog hair or drool on his pants.

Ashley saw my expression and wrinkled her nose.

"No, I guess not."

"Oh shi— sugar lumps!"

"Mom!" Katie gasped, her eyes wide and pleased. "You were going to say a bad word!"

"I wasn't," I lied grumpily as I climbed out of the car.

It was two days since Stan's surgery and I hadn't heard a word from Alex, so I assumed Stan was doing okay.

Ashley had convinced herself that Alex's lack of interest in her was because of his sexual orientation. I didn't want to believe that, but didn't say anything one way or another.

Dan had stopped by to say that he was still hearing rumors about illegal dog fighting going on in the area, and asked me to keep my eyes and ears open. He didn't comment on his interview with Alex, and I knew him well enough to know that he wouldn't tell me even if I'd asked. He was a real straight shooter, and despite the fact that we'd grown up together and were friends, he was a police officer first and foremost.

And although my thoughts had drifted to Alex more than once, and in ways that kept me awake at night, right now, I had other, more urgent concerns.

"Oh, jeez, a flat! Just what I need," I sighed.

It was my own fault. I knew that the tires were getting a little bald, but I'd hoped they could keep going a while longer. I didn't have a spare $500 to replace the whole set right now. Well, that plan was nixed. Just something else I'd have to put on the credit card.

My dad had made sure I knew how to replace a tire, so I dug the jack out of the trunk and worked up a sweat getting the car in the air. Then I remembered I was supposed to loosen the lug nuts before I did that, so I put it on the ground again and found the wrench.

By now, the back of my neck was burning from the noonday sun, and I was in a foul mood. But could I move those darn lug nuts? Nope, completely locked solid.

Defeated, I pulled out my phone to call for roadside assistance. Only there was no signal. I felt like swearing, but with my daughter in the car, I had to make do with furiously kicking the sagging tire.

It was a two-mile walk into town, but with Katie, it would probably take forever, and I didn't have water in the car.

I heard the sound of a vehicle coming up behind us, and suddenly realized how vulnerable we were out by the State Game Lands. I picked up the tire wrench and half-hid behind the car.

I nearly wept with relief when I recognized Alex's beaten-up truck.

"Alex! Oh, thank goodness! I've got a flat and my cell doesn't get a signal here..."

Then Katie's head poked out of the passenger window.

"Hi, Alex. How's Stan? Mom said he had to have a tooth out. I had to have that done once. It sucked."

"Katie! You don't use language like that!"

"All the kids at school say it, Mom."

"You don't."

Katie rolled her eyes, and as I looked at Alex, I suspected that he was trying not to laugh.

"Mom wouldn't let me eat candy for a week," Katie added with a woebegone expression.

Alex smiled at her and spoke softly.

"Your mom did a great job with Stan."

Katie rolled her eyes again. "Of *course* she did. My mom's really smart."

He chuckled quietly. The relationship between Alex and my daughter was so sweet I was almost jealous. I wished he could be that relaxed with me.

When he turned back to look at me, he was smiling broadly. *Yep, jealous of my eight year-old daughter.*

I blinked a couple of times then pointed at the flat tire.

"I was going to change it, but I couldn't turn the lug nuts to get it off."

"Mom was cussing!" added Katie in a loud whisper.

I threw Katie a mom-look that silenced her.

Alex picked up the tire iron that I'd been using. The muscles across his back writhed as he strained to loosen the lug nuts, and I was very much enjoying the view.

Finally, he fixed the donut in place and shook his head.

"I know," I said tightly. "It's just that new tires are so expensive and ... well, never mind." I paused, then smiled awkwardly as Katie bounded out of the car and threw her arms around Alex's waist, beaming up at him as if he'd just invented ice cream.

"You're like a knight saving people, except you don't have a horse. Or armor. Mom rides horses and I'm going to learn, too. Can you ride?"

Alex shook his head, a small smile playing on his lips as he gazed down at Katie.

"Mom can teach you. She's really good."

"Thank you for stopping," I said, annoyed that I sounded flustered.

He stared at me over Katie's head, his expression quizzical, but of course, he didn't say anything to me. He never did.

Sighing with frustration, I watched Katie chatting easily as she climbed back into the car, waving as we drove away.

For a moment, Alex just stood there, until finally, he raised his arm and waved back.

Chapter Six

NIGHTMARES

Dawn

This was a bad idea. Or maybe not. Probably yes. Bad. Very bad. In the history of bad decisions, this could be right at the top. Or the bottom. Definitely at the bottom.

I let the cell phone slide onto the table and stalked across the kitchen to the coffee machine, irritated with myself. But I'd promised Katie in a weak moment, and I made a point of keeping my promises to her. One of her parents had to.

Refueled with the strongest coffee I could bear, I picked up my phone for the tenth time, staring at it as if it might explode, then dialed, this time letting it ring. And ring and ring. And ring.

And ring.

I was considering it a sign not to bother, when Alex finally answered. Well, he didn't speak, but my phone was now silent and the call hadn't been dropped, so I assumed he was there.

"Hi, Mr. Win ... um ... Alex. It's Dawn."

There was a very long pause before I heard his voice, huskier now it was right by my ear.

"H-hi?"

"Yeah, hi! Um, look, I ... we were wondering ... if you're not doing anything tomorrow, would you and Stan like to come over for lunch? I always do a roast with all the trimmings on a Sunday. Sort of a family tradition."

I rattled out the words so rapidly, I wasn't sure if he'd understood.

"Uh..."

"It was Katie's idea," I laughed nervously. "She ... we wanted to thank you for helping us yesterday. God knows how long we'd have been stuck at the side

58

of the road if you hadn't come along, and there was no signal on my cell phone, and those lug nuts were just about glued on..."

His hesitation had me gripping the phone like I was choking it.

"*Oh...*"

"Great!" I said brightly, then cringed. Maybe he hadn't been saying 'okay'. Maybe he'd been trying to say something completely different.

"Uh, was that 'okay', you'll come, or 'okay', you'll think about it?"

"*N-no...*"

My heart sank and I felt sick. You couldn't get clearer than 'no'.

"Oh, well, that's fine. I thought I'd ask..."

"*Ah ... um ... I'm v-v-veg ... vegetarian,*" he finally managed to say.

"Oh! *Oh?* Oh, really? But you said you feed Stan bacon and hotdogs..." my words trailed off.

"*Y-yes.*"

"So, you're vegetarian but you cook bacon for Stan?"

There was another pause, and I imagined him nodding into the phone.

"I can work with that," I said. "Um, so, I'll text you the address. Okay. Great. See you tomorrow. And Stan. Bye. Tomorrow. Yeah, bye."

I hung up, flustered but relieved.

"I guess we've got a date," I muttered to myself.

No, no, not a date. I couldn't think like that. And for all I knew he was dating Stella. *Please, please don't be dating Stella.*

When I told Katie that Alex and Stan were definitely coming for lunch, she shrieked with delight, then immediately ran to her bedroom to decide what to wear. She was so much more like Stella than like me. But now I thought about it, I had no idea what I should wear. Which outfit said friendly (but not easy), cute (but not too cute, not trying too hard), interested (but not desperate). So ... that was a cute nun's habit. Right.

And then, of course, I couldn't sleep that night.

I second-guessed my decision to invite Alex for lunch. What if we were sitting there drinking coffee after coffee in awkward silence? Just because I was attracted to him, didn't mean it was right for me to invite him into our home. *Oh God! What had I done?*

Anxiety made me jittery. *What if he spends the whole meal mute? What if he's already regretting it? Does he just feel sorry for me, or maybe he just said yes because he feels obliged because I'm Stan's vet?*

At 4AM, I turned on my laptop and started looking up vegetarian recipes. I nearly passed out from shock when I saw how many ingredients were needed for a nut roast. I wondered if he'd think I was cheap if I just ran to the store and bought some veggie burgers. But then again, I had promised a home-cooked meal.

Finally, I found a recipe for vegetable lasagna that was near enough like the meat-based one for me to feel confident I could pull it off. Then I'd throw together a little tossed salad ... yep, that would do it.

Then I started wondering what he'd think of our home, which was a small duplex with a tiny front yard and a larger one in the back. His home was set on nine acres of the town's best real estate, and Spen said the cabin now looked like it belonged in a magazine.

That thought had me cleaning and tidying until a grumpy Katie traipsed down the stairs, scowling at the vacuum cleaner.

I had her straightening the throw pillows on the sofa and dusting the bookshelves before she got breakfast. Mom-style tough love.

Of course, the lasagna took longer to make than I'd anticipated, and I was running around like a chicken without its head, still getting ready when Katie yelled to tell me that they'd arrived. Five minutes early. Darn it!

I opened the front door before Alex had even rung the bell, only to find Stan with his leg cocked, watering my neighbor's flowerbed.

"Mom! Stan's weeing on Mr. Grimson's roses. He's gonna be mad!"

Alex reddened and whispered something to Stan who looked up at him with innocent eyes then bobbed his heavy head as if to say, *When a guy's gotta go...*

I couldn't help laughing as Katie pressed her hands over her mouth, trying to hold in a fit of giggles.

"Oh dear!" I said, smiling. "Mr. Grimson is very particular about his roses."

"S-sorry," Alex stuttered. "Stan, apologize to Dawn!"

Instead, Stan peered around to inspect his bottom.

"I think you'd better come in," I said, still chuckling.

But before Alex followed me inside, he reached into the truck for what looked like a box of candy. Damn, he had a great ass, his jeans clinging to him as he stretched and bent, those long, powerful legs straining against the worn denim. But instead of his usual ratty t-shirts, he was wearing a crisp white button-down. He looked delicious.

"Mom, you're blushing," Katie announced in her bell-like voice.

Alex turned around and caught my deer-in-the-headlights expression as my gaze dropped from his ass to the ground. Had he guessed that I'd been checking him out? I was mortified.

He took it all in his stride, but I was sure he knew what I'd been doing. He passed me a box of Swiss chocolates, and then rendered me mute by placing a sweet kiss on my cheek.

God, he smelled good, too.

"She really likes you," Katie said loudly. "She spent forever trying to decide what to wear."

"Katie!" I hissed.

"And she got the fancy guest towels out, even though Mom said she was saving them for when the President visits."

Whoosh! My cheeks flared with heat, and I threw an accusing look at Katie that said she'd be doing chores until she started drawing a pension. I snuck a look at Alex, and I was pretty certain he was trying to contain a smile, but was nice enough not to show it.

Then he gave Katie a present, too, taking the heat off of me.

"For you, Katie-kay," he said.

He used my pet name for her, and the few defenses I had left crumbled to dust. I closed my eyes, offering up a small prayer that he wasn't dating my sister. Or anyone else.

Katie held her book tightly, her eyes widening with happiness and surprise.

"Oh, wow! 'Walter the Farting Dog'! Oh, look at that picture. Aw, Stan, this one looks like you."

Alex seemed a little nervous, as if unsure how his gift would be received, and even though Katie's pleasure was evident, I rushed to reassure him.

"That was thoughtful of you, Alex. She'll love it. And thank you for the candy—we'll both love that."

He nodded and smiled, relief in his eyes.

It wasn't a beaming smile, it wasn't a grin, but it was a start.

I smiled back at him. "Well, come on into the house of crazy."

He stepped into the living room, his eyes taking it all in, and I wondered how it seemed to him. It was furnished in shades of blue and cream with the throw pillows cluttering up the sofa. It looked feminine and homey. A little tired, if I was honest. All of my child support was paid into a trust fund for Katie. I refused to touch my ex's money. It was all for Katie to pay for her college one day, and except for a weekend each month or thereabouts, I thought of myself as a single parent.

Alex followed us out to the deck where I'd set a small table next to the porch swing.

Stan plodded behind, then flopped down on the cool grass and stretched out, making himself at home. Katie immediately went to sit with him and started telling him some long, convoluted story about her friends and what they got up to at school. Stan yawned and snuffled happily as Katie stroked his ears, every now and then leaning down to whisper a secret to him.

And I was left alone with Alex. He chose to sit on the porch swing, his long legs out in front of him, relaxed as he rested one ankle on top of the other, his bent knees rocking the swing slowly.

I sat on one of the chairs I'd put by the table. Sharing a swing with him seemed ... too personal. Yes, far too date-like.

"How's Stan been? Any problems?" I asked in a friendly but neutral voice, reminding myself that for all I knew he'd been hooking up with Stella. *Please not!*

"N-no. No bones yet... "

"I'm afraid those days are probably over, but if he wants to try it won't do any harm either."

He sighed and looked down at Stan.

I hated to think of him getting old, too, but the evidence was there. His muzzle had turned from gray to white in the last two months, and he seemed to have slowed down a lot.

Alex glanced up at me and I realized that I'd been caught staring at him again.

"Where did you rescue him from?" I asked quickly, hoping my cheeks weren't as red as they felt.

"M-my brother. He was a Marine. Afghanistan. S-stan..."

"Oh," I said softly. "He's named Stan because he came from Afghani*stan?* That couldn't have been easy—bringing him over here."

He shook his head.

"You said your bother *was* a Marine. He's not anymore?"

He closed his eyes as his face filled with pain. And I had my answer.

"I'm so sorry," I said quietly.

A small piece of the puzzle fell into place.

He'd lost his brother, and all he had left of him was the dog that he'd rescued. It explained why Stan hadn't been neutered or microchipped. It might even explain why Alex seemed so alone, although I sensed there was more to his story. Not forgetting his startling transformation which left so many questions unanswered. If this now was how he usually looked, why had he let everything go? And what had made him change his mind and stop hiding behind all that hair and long beard?

Everything I learned about him intrigued me more. He was an enigma.

I could tell that talking about his brother had upset him, so hesitatingly, I laid my hand on his arm. He looked up at me and this time he didn't look away. It was just a moment, but it felt as if something important had passed between us. Something like friendship, maybe more.

"You're talking," I said with a sudden smile of realization as my hand fell back to my lap. "But you've always been able to talk to Katie."

"Yes. Stan, Katie ... and now you..."

My smile faded as his expression became serious, and he leaned in toward me.

"I ... I..."

Then my darn phone rang and I huffed in frustration, apologizing as I got up to take the call.

Did I imagine that? Had he been about to kiss me?

For once, I was actually grateful that a sales call had interrupted me. I needed to regroup. I couldn't let myself get carried away. *Could I?*

I poured a glass of water from the tap and took a long, cooling drink.

Katie was still chattering away to Stan, making me smile. But then I heard what she was saying and my attempt to relax and calm down came to a shuddering halt.

"If Mom and Alex get married, you can come and live with me," Katie was saying as Stan listened, his head cocked to one side. "And then they can have a baby and I'd have a little sister like my friend Marie at school. But I don't want a brother. Boys are a pain."

Emotions burned through me, a wildfire of sensations: embarrassment that Alex had heard her and might suspect my motives; but also loss. Katie's loss, my loss—the family we'd never had. The father she saw infrequently and paid her scant attention when he was there—a man who never put her first. The sister who'd given me up for reasons too painful to explain. And now Katie was weaving Alex into that tangled and knotted tapestry.

Why had she chosen him? What in her child's psyche told her that he was father material?

I reminded myself that I knew nothing about him. *Nothing.* For all I knew he could have a family already, maybe children of his own that he never saw. I'd made too many assumptions about him that had been wrong before. I needed to be wiser—or at least less trusting than my daughter.

Alex stepped down from the deck and Katie paused in her rambling, one-sided conversation. She wasn't the least embarrassed about what he must have overheard.

I watched for a moment, my heart beating too fast, as Katie showed Alex how to make a daisy chain. He listened to her carefully, nodded at her instructions, then patiently wove a long chain of tiny flowers that Katie hung around Stan's neck.

She clapped her hands in delight, although Stan's mournful expression was less enthusiastic.

It was a small, perfect moment.

"You really are multitalented, Alex," I teased, walking back outside. "From changing car tires to making daisy chains."

"I had to show him how to do it, Mom," Katie said, putting her hands on her hips.

He grinned up at me sheepishly, faint lines radiating from his eyes. I wondered again how old he was. Freshly shaved, he could have been anything from late twenties. Surely, he was at least mid-thirties. I hoped he wasn't younger than me. I'd heard Stella described as a cougar by more than one of my acquaintances in town. I didn't feel like carrying the same brand.

"Lunch is ready," I announced, smiling broadly. "Vegetable lasagna, and I've got a small plate of cold chicken and rice for Stan."

They followed me inside, Stan still wearing his daisy-chain necklace, and Katie led Alex to the sink so he could wash up. I was stunned into silence when she held his hand as she showed him to a seat at our tiny table. It was such an expression of trust, and I'd never seen her do that before. I wished I knew what Alex was thinking.

"Mom, you forgot the drinks," Katie said sternly as I sat.

"Katie," I admonished, "I didn't forget them. I thought it would be polite to ask our guest what he wanted. I've got beer, wine, juice or water," I said to Alex.

"W-water is fine."

Katie ran in to the kitchen and came back with three plastic cups and a bottle of chilled water.

"Please start."

Alex was about to take his first mouthful when Katie planted her elbows on the table and fixed him with a penetrating stare.

"Have you got a girlfriend, Alex?"

"Katie!" I snapped.

"But you wanted to know, Mom," Katie insisted crossly. "You said that you hoped he didn't have a girlfriend *or* a boyfriend."

My mouth dropped open. I *had* said that, but not to Katie. I'd been talking to Mom when she called last night, and I happened to mention to her that a friend was coming for lunch.

Katie continued with the interrogation as I gaped.

"Do you have a boyfriend, Alex?"

I managed to gather my scattered wits.

"That's enough, Katie!" I said, a clear warning in my voice as Alex shook his head, looking as if he didn't know whether to laugh or run.

"N-no."

Did he mean 'no' he didn't have a girlfriend, or 'no' he didn't have a boyfriend? It was so frustrating! Perhaps I should have let Katie continue.

Perhaps not.

I gave Katie another stern look and moved the conversation to easier subjects.

Thank goodness the lasagna had turned out well.

At first, Alex ate quietly, like a well behaved child at his parents' party, but then he began to open up—just a little.

"This is g-great," he said, as he ate everything on his plate.

"It's the first time Mom made it with just vegetables," Katie said cheerfully. "It's way better with meat. We have roast chicken or beef every Sunday. Unless I have to go to Dad's," and she pulled a face.

Alex seemed surprised. I'd never mentioned Katie's father to him, and from the look on his face I'd guess that he really hadn't heard the gossip about the whole wretched affair. In one way I was pleased, but in another, well, I'd have to tell him sometime, if whatever this was meant that we would be ... us...

Whether we became friends—or more—I wasn't looking forward to *that* conversation.

After finishing his chicken and rice in three mouthfuls, Stan parked himself between Alex and Katie, fixing his pleading eyes on each of them in turn as they finished their own food.

I'd warned Katie not to feed Stan from her plate, which meant I couldn't either, and Alex looked torn. Stan's mournful gaze grew heavier, until he rested his head on Alex's knee, his eyes following every movement of the fork.

Katie giggled.

"Did Stan do that when he was a puppy?"

"I didn't know Stan then," Alex explained quietly. "My brother rescued him two years ago and Stan came to live with me."

Katie's eyes grew huge. "Was he an orphan?"

"I guess, but not anymore."

She stroked Stan's head and accidentally dropped a piece of pasta onto the deck. I pretended not to see and didn't say anything. Besides, Stan was too quick and inhaled it before it was taken away from him. I smiled to myself: pretty good moves for an old dog.

"Why don't you eat meat?" Katie asked. "Bacon is soooo good, especially the way Mom makes it, really crispy."

"I like animals," Alex said simply.

Katie squinted at him, as if expecting something more. I think I was, too, because I realized that both of us were staring at him.

"We have apple pie and ice cream for dessert," I said, quickly changing the subject, and Katie gave a happy squeal, heading for the fridge.

Over pie and ice cream, I talked a little about life in Girard, explaining that I went to school at Penn State University.

We both tried to get Alex to talk about himself, but it was with extreme reluctance that he offered a few facts. He'd grown up in Minnesota and the mid-West, and had studied engineering and architecture at Northwestern. Of course, that left a significant gap between college and now, but I had a past that I didn't want to talk about either—Katie's dad, for one.

But the best part of the conversation was that Alex was hardly stuttering at all. I loved that he felt relaxed with us. Honestly? I loved it too much and I wanted to know so much more: what made it worse, what made it better? Had he always stuttered? From the little I knew of it, speech therapy helped some people. I wanted to know if he'd tried it, but I didn't think I'd earned the right to ask. Not yet.

"So, you moved here from Colorado?" I asked, hoping to learn little a about his life since school.

The ice cream slipped from his spoon as he frowned, then nodded. Silence reigned before he turned the conversation back to me.

"Have you l-lived here all your life?"

"Not yet," I joked.

Alex laughed, and it was wonderful to hear. But I guess after that maybe we did agree to save more personal questions for another time. *I really hoped there'd be another time, another not-date.*

After lunch, Katie took Stan for a walk around the garden. Mostly this meant that he would sniff at a shrub, pee on it, and Katie would shriek with laughter. I didn't mind. Besides, it gave me a chance to talk to Alex alone.

And I had one crucial question to ask him.

He helped me carry everything back into the kitchen, and was midway through stacking the dishwasher when I managed to work up the nerve to ask the question that had been burning on my tongue for the last two hours.

"Alex, I know this is none of my business, but I have to ask—are you seeing my sister?"

He paused and looked up at me, his gaze direct.

"No," he said firmly. "I'm not."

A small part of me wanted to cheer, but I hadn't finished yet.

"Did you ... date her?" I asked, almost afraid to hear that they'd hooked up after Spen's party.

"No, we never dated ... or anything else."

I bit my lip, frowning. "Because at the barbeque she said..."

"I know what she said," he interrupted, "but it was to get back at her ex-husband. You introduced us, remember? I p-promise you..."

What was he promising me? That he had no interest in my sister? That he was here because...?

"Sorry," I said uneasily, "it's just that things between me and Stella are ... complicated. I don't know if it's possible for it to get any worse, I just wouldn't want to risk finding out."

He sighed and stared into the garden, his eyes following Katie and Stan as they ambled around the backyard.

"Dawn, I haven't dated anyone in a long while."

I gazed at him skeptically. "Really? Why?"

He looked away. "Coming here has been ... a fresh s-start for me."

"You don't like to talk about your past."

"Neither do you," he said, raising one eyebrow.

I smiled thinly. "True." Then I sighed. "So where does that leave us? If anywhere..."

I was standing at the sink, my arms immersed in hot soapy water, when he closed the dishwasher door and stood behind me, resting his hands lightly on my waist. I jumped slightly, shocked, but very happy with this unexpected turn of events. He seemed so shy, I would never have guessed he could be so ... so...

His hands tightened on my waist and I felt his warm lips brushing the side of my neck as he kissed down to my shoulder. I rolled my head to the side and let out a long breath.

"Thank you for inviting us," he whispered against my burning skin, his breath cooling and igniting me. "It's been a good day."

I turned around so our bodies were pressed close together, my wet hands clasped around his neck.

Staring into my eyes, he leaned down and kissed my lips, searching, seeking.

"Is this okay?" he asked quietly.

"Um, it's been a while for me, as well," I said truthfully.

He started to move away, giving me some space, but I held him firmly.

"I didn't say no," I reminded him gently.

His arms circled me again as our eyes met, studying each other.

I watched, fascinated, as his irises shifted between several shades of golden-brown. They were a rich honey color when he was happy or laughing, which wasn't as often as I'd like; almost teak when he was concentrating on something; and a dark mahogany when he was aroused. Like now.

Faint lines radiated from the corners of his eyes; arcs curved into each side of his mouth, not quite dimples. And I could see a smattering of light brown hair where the buttons of his shirt were undone, decorating his firm chest and hard slab of muscle that I remembered so vividly.

Then he leaned down to kiss me again, and this time I kissed him back. As soon as I felt his mouth on mine, I couldn't stop myself. I kissed him until all I could see were stars bursting behind my tightly closed eyelids.

His lips were soft but firm, gentle yet certain, and when I opened my mouth, he didn't hesitate, kissing me with passion and determination, filling my mouth with a hungry surge, nothing hesitant or unsure. It was a man's kiss, a man who knew how to kiss a woman in a way that made her knees weak. I wouldn't have imagined he'd be so forceful, so assured, taking and giving in equal amounts. I didn't know what to think, but my body was way ahead of me.

His arms tightened on my waist and his hips pushed me backwards, pinning me to the sink. He was aroused, hard and hot against my body.

"Alex," I gasped into his mouth, as I tried to push him away.

I was a little embarrassed that I was behaving like a horny teenager on a first date, but mostly I was worried that Katie would walk in on us.

"Alex," I said again, asking him to meet my eyes as he stared at my heaving chest, "I liked it. Very much, but my daughter is just outside."

He nodded and took a step away from me, his eyes still heated and intense, an obvious bulge behind his zipper.

"It's okay," I said, forcing a smile and resting my hand lightly on his arm. "I just can't get carried away."

At which point Stan wandered through the kitchen and into the living room. I heard a soft thud and knew that he was lying on the carpet. Alex grabbed the drying towel to cover up his erection just as Katie waltzed into the kitchen. She stared at us critically.

"Were you guys making out?" she asked, wrinkling her nose.

My eyes went wide and I opened my mouth to deny it, but Alex's expression said it all.

"You shouldn't do it in front of me," Katie said grumpily, "I'm just a kid. I'm not supposed to see stuff like that. It could *scar* me."

Alex raised his eyebrows, evidently trying to hold back a smile.

I turned to watch Katie slump down next to Stan who was snoring loudly. She leaned down to whisper something to him, a smile on her face.

This was new territory for me, and I wasn't sure what to say, not in front of

Alex, at least. And the little minx who called herself my daughter, she knew it. She also knew that there'd be special 'mommy and me' time later.

But it reminded me—as if I needed it—that dating a man, any man, meant I was inviting him into my daughter's life as well as my own. And Alex had made it very clear there were things he didn't want to talk about. I should be wary, but with the memory of his burning lips on mine, I couldn't find it in myself to be distant or sensible.

Alex was watching Katie and Stan with a small, amused smile on his face. He seemed perfectly relaxed in my living room, content with our company, and easy in himself, which was something I'd rarely seen.

I checked my watch, surprised by how late it was.

"Katie, time for bed, sweetie."

"Mom!"

"Go on now. Brush your teeth, wash your face, get your pajamas on and jump into bed. I'll be in shortly."

Huffing and sighing, she slunk out of the room, giving me a taste of what teenagerdom would look like.

Alex turned his head and looked at me, still smiling, still relaxed.

"She's a great kid."

"I'm glad you think so. I do, too. Most of the time," I laughed. "When she's not embarrassing me, that is."

"I guess it comes with the territory," he said, sounding almost wistful.

"You never wanted kids?"

The words had just slipped out, and I wanted to stuff them back immediately and rewind the clock. But I couldn't.

Alex seemed to take the question in his stride, but when I thought about it later, his answer was evasive.

"Being a father is a big responsibility."

I wasn't sure what to say to that. Yes, he was right, but not all fathers felt the weight of that responsibility.

"I was surprised when you phoned me," he said.

I laughed a little, the sound embarrassed.

"Do you mind?"

"No, I'm really pleased you called. Surprised, but pleased. I..."

Katie interrupted whatever he was going to say. She was dressed for bed, wearing a pajama set with teddy bears on it.

"Alex, will you read to me? You promised."

I raised my eyebrows questioningly, but Katie wasn't looking at me.

"Will you? Please?"

Alex looked surprised but not reluctant. I figured if he didn't want to do it, he'd find an excuse not to. But I wasn't sure how *I* felt about it. If anyone else had said they'd let a man they didn't know very well in their daughter's bedroom alone, I'd nominate them for Worst Mom of the Year immediately.

"I'll tuck you in, and Alex can read to you," I suggested.

"Okay," Katie smiled, pleased that she'd gotten her way.

"Just ten minutes," I warned.

"Mom!" pouted Katie, but didn't argue further.

She knew I took bedtime seriously.

Still chattering at top speed, she took Alex by the hand for the second time that day and led him up the stairs into her bedroom with me following behind, almost redundant.

I saw Alex blink at the explosion of pink that was Katie's room, then manfully remove Barley Bear from a chair and pull it up to her bed.

I tucked her in and stepped back as she handed Alex a book.

"This chapter," she said imperiously.

"Please," I reminded her softly.

"This chapter, please, Alex, pretty please with a cherry on top," said my smartass daughter.

I threw her another look which she ignored, and I retreated to the hallway, pretending to straighten all the photo frames on the wall as I listened to the soft murmur of voices, and then the soothing tones of Alex reading to my daughter.

I felt a lump in my throat as I stood there listening to the rumble of his voice, the patience and pleasure expressed in every word. Katie's father didn't read to her, had never read to her. It wasn't fair.

I leaned against the wall, choked with unwanted emotions, memories of my own father reading stories to me, to Stella, his favorite part of the day, and ours.

As Alex read 'What Katy Did Next', diligently acting out the voices of genteel women-folk from a century in the past, my eyes blurred.

Was he the right man at the wrong time, or just the wrong man? I didn't know. Maybe there was no right or wrong, but just two people who were fumbling their way through life.

Finally, Katie was silent, and I heard Alex switch off her bedside light and tiptoe out of the room.

Wiping away a stray tear, I headed to the kitchen to make coffee.

When he appeared behind me, I'd managed to pull myself together.

"How did it go?"

"She didn't yell at me."

"Hmm, seems you passed the test." I looked at him thoughtfully. "You've never read a bedtime story before, have you?"

"Nope, a bedtime-story first-timer," he admitted. "Couldn't you tell?"

"No, you're a natural. Believe me, you'd know if Katie didn't like you."

"And she's given me permission to kiss her mom," he said.

I wanted him, but I couldn't have him. Not like this.

"I can't ask you to stay the night," I said, in a quiet but firm voice, "but I don't want you to go yet either."

He gave a small smile.

"Thanks. I wasn't sure when you invited me ... if it was a date?"

He ended the sentence as a question.

"I wasn't sure either," I said honestly, "but I think it is—if you want it to be."

We stared at each other across the room as I waited for him to answer.

But he didn't.

"Should I put some music on?" I asked, hoping to break the sudden awkward tension.

He nodded and retreated to the sofa while I knelt on the floor and flicked through my ancient CD collection. Rock was too loud, Country was too depressing—and he might hate it, Soul was too ... everything. Suddenly, I found the perfect accompaniment to silence.

"Do you like guitar music?"

He shrugged, his intense gaze saying he didn't care about the choice of music.

Soon the soft sounds of a Spanish guitar floated out through the speakers; it was emotional, beautiful, and the atmosphere in the room shifted, building, until I could feel it pressing down on me; or maybe it was spiraling out of me, and the way I felt was affecting the music. I couldn't tell.

When I'd gathered every scrap of bravery, I walked toward him slowly and lowered myself across his thighs, so my knees were pressing into the back of the sofa and my body was hovering over his.

He didn't smile and he didn't seem surprised. He simply rested his hands on my hips, his fingers twitching over the fabric of my skirt, and watched my face as if he could read the future in it.

I felt him hardening beneath me, and I wanted to say something, to tell him how unlike me this was, how much I wanted him, and how much that scared me. I couldn't find the words.

My mouth opened, but no sound came out. Frustration washed over me, and maybe that meant I understood what it was like to be him a little more.

His fingers dug into my hips as if he was anchoring himself in place. I raised my shaking hands, cupping his cheeks and lowering my lips to his.

Alex seemed frozen in place, so this time, I took the lead, teasing his mouth open until he responded, his hands gliding up to my waist and tugging me against him.

The intensity of our kiss increased until I was holding his face fiercely, and his fingers dug into the soft flesh at my waist with a grip that was almost brutal.

I whimpered when he lowered me to the sofa, noises coming from my mouth that I'd never heard before. He kept his weight on his arms so he didn't crush me, but I could feel the length of his body against mine, and the few inches between our hips didn't feel safe at all.

I ran my hands up his back, dragging his t-shirt with my nails, feeling the breadth of his shoulders, the strength in his bunched muscles. God, this was too much and too little. I was trying to stop, trying to take it slowly, trying to race ahead. My brain was scrambled.

I wanted to be brave, I wanted to be slutty, I wanted to be the woman who threw caution to the wind. But I couldn't. Shouldn't.

I pulled away slowly, and he started to reach for me again, but managed to stop himself. His eyes crinkled, as if he was in pain, as if that thin veneer of civilization was close to being stripped away, his baser instincts taking over.

He leaned his forehead against mine.

"I know," I whispered. "I'm sorry, but we have to stop. Katie could walk in at any second and I can't..."

His body eased away from me, but I could feel the tension in his arms as I gripped his biceps. I felt as taut as a bow string, my body tingling with suppressed energy. I breathed out slowly, calming my racing heart, but there was nothing I could do about the rigid flesh pressing between his jean-clad legs. He knew I could feel it, but I didn't say anything and he didn't move away.

We stared at each other, eyes darkened with lust, truth and lies hovering between us, an ocean of doubt.

Eventually, he sat up slowly, releasing me reluctantly.

"I want you to stay," I said softly, "and that's why you have to go. Do you understand?"

He nodded once, and I think he did understand. I was protecting myself— and Katie.

He scraped his hands over his hair, blowing out a long, frustrated breath, then surprised me with the smile that stole across his face.

"C-come over ... tomorrow. You and Katie. It's going to be hot. We can ... swim."

I matched his smile with relief and happiness.

Tomorrow was Labor Day, but the only plans Katie and I had included a gallon of Rocky Road and a 'High School Musical' movie marathon.

"A swim in the lake?"

He nodded.

"It sounds wonderful, and I'd love to see your place. Should we come in the afternoon?"

"For lunch."

I laughed softly. "I thought you said you couldn't cook."

"Not *well*. Stan likes my cooking."

"How reassuring. I'm sure Stan's a very discerning diner."

Stan opened one eye at the sound of his name.

He lurched upright, stretching out his spine with a faint popping sound, then he plodded to the sofa and rested his head on Alex's knee, gazing up at him adoringly

I probably had the same expression on my face. Which was kind of pathetic.

Alex stroked Stan's head, sighed and pulled his keys out of his pocket. I tried to look away while he discreetly adjusted himself. But the knowledge that he was still hard under those worn jeans heated my whole body with a blush of arousal.

"Time to go, Stan," Alex said quietly. "Say thank you."

Stan blinked, his tail wagging tiredly, then licked my hand.

I laughed.

"Love you, too, you big lug." I turned to smile at Alex. "So, we'll see you tomorrow. Both of you."

And my careless, thoughtless heart raced as the words etched themselves into my brain.

He kissed me chastely on the cheek, much the way he had when he'd arrived hours earlier, but a far cry from the scorching kisses of a few minutes ago. It did nothing to cool the heat I felt for him.

I watched him load Stan into the truck, and with a brief wave, he drove away.

I wrapped my arms around myself as his tail-lights disappeared into the night.

That was *not* how I'd expected today to end.

I admit that I'd been a little intimidated inviting Alex into our home. Not just because he was this large, brooding presence, but awful as it seems, because of his speech impediment. I'd wondered if we'd all be sitting there mute. Although his silence wasn't the deliberate aggression that Katie's father had wielded like a weapon, it was simply the absence of words. But Katie liked him and had conversations with him from the very beginning.

So, I'd taken a chance. And from the moment he arrived, he fit.

His thoughtful gift for Katie moved me. It was perfect. And I loved my candy. I'd planned to save it, but now I felt like eating it all in one go.

I sighed.

Admitting that I was attracted to him—that I liked him—it had raised the stakes. I wanted to be brave, I wanted to open myself to the possibility of love. But I had Katie's needs to consider.

His eyes had flared when I kissed him, and I felt like I'd lit a fuse that I couldn't put out. I'd definitely felt how aroused he'd been. I'd been so close to inviting him into my heart—and into my bed.

But no matter how handsome he was, especially when he remembered to smile, no matter how kind he was to Katie, or how much I was attracted to him, I couldn't take a risk tonight.

His beautiful eyes had seemed so wounded.

Telling him to leave was the right thing to do.

I felt awful.

And then relieved when he invited us over tomorrow.
Then worried.
And nervous.
God, what a mess.

Chapter Seven

ENERGIZING

Dawn

Katie was excited when I told her we were spending the day at the lake. And she did her happy dance when I said we'd be with Alex and Stan, although I couldn't tell you which of them she liked the most. She adored Stan, treating him somewhere between a child and the brother she'd never had. And Alex ... I knew she liked him a lot. Too much, when I thought about how few times they'd actually met. But I couldn't deny that both of us were excited to see him again so soon.

I packed the car with beach towels, sunscreen and bottles of water, then wrapped up as much of yesterday's leftover food as I could, and we piled into the car, singing along to songs from 'Frozen'. Not very seasonal, in my view, but Katie sang them all year round regardless of the weather. We knew them off by heart.

"Is Aunty Stella going to be there?" she asked suddenly.

"Not today."

Katie sighed, but didn't say anything else. I wondered how long it would be before she demanded answers—I had no idea how I'd explain why I'd fallen out with my sister.

The turning to Alex's cabin was half a mile past Stella's, but far less well signposted. In fact, I only made the turn at the last second because I spotted a gap in the trees. We bounced along the dirt until the tunnel of foliage opened into a sunlit glade.

It seemed magical, and the profound silence was almost unearthly, a quiet paradise, an Eden.

"Beautiful," I whispered.

The cabin was completely transformed and quite lovely—a two-story, white-painted clapboard cottage with a deep porch, protected by the wide branches of a large copper beech tree. As the sun struck the leaves, the whole house was bathed with soft, amber light, and in the distance, the lake glittered, welcoming us.

I was about to drive closer and park, when Alex came striding from the side of the house, his eyes stormy and a deep frown creasing his forehead.

He ground to a halt when he saw us, his expression distinctly unfriendly.

He held up his hand like a traffic cop, forcing me to halt.

The smile froze on my face and Katie looked shocked. Then Alex turned and stomped away from us.

"What's wrong, Mom?" Katie asked softly, clutching the packet of dog treats that she'd brought for Stan.

"I'm not sure, honey. Wait here a sec and let me go talk with Alex."

I opened the car door quietly and slid out, staring in the direction he'd gone.

I knew he heard me walking up behind him, my slow footsteps crunching on the gravel.

"You should stay in the c-car," he said tiredly, glancing over his shoulder.

He didn't seem angry anymore which I took as a good sign.

"Alex, you're scaring me a little. What's going on? Oh!"

Then I saw what he'd been trying to hide—a dead raccoon. Very dead. As in missing its body, one glassy eyeball swinging from its skull.

He shoveled the head into a garbage sack, an expression of revulsion on his face.

"Did ... did Stan do that?"

"N-no!" he said angrily, his stutter returning. "N-no!"

He took a couple of seconds to breathe deeply.

"No," he said again, more calmly this time. "I didn't want Katie to see."

"Okay. Um ... do you want us to go...?"

He shook his head, frowning again. Then without speaking, he stalked off, the garbage bag clutched in his hand. I didn't want to ask how he was going to dispose of the raccoon's grizzly remains.

Uncertain whether or not it was a good idea to stick around, I walked back to the car. But then Stan appeared at the front door, his tongue lolling out of his mouth in a wide smile.

Katie waved, almost as if she expected him to raise a paw and wave back, but he did wag his tail, and she giggled. I decided that we'd wait for a while. If Alex's strange mood didn't improve, we would leave.

Although I was disturbed by the dismembered raccoon. I knew that they were preyed on by bobcats and Eastern coyotes—but those were usually found in far more wooded areas and further away from humans. Something in the forest must have killed it, but what? It was odd.

Hiding my concerns from Katie, I parked in front of the cottage and she leapt out, skipping straight to Stan and talking a mile a minute.

I opened my trunk to pull out the picnic basket I'd brought, and jumped when Alex appeared suddenly behind me.

I held my hand over my heart, feeling the wild rhythm under my trembling fingers.

"You scared me," I said, attempting to laugh.

Alex grimaced and shoved his hands into the pockets of his shorts.

"S-sorry," he mumbled.

We stared at each other awkwardly, until he leaned over me, lifted out the picnic basket with one hand, plucked my beach towels from me with the other, and walked away toward the lake, Stan ambling after him, Katie by his side.

With nothing else to do, I slung my purse over my shoulder, locked the car and followed.

The track was thick with dust, sending up tiny puffs as I walked, and soon my white sneakers had turned a light brownish-gray.

Alex was wearing flip-flops, blue board shorts and a loose t-shirt. Even so, I could see that his shoulders were tense and he seemed far more anxious than yesterday. If it hadn't been for Katie chatting to Stan, oblivious of the strained silence between us, I would have turned around and left.

At least the view was worth the journey.

The lake sparkled in the sunshine, ripples lapping against the shoreline. The bright blue sky was cloudless, and a soft breeze made the tops of the trees murmur. It was very lovely, tranquil, and strangely soothing.

I glanced across at Alex whose lips were pressed together grimly as he watched me from under his lashes. When he saw me looking, he abruptly turned away.

I discreetly checked my phone, relieved to see that I had a clear signal. Alex was making me nervous.

He laid the picnic basket on top of a large blanket, and I could see three huge coolers and a portable grill next to a small campfire, all ready to cook with. Not only that, but he'd bought a set of pink paper plates decorated with rainbows and matching plastic cups. Even the plastic knives and forks were pink. And I knew he'd bought them especially for Katie.

All my unease dissolved, and I smiled at the thought of him trawling through Walmart for everything he could find that was pink.

"Thank you," I said sincerely. "This is amazing. Seriously, Alex. Thank you."

I was rewarded with the tiniest smile as he shrugged his shoulders. Then he kneeled down to place the grill pan over the fire, sitting back on his heels as it began to heat up. He'd ringed his cooking area with a circle of flat stones and he also had a bucket of water standing by. Three small cushions were laid out on the blanket, and there was a soccer ball and several of Stan's toys. I could see that he'd worked really hard to make today fun for us.

"Mom, Stan wants to go swimming? Can we?"

Stan yawned and flopped down on the blanket, his head on a green cushion, not the least interested in swimming or any other kind of activity.

"I think Stan would rather have lunch and take a nap," I pointed out. "I'll go swimming with you later."

"Mo-om!" she whined.

"I'll take her," Alex said softly.

"But you're getting lunch ready," I argued, pointing at the uncooked hotdogs and veggie burgers lined up next to the sizzling pan.

"It can wait ... and she shouldn't swim right after eating." He paused, glancing between me and Katie as if worried that he'd said the wrong thing. "If that's okay with you..."

Katie turned her pleading eyes to mine, and I knew I'd been outvoted. Not that I cared in the least.

"Fine," I said with a smile. "If Alex doesn't mind taking you now..."

Whatever else I might have said was drowned out as Katie screeched with pleasure and threw herself at Alex.

I almost laughed seeing the shock on his face as my eight year-old daughter clung to him like a baby koala. He definitely wasn't a man who'd been around children much, but he rallied at the last moment, cautiously patting her on the head the same way I'd seen him pet Stan.

I smiled encouragingly and he seemed to relax a little more.

Katie hopped on one foot as she kicked off her sandals then shimmied out of her shorts and t-shirt, her pink bathing suit almost neon.

I turned to say something to Alex, but my words dried on my tongue as I saw him pull off his own t-shirt and step towards the lake.

He was perfect. I mean his body was perfect. Better than I'd remembered. Smooth, tan skin; sculpted muscles and long, loose limbs. The smattering of chest hair that I'd seen before was almost golden in the sunlight, and where most men stowed their beer belly, Alex had a real six-pack, a ridge of defined abdominals. And then he held out his hand to Katie, and my remaining defenses crumbled.

They walked into the water together, hand-in-hand, Katie tiptoeing as the cool ripples lapped against her knees.

Her father had missed all her firsts: her first word, her first step, her first day at school. He didn't read to her at night, and to my knowledge, he'd never once taken her swimming during those once-a-month visits. And those were cancelled or postponed more often than not with short notice.

I smiled as Katie splashed water at Alex, braver than her mother, and her laughter rang out over the still lake.

He chuckled, wiping the water from his eyes, and waded deeper until it was up to his muscled thighs. He dived into the lake, leaving barely a ripple, and appeared several yards later, shaking the water from his hair. I watched, mesmerized, as his arms and chest glistened, droplets clinging to him; but it was his smile, a huge, happy smile that shot an arrow straight to my heart.

And I knew, right then, with the lake glinting in the sunlight, the scent of wood smoke drifting in the air, that I'd forever associate these things with Alex. The look in his eyes that said what his lips couldn't.

He was happy.

My throat contracted sharply and then I smiled back, a swell of joy filling me.

The rest of the day was just as perfect. After they'd swum and played in the water for nearly an hour, I watched Alex build up our small campfire again, snapping twigs with his strong hands to make more kindling, adding logs to the flames. It was the simple pleasure of seeing an attractive man doing physical work. The play of his muscles in the sunshine, the dappled sunlight across his back, his small frown of concentration, the color rising in his cheeks as his body warmed in the summer sun. The healthy glow, a strong, masculine man.

We talked about everything and nothing, and he barely stuttered, just occasionally tripping over his words in his eagerness to share something about his cottage in the woods, the animals he'd befriended, the fox cubs who visited nightly, or about Stan.

Katie was completely at ease with him, curling into his side and laying her head on his shoulder. Oh, and getting him to wear a mudpack on his face that she promised would make him handsome. And when the mud dried and cracked and Alex washed off the rest, Katie told him it had worked. Alex laughed. A real laugh, full of contentment and peace.

But as soon as he turned away, my smile slipped. How could I protect my own heart when Katie obviously adored him already? My daughter was the reason I guarded my emotions so carefully, but she was also the weak point in my armor. And a man who'd won my child's affections was close to winning mine.

I was dozing off, well fed and contented, with Katie taking a nap next to Stan, when I cracked an eye to see Alex walking back along the track from the cottage.

"I didn't hear you leave," I said, yawning.

"Had something to do," he said, a glint of mischief in his eyes.

I sat up, more awake now.

"Hmm, that sounds suspicious! What have you been up to?"

"Don't be mad..." he began.

"Um, okay, but why would I be mad?"

He winced slightly.

"I ... I b-b-b-bought new tires for your c-car."

My eyes opened wide.

"Alex, I can't possibly accept..."

"P-please! I need you and Katie to be safe."

"I ... but ... thank you, but ... tires are expensive. I can't let you..."

"Please. Anyway, I've already put them on."

I didn't know what to say. It was one of the sweetest things anyone had ever done for me. But I didn't feel comfortable accepting such an expensive gift.

"That's really nice of you, Alex. But I'd feel better if you'd let me pay for them."

His lips turned down.

"They're a g-gift," he said quietly.

I swallowed my pride, not wanting to hurt his feelings any further.

"Thank you," I said, smiling and shaking my head at the same time. "Thank you very much."

He grinned at me and winked.

As the sun began to sink, Katie was dragging. We packed up the remains of the food and Alex promised he'd come back for the coolers later as Katie climbed onto his broad shoulders, riding back to the cottage in style.

I'd thought the outside of his house was beautiful, but the inside was astonishing. Antique hardwood floors gleamed in the muted light, and the furnishings were all new and top quality. It made my duplex seem small and shabby by comparison.

"Oh, Alex! It's so beautiful! It looks amazing. Wow! I can hardly believe it. You did all this yourself? Oh my, you should do it professionally."

I stopped and looked over at him.

"What *do* you do, for a job?"

He shrugged uncomfortably.

"Now, just this."

"Hmm," I said, narrowing my eyes. "And you went to school to study architecture and engineering?"

He looked away and didn't reply.

By now, Katie was sound asleep on the wide sofa, the deep, drugging sleep of a child who has spent the day in fresh air and sunshine, the sleep of the innocent.

Carefully, quietly, Alex covered her with a blanket, tucking in the ends so her feet wouldn't get cold. I imagined him lying there on that sofa, his large frame stretched out, Stan beside him as he watched TV or read one of the many books dotted around the living room. And I imagined lying there with him, cuddled together, the fire lit against the chill of winter.

Dreams are dangerous things—they tempt us with all the things we shouldn't want.

I had a home, a mortgage I could afford and a job I loved. And I had Katie, the bright star in my life.

But now, I was dreaming of *more*—what the woman in me wanted, and not the mother.

I'd been dismissive of friends who said that they'd experienced a soul-deep, chest-squeezing urgency for another person. An unnamed yearning. The desire to be so ridiculously, inexplicably desperate for one particular person.

But now ... now I began to understand.

I wanted Alex's body, but I wanted his smile more. I wanted his laugh, his eyes dancing with happiness, because it was so rare, and once seen, never forgotten. I wanted the closeness, the intimacy of two adults sharing a life together. I wanted someone to reassure me in the small hours of the night, to remind me that Katie was doing okay, that I wasn't a total disaster as a mother.

I was here, so close to having what I hadn't known I'd wanted until this moment ... it terrified me in new and creative ways. I wanted him. I shouldn't. But I did.

I want, I want, I want.

Alex offered me coffee, and glad of the reprieve from the intensity of his expressive eyes, I followed him into his charming, rustic kitchen, lined with new cabinets and an unlit wood-burning stove.

He made two cups of rich, aromatic coffee, and carried them out to the deck at the back, where we sat in silence, enjoying the solitude as the sun sank beyond the lake.

He sat staring out into the forest, allowing me to study his sharp profile, silhouetted against the rising moon.

Then he nudged my arm, pointing into the forest's deep shadows. Three, no four pairs of eyes gazed back at me, glittering as the porch light reflected their nervous stares. I saw Alex smile at the fox cubs who darted out, heading for Stan's food bowl.

"Oh, he won't be pleased," I whispered.

Alex smiled.

"He's used to sharing. They've been coming here every night for a while now."

"Forest foxes are usually shy."

Alex shrugged. "I started feeding them after their mother was killed."

His mood turned somber again as he watched the cubs inhale their meal and slink back to the thickening shadows.

"I had a really nice time today, Alex. We both did."

He nodded slowly, seeming to ponder my words.

"Nice. Nice?"

"You don't like that word?"

His reply wasn't acerbic, if anything, he sounded thoughtful.

"I haven't had a whole lot of nice."

I wondered if I should take his words as an opportunity to dig deeper, but he seemed more closed off now and a little sad, and I didn't want to spoil such a lovely day.

"Nice is good," I agreed evenly, and was happy when he forced a small smile. "Thank you—for everything."

I leaned across to kiss him on the cheek, surprised by my own boldness. His eyes widened and he sucked in a quick breath.

Was the world still spinning or had time frozen as we sat there, creatures in the dark our only witnesses?

Is love a disease? An affliction? Or is it something catching? Can you catch love, can you hold it in your hands, can it be communicated like a plague? Or is it like an infectious laugh that makes your eyes water and your stomach hurt, even though the joke isn't funny?

I'd begun to believe I was immune to love—the kind that exists between a man and a woman. Instead, I'd been gifted an ocean of love for my daughter. I thought perhaps that had filled me full, leaving no room for other love. Other loves.

My lips tingled from the roughness of his day-old stubble.

And is it love when you want someone's smile as much as you want their body? When their laughter softens your words to a prayer?

My heart began to race.

Or is it sheer animal lust, a torrent of hormones assaulting your blood, heating you from the inside out?

He reached out to touch me, questions in his shadowed eyes as he cupped my cheek. I sighed and leaned into him, eyelids fluttering.

My mother always says it's the softness of men that she loves most, because it's at the center of them. Their outsides are hard with muscle; their bodies large, larger than hers—or mine—heavier, stronger. So when a man's touch is soft, when his fingers drift across your skin like sunbeams, then you're seeing into his soul.

I never understood. I never believed her.

Until now.

So gently, so very gently, he pressed his dry lips against mine, and I wrapped my arms around his neck, kissing him back.

He tasted of coffee, and he smelled like sunshine and pine forest.

Gentleness turned to want, and want turned to need, and I thought my mother was wrong. I wanted to feel the strength of his body surrounding me, on top of me. I wanted to feel his hardness against me, inside me. I was wearied by supporting the weight of my family alone. I wanted someone to carry me. For just a little while. A single moment.

The wooden arm of the chair pressed into my ribs as I leaned across, and I tried to ignore it. But Alex lifted me onto his lap, shocking a gasp out of me that ended with a soft laugh, because maybe he'd read my mind, because maybe he wanted the same things I did. And then we were kissing again.

Again and again for the longest time, hesitance turning to urgency, and long languid kisses to heated mouths and hot sighs.

My fingers fumbled to find the hem of his shirt as I floundered my way down his chest, sliding my palms across warm skin that left shivers in their wake. I started pushing the material upward, and Alex leaned forward and dragged the shirt off, tossing it to the ground impatiently.

All day, I'd longed to touch, yearned to taste, feared to want. I was tired of caution, weary of wading through life alone. If this was just one night, I'd celebrate it forever, and if it was more ... well, that was a bridge still to be crossed, a land waiting for discovery.

My hands swept down his back, reading his skin with my fingers as if sight didn't exist, while we continued to kiss, tongues tasting, learning and teaching. I gripped his biceps, my fingers digging into the ridge of muscle, shuddering with pleasure as he cupped my breast with one hand, the other anchored behind my back to stop me from falling.

Too late.

I'd already fallen for Alex Winters, man of mystery, animal lover, gentle soul, wounded warrior in the battle of life. Or maybe that's just life. We're all survivors, one way or another.

My fingers drifted down to the waistband of his shorts, and his stomach contracted as his eyes closed, his groan guttural.

It was a sensual game of chess: my move, his move, mine, his, each working toward the moment of checkmate, and I'd be hoping for defeat.

His lips whispered wordlessly down my neck, kissing my throat, lower, lower, running his tongue along the scooped edge of my t-shirt.

But I was still me, and my daughter was sleeping on his sofa, just a few feet away. And what I wanted wasn't the most important thing.

I pushed lightly on his chest.

"Alex, wait."

It took a long moment for him to catch the meaning and tone of my words. His reluctance to pull away won my approval, and when he let me go without question, he won my heart.

"Katie can't see us like this."

He nodded, his face solemn in the shadows. As he stood, I slid against his body, and he held me for a second as my toes touched the wooden deck.

And then he held my hand as we tiptoed into his living room.

Katie was sprawled on the sofa, snoring softly, one hand tangled in the blanket, the other resting on Stan's thick fur.

His wise old eyes watched us as we crossed the floor, but he didn't move.

I'm on duty, he seemed to say. *Her dreams are safe with me.*

Katie was sound asleep, lost to the world, awake only to her imagination. And so I had a choice. My mommy-senses were satisfied: my daughter was well, warm and happy.

But the woman in me...

Alex sensed my hesitation and squeezed my hand, his eyebrows rising in silent query.

"She's fine," I whispered. "I just needed to see."

He smiled, his eyes resting on my daughter and then on Stan, before commanding my gaze again.

"I ... I w-want ... t-to make love. To you."

His voice wavered, but his eyes were burning with intense desire.

"Yes, I..."

Those were the only words I had time to speak, slayed by the smile of joy that lit him from within.

He kissed me deeply, big hungry kisses, his arms gathering me against his warm body. And I held my breath as he led me toward the stairs, then up, up, up.

To his bedroom.

I want. I want. I want.

Cool, white sheets touched the backs of my legs as Alex walked me to his bed, the door locked behind him.

I reached for him, pulling him closer. As I flicked my tongue at the base of his throat, he growled a quiet rumble of appreciation.

Then I moved lower, greedy for his perfect body, touching his stomach with my lips. His eyes closed and fists clenched at his sides.

As I continued to kiss all the flesh I could reach, his hands lifted my hair, reverently stroking his fingers down to the blunt ends that clung to my cheeks. Tucking the unruly strands behind my ears, he kissed my jaw, his tongue lapping against my racing pulse, then sucking not so gently.

I squirmed, and he immediately slid lower to the juncture between neck and shoulder, nipping the skin, making me jump. He laughed softly, his nose nestled in my t-shirt. Abruptly, he stood upright, and lifted me further up the bed as easily as if he was lifting a child, not 130 pounds of full-grown woman.

His dominance surprised me. Oh yes, and definitely aroused me. I hadn't expected this. Another layer to the mysterious man who was slowly peeling my clothes from my body.

He lifted my breasts to his mouth, kissing all around, plucking the nipples with his teeth, pain close to the pleasure.

I reached for the straining material of his shorts and he batted my hands away, but not before I'd felt the hot core pulsing against the thin fabric.

"But I want to..."

Undeterred, he kissed under my breasts, across my ribs, my hipbones, then pushed my thighs wide apart and pressed his face against my mound, his tongue, so stubborn in its consuming silence, now consuming me. His tanned hands against the pale flesh of my hips, the scrape of his stubble on my inner thighs.

Weeks of wondering, months of wanting, years of waiting. My body ignited, erupted, a volcano, a wildfire burning and crackling, racing across an arid landscape. I mashed my lips together, willing back sounds in the towering silence, as he whipped my pleasure higher.

All the tension inside me broke. Hotter than a comet, bright lights burst behind my eyes and my body flooded with heat, trembling from my outstretched toes to the tips of my fingers. I shuddered, my back arching as blind pleasure swept through me.

I stole a breath, and then another, as fluid and limp as seaweed after a storm.

I could smell my own arousal, and the thought sent another jet of heat blasting my blood. I opened one eye.

Alex was standing over me, his gaze serious, as if he was waiting for a verdict.

Suddenly I understood the look in his eyes: longing, desire, want. Maybe need. And the intensity of his scrutiny burned a path across my body.

I didn't have the words, so I reached for him, tugging at the waistband of his shorts. His erection had leaked, leaving a darker patch, reminding me of an essential point.

"You have protection?"

His eyebrows shot up and he spun on his heel, large hands fumbling through a drawer in his dresser. And then, triumphant, he returned, a small package in his hand and oh my God, he was smiling so brightly, his white teeth glinting.

He ripped off his clothes, urgent now, hands sheathing himself swiftly. In the moonlight, his body was a sculpture, the shadows caressing his edges, the light silvering his skin.

I grabbed his hips, tugging him closer, digging my nails into the firm globes of his ass.

Half stumbling, he lay full length against me, then began kissing my neck. My body arched, willing him closer and my thighs pressed against rigid flesh.

I wrapped my hands around him, closer, closer, and suddenly his control snapped. An 'Oh shit!' moment before plunging into a storming sea, he devoured me. And I was shocked by my own utter abandon.

He pushed against my opening, firm and insistent, bordering on desperate. It had been so long and he was so much a man, my body surged even as it protested, and then he was inside and everything became a driving need as his thrusts grew bolder. The seductive sounds of him inside me, skin slapping against skin. His woodsy musk mingling with the scent of sex. This beautiful man hammered his way into my life, one wild thrust after another.

It seemed to go on and on, thrust after thrust, a fierce frown notched between his eyebrows, his fingers gripping my hip tightly, his other hand fastened on the mattress as the bed rocked beneath me. A hurricane roaring under my skin.

Thinking absolutely nothing, feeling absolutely everything.

I hadn't expected this—Alex was usually so gentle. He'd been tender and considerate when we'd kissed. But now, his body was taking over. I could see it in the darkness of his eyes, the intensity of his expression, the taut pleasure in his face, the low grunts as his hips pounded into me relentlessly.

His voice was silenced, but his body roared.

Wild, wild passion.

He didn't, wouldn't, couldn't speak, and that made the intensity of sex with him so enthralling.

He closed his eyes, a helpless groan rolling from his throat, the cords of his neck tightly drawn. A deeper thrust, he stiffened, rigid above. And me? I was shocked out of my skin—the way he'd taken me, the ferocity and passion. And I was lost in the storm, a shipwreck survivor.

His sweat dripped onto my chest and his arms shook, but he placed a trembling kiss on my lips before he flopped onto his back.

I lay on the bed, breathless, as if someone had poured me there, my brain scrambled like cooked eggs.

My silent lover lay next to me, and without a single word, the rock steady continent of my life had become a shifting, boiling tectonic plate. The land under my feet rippled like a desert's mirage.

I was almost afraid to move in case I fell into the deep rifts our love making had created. It couldn't just be lust, could it? Unconnected to emotion?

And I was too conscious of a rising silence, so I forced myself to speak.

"That was ... amazing," I said feebly, the words inadequate for what I felt, what I'd experienced.

He rose onto one elbow, staring down at me, his eyes soft and sated.

"Because it's you."

I glowed with joy, but said nothing.

Acting like it didn't mean anything didn't alter the fact that it did.

Chapter Eight

RESOLVING

Dawn

"I was wondering…"

Alex rolled onto his side, watching me with that small, familiar smile on his face. He raised his eyebrows, waiting for me to continue.

"It's not important," I sighed.

And at that moment questions weren't important. We'd made love several times and my body was tired, or rather, deeply relaxed, but I felt so wholly alive. Electricity hummed along my nerves and sinews, and a fizz of constant arousal hovered under my skin.

The contradiction was dizzying.

Alex stroked my stomach, tracing his fingers downward, following the thin, silvery lines of stretchmarks. He'd already kissed every one of them, and made me cry when he said they were beautiful because they honored me as a mother.

I shivered with pleasure as the tips of his fingers drew patterns around my hip, then he looked up at me.

"Ask," he said.

What? Oh yes, I had a question. I wish I hadn't mentioned it now.

"Ask," he said again. "Anything."

I hesitated, not wanting to spoil the moment, but then again, he'd said I could ask him anything…

"Okay. Well, I was wondering … why did you cut your hair? And shave your beard? It seemed like … well, like you were hiding. So I wondered … what changed your mind?"

I finished lamely as his hand stilled.

Then he pulled his hand away and rolled onto his back, staring up at the freshly painted ceiling.

"I'm sorry, I..."

"No," he said. "No, don't be ... it's hard t-t-t to talk about."

"Then don't."

His head turned toward me and he smiled sadly. Then he closed his eyes.

"I didn't remember to shave," he explained simply.

I waited, expecting more.

The silence stretched uncomfortably, and I wished again I hadn't brought it up. But then he started speaking.

"When Carl died, I was devastated. He was my only brother, my own family really. And ... several other things happened at the same time, at work and ... but Carl's death was the worst. I guess I went a little crazy. I stopped going to work, stopped living, I think. I didn't shave or cut my hair for 18, no, 19 months. And then, when I started to ... wake up ... I liked that the way I looked made people think twice about talking to me. My ... my stutter was bad, so keeping people away seemed easier than trying to communicate with anyone. I think maybe you're right. I was hiding. Anyway, I just let it grow."

"You're not stuttering anymore."

He smiled softly.

"Not with you."

I chewed my lip uncertainly.

"I don't really understand. Why does it come and go like that? You don't have to answer if you don't want to."

He frowned.

"I'm not sure I can answer that in any way that makes sense. Stress, I guess. But not always. It started when I was a kid. I was about Katie's age when my mom left us, so I don't need a shrink to make that connection obvious."

"That must have been hard."

He shrugged.

"If you want the clinical definition, it's called psychogenic stuttering. The shrink told me that onset usually begins suddenly following an event that caused extreme psychological stress," and he gave me a dry look. "Characterized by repetition of the initial or stressed syllables."

"Will it go away? It has now, hasn't it?"

He shook his head.

"I don't know. Nor does anyone else. It might go, or it might be for life. I'm assuming it's here to stay, but I can't be sure."

"I can't imagine how difficult that is."

"People get impatient, finishing your sentences. It's humiliating, having someone talk for you, assuming they know what you want to say. With you and Katie, I feel ... safe is too strong a word, but I know that you won't judge me for it."

I leaned on my elbow and touched his stubbled cheek, brushing my fingers over his short hair, barely more than bristles covering his skull. His lips turned upward, and he hummed with pleasure, making me laugh quietly.

"You like that?"

"Yes," he sighed with contentment, opening one eye as he grinned up at me. "You could do that all day and I wouldn't want you to stop."

"I'm glad you cut it," I said. "In my mind, you weren't 'Mr. Winters', but 'the Mountain Man'."

He laughed. "What, like Grizzly Adams?"

"Yes, but with Stan instead of a bear."

"I think Stan would like that."

"You did seem rather unapproachable, forbidding."

His smile dropped.

"I know. That's why I cut it. That girl in the forest..." his forehead wrinkled as his face contorted at the painful memory. "I scared her. Terrified her! I didn't mean to. I hadn't thought about the way I looked for so long. I liked that people stayed away from me, but I didn't think ... I kept hearing her screams. Her parents ... they looked at me like I was some sort of monster. It really shook me up. Badly."

His face smoothed out, but he seemed so sad.

"If it hadn't been for the kittens I would have ... after I dropped them off with you, I was just so tired of it all. Being on the outside, living a half-life. I knew I had to start making an effort to ... to reintegrate ... or I'd end up being this crazy hermit who scared kids forever."

He turned to look at me.

"And by then ... I'd met you."

"Me?"

I blinked, surprised. I hadn't thought that he'd even given me a second glance.

Alex smiled.

"You were kind. Kind to Stan, kind to me. I didn't imagine this exactly," he said, waving his finger between us. "But I didn't want you to be afraid of me either. You were special."

He needed to be kissed for that.

We made love, we slept, we made love again, the whole night through. By morning, I was the worse for wear. And better. So much better. Sleep deprived and sore, but smiling stupidly.

Of course, it had to end. I had to get to work and Katie was going to spend the day at Holly's house. I'd been a very bad mom, keeping her out. And when I tried to plan what to say to her ... explain why I'd stayed the night with Alex, the words caught in my throat. I'd have to tell her *something*. But what?

Alex tugged me into the shower with him, and we enjoyed each other's bodies again in the steaming water. We didn't speak, but he was touching me the whole time, his lips curving upwards. And besides, he was a man at ease with silence.

"I have to go," I said sadly as I dressed in yesterday's clothes. "Katie is going to her friend's house, and I have work. We both need to get home and change, eat breakfast..."

"I have food."

"Ah, yes! Bacon and eggs for Stan, right?"

He grinned sheepishly.

"But unless you have Mini Wheats with Maple Brown Sugar, you'll see Katie combust."

He raised his eyebrows, skeptical.

"You've only seen her sweet side, but my daughter has a temper, believe me!"

He seemed bemused by the idea, but Katie was so like Stella, she could go off like a rocket. I sometimes wondered how she ended up being my daughter.

He scratched his chin, his fingers rasping against the coarse hair.

"The diner?"

"You want to take us to breakfast at the diner?"

He nodded.

I wanted to say yes. I wanted to delay the moment when I had to say goodbye to this perfect point in my life, but was I ready to announce to Girard that Alex and I were ... wait ... were we dating?

My cheeks colored, and Alex threw me a puzzled look.

That was a conversation for another time.

"How about we wake Katie, and you and Stan come to breakfast at our house?"

He accepted by dropping a passionate kiss onto my lips, his hands tightening on my hips. And we went from zero to sixty in less than a second, the flames of passion that I thought had been exhausted, fanned into a blazing fire.

And then Stan farted—a long, satisfying, bass rumble.

I laughed and the mood was truly broken, and a putrid smell like rotten eggs wafted through the room. I pushed away, as Alex threw Stan a dirty look.

"Not exactly mood music," I chuckled.

"That mutt is going to find himself in a goddamn kennel," he muttered.

Stan grunted, surprised that he'd woken himself up. Then he closed his eyes again, huffing quietly.

Still laughing to myself, I went to wake Katie.

She was usually grumpy in the morning, but as soon as she saw Stan, she was all sunshine and smiles. And when she saw Alex, she ran over and hugged him tightly around his waist, snuggling into his plaid shirt.

His eyes widened, and he glanced at me above her head as he cautiously lowered his arms to hug her back.

"Alex and Stan are coming to breakfast with us at home," I said casually, wondering how Katie would react to that.

"I'm hungry," she said simply.

Then she climbed the stairs to Alex's bathroom as if she'd been doing it her whole life.

She hadn't asked for any explanations, hadn't wondered where I'd slept—instead, she seemed perfectly at home with all of this. For now. I knew that I'd have to give her some answers later ... I just didn't know what they'd be.

Minutes later, after Katie had decided that Stan wanted her to ride with him, Alex loaded them both into his truck and followed me as I drove through the town.

I had to stop at Walgreens to pick up a gallon of milk, then we had a fun, if chaotic breakfast, before I had to drop Katie at Holly's house and head to work.

While Katie was getting changed, Alex grabbed my hand, but refused to meet my eyes. We sat there in silence for some minutes, his thumb drawing hesitant circles across my wrist.

"So," he said slowly, drawing out the syllable, "c-can I call this a date? Because I'd like to take you on a real one—dinner, a movie, whatever you'd like."

I'd hoped to hear those words. Feared them, too, but hope glowed brightest.

"Yes," I said. "I'd like that."

He grinned at me and placed a soft kiss on the inside of my wrist, making my pulse leap.

Then Katie raced down the stairs, kissing Stan on top of his furry head, and earning a lick that made her giggle.

"Can Alex take me to Holly's?" she asked.

I blinked with surprise, not expecting that question.

"Not today," I replied, my voice flat.

"What about tomorrow? You're working tomorrow, too, and school doesn't start till Monday."

"We'll see."

She pouted, her expression growing thunderous.

"That means no. Why can't Alex take me?"

"Katie! We're not having this conversation now. Here's your bag. Now, say goodbye to Stan and Alex and go get in the car."

She snatched her bag and stomped outside, slamming the door behind her.

Alex raised his eyebrows.

"Sorry about that. Welcome to Parenting 101."

"She's a great kid."

"Mostly, yes. Give or take three years of sleepless nights, teething, tantrums and ... yep, motherhood is wonderful."

"You're l-lucky," he said, looking down.

"Yes," I said quietly. "I am."

It was later that day, when tiredness was catching up with me that the other shoe dropped.

Dan stopped by to see me at work.

"Can we talk?" he asked, looking serious.

"Is it Katie?" I gasped, my hand flying to my chest.

"No, no, nothing like that," he reassured me quickly. "We just need to talk. In private."

Ashley rolled her eyes and went back to reading a magazine as I ushered Dan into one of the empty consultation rooms.

"What's this about?"

He grimaced and slowly lowered himself into a chair as he set his hat on the desk between us.

"I saw you this morning," he said at last. "At Walgreens."

My mind raced. *Where is he going with this?*

"Okay?"

"I saw Katie in Alex Winters' truck," he said accusingly. "Real early."

I was taken aback. First, by his hostility, and second, I wasn't ready to discuss our relationship. It was too new, too untested. But Dan was an old friend, one of the few who'd stuck by me after...

"So?" I asked testily.

He leaned forward on his elbows.

"So, you didn't look like you were meeting for breakfast."

"That's really none of your business, Dan."

He ignored my clipped tone and plowed on.

"You stayed the night with him, didn't you?"

My cheeks flushed and I bridled at his disapproving tone.

"Are you asking me or telling me?"

"Dawn..."

"And just for the record, is this visit as a police officer or as my friend?"

"I'm both, Dawn. Always."

I sat back in my chair, crossing my arms defensively.

Dan settled his service revolver more comfortably against his hip and frowned at me.

"Then you were with him. God damn it, Dawn! You hardly know this guy!"

"How dare you!"

He winced and backpedaled immediately.

"I mean, he's only been in town a couple of months. That's not like you. And with Katie to think of..."

"Well, as my *friend*, I would have thought you'd be pleased that after all this time I've met someone that I ... like."

He pushed his hands through his hair, anger and frustration marking his face.

"Not him."

"Why not him?"

"Jeez, Dawn! We've been friends half our lives. After what Matthew did to you ... can't you just take it from me that Winters is bad news?"

I swallowed, my mouth suddenly dry. *What wasn't he saying?*

"What do you mean? You're going to have to give me more than that, Dan."

He growled with irritation.

"My word not good enough for you?"

"You know it is. But I'm not a child, so whatever it is, just tell me what you know."

He sighed, regret and resentment coloring his voice.

"I can't tell you everything ... but after he brought in that dead dog, I did some checking." He paused. "I didn't know that you were ... how long has it been going on?"

A night, a month, my whole life? I had no way to answer him. Alex had become important to me. I'd fallen for him.

My voice was quiet when I replied.

"It's recent."

"Good. Then you won't get hurt," he said briskly.

Too late. Much too late. This conversation is hurting me.

"What did you find out?"

My voice trembled, and Dan looked away discreetly.

"All I can tell you is that Denver PD have a file on him a couple of inches thick. There was a lot in it. Bad stuff. I can't tell you more because part of it is an ongoing investigation..."

Cold sweat trickled down my spine, and my hands shook.

"Shit, Dawn! We've been friends a long time. You know I care about you and Katie..."

I did. I did know that, but I didn't want to believe the things he was saying about Alex—*couldn't* believe them. It just didn't seem possible. But then again I didn't have a great track record in picking men. I didn't *want* to believe what Dan was telling me, but at the same time...

"Is ... is Katie in danger ... from him?"

He blew out a long breath.

"Honestly? I don't know. All I can tell you is that the guy isn't stable. You remember what he was like when he first came here?"

I did remember, only too well. But he was grieving at the time and having a tough time at work. But he'd also admitted that he hadn't been in his right mind. What would it take for him to relapse? Would he be dangerous?

"Do you really want someone like that around her?" Dan continued. "Around you?"

Tears stung my eyes and I shook my head.

"Is ... is it bad?"

Dan gave me a look full of pity.

"Seriously, Dawn. The guy is looney tunes." He sighed. "I'm sorry, but you had to know. And in any case, you can do better than a man like that. You *deserve* better."

He stood up, running his hands along the brim of his hat as he stared down at me.

"You let me know right away if he gives you any trouble. Any time, day or night. I..."

Whatever else he was going to say was bitten back and he shook his head.

"I gotta get going."

Having delivered his message, he slid his hat back on his head, adjusting it to a jaunty angle, then touching the brim with his finger.

"You have a good day. Crystal says hi."

And he walked out of the office.

I sat stunned, unable to move, thoughts racing through my mind. I tried to recall all the things Dan had said: *unstable, a police record.*

I didn't want to believe it.

Images of Alex with Katie, playing with her, reading to her, tucking a blanket around her as she slept. And with Stan, those large hands so gentle and caring.

And with me, my God, the way he was with me—passionate, intense, focused. And loving. When he looked at me, I felt loved.

But I couldn't deny the times I'd seen him anxious, unable to communicate, falling apart. And angry. I'd seen him shake with rage. I'd seen his eyes darken murderously, and even before I'd known *this*, I'd felt him capable of violence. I'd *seen* his bloody knuckles the night he'd brought in that poor dog. I'd seen, and refused to believe.

Tears of frustration leaked from my eyes and I swiped them away angrily.

So unfair!

But Dan was my friend and a police officer—he'd always supported me.

I'd been taken in, lied to by another man. So what was new? Just another woman who'd believed what she wanted to believe, seen what she'd wanted to see.

No, nothing new under the sun.

It had only been one night.

Not enough time to fall in love.

The lies we tell ourselves when our hearts are breaking.

. . .

93

I went through the motions for the rest of the day, but I felt numb. And when I picked Katie up from Holly's, I hugged her extra tightly.

She squirmed out of my grip.

"Mom!"

I forced a smile. "Sorry. I forgot my little girl is all grown up now."

She gave me a funny look, then started telling me about her day. I only half-listened, putting 'yes', 'no' and 'wow' into more or less the right places.

Finally, she pinned me with fierce scrutiny.

"What's wrong, Mom? You're acting all weird."

"Oh," I laughed uneasily. "I'm just tired. Long day. How about a Disney marathon tonight. Only girls allowed."

"What about Alex and Stan?"

My fake smile froze.

"I don't think they'd like Disney," I said lamely.

"No, Mom," she huffed, as if explaining to a two year-old. "That's because they're boys."

"Don't you want to watch movies tonight?"

She shrugged.

"I'd rather go to Alex's house. It's cool."

All the insecurities, all the anxieties I'd ever had about my abilities as a mother came crashing in. *Just one day, and she'd rather be with him ... a crazy man.*

"We're not seeing them tonight," I said, more coldly than she deserved.

Katie huffed some more and we rode home in stiff silence.

When my phone rang and Alex's name came up, I jumped so much that I jerked the steering wheel, making Katie squeal.

"It's Alex," she said, pointing at my phone holder on the dashboard.

"I'll get back to him later," I lied. "It's dangerous to be distracted when you're driving, even with a hands-free phone."

She gave me a look that said she wanted to call me on my bullshit, but didn't say anything.

A minute later, a text came in.

* Dinner tonight? Stan's cooking. *

"Mom?"

"I'll text him later."

Katie stared thoughtfully. "Are you mad at him?"

"That's enough, Katie. I said I'll text him later."

She refused to speak to me for the rest of the journey, only thawing out when I offered to make her favorite pancakes for supper.

Alex texted me several more times before the phone fell silent.

Each one hurt my heart a little more. I knew it wasn't fair to leave him wondering what he'd done, when he'd done nothing ... or maybe something. Something terrible enough to worry Dan. It was all so confusing.

I decided to sleep on it.

That plan might have worked if I'd actually gotten any sleep, but I spent the night tossing and turning, trying to banish the images of his hands, darkly tanned against my pale thighs, spreading them open as his tongue lashed me.

I was adrift the whole night, lost in that stormy sea of caring, but by morning, I was drained and miserable—and no closer to knowing what to do.

I found myself lying to Katie again as she inspected my red eyes and swollen eyelids.

"I'm fine," I muttered. "I might be coming down with something."

She looked so worried, hugging me tightly, that I had to pretend there was nothing wrong. It was the worst sort of lie.

"It's not that bad. I'll be fine."

I stumbled through the day, making mistake after mistake, until Gary sent me to the medicine cabinet to do inventory, something that was usually Ashley's job.

But when I got home after collecting Katie, I wanted to turn around and go somewhere far, far away.

Alex's battered truck was parked outside my house, and Alex and Stan were sitting on the doorstep.

"Alex!" yelled Katie happily, leaping out of the car and running to throw her herself at him.

He caught her easily, twirling her around, making her shriek with laughter. Then she scooted down next to Stan and rubbed his belly while he panted with pleasure.

Alex was watching me warily, his hands shoved in his pockets.

He was wearing a white shirt and those soft worn jeans again, and my mind was assaulted with memories of what it felt like to run my hands over the thin material, feeling his heat, watching those sensitive honey-colored eyes darken to teak as arousal took him.

I breathed deeply and steeled myself. Time to be an adult and stop hiding. The ostrich approach to relationships was not one I'd recommend ... from bitter experience.

"Hello, Alex. How are you?"

He gave an awkward half-smile and shrugged his shoulders.

"Have you got time for a coffee?" I asked coolly.

His smile slipped at my tone, and his shoulders slumped. He glanced at Stan and Katie, then nodded uncertainly.

I sent Katie to play with Stan in the backyard while the coffee machine gurgled and hummed. Alex watched me silently from the tiny table, and it didn't escape my attention that he hadn't tried to touch me. I poured the coffee and handed him a mug.

"We need to talk," I began, aware that my current coolness and prior behavior meant talking was probably beyond him right now.

His expression hardened and he set his untouched coffee on the table, waving his hand, indicating that I should begin.

"I'll be straight with you, Alex. Katie is the most important thing in my life and I don't want her upset. Her father is barely present in her life, and she gets attached to people. But you should know that ... my daughter always comes first. Always."

His eyes lit up and he smiled, nodding in agreement.

"G-g-great k-kid."

I hesitated, searching his face for any hint of dissembling, but there was nothing. *Oh God, this was so hard.* Hope blazed in his eyes as I sat on the edge of my chair, tense and uncomfortable, taking several deep breaths before I continued talking.

"Alex, is there anything I need to know? I don't know anything about you, not really. You never talk about yourself, and it makes me feel like you're hiding something..."

He sat unmoving, his expression frozen in horror as I plowed on.

"So, if it affects Katie *in any way*, I want to know. Or at least give me the chance of ... of walking away—before I get in too deep."

It was a partial truth, but it was as close as I could get without explaining that Dan had visited me. I was desperate for ... something. But I wanted it to come from him. I wanted, no, I *needed* Alex to explain it to me.

He screwed his eyelids shut, a deep sigh tumbling from him, and he appeared to be in pain. Then he opened his eyes, naked with emotion, and his piercing gaze seemed to push under my skin like a surgeon's blade. I had a sudden and urgent desire to hug him and tell him that everything was going to be alright.

Then I realized that his hands were shaking and he was sweating heavily, his breath coming in short pants. His skin was ashen, with an unhealthy sheen across his forehead.

Oh my God! I think he's having an anxiety attack! And I remembered that Dan had said he was unstable...

"Alex? Are you okay?"

He shook his head and stood abruptly, pacing the room, wrapping his arms across his chest as if he could physically hold himself together that way. He took deep, gulping breaths, and gradually, after several minutes, his color returned to something near normal.

I poured him a glass of water and he drank it quickly, wiping his hand across his mouth.

"I'm sorry," I said softly, guilt churning in my stomach. "I didn't mean to ... it's just that Katie..."

My words tailed off.

Stan poked his head into the kitchen and trotted over to Alex, gazing up at him anxiously.

He crouched down next to him, burying one hand in the soft fur that grew in a thick mane around his neck.

"I was m-married," he said, his voice almost inaudible.

Married?

Whatever I'd expected him to say, it wasn't that. I sat back in my chair.

He didn't look at me as he continued speaking, his voice a low, colorless monotone, the robotic voice he used when he was trying to force words past his stutter.

"When she left, I started drinking and..."

"Oh! You drink? A lot?"

My sudden interruption threw him off track, and he paused to gather himself, but after two shocks in two sentences, my heart was beating wildly, wondering what else he was going to reveal.

He swallowed, and continued kneading Stan's fur.

"I did drink. I'd had a really bad time at work, and I lost my job—and my brother ... it was a way of coping. I've stopped now. I haven't had a drink for nine months. I just find it ... hard to talk about."

This time he met my eyes, begging me to hear him, but I was afraid of what he'd see in my face as I turned away.

"I ... I didn't know. I'd never have guessed..." I stammered.

"Stella..."

My eyes opened wide.

"Stella? What about my sister?"

He looked back at Stan who was whining softly.

"She hit on me..."

"That doesn't surprise me." I laughed unhappily.

He plowed on ruthlessly, but by now his reckless honesty was too much. *Too much.*

"But after I'd seen her at Spen's party, I told her I couldn't be around anyone who drinks. She didn't take it well."

"So Stella knows?"

He nodded.

"Thank you for telling me," I said stiffly.

The silence seemed to take on a mass and volume that weighed me down. When I forced myself to meet his gaze, my protective gates had already slammed shut, leaving Alex on the outside. And I still had no idea what any of this had to do with a police file in Denver, but I'd already heard enough. He'd thrown so much new and worrying information at me in the space of a couple of minutes that I had no idea where to start.

Divorced. An alcoholic. Fired from his job.

He sank back into the chair, his head in his hands, and when he looked up, his eyes were bleak.

"D-do you want me to go?"

No! my heart shrieked.

I wanted him and I was desperate for him to stay. But I couldn't.

I couldn't be that irresponsible.

Not for me and certainly not for Katie.

"I think that would be best," I agreed quietly, my voice surprising me with its firmness. "I need to think about this."

He nodded, as if expecting my answer, although he may have hoped for a different one. His expression was cold and shuttered as he straightened up and turned away from me. As Alex walked toward the door, Stan followed, moving stiffly, pausing next to me so I could scratch behind his ears.

"Bye, Stan."

Alex hesitated, his shoulders rigid, but he didn't speak again, and he didn't look at me.

Then he walked outside and loaded Stan onto the passenger seat.

I stood by the front door, watching until his truck was swallowed up by the distance.

Katie came running through the house.

"Where's Alex?"

"He had to go home," I said quietly.

"When's he coming back?" she asked sharply.

"He's not."

"Why not?"

"Just because."

"Because what? When are they coming back?!"

"Katie..."

"What did you do?" she cried, her lips trembling as she searched my face for answers.

"I'm sorry, Katie, but it's for the best."

"No, it's not! It's not best! It sucks! I hate you! You make everyone go away!"

And with tears pouring down her face, she ran upstairs and slammed her bedroom door. I could hear her crying, great heaving sobs.

My stomach flip-flopped and I felt sick. Was she right? Did I make everyone go away? Her father? Stella? And now Alex? I realized that I'd been too upset to even ask about his encounters with the police. And he hadn't mentioned them. So he was a liar, as well. I had to remember that.

I felt like crying for both of us.

Chapter Nine

SUSTAINING

Dawn

Did I just made the worst mistake of my life?

Did I? Did I? Did I?

That's the thing about being sensible, responsible—it assumes that emotions should lose out to rationality. But is that the right thing to do? Who ruled that emotions are less important? Who said that reason weighed heavier in the evidence? Since when is the head mightier than the heart?

Love is not love which alters when it alteration finds.

Shakespeare wrote sonnets about love, but if he wrote about the importance of being sensible, my high school English teacher never mentioned it.

Or maybe I was an idiot and hopelessly addicted to the wrong men. Maybe I knew deep down that I couldn't trust my own judgement.

But if I'd done the right thing, why did it feel so wrong?

Unstable.

What did that even mean? Had Dan been referring to Alex's drinking? And if so, why didn't he say that? What had happened? What had Alex done to have a criminal record? If he *had* a criminal record—Dan said they had a file on him, but he didn't say he was a criminal. But why would the police keep files on someone who *wasn't* a criminal ... and an ongoing investigation, no less?

Dan didn't have an axe to grind. He was a good, fair police officer, trusted and well liked. He was the person who told the gossips to shut the hell up when Alex first came here. Now he was telling me to stay away from him.

I was so confused.

Dan was my friend and I knew that he was looking out for me, but he was thinking like a police officer.

What have I done? The question rattled around my head all night, leaving me wretched and wrung out.

Why was I such a mess? The man admitted that he's an alcoholic! I should be running in the opposite direction. But his kisses—I didn't think I'd ever recover from those. The look in his eyes was pure desire, and I felt the same. I hadn't felt anything like that in so long, if ever.

And he was so sweet with Katie—I already knew that she liked him a lot. And I didn't have to guess what she was thinking, hoping for.

I felt horrible when I'd told him to leave. The look of devastation on his face was bad enough, but it was the quiet acceptance that ruined me—like he'd expected it all along. I cried non-stop for nearly half an hour after I went to bed, and I hardly ever cry.

Unstable.

And his house! It had been such a surprise. It looked like it belonged in 'Better Homes & Gardens'—it was stunning. He'd transformed a ramshackle hovel into a show home that wouldn't look out of place in the Hamptons, and Spen said that Alex had done all the work himself. The man has skills, but says he's not in construction. Why wouldn't he tell me about himself, about what happened with the police? What could be worse than admitting you're a divorced, unemployed alcoholic?

A platoon of horrible answers marched through my mind, but certainties disappeared in a cloud of smoke and mirrors.

I spent the night thinking about what Dan had said, and how much his picture of Alex differed from the man I knew. I prayed for sleep. I begged for a little peace, a break from this remorseless doubt.

The next morning wasn't much better. I'd barely closed my eyes all night, because each time I did, the relentless images of his touches, his beautiful expressive eyes, played continuously, a never-ending movie reel.

Katie still wasn't speaking to me. I knew from experience that she could keep this up for days. So I continued a cheerful monologue that she ignored in stony silence, all the way through breakfast and during the journey to Holly's. I didn't have the energy to fight with her about the attitude.

After I dropped her off, I took the long route to work, stopping to get a latte with extra kick. It wasn't enough caffeine to get me through the whole day, and by lunchtime I needed a break. I headed back into town to buy some groceries and try to clear my mind.

I also had a check for $500 in my back pocket to pay for the tires Alex had bought for me. I still hadn't decided what to do with it.

And then, as if my imagination sprang through some portal of reality, I saw him, and my mouth dropped open with shock.

He was coming out of Home Depot wearing the same clothes he'd worn when I'd found him sitting on my doorstep yesterday evening. But now, the crisp white shirt was torn and muddy. His jeans were filthy, coated in dirt and cement dust; he had mud smeared across his cheek, and his hands were caked with grime.

I noticed his bloodshot eyes, and my first thought was that he'd been drinking.

When he saw me, he clenched his fists, and I took a worried step backwards.

I witnessed the exact moment when despair suffused his whole body, and he turned away from me.

Guilt, regret, more guilt, worry and concern drove me forwards, despite my racing pulse and fight-or-flight adrenaline rush.

"Alex!"

He froze mid-step when he heard me calling his name, but he didn't turn around.

"Alex," I said again, my voice uncertain. "What happened to you?"

He stared at me over his shoulder, his eyes cloudy, his brain fogged by tiredness and incomprehension.

"You look like you've been rolling in mud."

He glanced down at his clothes, as if seeing them for the first time.

He gave a helpless shrug. "L-landscaping."

A sharp pain gripped my heart, and I realized that once again my assumptions were way off base. I suspected, I guessed, I knew that he'd been awake all night, working out his frustrations on the land. He hadn't been drinking—he'd been digging, shoveling mud ... landscaping, he called it ... wearing the new white button-down shirt that he'd worn to see me yesterday.

I wanted to apologize, but I also wondered if I should give him a chance— give myself a chance. But now I was doubting myself again. He looked terrible this morning, and he clearly hadn't slept or even stopped to change his clothes.

But that was beside the point—it wasn't normal to do landscaping in the middle of the night.

Unstable.

But a small voice reminded me that at least he didn't turn to a bottle for company.

I did this to him, I know I did.

My harsh dismissal ... I'd nearly broken him.

And in that split second, seeing how much this ... us ... meant to him, my heart told me not to give up, not to listen to Dan's edited truths.

Silly old heart. Thoughtless, careless, reckless heart.

I paused, wondering what to say, how to begin, how to find our way forward...

"Alex, I..."

His eyes were sad and distant, their honey-colored depths clouded with lonely despair.

"Can I talk to you, Alex?"

He nodded wearily, hopelessly.

"I want to apologize for the way I behaved yesterday. I ... You were honest with me—which is what I'd asked for—and then I told you to leave. I'm sorry."

He stared at me with confusion in his eyes, as if he didn't understand what I was saying to him. I hardly knew myself. But this was gut instinct, emotion, call it what you want. I was giving him ... me ... us ... another chance.

"So, I was wondering if we could start again?"

He shook his head, and disappointment ripped through me.

"N-no! I w-want..." He hesitated, trying to enunciate as clearly as possible. "W-want ... can ... c-coffee?"

The oppressive weight of doubt lifted and relief made me feather-light. I laughed because I was filled with hope and that made me happy. Alex offered a tentative smile in return.

"Yes, I'd love a coffee. But I've only got a few minutes before I have to get back to work and, um, maybe you should go home and clean up. You look awful, Alex. No offense."

He stared down at his mud-covered body, and shrugged like he didn't care. We found an unoccupied bench opposite the playground and sat down, ignoring the curious stares of people driving by.

I gazed into my steaming coffee as if it contained the meaning of the universe.

"I meant what I said, Alex," I said softly. "I am sorry for how I was yesterday afternoon."

"It's o-k-kay."

I shook my head, upset that he accepted my horrible treatment of him so easily, as if he expected it, was used to it, deserved it.

"I don't want Katie to get hurt, but I know that I use her as a defense, as well, to keep people—men—from getting too close. Yes, the whole drinking thing bothers me, but you say you've stopped ... and I believe you."

He wasn't looking at me. Instead, he was staring at his hands clasped in front of him, but I could tell that he was listening.

"Maybe we could ... take it slowly. Maybe ... go on a date, like you said. If you want. Just the two of us?"

He nodded, a sweet smile spreading across his face.

"Okay, that's great," I said, breathing a sigh of relief. "So ... I need to get going now. I just came to do a little shopping and grab a coffee. I guess, well ... I'll call you."

We both stood up

"D-dawn...?"

I turned quickly, half wary, a lot hopeful.

"Yes?"

His eyes squeezed shut and his face contorted as he tried to force out words. Only a few strangled sounds made their way out, and his face reddened with frustration and embarrassment.

"It's okay," I said as my eyes began to water. "I'll text you. Bye."

He nodded again and shoved his hands in his pockets as I walked back to my car.

He was still watching me as I drove away.

I hoped I wasn't being naïve by giving him, me, us a second chance.

The day passed slowly after that. I picked up my phone a dozen times to text him, but I couldn't think of what to say. In the end, I decided to wait until my brain was less fried, after two sleep-deprived nights.

I picked up Katie and we stopped at the bakery to buy freshly-baked donuts and go eat them in the park. A peace offering, and something we did when we needed cheering up.

The woman in front of us seemed to resent the slow speed of the line. She huffed and muttered to herself, glancing at her heavy gold wristwatch several times.

I smiled to myself. Those tactics wouldn't work—I knew because I'd tried them once, long ago. The bakery owner, Mavis, was in the habit of chatting with everyone who came in—it was how she picked up so much gossip about the whole town. I don't think anyone would willingly put up with the glacial speed she served people, but she made the best cakes and pastries in town, and her coffee was to die for.

I watched the woman's narrow shoulders stiffen as Mavis addressed her as 'honey', the designer suit jacket, tightening across her narrow back.

She was blonde, petite, with a tiny waist and large boobs. She looked like a miniature Jessica Rabbit with her huge eyes and perfect mane of long, glossy hair—the polar opposite of me.

Katie's eyes took on a glaze of admiration as she surveyed the woman's expensive clothes and five inch heels. My eight year-old daughter had put a subscription to *Vogue* on her Christmas list. Not even *Teen Vogue*. What was wrong with *American Girl*? Where had I gone wrong?

"I wonder if you can help me?" the woman said, her accent hinting at New York.

"I can help you with coffee, hon, and we do awesome donuts."

The woman grit her teeth.

"Fine. Black to go."

Mavis calmly poured coffee into a take-out cup, and put the woman's change in the tip jar. I could tell that she was making the most of this.

"I'm looking for a property called *Tanglewood*," the woman clipped out. "Do you know it?" And she gave an affected laugh. "It's not like finding your way around a city, that's for sure. So many unmarked ... roads ... that aren't shown on GPS."

Mavis's eyes glittered with interest.

"You want Old Joe's place, down by the lake."

"Old Joe? Is the property you mentioned named *Tanglewood?*" she asked impatiently.

"Why, yes it is. Do you have business with Old Joe? Because you know he passed on ... quite a few months ago now."

"If you could give me directions..."

"The new owner isn't fond of strangers," Mavis said, her smile telling me that she was being deliberately evasive. "Isn't that right, Dawn? She's met the new owner quite a few times." And she smiled at me. "How are you doing, honey? And how are you, Katie?"

The woman turned to examine me, her hard eyes skating over my jeans and t-shirt, her gaze critical. She glanced coldly at Katie, obviously dismissing her, and my hackles rose.

"You know Alex Winters?" she asked, her voice flat with affected boredom.

"Yes, I do," I said, lifting my chin. "I've treated his dog, Stan."

"Oh God, he doesn't still have that smelly mongrel, does he?"

Katie gasped.

"Stan's my friend and he's *not* smelly!"

The woman's eyes narrowed.

"Alex is a friend of ours ... me and my daughter," I said, tugging Katie closer to me as she scowled up at the woman.

The woman gave me a superior smile.

"Then you've met my husband," she said.

Chapter Ten

UNCERTAINTIES

Alex

She's going to give me another chance.

The words thrummed through my mind in a tangle of half hope and half despair. After the way this day had started, slipping tiredly from night to day, I would have bet my left nut that it wasn't going to improve. Her subtle scent seemed to be everywhere in the cabin. It drove me to distraction.

Being with Dawn, spending the day with her, spending the night—it felt easy and incredible all at the same time. Getting to know her as a woman and as a mother, I'd started to imagine a future again. It felt right. It *was* right.

What was happening to me, to my life? I was cracking open, and Dawn was the light, blasting through to all my darkest places. It was terrifying.

Touching her, tasting her, being with her, inside her, it was a different dimension. It was lust and need and want and heat. It was fucking in the dark, it was loving in the light. It was warmth in the morning when we'd woken up together. It was exploring her body, trusting her to explore mine, to let her into my shadowy world.

That had nearly ruined everything. Nearly.

I had few possessions and, arguably, dignity wasn't one of them. She'd walk away at some point. I always knew that.

Running into Dawn today, I'd anticipated the disgust in her eyes, been afraid to see her repelled by what I'd said, the little I'd told her about myself. Instead I saw compassion mixed with wariness, and every emotion played out on her face was reflected in mine. I hated feeling like this—as if I was made of glass, and all my thoughts and hopes, dreams and fears were visible, but just out of reach.

She'd been sitting close enough today that I could smell the fresh, floral scent of her shampoo. Her dark hair looked thick and glossy, and I longed to touch it again. But when she looked up, her eyes were hesitant, guarded. There was some new knowledge behind her expression that I didn't understand.

I'd wanted to tell her that we could take it as slowly as she liked—whatever she needed from me to feel safe. I hadn't wanted to let her go without explaining that being with her made me feel alive, that I'd felt the soft swell of contentment, the excitement of possibilities. I wanted her to know how much Katie meant to me, too, that I'd protect them both with every breath in my body. I wanted to tell her everything.

But the words wouldn't come. They never did when I needed them. Not anymore.

I could have sent her a text, but that didn't feel right. Maybe I should write a letter. But the truth was I wanted to be able to say the words, to explain what I felt, to speak like a normal human being.

Unwilling memories spilled into my thoughts. Most of my childhood was spent hiding. It's amazing how you can hide in plain sight. If you don't speak, eventually you fade into the background, you become invisible. I thought I'd put all that behind me, but life has a way of kicking you in the balls when you're already on your hands and knees.

I hate my stutter, hate that it minimizes me, but the angrier I get, the worse it is. I try to speak, but nothing happens, no sound. I see the confusion and pity on their faces, and people try to finish my sentences, assuming they know what I want to say, what I'm thinking. I see it in their eyes—*what's wrong with him? He's not normal.*

I'm not. It feels like I'm missing a limb, except no one knows but me. For a hundred-thousand years, humans have communicated with their voices. But not me, not anymore.

And it gets worse.

The frustration, the rage. The despair.

But with Dawn, I touched normality, humanity ... and she'd promised to call me...

Stan licked my hand, then leaned against my knee, gazing up with concern in his eyes.

My brain spun in loops, hopeful and hopeless, resigned and defiant. I wanted to fight, but the war was inside my head.

What the hell had I expected yesterday? Did I really think that she'd be okay having a fucked up alcoholic around her daughter? And that was only half the story. I must have rocks in my head. *I* wouldn't want me. I'd been so blind playing happy family for the day. Why would an attractive, intelligent woman like Dawn bother to go anywhere near damaged goods? I couldn't blame her. I didn't blame her.

I'd just felt some ridiculous, pathetic need to tell her the truth—or some partial, edited version of it. Because she'd asked. Because I'd felt that elusive connection with her. Why hadn't I kept my damn mouth shut? Why hadn't I been more careful with my truths?

She was half-scared of me now.

So, what was the alternative? A relationship built on lies—more lies? No sane woman would want me.

It wasn't enough, and being with Dawn and Katie, I'd thought of other possibilities.

After she'd kicked me out yesterday, sleep was the furthest thing from my mind when I'd walked into the cabin. Knowing what was coming, Stan had taken himself off to one of the spare rooms. He sighed and gave me a look, almost shaking his head. *Boss, women ain't worth it.*

I wouldn't have been surprised to see him with his paws over his ears and his head stuck under a pillow.

I'd slammed through the house, looking for something I could hit with a hammer, but the damn place sneered at me in pristine condition.

Then I remembered I had some logs out the back that needed splitting into kindling for the log burner that I'd installed in the kitchen, ready for the winter.

I snatched up the axe and smashed the fuck out of pieces of wood until sweat made my eyes sting.

At 2AM, I'd decided that I was going to build a path down to the lake. I'd been thinking about making a mini quay so I didn't have to wade through mud every time I went for a swim. The middle of the night had seemed like a good time to start it.

Grabbing a hurricane lamp, a shovel and pickaxe from the shed, I'd made my way through the trees down to the lake.

I worked furiously, not caring how much my muscles ached, or how filthy I became. Gradually, exhaustion began to work its way into the edges of my brain, giving me some relief from those poisonous, destructive thoughts.

It was the best way of coping that I'd found—safer than booze or drugs. Safer than women.

Everything bad that happened in my life was because of a woman.

If God made a good woman, I haven't met her yet.

Dad used to say that after Mom walked out on us. What kind of woman walks out on her kids without a word? No birthday cards, not even a Christmas card. She wanted to 'find' herself. I guess she didn't want to find she was a wife and mother.

That's when I started to stutter—after Mom left.

I'd gone from being popular and happy to miserable and withdrawn. It only took a couple of times of being called 'A-a-a-alex' to make me almost mute.

My school arranged for me to see a speech therapist. I think I a few hours a month. It didn't help. I only started to gain confidence when I was 13 and began training at the gym with Carl. I've been working out ever since, and by the time I was a sophomore in high school I stopped stuttering. Until Charlotte and Warren.

And after what happened with Dawn, I thought I'd be lucky ever to string two words together again.

By first light, I'd fashioned the bank down to the lake into a series of broad steps. I just needed to mortar in some paving slabs, and I'd have a pretty good landing platform. It would be the perfect place for a bench, too.

A bench for your sad, lonely, loser ass to sit on all alone.

I didn't even bother to change my clothes before I headed out to Home Depot to place an order for paving slabs. Better still, the delivery driver wasn't busy, so two tons of sandstone was on its way to my house.

The guy backed his truck as far up my driveway as possible, but it still meant I had to use a wheelbarrow to ferry the rest. I didn't care. More exertion, anything to stop me thinking.

Stan watched from the sidelines, yawning every now and then and practically rolling his eyes as I staggered backwards and forwards, carrying paving stones. He was used to my brand of weirdness.

Wake me when you're finished, boss.

By then, I'd been getting a slight brain buzz from lack of sleep, but it felt right—sort of numb, like nothing else would fit in my head—which had been the point of the exercise. I just needed the mortar between the slabs to harden and it was finished. Hell, maybe I should just pave the whole nine acres that I owned. That would stop me feeling anything for a couple of years.

I'd headed back to the store to buy a bench.

And then ... I'd spotted Dawn.

I hated the new wariness in her eyes, but despite everything I'd told her, she was going to give me, us, a chance.

When I heard the engine of a car drawing closer, unexpected hope swelled inside my chest. *Dawn was coming back.*

But when I opened the front door, a tentative smile on my face, I had a sudden urge to slam it again.

The woman in the car was shorter and curvier than Dawn, arguably sexier, and most men's definition of hot. And the most manipulative, lying bitch I'd ever had the fuck awful luck to meet. Also known as my wife.

Charlotte was climbing out of a rental car, scowling as the new gravel marked her designer pumps.

My stomach clenched, and I knew my eyes were wide and wary, wondering if I had time to retreat.

She saw me watching and pasted a phony smile onto her face.

"Hello, Alex."

I stared at her, all my words fleeing the scene of the crime.

"You've cut your hair. And that awful disgusting beard. Much better."

I scowled at her.

"Nice place you've got here. It's very ... folksy."

What did she want? She'd already taken everything.

She put one hand on her hip and thrust it out, the painted nails tapping impatiently against the tight fabric of her linen skirt.

"Aren't you going to invite me in?"

Powerful anger pulsed through me. I folded my arms across my chest and shook my head slowly. I didn't want memories of her tainting my new home.

Her smile vanished, and I was amused to watch the struggle as she tried to hold back her irritation.

"I just flew halfway across the country to see you!"

She sounded so indignant, I almost smiled. But no, she didn't deserve my smiles. She didn't deserve any of me, and certainly not my time.

I turned and walked back inside, closing the door firmly behind me.

Yeah, well. I should have bolted it, locked the windows, and tossed Holy water over the whole place, because thirty seconds later, she was standing at the backdoor looking really pissed.

Stan growled softly, his hackles rising in a stiff ridge of fur along his back. I placed my hand on his head to reassure him, and he raised his eyes to me in a worried frown.

Charlotte shot him a dark look, then took out her annoyance on me—a tactic I'd gotten used to.

"You just slammed the door in my face! I can't believe you did that!"

"D-don't w-w-w..." I took a long breath to allay the rising fury, and tried again. "I d-don't want t-to ttt t-to t-talk to you."

She reached out to touch my cheek, but her hand fell into empty space as I took a quick pace back.

"You're still stuttering. I thought you'd have gotten over that by now."

If I hadn't been glaring at her, I would have missed the wash of guilt that passed across her face. But it was brief, and in an instant, she was back to business.

"I do need to talk to you," she said, softening her tone minutely. "It's important."

Behind the power suit, the spike heels and the harlot red lip gloss—somewhere under all of that was the 20 year-old college student I'd met and fallen in love with. And even though I didn't owe her a damn thing, I thought maybe I owed it to myself to hear her out. Maybe what she said would answer the question *why?*

I stood aside and let her through to the kitchen, watching her warily as she looked around, taking it all in.

"You know, you've done a great job with the place," she said. "I really like the detail, especially the chair rail and paneling. Original oak floors—very nice."

I doubted she'd come all this way just to critique my house, although it didn't surprise me that she knew I'd bought a fixer-upper. She always said that knowledge was power. I raised an eyebrow.

"W-what ... w-what do you want?"

"Do I need a reason to see my husband?"

My heart shuddered to a halt. *Un-fucking-believable!*

"Ex. H-hus b-band."

Her eyes met mine, then she pulled out a kitchen chair and placed her briefcase next to it, crossing her legs so her skirt slid up her thighs, and composing herself as if for a business meeting.

"We'll get to that. We never got a chance to talk. You were drunk or high all the time. You wouldn't return my calls."

That was true. Being numb seemed like a good idea after my brother was killed and I found her fucking Warren.

"But ... I'm sorry about Carl. I never got to say that."

I couldn't help noticing how she still glossed over the fact that she was screwing my best friend in our bed. And yet her blue eyes shone with sincerity. She was always good at faking that.

"You d-didn't like Carl."

"No, but you loved him, so he was important to me, too."

I didn't know how much of this to believe. But I think I wanted to. I hated the feeling that our whole marriage had been a lie. I didn't want her back, but I didn't want to have been wrong from the start.

"Warren was a mistake. I want us to try again."

She didn't even blink.

"We were good together once. Remember when we met? We were Juniors. We were so in love. You couldn't keep your hands off me," and she laughed lightly. "Do you remember our first vacation in Aspen, when we skied all day and screwed all night? I must have lost ten pounds. Or what about when we won the Monaco Street contract? We fucked on the boardroom table? Remember? Good memories, Alex. I think that over the years we just got caught up in the business, but we have all these amazing memories, too."

She was right, partly. I had loved her, with all my heart.

And she'd crushed me. It was terrible to love someone. Terrible to love the wrong person, the wrong people. And be fucked up, fucked over, and just plain fucked.

I thought about Warren, my former friend. Also former Best Man and former business partner. And when I thought about him, I imagined marzipan around a turd: sweet on the outside, shit on the inside.

Caught up in the business? She still thought I was a pathetic idiot. Maybe I was. But I wasn't *her* pathetic idiot.

"C-caught up in the sheets of our bed with W-warren."

"There's no need to be crass."

I laughed without humor and stood up, willing her to leave.

"I never ch-cheated on you. Never."

"Yeah, you're a saint, I'm a slut." She rolled her eyes. "I just met your little *friend*. Dawn, I think she said her name was."

I scowled at her as she smiled, a pleased cat-like moue of amusement.

"Does she know about you?"

I gave a brief, jerky nod, enjoying the flicker of surprise on her face, followed by calculating indignation.

"Is it the daughter? Is that what you want? We can have children, Alex. You always wanted to. Well, I'm ready now."

I was speechless. She couldn't find an unprovocative topic of conversation with a GPS. But that was her M.O.

Charlotte trailed a manicured finger down my arm.

"With your talent and my business sense, we'll make Denver ours. Hell, why stop at Denver? Children don't have to get in the way—that's what au pairs and nannies are for."

"N-not interested."

She leaned back in the chair, appraising me silently.

"You loved me once, Alex."

I did. But I don't think you ever loved me. Not really.

She gave a long sigh.

"I can see that you're not going to forgive me right now, but don't hold a grudge believing that I never loved you."

I wasn't sure she was lying, but actions spoke louder than words. And she'd loved the business more.

"L-liar! P-p-police!"

"Good grief! Are we back to this? I did it for *your* sake, Alex! You were completely losing it—giving away *our* money, tossing it in the street like confetti."

Only one time, and it had felt damn good. I smiled at the memory.

"My God, you were giving away the clothes off your back to street people —you were having a breakdown, you just didn't want to admit it. Getting you into rehab probably saved your life. What happened afterward with the police, that was all you, nothing to do with me."

I gave away my coat to a homeless man, I wasn't naked in the damn street. Okay, so I gave him my shoes, too. But I had others, and he didn't.

"Do you know what they called you?"

Yes, I knew.

I also knew that she'd been the one to involve the police in the first place, the one who'd sent Stan to a high-kill animal shelter.

Yeah, she'd done me a favor, because she'd targeted the one thing, the one creature that I still cared about.

I was sickened that she could convince herself that she'd done it all for my own good. Charlotte was an expert editor of her own history. But there was one thing she couldn't edit, although I wished she could—the image of her with...

"W-warren," I said flatly.

She shook her head.

"I lost my way. You were working those crazy hours, you never had time for me. I wasn't your wife—I was your business partner. I saw you more in the Boardroom than the bedroom. I was lonely."

I shook my head derisively, and Stan's worried gaze ping-ponged between us. He'd stopped growling, but was glued to my side, his muscles balled with tension.

"You think you lost everything and that I took it, but I've lost too, Alex." She gazed into the distance. "Not a single architect we've hired can match your flair, your vision. Look at what you've done for this dump. It would be a waste for you to bury yourself in Nowheresville. Come back. As a partner, or as a consultant—no strings and a six-figure salary. Not to me, if that's not what you want. Come back to the company. Hell, it's still got your name on it—that must mean something to you."

"It d-did."

"It could again. Just think about it. I'll get my lawyer to draw up any contract you want. Or use your own. Your terms."

After what Charlotte had done to me, the word 'lawyer' scared me more than 'zombies are real'.

"S-stan."

She wrinkled her nose. "What about him?"

I cocked my head on one side. She hadn't changed.

Charlotte rolled her eyes.

"Fine, bring the mutt, too."

"L-like it h-here."

She fumed, her barely suppressed frustration ready to boil over. She hated anyone telling her no. For once, I was finding it surprisingly enjoyable.

"Is it that woman? Is it serious?"

I thought of the way my heart hammered when Dawn looked at me. Yeah, it was serious.

Probably fatal.

"Then work from here!" she huffed out. "Fly in once a month for meetings. The company will pay. The best hotels—all your expenses."

My eyes narrowed. Why was she so desperate? What wasn't she telling me?

She took a deep breath as I shook my head again.

"I can't do it without you, Alex," she said softly, her large blue eyes gazing up at me, tears making them glisten.

And despite telling myself it was part of the act, I couldn't help feeling my conscience twinge.

"The business is failing," she sniffed, delicately wiping her eyes so that she didn't smudge her mascara. "It's *your* designs that made it work. We'll lose the

Lockheed contract without you." She took a shuddering breath and stared straight at me. "Fine, I'll say it: I need you, Alex. The company needs you. All those people—your friends—they'll lose their jobs if you don't come back. Do you want that on your conscience? Knowing you could have done something about it?"

She really was a piece of work.

If she'd come clean at the start then I might have considered working from home to help out until they found someone else. She was right—I had cared for my staff, valued and respected them. But they'd known about Charlotte and Warren, and not a single one had told me. They'd sold me out as quickly as she had. I didn't owe her or them anything, and her attempts at manipulation enraged me.

She never had understood me. I suppose the evidence would say that it was mutual.

"Warren?"

She looked uncomfortable. "You wouldn't have to see him."

I stood up and walked to the front door, opening it and waiting for Charlotte to catch on.

After a few seconds, I heard the clack of her high heels across the wooden floor.

"So, you'll do it?"

"Find another s-sucker."

"But the company...?"

"Fuck the company!" I said bitterly.

A company can't keep you warm at night. An office won't grow old with you. A paycheck isn't a friend.

"I l-loved you, trusted you. You nearly killed me. For a while I hated you..."

Her face paled. "And now?"

"S-sorry. I feel sorry for you."

She looked as if she might say something, but then she leaned forward and kissed my cheek. I paused, feeling the weight of nine years of marriage, thirteen years of being together, and now all that was left was goodbye.

It was sad because I didn't care.

She pulled an envelope out of her briefcase and pushed it into my hands.

Then she frowned at the leather bag, dropping it suddenly.

"Your mutt peed on my briefcase!"

A broad grin broke out across my face as I glanced at Stan who was watching from the kitchen, his head cocked to one side, the picture of innocence.

"Oh my God!" she screeched. "That's disgusting! That cost me $3,000! It's Gucci!"

I couldn't help laughing.

Charlotte picked up the briefcase with the tips of her manicured fingers and strode through the door, her lips flattening.

As she slid into her rented Benz, she looked out of the window at me.

"You're a loser, Alex. You always will be. You're pathetic—and you have a fucking ugly dog."

Tires spun on gravel as she shot out of the driveway and out of my life.

I watched her leave, closing the final chapter in our lives as Mr. and Mrs. Winters. All in all, it had gone better than I would have imagined.

Had she given me answers? Yes and no. But I felt as if I was seeing her clearly for the first time ever. Maybe she felt that way, too. We definitely weren't the same people we were at 20. We'd changed, but we hadn't grown together. Looking back, I think I was trying to find a family, something to be a part of when I married her. But now when I had those sorts of thoughts, Dawn and Katie slipped into my mind as if they belonged there.

I looked down at the envelope in my hands, opening it, wondering what new wrath Charlotte's lawyers could rain down on me.

The letter was headed 'Dissolution of marriage'. It sounded so clinical, so cold. But it also felt like I'd stepped out of the center of the hurricane—not our marriage so much, but the aftermath, definitely.

Looking at the document in my hand, I felt relief, maybe … deliverance. Yes, it was something else I'd failed at—like life—but at least I was free.

I waited two days for Dawn to call me, two long days before it occurred to me that something was seriously wrong. And I had a creeping suspicion that I knew what, or rather who, was the problem.

Charlotte had known about Dawn and I hadn't even thought to ask her where she'd come across that information. After all, we'd only had two not-dates, so how the hell could my ex-wife have known?

But I was more worried about what Charlotte might have said to Dawn rather than how she found out about us. If there was an 'us'—which was beginning to seem less and less likely.

Stirring things up had always been second nature to Charlotte. Had she said something to Dawn?

When my first text went unanswered, the trickle of unease kept me tossing and turning all night.

So I sent a second text asking if we could meet, and this time Dawn did respond.

> I don't think that's a good idea, so I'm going to say no. Please don't ask me again. Good luck in the future

I cursed loudly when I saw the answer. I *knew* that Charlotte had fucked things up for me again. There was no point even wondering about *why*, but *how* had me pulling my hair out.

I texted Dawn several more times, but she never replied. One day, I tried to call her, but by then she'd changed her number.

I thought about going to see her, somehow convince her to change her mind ... but what was the point? She'd made it very clear that she didn't want me around.

Desperation turned to anger, and anger turned to crushing despair. I thought Dawn was different, special. I really shouldn't trust my instincts about women, they were obviously broken.

Stan rested his head on my knee and sighed heavily as I pulled his ears gently.

"Just you and me again, buddy. You and me."

I decided there and then that relationships were a distraction I didn't need. Instead, I'd concentrate on the next mission.

And that gave me a newfound desire not to die. Unexpected, but true.

But the following day, I came home and found a check from Dawn for $500 in my mailbox, and a brief note saying it was to pay for the tires I'd put on her car.

I tore it into pieces and let it scatter in the wind.

Stan

The boss was sad, but at least he didn't get sick like last time.

He spent a lot of days by himself. Humans are pack animals, like dogs, so it worried me that he was alone so much. And I wasn't getting any younger. I wouldn't be here forever.

I missed them—the woman and the kid. Even when she was putting daisy chains around my neck, she was a sweet little pint-size.

I didn't know what had happened with the boss and his woman, but I had a suspicion it was something to do with that hell-bitch he'd been married to. I wished I'd bit her in the ass while I had the chance, but I did get a buzz out of pissing on her briefcase.

Chapter Eleven

RETRIBUTION

Alex

There was nothing left to do on the house. I needed a new project. I'd been avoiding Cleveland since that night, trying to convince myself to stay away, but the draw was becoming stronger. I knew I shouldn't go back, but with nothing else to distract me, it was just a matter of when, not if.

I loved it—and missed it—the chaos, the adrenaline. It made me feel alive, real, like there was a point to living. And it was the only thing bigger, crazier, more fucked up than me. It felt good to be someone who banished the dark, if only for a single night. But life is made up of a lot of moments, a lot of nights. And a single second could change your life forever.

I'd make the most of it.

Giselle wasn't expecting me, but when she saw me, she smiled, anticipation making her eyes glitter.

She was standing under the same streetlight, wearing the same uniform of leather miniskirt, low-cut tank-top and high heels. From a distance, she'd pass for thirty; close up, my guess was sixty, maybe more.

I hung back, staying in the shadows as I lifted my chin in greeting, smiling when she sauntered across to me.

"Well, well! I wondered if I'd see you again, lover. You here to give me some more of your hard-earned money?"

I grinned and nodded, handing her fifty bucks.

"Same again?"

My smile faded and I felt my expression harden as she slipped the fifty inside her bra.

Then she put her hands on her hips and stared at me.

"You gonna be more careful this time?"

My lips twitched as I shook my head.

"You got anyone waiting for you at home?"

"St-st-stan."

Her eyebrows shot up. "You're gay?"

I shook my head and pulled out my cell phone instead, showing her a photo of Stan sleeping, curled up in his bed.

They say a picture tells a thousand words. Comes in handy when you're a mute freak.

Giselle laughed.

"Figures. You're a regular Saint Rocco."

I peered at her in the dark, puzzled.

"What? I went to Catholic school. A third of us become nuns, a third become whores, and a third become school teachers. The words 'morning Mass' still makes me break out in hives and I hated school."

"Wh-who?"

"Saint Rocco? Look him up, handsome."

I grinned at her, and she winked.

"So, you're in the market for a little disorder and mayhem? A few broken laws, a lot of broken heads? Because it just happens that I know a place where you can get your fix."

She pulled a cigarette out of her purse and lit it, blowing the smoke away from me.

"I heard there'll be your kind of action on E55th Street, Friday next week. Funny, I was just thinking of you, and here you are. Does that make you my dream date?"

She laughed out a hacking cough, gripping my shoulder with her blood-red nails as she wheezed helplessly at her own joke.

I held onto her until she steadied herself, raising an eyebrow when she slid her hand down my arm and squeezed my bicep.

"You know where to find me if you want to work off some of your ... energy ... later."

I shook my head, and she gave a theatrical sigh.

"Whatever. So, I heard that there's this abandoned building—used to be a bowling alley. That's where the action is. But..." and she gave me a serious look. "I also heard that the dudes running the joint maybe have *connections*, ya know? I hope you can stop them but ... don't get caught."

I crossed my heart with one hand, and she rolled her eyes.

"See you around, lover."

And she strolled away, weaving around the cracked paving stones with familiarity and expertise.

I climbed back in my truck and programmed the address she'd given me into my GPS. It was only a few blocks away across the city. I also looked up Saint Rocco: *patron saint of dogs and falsely accused people.*

Both fit. *Funny lady.*

As I drove, the neighborhood became more and more rundown. Abandoned buildings with broken windows butted up to empty lots, or shops so heavily fortified with metal roller screens on doors and bars fitted to windows that only a Sherman tank could have broken through.

The bowling alley was on a corner, its cracked neon sign hanging loosely. I parked the truck half a block away and circled the building on foot, checking the legitimate access points as well as the unadvertised ones. The building was locked solid and from the look of it, I'd guess it was used fairly often for purposes that escaped the tax man's notice. My heart beat faster at the thought of what this place was used for now, and the familiar heat of rage pulsed through me. It was the most alive I'd felt since Dawn.

I worked my way around to the back and found a fire escape about seven feet from the ground. With some effort, I managed to climb onto it, and I dragged myself through a smashed window, avoiding the shards of glass that pulled at my clothes like claws.

This would work. I'd throw the grenades from here, then I'd wait and watch, figure out who was in charge. Once I'd made them, I'd head back to my truck and make the call. Yeah, smoke grenades. It's amazing what you can buy on the internet.

I studied the rest of the crumbling building, one room at a time, seeing only the red of rats' eyes glittering in my flashlight, their nails scratching on the floor as they scurried away. When I was satisfied that I could find my way around, I climbed out of the broken window silently.

I'd be here next week. And then I'd make the bastards pay.

When I arrived back at the cabin, Stan opened a sleepy eye, sighing with relief as I sat down next to him.

I stroked his fur, my fingers lingering over the ridges of his scars, fingering the rip in his ear that had healed off-center.

We'd both been damaged by life, but I'd get revenge for what had been done to Stan.

I spent the rest of the week, prowling the forest. I'd become so used to wandering along the paths, that I could find my way even on the darkest nights, and whoever had been setting snares on my land hadn't been back in a while. I frowned, thinking of the raccoon's head that someone had left at my front door when Dawn and Katie visited. I didn't know if it was a warning or just someone who didn't like me. Whatever the reason, the dismembered animals had started to appear from the first day I'd moved in. I had my suspicions ... I just needed to catch them in the act.

But whoever it was seemed to have suspended their activities. Or maybe gotten bored of tormenting me. At least I didn't have to worry so much that Stan would get caught in one of the traps. It was bad enough when I found other animals, but the latest injured creatures were all from natural causes. When I found them, I still took them to the veterinary office, but I went before sunrise, when there was the least chance of being seen. I was forcing myself to go cold turkey when it came to the woman I still wanted.

The week passed at a torturously slow pace. Only the lure of Friday night kept me from doing something really crazy like going to Dawn and begging for another chance.

By Thursday evening, I was wound so tightly, I was little more than a ticking time bomb, waiting to unleash my insanity.

With Stan by my side, I sat on my new bench on my newly built dock, watching the sun set behind the lake. *Twenty-four hours from now…*

I'd planned carefully so I wouldn't get caught, but if I did, I hoped that Dawn would take Stan. I hoped. No, I couldn't think like that. I couldn't trust her either.

As day sunk into night, giving the illusion of being shrouded by darkness, I stood and walked back to the cabin. It was quiet, but the forest is never completely silent. Stan followed me, his tail swishing as his shoulder bumped my thigh, his breath clouding in the cooler night air.

He wasn't doing so well. He'd slowed down even more, and had been suffering from a persistent cough all week. I'd even taken him to the vet's when I knew Dawn wouldn't be working. Gary had prescribed steroids, and they'd helped a bit, but not as much as I wanted or as much as I hoped they would.

He should have been putting on weight, but instead he was getting thinner. It scared me. I couldn't lose Stan as well. I couldn't. I felt my grip on reality slipping away the harder I tried to hold onto it. Stan was my anchor, and I needed him.

At the cabin, I carried him upstairs to his dog bed which was next to mine in a corner of the bedroom. With a deep sigh, he stiffly climbed inside, curling into a comfortable position.

I tucked the blanket around him so no cold draughts could find him, and muttered that he was getting spoiled in his old age. He panted softly and closed his eyes while I stroked him.

Not long after that, we were both asleep.

I sat up, shivering.

Other unexpected wake up calls had included my ex-wife smashing me in the face with her elbow (I was taking up too much room in the bed), and Carl calling in the middle of the night because it was the only time he'd been able to get to the Comms room when he was away on deployment.

But hearing someone vomit … never a good start to the day.

My body still felt tired from yesterday's patrols, and my brain definitely wasn't firing on all cylinders.

I switched on the bedside light and stared at the mess: by Stan's bed, on his bed, and seeping wetly across the floorboards of my bedroom.

His head hung down and his flanks were heaving as if he might vomit again.

"Have you been eating grass, buddy?"

He lifted his head slightly, licking his lips and drooling.

"Come on, time to go outside if you're going to hurl again."

But he sat on his haunches looking at me pathetically.

"You can manage the stairs going down, fella?"

When he still seemed reluctant to tackle the stairs, I heaved him up and carried him downstairs, really worried now. He'd always been able to get *down* the stairs before.

I opened the kitchen door and set him on the dirt beyond the deck, watching worriedly while his body convulsed.

My gut twisted in sympathy and fear.

I crouched down next to him and stroked his head.

"You really are feeling rough, aren't you, buddy? Was it something you ate? Maybe you have stomach flu?"

He leaned against me and I could feel that he was trembling.

The knot of anxiety twisted a little tighter. I wondered whether I should call the Petz Pets emergency line.

Maybe it was just gas? I was guilty of feeding Stan his favorite treats, although I'd been trying to cook healthier meals for both of us.

I encouraged Stan to walk a little because sometimes that helped, especially if he needed a dump. He stood on shaky legs, took a few steps toward me then sat down again, shivering in the light drizzle that was misting the dawn air.

I tried again, encouraging him with whistles and calls. He managed just one step.

It broke my heart to see him so willing to please me but not being able to manage more than a single, painful pace.

After a few minutes, he seemed easier, so I carried him inside, drying him gently with a towel and settled him onto the sofa. But he started licking his lips again and panting heavily.

I sat on the floor and rested my back against the couch, stroking his head. He closed his eyes and sighed, then blinked and stared straight at me.

I'm not doing so well, boss.

"I know, buddy. I think you're going to have to see the dog doctor again, but they're good guys, so it shouldn't be too much of a problem. Maybe you'll even walk in by yourself this time so I don't have to carry your heavy ass."

Sure thing, boss.

And he closed his eyes.

I decided it wasn't worth going back to bed, so I threw on a t-shirt and a pair of jeans, then cleaned up the mess in the bedroom.

When I ran back down the stairs, Stan looked like he was about to throw up again. I only just managed to carry him outside in time. His sides quivered as he coughed up a thin stream of bile—he looked so sorry for himself that I decided not to wait any longer. This wasn't something that could be fixed by kind words.

It was nearly 5AM and light was filtering through the trees, turning the lake to silver. But the beauty was lost on me this morning.

I grabbed my cell and dialed the vet's emergency line.

I hadn't expected Dawn to answer. What were the odds she'd be on duty tonight? Not that I cared. I didn't.

"Petz Pets Emergency Line, how may I help you?"

"D-D-D!"

"Alex? Are you okay?"

"S-S-Stan!"

She was instantly alert. "Bring him to the office. I'll meet you there in 20 minutes." Before the phone clicked off, I could hear her running through the house and calling to Katie. *Why was she there when Dawn was on night duty?*

I didn't have time to worry about that, so I tucked my cell in my pocket and ran out to the truck. I covered the passenger seat with several thick blankets, making a cozy nest for Stan.

When I picked him up, he laid his head on my shoulder, his eyes closed.

A cold fear began to seep through me.

"Hang on, buddy," I murmured, trying to keep the anxiety out of my voice. "It's going to be okay. I know you're sick, but Dawn will fix you up."

Stan's eyes were still closed as the breath wheezed out of his lungs too fast. *It hurts, boss.*

"I know, buddy, I know. Just hang in there."

I broke every speed limit and drove through every stop sign, getting to the vet's office in record time. I was there first and already going crazy with waiting when I saw Dawn's car coming up the street.

I ran around to pull open her door and then saw Katie bundled up on the back seat.

"Are we there, Mom?" she said sleepily. "Is Stan okay? Hi, Alex."

"I don't know yet, honey. Try to rest."

Instead, Katie sat up and rubbed her eyes.

"Can I see him?"

Dawn was already opening the doors to the practice and turning off the alarm. "Okay, but be quick," she called over her shoulder.

I saw that Katie was still wearing her pajamas when she peered into the truck. She was so small, she could barely reach Stan with the tips of her fingers. I lifted her up so she could stroke his head.

"Don't be sick, Stan," she whispered softly to him.

Her lips trembled and tears glistened in her eyes as she looked at me.

"He wagged his tail," she said, her voice wobbling, "but it wasn't a very big wag. Mom says a dog's tail is like his smile. I don't think Stan is smiling, Alex."

I had to swallow a lump in my throat before I could reply. "I don't think so either, Katie-kay. But your mom is a great vet, I'm sure she'll fix him up."

"Okay," she said, her eyes wide and worried.

I carried Stan in my arms and Katie went ahead, holding all the doors for me, until I laid him down on Dawn's examination table.

She already had his notes up on the computer screen, scanning through them rapidly.

Stan licked his lips, then coughed up a thin stream of stomach acid.

"When did he start vomiting?" Dawn clipped out.

"The f-first time at 4AM and the s-second time just before I called you."

Dawn looked up sharply. "Any weakness or lethargy?"

"He's been slowing down for a while now. I thought it was just old age. Gary gave him steroids for a cough. He's had that for the last w-week..."

Dawn frowned and looked at Stan's tongue. It had a bluish tinge to it that certainly wasn't its usual healthy pink color. My palms began to sweat and I had to wipe them against my jeans.

"Katie, wait outside, please," Dawn said, her voice crisp and authoritative.

"Mommy, no! Can I stay with Stan, please, Mom? I'll be quiet. He likes me being here."

Dawn looked at her daughter thoughtfully and opened her mouth as if she might say something else, but then she simply nodded quickly. "You can stay, if it's okay with Alex."

Katie's pleading eyes turned to mine and I nodded. Stan was her friend. I understood that, all too well.

Dawn placed the stethoscope against Stan's ribs and listened intently. When she finally met my eyes, I could see her concern.

"Stan has some fluid building up in his lungs and he has an abnormal heart rhythm. It seems likely that he's had a heart attack."

I hadn't expected to hear that. I didn't want to hear that.

Please God, no.

Katie whimpered and buried her face in Stan's thick fur. I felt like doing the same.

"But you can make him better, right? People—uh—dogs ... they have heart attacks all the time."

Dawn took a deep breath.

"Stan is pretty old for a dog of his size, Alex. It's remarkable he's done so well, especially given his difficult start in life."

"No," I whispered. "Don't say that. He's not ready to go. I'm not ready to let him go. Christ, Dawn! Please."

Her gaze dropped back to Stan and she nodded slowly. "I promise I'll do everything I can."

When Katie's tears started to wet Stan's fur, Dawn sent her to the waiting room, then left herself to prepare Stan's meds.

I leaned down and let my fingers sink into the thick ruff around his neck.

"Come on, buddy. You can do this. You've just got to do what the doc says. Maybe lay off the hotdogs, pal. I know that sucks, but I'll make it up to you, right?"

Stan's tail wagged once then fell limply to the table.

I don't know, boss. I ain't doing so good.

I tried again.

"Just think of all the cool stuff we're going to do for the rest of the year. And I'll roast you a turkey for Thanksgiving, and ... and we could go on a road trip in the Spring—somewhere warm. I don't want to do that without you. Come on, Stan, you've got to try."

Dawn reentered the room and laid her hand on my shoulder.

"Okay, I have his meds, Alex."

"What are you giving him—it's going to work, isn't it?"

She only answered the first part of my question.

"I'm giving him a combination of Digoxin to help his heart; there's also a diuretic, Furosemide, that will help clear the fluid in his lungs. If we can do that, it'll make it easier for him to breathe. Because Stan's heart isn't working properly, the flow of blood is sluggish."

"Okay," I said, my voice gravelly.

"This won't hurt, Stan," she said as she grabbed the scruff of his neck and carefully inserted the needle.

Then she rubbed the site of the injection and stroked his head.

"We'll put him in an oxygenated cage now," Dawn said. "Bring him through here."

I picked him up carefully and carried him into the area that the public didn't usually get to see, although I'd been there twice before.

There was a row of cages in varying sizes. Stan's cage was one of the largest. But instead of a normal cage with thin bars, this one was a clear plastic box, with tubes pumping pure oxygen into it.

There was already a blanket in the bottom, but I thought Stan would prefer one from home. Dawn agreed and sent Katie to get it from my truck.

"How's that for you, buddy? Smells like home, right? At least it doesn't smell of disinfectant. You'll come home smelling clean, but don't worry, it won't last."

Stan raised his head and let me pillow the blanket around him. Then he licked my hand.

Thanks, boss.

"Love you too, buddy."

Dawn laid a gentle hand on my shoulder as I knelt down next to Stan.

"Alex, come and wait outside now."

I shook my head. "I'm not leaving him."

"It's really for the best. Stan needs to rest and right now he's feeding off your anxiety. Just come out to the waiting room. I'll make us both a coffee."

I didn't want to go, but if it was best for Stan…

I stroked his head again.

"Gotta go for a bit now, but I'll be right outside. You just take your time, get some rest. Okay? Okay, Stan? I'll be right outside, I promise." I turned around to look at him once more. "You can't leave me, buddy. You hear me. You've got to fight this—you can't leave me."

As I walked out of the room, Stan lifted his head, his chocolate eyes fixed on me as if he was giving me a message. *I'm awful tired, boss.*

"I'll be back soon," I said, my voice cracking.

Entering the waiting room, I forced myself to get it together. Katie's eyes were wet, and she kept sniffing.

Her usual rapid fire chatter had ceased and she sat in silence, looking very young and very scared.

Dawn passed me a chipped mug steaming with hot coffee.

"I've called my neighbor and she's going to come and take Katie home," she said quietly.

"I was surprised to see her. Nice surprise," I said weakly, ruffling Katie's hair.

"Her fa— sitter let us down at the last moment, so…"

"I want to stay with Stan," Katie whispered, her bottom lip trembling.

"You need to go home and get ready for school, Katie-kay."

"Mommy, Stan wants me to stay with him."

Her lip wobbled and tears sparkled in her eyes. I could see Dawn softening.

"Okay, but you have to go put some clothes on, and when you've had breakfast, Mrs. Lendl will bring you back here if you want to. Alright?"

Katie looked mutinous.

"I'm serious, Katie. I need to focus on Stan right now."

"But I'll be good, I promise, Mommy."

Her voice was so small.

"I know, honey. You can come back as soon as you've eaten something."

Katie sighed, looking down, defeated.

I felt the same.

I hated sitting in the waiting room knowing that Stan was just next door, hovering on the edge of this world. I couldn't let him go. I wasn't ready to say goodbye. I never would be. *Come on, Stan*, I said to myself. *Don't leave me like this, buddy.*

And for the first time in a long time, I prayed.

> *Dear God, if you're really there, if you're really listening to me, please don't take Stan. He's one of the good guys. He never willingly harmed anyone in his whole life, and he saved mine over and over again. It's*

not fair that this is happening to him. Please, please let him get better. I know I don't have any credit with you, and I'm not asking for myself, or maybe I am, but I'm asking for Stan.
   Please.
   Amen.

I didn't know if would make a difference, but at least I'd tried.

Twenty minutes later, Dawn's neighbor collected Katie. She didn't want to go.

Dawn went to check on Stan, but when she came out, her face told me everything.

"I'm so sorry, Alex," she said. "Stan's not doing very well..."

"W-what ... what does that mean?"

"It's time." Her eyes were glassy with unshed tears. "He's dying, Alex."

"No!"

I didn't want to believe her. I couldn't. I shook my head.

"You should say goodbye."

I pushed past her and squatted down next to Stan. His chest was heaving, his breath coming in short pants, and his eyes were closed.

When I stroked his head, his eyes flickered open but then closed again.

I stroked him and held him and buried my face in his warm fur, but I knew Dawn was right. He wasn't coming back from this and it was time to say goodbye.

"It's okay, Stan. I'm here. I'm here."

Stan

I hurt so bad. Every breath was painful like a clamp across my chest. But the worst was seeing the pain in the boss's eyes.

He squatted down next to my cage and ran his fingers through my fur, talking softly, his voice scratched and broken.

I licked his hand and tried to wag my tail, but I was tired. So tired. All I could manage was a limp thump of my tail against the floor.

My last job on earth was to let the boss know that he was loved, and I was leaving him in good hands.

My job was done.

I hoped he knew that he'd never let me down, that he was a good boss, a kind and careful owner, a true friend.

I hoped he knew, but it was getting darker and the light was fading from my eyes.

I sensed Carl waiting for me, not far now, just across the river and over the great divide.

No more swollen joints or blurred vision. No more shortness of breath. No more pain. I was going home.

The rest is silence...

Alex

Dawn touched my arm gently.

"I'm sorry, Alex. He's gone."

"No," I whispered.

"Alex..."

"He wouldn't leave me," I said, incredulous. "He wouldn't do that."

"It was his time."

"No, it wasn't his fucking time! He's not supposed to leave me!" I shouted.

I wanted her to yell back at me, to be angry, but she wouldn't. Instead she held my hand, her warm fingers curling around mine.

I couldn't look at her, so I turned my head to stare at Stan.

He was lying with his eyes open and his tongue lolling from his mouth. The life force, his spirit, the easy friendship he brought to every place he went was absent. His chocolate eyes were fixed and glassy, the light gone forever.

His spirit had already left his battered old body. My friend was gone.

I fell to my knees on the concrete floor.

"I should have been with him!" I cried. "I wanted to stay the whole time but you made me wait outside. Stan was dying and it's your fault. I will never, ever forgive you for that. I should have been here for every second, for every breath!"

Part of me knew my words were cruel and unjust, but I couldn't bear the pain of knowing my best friend was dead.

I pushed my fingers into Stan's fur. He was still warm. It was wrong. Just wrong.

"I'm so sorry I wasn't here, buddy. You were the best dog ever. You were my friend. My only friend. You saved me when no one else could and I'll always be grateful for that. I am going to miss your stinky ass so much. So much."

I reached into the cage and closed his eyes, but there was nothing I could do about his lolling tongue, and that just didn't seem right. With shaking hands and clouded vision, I wrapped Stan's body in his blanket and lifted him out of the cage, ignoring the words of comfort that streamed from Dawn's mouth.

As I headed out of the office, I nearly barged into Ashley who was coming in ready to start her day.

She jumped when she saw me and her mouth fell open. If she spoke, I didn't hear her.

I laid Stan onto my truck's passenger seat.

"I'm taking you home now, buddy. I'm taking you home."

Dawn tried to touch my arm, but I shook her off. I wanted to rage at her, blame her for everything. At that moment, I hated her ... for losing those precious seconds, because she couldn't save him.

I started the truck and drove back to the cabin, although I knew it wouldn't feel like a home without Stan in it.

I didn't know what to do when I parked in my driveway. I should bury him, I knew that, but the thought of putting him in the soil, of laying heavy rocks over the top of his grave, it was more than my breaking heart could bear.

But I would do it. My final act of friendship to the creature who'd come to mean more to me than just about anyone in the whole damn world.

I gripped the spade, shoveling dirt until sweat bloomed under my arms and dripped into my eyes, already gritty from lack of sleep.

I dug the hole deep, really deep, making sure that no one would disturb his eternal peace. Then I loosened the blanket around his body and carefully unbuckled his collar. It didn't seem right for him to wear it now he was free.

And then I heard a car crunching up the gravel driveway. I knew without looking that it would be Dawn.

Brushing my filthy hands on my jeans, I walked around to the front of the house.

She was just getting out of her car when she saw me, and she hesitated. I frowned, then realized belatedly that Katie was with her.

She walked up to me and spoke quietly, staring at somewhere just below my chin.

"Alex, I ... I didn't want you to have to do this alone. So, please ... and for Katie. She needs this. She needs to say goodbye."

And I didn't say it aloud, but I understood, because I needed it, too.

"I know you're mad at me. We've had our ... differences, but Katie wants to have a funeral service for Stan. I know you don't believe ... well, I'm not sure what you believe, but ... Alex, it would really help her."

"It's fine."

She swallowed and ran her tongue over dry lips.

"This is the first time she's been faced with the death of someone she loves and..."

"I said it's fine."

"Thank you. I really appreciate ... and, um, she wants to have a plaque made, for Stan."

"A plaque?"

"She loved him, too."

Katie was crying quietly as she climbed out of the car, tears streaking her face. She wiped her sleeve across her nose and mouth, then stumbled toward me and threw her arms around my waist, hugging me tightly.

"It's not fair," she cried. "I don't want Stan to be dead."

I didn't have the words. I just didn't. So I hugged her fiercely, wishing I could protect her from all the bad things that happen in the world. But no one can do that. Not even God, apparently.

Dawn joined us, running a finger under her eyes to wipe away tears, and I wrapped my arms around her, too. Because I needed it, because she wanted it, because it felt like we were a family, just for a little while.

"I've brought Stan some biscuits," Katie sniffed, staring up at me with her puffy eyes.

I glanced at Dawn, confused.

"She's been studying Greek mythology at school," said Dawn quietly. "You know the one about Charon?"

Then I understood: a biscuit to pay the ferryman. Stan would like that.

"Thank you, Katie-kay," I said, kissing the top of her head.

We buried Stan under his favorite tree, the copper beech. I stroked his fur for the final time and wrapped the blanket around him once more. His body was cooler now, and that hurt so badly.

I laid him to rest and said my final farewell.

"Goodbye, buddy. I love you, man. You're my friend and I am so mad at you for dying. I hope Heaven has bacon sandwiches and hotdogs, because I know you loved them even if they weren't good for you. Bye, Stan. Thanks for always being there."

Katie was sobbing the whole time, but when her turn came, she whispered something to Stan, then carefully laid three large dog biscuits on top of the blanket.

And then I filled in the hole, feeling tears on my face as the dirt fell on my best friend.

When I was finished, Katie placed a cardboard plaque with her large, childish handwriting on top of the mound, and she cried, telling Stan it would be replaced by a real one soon.

Stan

10 years old

Our friend

I gave Katie a quick hug and promised to see her soon.

I didn't keep my promise.

Chapter Twelve

RELEASE

Alex

After they left, I paced the house restlessly.

It was too quiet, and the silence became unbearable. In every room Stan's ghostly presence hovered, just out of sight. His blanket on the sofa, his bed in my room, his food in the kitchen, his bowls outside on the deck. If I closed my eyes, I could almost feel his soft breath on my hand.

Katie had wanted to stay, but she was tired and upset, and I agreed with Dawn when she said they should go home.

But now I was alone, my rage grew with every angry step.

Hadn't the world taken enough from me? My mother, my father, my brother, my wife, my life, nearly my sanity, and now even my dog. When was the universe going to stop shitting on me?

I wanted to go to Cleveland and spill some blood, but more than that, I wanted a drink.

Alcohol was always there, always willing to spend an hour or four listening to you bare your soul.

I wrestled with the want, the need, for nearly an hour, and then I broke. Just one drink before I went to Cleveland. Just one.

Scooping up Stan's collar, I shoved it in my pocket before striding to my truck. Not giving myself time to think anymore, I accelerated out of my driveway with a spurt of gravel as the tires skittered across the loose surface, and the trees were just a blur of color in the side mirrors.

I swerved onto the highway, ignoring the angry honking of cars, then sped down the road.

I needed to be numb. I needed the feelings to just fucking *stop*. But I'd settle for taking the edge off.

Just one drink.

As soon as I hit town, I headed for the first bar I could find and dumped the truck on the street in front of it.

It was late afternoon, so it wasn't empty but it wasn't packed either. A few old guys were propping up the bar with slow-eyed familiarity, as if they'd been collecting dust there forever.

I ignored their open curiosity, slapped down five dollars and asked for a shot of Jim Beam.

I hesitated, thinking of all the reasons why this was a bad idea, trying to remember why I'd stopped drinking nearly a year ago. But the truth was Stan. Stan had stopped me the last time, Stan had saved me. And now Stan was gone.

I tossed the drink down my throat, my eyes watering at the fucking fantastic burn.

"Another?" asked the bartender.

Just one more.

I answered his question by placing another five-dollar bill on my empty glass and sliding it over to him.

He filled the glass again and leaned on the bar top, watching me as I tipped the whiskey into my mouth.

The double shot on an empty stomach after nearly a whole year of sobriety hit me hard. And I fucking loved it. I forgot about Cleveland, forgot about my plans, forgot about the promises I'd made myself. I was going to drink until I couldn't feel anything—maybe never again. That was the new plan.

"B-bottle," I stuttered, pulling a fifty out of my wallet.

The bartender raised his eyebrows.

"You driving?"

I hesitated: I had things to do, places to be, souls to save. But the whiskey called to me, making promises that everything would be better with just one more drink...

I shook my head and tossed the bartender my car keys. I'd never been the kind of a dumb asshole to drink and drive—every other kind of asshole, hell yeah.

The bartender gave me a searching look, but didn't argue. *Wise move.*

I took the bottle from the bar, weaving my way over to a dark corner where I could drink in peace.

As I opened the bottle, the rich malt aroma hit me between the eyes. I licked my lips, almost salivating at the thought of the next pleasurable bite that was just seconds away. My hand shook as I poured the dark amber liquid into the glass, and I sloshed some onto the table.

I had no one. Nobody who'd care, nobody who'd miss me. Well, maybe Charlotte would miss me—she needed a damn good architect to save the business. I laughed at the irony.

The burn of shot number three hit the back of my throat, making me cough slightly, followed by the sweetness of corn and the scent of oak barrels. I wiped my eyes again and took another shot. And another, and another, until I lost count. Drinking until the feelings would be distant and bearable.

You're weak, one tiny corner of my brain was screaming. *You've always been weak. You're a fucking disgrace. WEAK! WEAK! WEAK!*

But the more I drank, the quieter the words became, slurred and indistinct as I slumped in my seat, retaining just enough focus to keep on pouring, keep on drinking.

When I tried to make my way to the bathroom, the floor was bucking and rolling like the deck of a ship in a storm. My empty stomach churned in sympathy and I wondered if it was possible to piss whiskey. Man, that would hurt.

The afternoon passed and the evening rush started to fill the room. I ordered a second bottle before the first was finished.

"You might want to slow down a bit, dude," said the bartender. "Have some water with it. Eat something, maybe."

I pushed a pile of bills toward him and he shrugged.

When I made my way back to my table, I was followed by a blonde with pneumatic tits and glaringly-red lipstick that made me squint.

"You want some company, handsome?"

I pointed at the bottle—I had all the company I needed. But she took that as an invitation to join me and poured herself a glass then tapped it against mine.

"Here's to new friends. I'm Harper."

I carried on drinking.

"Is that a dog collar you've got there? I guess you like some kink, huh? That makes you my kind of guy."

She laughed coarsely and dug her nails into my arm when I pushed Stan's collar back into my pocket.

I felt her tongue in my ear and shook her off as I took another shot.

At some point she must have gotten bored, because next time I looked up, I was alone. *Much better.* I was alone and surrounded by people. Stan had been my people, Stan had been my crowd.

I rubbed my eyes. *Not drunk enough yet.* I poured another glass. I drank it.

Pour, drink. Pour, drink. Until my head felt like it weighed a thousand pounds. I decided to rest on the table, just for a moment.

I don't know how long I was out, but the next thing I remember was someone shaking my shoulder.

"Alex, come on, wake up. Time to go home."

A woman. She smelled good.

I smiled and looked up, my vision blurry. Dark hair, dark eyes, tall. Dawn? No, not Dawn. I was surprised when I recognized Stella.

"Home's empty," I slurred.

"Where's Stan?"

I pointed upward.

"Stan's upstairs?" she asked, her voice confused.

"Yeah, golden stairs," I muttered.

She huffed quietly. "Alex, you're not making any sense. Do you think you can walk to my car?"

I doubted it. I couldn't feel my feet.

She tugged on my hand, helping me get upright, and slung my arm around her slim shoulders. Together we staggered and weaved across the parking lot to her car. She propped me against the door but I slid down, the cold metal scraping across my back as my t-shirt snagged on the side mirror.

"Give me some help here, Alex!" she complained. "You weigh a ton."

She fought to help me to my feet, opened the door, then pushed me inside. I was splayed out across the stick shift, ignoring the way it poked uncomfortably into my side.

"Oh for God's sake! Can't you sit upright! You'd better not hurl. Do you have any idea how much it costs to clean this car? I'll open the window: if you're going to be sick, stick your head outside."

I tried, I really did, and for most of the journey I was fine. But when we started bumping down my potholed driveway, my stomach rebelled, and I vomited whiskey and stomach acid all over the fancy leather.

She screeched. "I can't believe you did that!"

"Sorry," I slurred.

She parked the car, and when I opened the door, I fell out, crawling on my hands and knees to the front door.

"Do you feel better now?" Stella asked tartly.

I belched loudly.

"Oh, God!"

"Gonna go sleep now."

"Not like that!" she snapped. "Take off those disgusting clothes and get in the shower."

I yanked my shirt over my head, vaguely aware of ripping sounds as I crashed against the doorframe. Stella had to reach into my pants pocket to wrestle my keys free.

I laughed and thrust my hips at her.

"You're drunk and you stink."

I nodded in agreement.

I fell over trying to kick off my boots in the hallway. One landed in the living room and the other ... I have no fucking idea where that one went.

Then I unzipped my pants as I started up the stairs, tripping and falling to my knees.

I dropped the pants halfway up the stairs and used the banister to haul myself up the rest of the way.

The boxers were left somewhere else, and then I found myself in the bathroom. It took two attempts to turn on the shower and then I stepped inside and slipped, banging against the soap dish and kicking over a bottle of shampoo. I guess wearing socks in the shower was a big no-no.

I tried to dry myself with a towel, but it seemed like too much effort so I stumbled out dripping wet.

I heard a sudden intake of breath behind me, but by then consciousness was a losing battle. I fell onto my bed and passed out.

Waking up the next day was one of the worst experiences of my life. My mouth tasted like I'd eaten something puked up in Hell.

The thumping hangover was bad, but the shame was far, far worse. I felt bitterly disappointed that after all this time I still didn't have a better control of myself.

Then the pain of losing Stan spiked through the fog, and the wound felt fresh. I remembered everything in vile clarity: Stan, Dawn, running away, the whiskey and ... my throbbing head and stomach rolling with nausea was a stark reminder of how lost I was, how screwed up my world, how pointless my existence.

I lay there feeling sorry for myself when I heard the soft rush of water in my bathroom, and I sat up.

That was a mistake. My head felt so fragile I was half afraid it was going to shatter if I moved again. I reached out cautiously and felt the sheets next to me. Shit, they were still warm.

How the hell had I gotten home last night? And who the fuck was in my bathroom?

The answer walked out wearing one of my t-shirts.

Stella.

What the fuck had I done?

I screwed my eyes shut and groaned.

"Jeez, Alex, you don't have to look so happy to see me!" she snorted, her hands on her hips and an amused expression on her face.

I eyed her warily and her gaze softened.

"You look like hell. How are you feeling?"

I tried to speak, but my voice was so hoarse that I sounded like I'd smoked ten packs of Marlboros as I grunted at her.

She smiled and shook her head.

"That was some bender you were on. I have to say I was pretty surprised to see you in a bar. The bartender said you'd been there all afternoon drinking your body weight in whiskey. What set it off?"

I looked away from her, almost amazed that she couldn't see blood dripping from my wide open heart.

"S-stan d-d-d d-died," I said, my voice breaking on the second syllable.

"Oh," she said quietly. "I'm so sorry."

There was no possible response.

She paused, then handed me the glass of water she was holding.

"I can't make that better, but I can help your hangover. It must be horrendous."

I took the water with shaky hands and swallowed down the two pills she held out.

"You should take another shower," she said firmly. "You've been sweating whiskey all night, and I have to say it isn't pleasant."

I shifted my legs to the side of the bed, willing my stomach to quit heaving.

"Oh God, not again!" Stella yelped, turning around and shielding her eyes. "I saw enough of your dick last night. I don't need a repeat performance!"

I froze. As if the morning wasn't bad enough.

She looked over her shoulder at me, peeking through her fingers.

"Oh, don't look so worried—we didn't have sex. You just decided to do a striptease on your way to the shower last night. And by the way, I'm officially insulted that you look disgusted at the thought of sleeping with me. There was a time when ... well, never mind. Just let me get out of the room first."

The door closed and I heard her yell, "And put some damn pants on!"

My head hurt too much to process why she was here, so I took a long shower, emerging feeling cleaner and slightly more sober. Or slightly less drunk.

My mind cleared, too, and grief threatened to overwhelm me. But there was shame, so much shame. For nearly a whole year, I'd been sober. Eleven long, hard months. And now I was back at square one. Stan hated me drinking. He'd be pissed at me for last night.

Christ, shamed by my dog. I needed therapy. Well, I'd tried that already, but in the end, Stan had been the best therapy.

I lurched back into my bedroom to dress.

Stella had opened the window to the frigid air, but she was right: the room smelled rank and I knew I'd have to change the sheets before I could sleep in that bed again.

Then I glanced down at Stan's bed next to mine. The blankets were cold, but they still smelled like him. I'd always loved the way his fur smelled when he'd been sleeping in the sun—warm and rich like fresh bread or baking cookies.

Tears stung behind my eyes and I swiped them away angrily. Better to be angry than sad.

I listened to Stella moving around my kitchen and wondered again what she was doing here ... and whether I would stomach the coffee that I could smell wafting up the stairs.

Suddenly, there was a frantic pounding on the door. It was too early and too loud and it made my head throb even worse as I tentatively made my way down the stairs. At the same moment, Stella came out of the kitchen.

"I'll get it," I muttered, groaning as the thunderous knocking started again. I pulled the door open and saw Dawn.

"Oh, thank God! I didn't know..."

She stopped mid-flow, her eyes narrowing and her mouth clamping shut. "Stella," she said, her voice dripping ice.

I glanced over my shoulder at Stella, still wearing my t-shirt, her legs bare and hair mussed.

Stella's eyes were wide with shock and alarm.

"Oh, shit," she murmured.

Dawn didn't stay to listen to excuses. She threw me a venomous look as I tried to force out words, but before I could say even a stuttered syllable, she turned on her heel and left. I was in no shape to chase after her.

Stella walked up to me and rested her hand on my shoulder.

"I'm so sorry. I promise I didn't want to mess things up for you. Either of you."

I let the door slam, wincing at the noise, and staggered into the kitchen where I slumped into a chair.

"Why are you here, Stella?"

She sighed and sat down on the opposite side of the table, pushing a cup of coffee toward me.

"I saw your truck outside Mike's bar. I was surprised because, well, after what you told me ... you know ... that you were an alcoholic. When I found you, I could see you were in pretty bad shape, so I thought I'd better take you home. I would have called Dawn ... well, I probably wouldn't, but I knew that you couldn't get home by yourself." She paused. "I'll take you to get your truck when you're sober ... which isn't yet."

I squinted up at her. But then I wondered why she was wearing one of my t-shirts. I raised my eyebrows.

She rolled her eyes.

"You threw up in my car and all over me."

I hung my head.

"I didn't dare leave in case you were sick in your sleep. So I grabbed this. You weren't quite so modest. You have a very impressive dick, by the way. I didn't really mind you showing it to me."

Her laugh was soft.

"I'll talk to Dawn," she said, although her expression wasn't very reassuring. "She thinks I'm a slut, but she knows I'm not a liar. I think she'll listen when I tell her the truth. There's a chance she might believe me."

I was so confused. Why was she being so nice to me? The last time I'd seen Stella it had gotten very ugly...

135

It had been a few days after Spen's party, and I'd been working on my truck when Stella had driven up to the cabin. She said she was just being neighborly, but I'd recognized the calculating look in her eyes. I recognized it because it reminded me of Charlotte.

But she was also Dawn's sister, so I'd given her the benefit of the doubt. Against my better judgement, I'd offered her coffee. She'd wanted a lot more than my best Colombian with cream and sugar. And then she'd invited me to dinner.

When Dawn had asked me about Stella two months ago during our not-a-date, I'd admitted that her sister had hit on me—but it had been a lot more than that.

The memory was unpleasant, and I felt demeaned by what had passed between us, by the way I'd behaved.

We'd been sitting on my deck, and I remembered her watching me that afternoon, a hungry expression on her face...

"I was just wondering if you'd like to come over one evening. No strings, Alex. I just get ... lonely. And you're out here all by yourself..."

I was blunt. I'd told her I couldn't be around anyone who drinks. It had gone downhill from there. Like most alcoholics, she didn't want to believe it when faced with the ugly truth.

"Oh for God's sake," she'd said, her voice strident with irritation. "I have one or two glasses of wine in the evening, that's all. It's not like I'm an alcoholic or anything."

"I am," I said, meeting her eyes.

Several seconds passed as she stared at me, her eyes widening. She seemed stunned. "You?"

I nodded and I could see awareness sweeping over her.

"But you're so ... you seem so..."

"S-s-sober n-nine months now," I'd said, staring out at the lake again. "It's been h-hard."

She gazed at me appraisingly.

"We all knew you were running away from something. My guess was divorce."

I winced and she smiled coldly, knowing she'd made a hit.

"So, I was right about that. I'm not surprised—you've got the look. Hell, I've been there, Alex, I know."

She'd leaned forwards and run her hand through my hair. I ducked my head away and frowned into my coffee.

"Sure I can't persuade you? Have a bit of fun for a change? Or did my little sister get there first?"

I glared at her, my anger building.

"Oh, come on!" she laughed. "I saw the way Dawn was all over you. The frigid little bitch is never that friendly. It was obvious. Does she know? About you?"

I was really regretting telling her anything, and I shook my head.

"N-no! N-n-n-no one!"

"Oh, don't worry that I'll say anything," she said huffily. "I can't stand all those gossiping hens. I've been their target too often, believe me." Then she paused. "So, if my little sister isn't pressing your buttons, who is?"

She was refusing to take a hint.

I stood up and poured my untouched coffee on the ground, hoping she'd realize it was time for her to leave.

"Why so coy? Am I shocking you?"

"Don't p-push me," I warned.

Instead she laughed again.

"Come for dinner. I'll keep the wine on my side of the table."

She was igniting the fury that burned inside me, and she didn't even realize it.

"You know you want to," she said, stroking my hair again.

I gripped her arms suddenly and she jumped.

"You want sex, Stella?" I said, my voice low and hard. "You want a quick fuck, no emotions involved? Then let's go."

"Well, I didn't say 'quick'," she said, her eyes flaring with excitement.

She took my outstretched hand and I pulled her up. As soon as she was vertical, I pushed her backwards hard, hearing her body thud against the side of the house. She didn't even notice.

I pinned her against the wall with my hips and forced my mouth down onto hers. Her hands clawed against my back as her tongue fought with mine. I pulled her hair hard with one hand, forcing her head back, then roughly dragged my other hand up between her thighs. She groaned and writhed.

Then I yanked on her panties until they slid down past her knees.

"Not here! Not on the deck! Alex, please!"

I didn't stop, fury and rage burning away my humanity.

I saw the slap a split second before it made contact and raised my arm to block her.

"No!" she yelled.

I backed away, staring at her.

"Isn't this what you wanted, Stella?" I said, ice freezing my voice. "No emotions, no connection, just sex? Isn't that what you've told everyone anyway, that you've already fucked me? You're just using me, right? Like you said. No strings."

"You bastard," she hissed. "I'm not surprised your wife left you! I can't believe I thought you were a nice guy."

"No, you didn't," I said evenly. "You thought I'd be grateful and you thought I'd be easy. Or maybe just convenient."

With a look of utter loathing, she ducked down to pull up her panties, trying to maintain a few shreds of dignity.

"Fuck you!"

...She hadn't spoken to me again after that, and I hadn't seen her since that day. I assumed that was deliberate.

It was awkward and humiliating for both of us, remembering that day. We'd both traveled a long way since then, weathered the storms, grown older, maybe grown wiser.

"You h-hate me?" I muttered questioningly.

Stella stared out of my kitchen window. "I did, for a while. You were a complete bastard, but I had to admit that my own behavior wasn't quite as pure as the driven snow. It was as if you held up a mirror—and I didn't like what I saw in the reflection." She shrugged. "I feel bad for what I said and did that day. And despite everything, I'm glad you and Dawn are together."

"We're not."

"Really? But Dan ... I heard that you two were dating..."

"It's a long story."

"Perhaps you'll tell it to me sometime. I'm not a complete bitch."

I frowned, and she laughed sadly.

"I've been doing a lot of soul-searching since the last time I saw you. I suppose I should thank you. Although the home truths have been a bitter pill to swallow. If I can fix this..." and she waved her hand at me, "then maybe I'll get my sister back, too."

Her voice was wistful.

"I miss her, and I've missed out on so much of Katie's life." Then she slapped her hands on her knees. "But before that, we've got a busy day ahead of us. So drink that coffee ... unless you're going to throw up again."

My head was still pounding and Stella's fizzing energy was making me dizzy.

I took my coffee, staggered into the living room and slumped onto the sofa.

Stan's folded blanket was laying on the corner. Every room reminded me of him.

Stella came and sat next to me as I fingered the soft material of his blanket.

"I'm sorry about Stan," she said quietly.

I couldn't speak, so I just nodded. Stella wrapped her arms around my shoulders and hugged me. It felt good, and there was no judgement in it, no motive other than friendship. After a minute, she let go.

"I know he was important to you. Perhaps you'll tell me why. One day."

I nodded wordlessly.

"Now, I'm going to go home and get some clean clothes, but I'll be back soon. We have somewhere we need to be."

"Today?"

She nodded.

"Today." And she smiled sadly. "Trust me: Stan would approve."

Stella wouldn't tell me where we going. We drove for nearly an hour and were on the outskirts of Cleveland, which made me twitchy, reminding me that I'd missed my date last night—something else to feel guilty about. Then she shocked the hell out of me by pulling into the parking lot of a rundown church.

I gave her an incredulous look.

"Come on," she said firmly.

The discrete poster on the door clued me in.

> DO YOU CONTROL YOUR DRINKING OR DOES YOUR
> DRINKING CONTROL *YOU?*
> Alcoholics Anonymous
> Every Friday, 11AM

"I come here sometimes," she said quietly. "It helps."

I took a deep breath and told myself this was something I'd done before and that I could do again. I knew Stella was right and I knew I was weak. Maybe this would make me stronger. I clenched my fists and walked inside.

At the side of the church there was a gloomy room with dirty windows. Eleven people sat in hard wooden chairs laid out in a half circle. There were two exit points as well as the dingy entrance. I automatically counted the people: eight women and the rest were men. One was a woman in her twenties who looked broken and hopeless, her hair lank, her skin blotchy and greasy; there was a man in his seventies who wore a shirt and tie; the rest were in their fifties. I stuck out like a sore thumb—but really I fit right in, too.

The man leading the meeting smiled but didn't ask any questions, waving us into seats. Stella gripped my arm and stayed close.

I glanced at each face, knowing that every one of them had done the sort of things I'd done; we'd all fucked up in our different and individual ways. We were all the same.

When the speaker asked if anyone wanted to start, Stella gave me a quick smile.

"Hi, I'm Stella and I'm an alcoholic."

"Hi Stella," everyone replied with varying degrees of interest.

My stomach churned and I started to sweat. I hated being here, but maybe I needed it, too.

She squared her shoulders and began speaking.

"I used to think I was just a social drinker until a friend slapped me in the face with the truth," and she glanced down at me. "I've blamed it on a lot of things, my divorce, my ex-husband trying to take the house." She sighed. "But really it goes back further ... when I found my fiancé cheating on me ... with my little sister."

My eyes darted to hers and I drew in a stunned breath. Stella grimaced and carried on.

"She was always the clever one and I was the popular one, you know?" and she laughed awkwardly. "My sister became pregnant and I turned to my new best friend whiskey and soda. I said some terrible things to her ... really bad ... things I'm ashamed of. I blamed her for the way my life was falling apart, but it turned out she had no idea that the father of her child was my fiancé. The asshole had been dating us both at the same time. But by then the damage was done, and I was too proud, too stupid to admit that he'd played us. Then I met Bob, and I thought marrying him would fix everything, but really it just made it worse. I knew I'd reached another low when I hit on my sister's new boyfriend. He turned me down and told me ... he told me I had a problem."

She took a shuddering breath, and I reached up to squeeze her hand. She glanced down gratefully, then continued.

"He was right, although it took me a while to realize it. And I also realized that I'd been angry for a long time. And it helped when I forgave my sister, but most of all, I'm working on forgiving myself. Well, this week I'll have gone 100 days without a drink."

Everyone murmured congratulations, and Stella gave a small, embarrassed smile.

"I can't fix everything I've done wrong, but I'm going to try."

Chapter Thirteen

ENDINGS

Alex

The drive back from the church was quiet. We were both lost in thought. I was still tired and my headache had come back.

Stella switched on the radio, tuning it to some jazz station, but after a minute she turned it off.

"People love to gossip. They'll all have an opinion. It didn't go unnoticed that I picked you up from Mike's bar last night. Besides, you've been a favorite topic since you arrived in town."

I stared out of the window. All I'd ever wanted was to be left alone—just me and Stan. Well, the joke was on me. I didn't think I could feel more alone.

"Some people will never accept you. I'm speaking from experience, of course."

I glanced at her sideways, but she was staring straight ahead.

"Because of Katie's father?"

She shrugged.

"Yes. It made the most fascinating gossip: two sisters, one man, a child out of wedlock, and the aforementioned sisters screaming at each other on Main Street. Riveting."

Her voice was sarcastic, but I heard the pain beneath it.

"And now it's happening again—the same two sisters, but a different man. You."

"How the hell did anyone come to that conclusion?"

"Well, my very public display at Nancy and Spen's party was the starting point, but also..." and she sighed, "Katie told her friend Holly that she and Dawn had stayed the night at the cottage. Holly is Gary Petz' granddaughter and Ashley's niece. Small town, you see. Word gets around and people draw conclusions, wrong or right. "

I grimaced, but not because I thought she was wrong. The words weren't exactly cheerful.

"Don't go into counseling, Stella. It's not your calling."

She snorted, and when I glanced at her she was smiling.

"I'm just saying you're going to have to listen to some garbage and sometimes you're going to have to walk away from it. But I say screw 'em. If their lives are so pathetic and unfulfilling that they've got to get their kicks by gossiping, then that's sad. I think you should stay—you haven't done anything. You've got nothing to be ashamed of."

That wasn't true and I shook my head.

"I don't want to run anymore. But everything with Dawn got so messed up."

"What happened?"

I rubbed my hands over my unshaven face.

"She asked me if there was anything in my past that she should know, anything that might affect Katie or..."

"And you told her you're an alcoholic."

"Yeah, and that was enough to make her walk away. And this morning ... she'll think ... hell, you saw the look on her face. She'll know that she made the right decision and..."

I couldn't finish the sentence, but I didn't have to.

"Alex, right now she feels betrayed—by both of us. To her, it must seem like history is repeating itself. All we can do is tell her the truth and hope that she believes us. I'm tired of fighting with her so I need to fix this for my sake as much as hers ... and yours."

"Do you think she'll listen?"

"I'll make her listen," Stella said, her voice determined. "Whether she believes me ... I think she'll want to believe you..."

"I know she cares about you," I began. "She told me you were close as kids, but grew apart when you went to college. Now I know why. She admired the fact that you didn't drag Katie into any of your issues. She appreciated that. And Katie likes you, so that's a good start."

"Don't tell me *you're* going into counseling."

I shook my head, smiling. "Nah, I don't think so—anyone who got counseling from me would be really fucked up, even if they weren't when they came in."

Stella laughed but elbowed me in the ribs at the same time.

"Smartass! But seriously, what are you going to do, now the cottage is finished?"

I frowned and shook my head. "I need to do something. I just don't know what that is yet."

I was lying. I knew exactly what I'd be doing later on this week—I'd be going to Cleveland to talk to Giselle again. I knew from experience that although the venue might move around, most events were monthly. That helped to build an audience. I just needed to wait.

Stella patted my knee.

"You're a smart man; you'll figure it out."

"What about you, what are you going to do?"

"Fix things with my sister."

I watched Stella's tail lights as her car bounced away down the road away from the cabin.

Home. Now there was a misnomer. Without Stan, it didn't feel like anywhere special, it was just another place to sleep. I stripped the sheets off my bed and tossed them in the washing machine, puttered around tidying up, but after a while, I couldn't bear to be in the house without him, so I wandered outside and sat down next to his grave.

"Hey, buddy. You probably know all about last night by now, and you're probably pretty disappointed in me. That makes two of us; three, if you include Stella. She turned out to be okay—she even dragged me off to an AA meeting."

I sighed.

"You were a good friend, Stan, my best friend and a great dog. I have never regretted having you in my life for one single day—not even when you pissed on the carpet and chewed the hell out of the furniture. Without you, I'd probably have drunk myself into a ditch two years ago. I'm kind of mad at you, though, leaving me like this, but I guess when your number is up, that's it. I'll miss you every moment of every day, buddy. I hope it's good wherever you are, and they're serving heavenly bacon sandwiches. Say hi to Carl for me."

I rubbed my eyes, and waited. I'm not sure for what—a sign that he'd heard me, something.

The sounds of the forest were all around, and in the distance I could hear a powerboat on the lake. I leaned back against the broad trunk of the copper beech and stared up through a patchwork of russet leaves at the dull, iron-gray sky. Maybe I was waiting for the sound of barking, but it never came.

Dawn

Betrayed. By someone I cared about.

Again.

Betrayed. By my sister.

Again.

Seeing her standing at the cottage door, dressed in Alex's t-shirt, I'd felt crushing pain deep inside my chest.

I wanted to hurt her. I wanted to throw up. I wanted to hurt him. I wanted to run.

Why did she hate me? I'd been just as much Matthew's victim as she had. Why had she done this to me now? Why!

It was too cruel.

So I'd run. And then I'd broken down in tears on the way home and was forced to pull over because I knew that I wasn't safe to drive.

All the years of hurt and pain, anger and regret were released in a river of tears. I cried for myself, for the loss of my sister, for my fractured family, for the man I dared to believe in, for the future we'd never have.

I wanted the tears to be cathartic, to wash me clean, to leave me with a new place to start, but all I felt was empty.

I stumbled through the front door, relieved that Katie was with Holly, and I curled up on the sofa, cold and numb and so alone.

I heard Katie's voice in my head, *You make everyone go away*, and a fresh wave of tears swept through me.

It all seemed so pointless. Why try so hard, when failure hurt so badly? Why bother to dream, when it all turned to nightmares?

It was early evening when I heard a knock at my door. Night had fallen, and there wasn't a single light on in the house. Dully, I stared at my watch. Katie wouldn't be home for another hour—time to pull myself together.

The knocking began again, louder this time.

I hauled myself up from the sofa, a pounding headache making me slow and listless.

When I pulled open the door, Stella was standing there.

Stunned, I stared at her, then started to close the door immediately, but she pushed it open and stuck her purse in front of her so I couldn't slam it shut.

"I didn't sleep with him," she said abruptly.

I stared at her disbelievingly.

"I didn't," she said, her voice quieter now. "Alex loves you. He loves *you*."

A bitter laugh bubbled out of me. "This is low, Stel, even for you," and again I tried to close the door.

Surprising me with her strength, she shoved it wide open, pushing me backwards and inside.

She pointed at me with one perfectly manicured finger.

"Dawn, that man is in pieces because he thinks he's messed up with you. And right now, he needs you." Her hand dropped to her side. "So, please! Before you make a huge mistake, just ... just hear me out. Please."

I folded my arms across my chest, trying to hold inside the hope that dared to bloom.

"Why are you here, Stella? Really?"

Her tough façade crumbled and she pressed her lips together.

"I miss you. I want my sister back."

Nonplussed, all I could do was stare at her warily.

"It's true," she pleaded. "I miss my sister. I know I blamed you for what happened with Matt, and that was wrong of me. I'm so sorry, Dawn. It's not a great excuse, but I felt so humiliated and hurt, and I didn't want to believe that he'd never cared about me. I let my pride get in the way of the truth, and I was angry with the wrong person. You're my sister and I love you." She took a deep breath. "And I'm so sorry."

Tears threatened, and I forced myself to swallow the lump in my throat. I'd waited to hear her say those words for more than eight years. I badly wanted to believe her, but...

"Matthew ... Matt ... he played us both," I said, my voice shaking. "I know that. I never wanted any of it to happen, but I have Katie, and she means the world to me."

"And to me, Dawn. She's my niece and I love her to pieces."

"I know."

And I did know that. Stella had never let any of the bitterness or hurt affect how she behaved toward Katie. I'd always respected her for that.

"I want to be a part of her life, Dawn. A real part of it before she gets too much older. She's going to ask me why we're always fighting and I can't *bear* the thought of that. I want to be her Aunt Stella. Well, her cool Aunt Stel," and she gave the ghost of a smile.

It sounded wonderful. I ached to have my sister back, but the doubts wouldn't be silenced.

"I saw you, Stella. This morning. You were wearing ... you were wearing Alex's t-shirt. You'd spent the night."

Stella grimaced.

"I did, but it's not what you think. I promise. I promise you! Nothing happened. Look, will you let me come in and sit down? I don't need any more gossip in town about the battling Andrews sisters."

Silently, I stepped back, and with a final, searching look in Stella's face, I walked into the living room, leaving her to follow me.

She perched nervously on the edge of my battered sofa, her eyes wide, as if surprised that I'd allowed her in.

"Thank you," she murmured, glancing around the room.

I nodded, waiting for her to explain.

"It's not what you think," she began.

"You already said that."

"Yes, but it's true. I ... I'm not sure where to start..." she took a deep breath. "I'll start at Nancy and Spen's party. I was miserable. Bob had been giving me a hard time and the lawyer's fees were stacking up. I was drinking too much ... and then I saw you with Alex. You looked so happy, just so *right* together. I was jealous. I've always been jealous of you, Dawn."

Her mouth turned down with her admission.

I was stunned. I'd always believed that she was the charmed sister, the lucky one. I'd always been jealous of *her*.

She cleared her throat.

"When I saw you with him, I wanted to prove that I could be the sister men wanted after all. I realize now that I'd been holding onto all my anger over Matt for a long time. I still blamed you, even though I knew that Matt was a bastard. Anyway, as you know, Alex drove me home and that was that. He wouldn't even come in for a drink. I know why now," she said sadly. "Although there was more than one reason, of course. Anyway, shortly after that, I went to see him and ... I made it pretty clear that I wanted to sleep with him."

Even though Alex had told me himself that Stella had hit on him, a hot bolt of anger had me clenching my fists. Stella licked her lips and hurried on.

"He turned me down, of course. He wasn't the slightest bit interested in me, and I admit that hurt my pride. He told me that he couldn't be around anyone who drinks. I was so shocked! I'd never thought of myself like that. But it was the wakeup call I needed. I took a long, hard look at myself ... and I didn't like what I saw."

Her expression was pleading again.

"I had a failed engagement and a failed marriage behind me. I was a thirty-six year old divorced alcoholic whose sister wouldn't speak to her. I've failed at everything that's important. So..." she took a long, shuddering breath. "I started going to AA meetings, and I began to see things more clearly."

I interrupted her quietly.

"Did Mom and Dad know about this?"

"Yes, but I only told them two weeks ago. I needed to know that I could keep it up—the sobriety. They were pretty mad that I hadn't told them before. But I didn't want to fail in public again, you know? I wanted to be able to say that I was a *recovering* alcoholic, and for it to be true."

She stared down at her hands.

I knew how much it cost her to tell me all of this. She was stripping her soul bare, and her braveness confounded me.

"And is it true? Have you stopped drinking, Stel?"

She nodded, a small smile of pride lifting her lips.

"A hundred days sober, Dawn. A hundred days."

"Wow! That's amazing ... congratulations."

"Thank you. That means a lot to me."

I smiled at her tentatively. It felt new and slightly awkward. But good. It felt good to smile at my sister and mean it.

"It hasn't been easy," she continued quietly. "I wanted to come to you a million times, but I needed to get through this first."

"You didn't have to do it alone, Stel."

"Yes, I think I did. But thank you for saying that. I wanted to fix things with you. I didn't know how, but I wanted to try."

I licked my lips.

"Where does Alex fit in?"

She gave me a worried look.

"I was driving through town last night and I saw his truck outside the bar. He'd told me he was an alcoholic, so as soon as I saw where he was parked, I was concerned. I thought ... I'm not sure what I thought, but then I saw him, and he just looked so ... so broken."

I sucked in a deep breath.

"Stan died. His dog."

"I know. Well, I figured it out eventually—he wasn't very coherent. So I got him in my car and drove him home. On the way, he threw up all over me and all over the interior of the car. I just hope the detailer can get the smell of vomit out of the car," and she wrinkled her nose, startling a laugh out of me.

Her eyes lit up and she smiled back.

"It was totally disgusting! I made him get in the shower and go to bed. But he was so drunk, I was afraid he'd be sick in his sleep. So I stayed..."

"And you needed something to wear."

"Yes! And that's all! I promise! The man loves you, Dawn. Really loves you. And he's devastated because he thinks that he's ruined everything with you. But I can see that you care about him, so please don't let him go because you think I did something ... he loves you and so do I. All I want is for you and Katie to be happy. And, like I said, I want my sister back."

I wanted to believe her. Sincerity shone in her eyes, and I could see the hope trembling behind them, the desperation that I believe everything she'd said.

I stood up and walked across to my sister. And then we were hugging each other and crying, apologizing and crying some more.

Stella hugged me tightly, and it felt good. It felt right.

When we untangled ourselves, Stella whispered in my ear.

"Go to him, Dawn. Give him a chance. Give yourself a chance."

Alex

I must have fallen asleep outside by Stan's grave, because when I jerked awake, bone cold, the sun had shifted several degrees and the shadows were deepening across the forest.

Then I saw what had woken me.

"Dawn," I croaked, trying to sit upright, wincing when a sharp pain shot up my neck from the awkward angle.

"Sorry I woke you."

I rubbed my eyes, unable to believe that she was here. I didn't need to explain what I'd been doing outside. She'd been there when I buried Stan.

I stared up at her, but then she sat on the ground opposite me, her knees pulled against her chest.

"How are you feeling?" she asked cautiously.

I sighed and rubbed my hand over the scruff on my jaw.

"Ashamed. Stupid. Disappointed in myself. Missing Stan. Hung over."

She didn't say anything, she just continued to stare.

"Stella came to see me," she said at last. "I want to believe her..."

"I didn't sleep with her." I shook my head. "No. You're the person I want to be with."

"You didn't come to me," she said sadly, her voice tired, worn paper thin. "You didn't give me a chance to help you. You went to a bar and got drunk instead."

I winced.

"That was ... I wasn't making good decisions. I'm sorry about that. Hell, I'm sorry about everything that I did yesterday. It was just ... too much."

"I know, I could see that."

I let my head thud backwards against the tree trunk. "Dawn, I'm an alcoholic. My first instinct will *always* be to drink. I've just got to keep fighting against it. I'd been sober for nearly a whole year, but after everything that's happened, I broke, and I can't tell you how angry I am with myself."

She sighed.

"I really am sorry about Stan. I know how much he meant to you. I'm so sorry that I couldn't do more. I tried everything, but..."

"It was his time. I know. And I'm sorry, too. I didn't mean those things I said. I don't blame you."

Her shoulders slumped, some of the tension leaving them.

"Thank you. I wish ... I hoped..." and her eyes met mine. "Ever since Stella came over ... even before that ... I've been thinking about you, about us, pretty much nonstop. But I can't risk *this* with Katie."

I didn't think it was possible to feel worse, but then Dawn went and proved me wrong.

As we stared at each other, doubt clouding her eyes, I abandoned any scraps of pride.

"Will you give me another chance?" I said at last.

She sighed and looked away.

"I want to, but I don't know if that would be smart. Not right now. It's too soon. I think ... I'd always be waiting for it to happen again, walking on eggshells. I can't live like that."

A sharp pain jabbed at my battered heart.

Hadn't she said enough already? Did she really think she needed to wield her sword of truth again? I only had one neck, and I'd stuck it out far enough already.

I wanted to tell her that she'd already given me more than I'd ever dared to hope for or deserved. But I didn't. Couldn't.

Instead, my voice was bitter, accusing.

"I'm not blaming you. I wouldn't take a chance on me either."

Her eyes were sad as she pushed herself upright.

"I'll see you around, Alex."

"I doubt it. I don't need a vet anymore."

Her jaw snapped shut and she walked away.

And yes, I could make the day suck even more by being a complete asshole. But I didn't follow her.

The weather grew colder and the ice in my heart that had begun to thaw had frozen again with Dawn's words. She couldn't be with a man who'd been an alcoholic. The End.

I did a lot of thinking during the next couple of weeks. There wasn't any work left to do on the house other than regular cleaning. It only took one morning before the place could have passed muster by a Drill Sergeant at boot camp.

I missed Stan. The house was so silent. Even when Stan had been asleep, his quiet presence had filled the place. Now only his memories lived here.

I missed Dawn, and Katie, as well.

The empty burn inside was painful. I wanted to fall apart again. What was the point of fighting so hard when it all turned to shit?

But there was one bright spot, a ray of hope—from the unlikeliest of people.

Stella came over each evening and I made her supper. I'd told her that the evenings were the toughest time of the day, when I was at my weakest, so she made sure I was kept entertained. Plus, she was a lousy cook and had been living on takeout since her divorce.

She told me more about growing up with Dawn, and about the douche Matthew who thought it was a big game to date sisters without either one of them knowing. Bastard. I already knew he didn't have a lot of interest in Katie. Stella said he did the bare minimum.

"The irony is that I met him when I went to visit Dawn one weekend at Penn State University. She'd stayed after class to talk to her professor and that's when I first saw Matt. He taught at the Behrend campus, well, he still does. We started dating, and then he asked me to marry him. He was suave and sophisticated, and it seemed like a dream come true. You have to remember that at the time, I had a very dull office job in Erie. I suppose it was a way of escaping. I had no idea that he was seeing Dawn during the week and me at weekends.

"I don't know why Dawn bothers with him. I think she's still trying to do the right thing," she sighed. "She thinks Katie should have her father in her life," and she shot me a quick look which I ignored. "A male role model. Spen is great, but he'll be knocking on 80's door in a few years."

Thankfully, she dropped the topic after that.

And there was more bad news. The asshole who'd welcomed me to Girard with the gutted torso of a dead fox on my doorstep last summer ... he was back to his old tricks. This time I was going to catch him.

I'd just driven from the grocery store with ingredients to make risotto for Stella. I'd only been gone an hour, but in that time, the asshole had strung up a dead rabbit and hung it on my porch.

I pulled Carl's old Swiss Army Knife out of the truck's glove compartment just as I heard Stella's car crunching over the gravel.

"Ugh! What is that?"

I didn't bother to answer, cutting it down quickly and tossing it into the forest. My fox friends were now all grown, but they wouldn't turn down a free meal. I'd always thought it must be their mother who'd been sacrificed to make a point when I arrived in town. I just didn't know what that point was. Except that I wasn't welcome. Usually people had to get to know me before they hated me.

Stella had made herself comfortable in the kitchen and was filling the coffee machine with water.

"What was that all about?"

"Someone trying to intimidate me. I'm not sure why, but it's been happening on and off since I moved in."

"Seriously? Does Dan know?"

"Yeah, he was here once when someone had tied a dead crow to the porch. I'd guess it's the same person who was setting snares in the forest."

"What did Dan say?"

"Not much. Just to let him know if it continued. It seemed to stop for a while, so I didn't bother and besides," I said, looking at her sideways, "I don't mix well with police."

"Hmm, no, I don't suppose you would, but Dan is one of the good guys."

I shrugged. Whatever was happening on my land, I'd deal with it my own way.

"What about you?"

She snorted. "You mean my stalker? Yes, Bob is still around, still trying to get me out of the house."

"Can't your lawyer help?"

"The divorce settlement is done. I get to keep the house in lieu of any future alimony, but I'll need to pay for the taxes and upkeep. I'll have to get a job soon, but the house is mine and I'm not giving it up. I don't even know why he wants it now—he never liked living there. He said it was creepy being in the woods. Well, he's the only creep around."

She paused, deep in thought.

"You know what, I just realized something..."

"He's not a creep?"

"Don't be ridiculous—he's the biggest, creepiest thing ever. No, I think I've just figured out why he wants the house after all this time. Can I use your computer? My phone never works on your wifi here."

I gave her my laptop and she smiled at the screensaver—a picture of Stan sunbathing on the deck.

"Soppy old mutt," she said affectionately.

Then she pulled up a story from the local newspaper about the potential for property development along the lakefront.

"I can't imagine they'd get planning permission."

"Not in the State Game Lands, no. But my house isn't protected by that." And she gave me a worried look. "And neither is yours."

I knew how much property with a lake view would be worth with planning permission for development, and suddenly it all started to make sense.

"At Spen's party, he started trying to talk to me again about selling. That's what kicked it off. Well, that and the fact I'd been drinking all afternoon." She gave me a wry smile. "And he's been very persistent."

"Spen told me that someone else had put in a bid for Old Joe's place, but it was way under what I paid." I shrugged. "I didn't care what I paid—I just wanted somewhere quiet."

Stella was thoughtful.

"I can't believe I'm even thinking this, but ... you know, Bob likes to hunt. Every year, he'd go off with his buddies when the hunting season started and shoot some poor caribou. He'd know how to lay a snare." Then she sighed. "Even though the guy is a louse, I hate to think that he'd be capable of leaving dead animals on your porch. But the timing..."

"If he is, I'll catch him."

"You love all that macho stuff, don't you? Well, go and show me how domesticated you can be in the kitchen. It's all good practice for when my dumb sister comes to her senses."

"Stella..."

"Shoo! Off you go! Cook for me, Alex."

Fall was fading quickly and winter was just around the corner. I could measure the passing time by the color of the leaves turning from dark green, to reds and oranges and yellows that made the forest blaze, even as the temperature began to drop. I was still undecided whether to stay or sell.

But if I did sell, it wouldn't be to Bob. The more I thought about what Stella said, the more I thought she was right. The timing was too convenient.

Whatever his plans were, I'd counter them. But right now, I had other business to take care of.

I'd been to Cleveland twice, looking for Giselle, but she'd disappeared, and I didn't have any other contacts to find what I wanted. Hanging out in bars, hoping to hear something, to find a clue, yeah ... that probably wouldn't be the best plan B. So for now, that project was on the back burner. If I'd spent time hanging around the right bars, I might have got the information I needed, but that would be like sprinkling gasoline then walking around tossing lit matches. And although I was miserable, I wasn't suicidal.

To keep my mind active, I started working on some architectural sketches, ideas for other cabins like mine—a far cry from the industrial scale I used to do, but it was something.

Dawn still hadn't contacted me. I tried to call her once, but her phone went to voicemail and I didn't leave a message.

I enjoyed hanging out with Stella. I liked having a friend, someone who knew the painful parts of my past, and didn't judge.

We were sitting in my living room watching the flames leap in the fireplace, the logs popping and giving off a scent of cedar and oak. It was comfortable, domestic even. And it was peaceful. Since I'd been sober for the second time, I'd learned a new appreciation for life without drama.

Stella was drinking coffee and I was drinking some herbal tea. I used to laugh at anyone drinking that shit, but I was avoiding all stimulants, even caffeine.

"You know that I went to see Dawn the day after Stan died," she said out of the blue.

We'd both avoided mentioning Dawn's name, so Stella had surprised the hell out of me.

I paused, my cup halfway to my mouth, then I carried on sipping my tea. I knew that she'd seen my hesitation.

"I know," I said, at last. "She told me. Thank you for doing that."

Stella gave me a sad look.

"It didn't help though, did it?"

I grimaced.

"Stel, I'm completely capable of fucking things up by myself. You were trying to help. It *did* help. At least she knew the truth and wasn't thinking the worst."

Stella sighed.

"I had to do some begging outside her house before she opened the door. At one point, I thought I was going to have to swear on my entire collection of Chanel purses before she let me inside. I think I only got through the front door because she was embarrassed about what her neighbors might hear." She glanced across at me. "I'm not very good at taking no for an answer, but I think you already know that."

I smiled weakly at her.

"True."

"I've tried to talk to her about you since then..."

"So you're still seeing her?"

"Yes, we meet for coffee. Sometimes she brings Katie."

"That's ... good. Really good. How is she?" I asked as calmly as I could.

I was pleased that Stella and Dawn were mending their relationship, especially if it meant I got to hear about her, as well.

"It's good with you both now?"

Stella gazed at me appraisingly.

"She misses you. She's worried about whether or not she's made the right decision. For the record, I told her she was making a mistake and that what you two have together is rare enough to deserve a second chance, or a third chance, or as many chances as it takes for you to work it out."

"How's Katie?" I asked, sidestepping the rest of her point.

"The same: missing you, missing Stan."

"Yeah."

Stella took one look at my face and changed the subject.

"Are you sure you won't come to Florida with me for Thanksgiving? I made a reservation at a hotel so it's not like you'd have to stay with my parents."

"No, but thanks for the offer. I'd rather forget about the holidays. Anyway, I've got some research I need to get on with."

"Research, huh? I don't think I want to ask. Just be careful." Her voice was skeptical. "Are you sure you don't want to change your mind? Save me from my parents?"

I smiled at her. "Another time."

"I'll hold you to that," she laughed. "Dawn has already said she's not coming because the asshole wants to see Katie for part of the holidays." She rolled her eyes. "He's not doing it because he cares; he only does it because it disrupts things for Dawn. They're both staying in town."

She'd already made sure I knew that, and yes, it was part of the reason I was staying, too. I didn't tell Stella that, but I could tell she guessed by the amused glint in her eye.

"You know, I've been wondering..." she said, her smile growing even wider. "That day on your deck, you were really going to fuck me, weren't you?"

I winced. "Stella..."

"Come on, Alex, I'm not going to leap on you and steal your virtue ... what's left of it ... but we're friends. You can tell me."

"Christ, Stella!"

"Tell me!" she insisted.

"Okay, yes. I would have fucked you on the deck. You kept pushing me, and I lost it. I feel bad about it—really bad and I'm sorry, okay!"

Stella laughed. "Oh don't apologize, it was hot! Besides, it's nice to know that you don't find me completely physically repulsive."

"You're busting my balls," I said flatly, and she cackled loudly.

"Why, yes I am. But only because it's so much fun. Don't worry, handsome, I know you're spoken for, and hopefully one day soon my idiot of a sister will come to her senses."

I smiled and shook my head. Stella was one of a kind.

Stella flew down to Florida the next day and I felt her absence acutely. The temptation to drink intensified as I found myself alone; it was a constant shadow, an ache, a need that grew more toxic the more I tried to ignore it.

I compounded the misery by getting rid of Stan's old blankets and tossing out the chewed toys and half a bag of dog biscuits that were still in the pantry. Then I changed my mind and dug the biscuits out of the trash and scattered them in the forest for the foxes and other wild animals. Stan would have approved.

I hated the fucking holidays, period. It had been a God-awful time when I was a kid, Mom and Dad stuck in the house together, locked in their mutual unhappiness.

It hadn't been so bad in college. A couple of times I'd been invited to my roommate's family in Detroit, until I met Charlotte. Not that she'd been much into holidays either. Her idea of a good time was to go to Acapulco or Maui—somewhere expensive with sunshine.

For the last two years, me and Stan had developed our own traditions: soda and pizza—double cheese for me, pepperoni for him. Hell was other people. That had become my motto, but this year ... fuck ... this year, I'd hoped for other things, other people, a family. With Stan. Now I didn't even have the alternative of getting wasted and passing out.

When I woke up reluctantly on Thanksgiving, a sudden frost dusted the world with white, and the forest around the lake was locked in glittering ice. I shivered. It was probably time to crank up the boiler, but I couldn't seem to care.

I stared out of the window, wondering if I should have gone to Florida with Stella and grabbed some winter sun while I could. But there would have been too many questions from her parents, and I didn't want to be so far away from Dawn, even if she wasn't talking to me.

I shook my head: I couldn't think like that. Instead, I pulled on sweats and my running shoes and headed out into the forest.

My breath turned to steam as I dragged frigid air into my lungs, the icy burn making my throat sting. I ran through the forest, my footsteps crunching loudly on the fallen leaves. I pushed faster and faster, until sweat was dripping from my body and the muscles in my thighs were trembling. I slowed down to a jog then leaned against a tree to catch my breath.

Something was changing inside me, I just wasn't sure what it was.

Returning home, whatever that meant, the creeping stillness choked me. I needed to stay busy. So, I spent the rest of the morning hanging drapes that Stella had helped me choose, because the temperature drop meant that I could see my breath in the bathroom mirror.

I hated to think of Stan cold in his grave, so I pushed the thought away.

I'd find ways to occupy myself for now, but on the night of Black Friday, I was heading to Cleveland. I'd finally found Giselle—and she had the information I'd been waiting for.

Chapter Fourteen

CHANGES

Alex

It was Thanksgiving, and I'd spent the morning going for a run along the lakeshore, and the afternoon changing the oil on my truck. Lunch had been cold cuts and a baked potato.

I'd just about finished, but was up to my elbows in grease and oil, when my cell phone rang, scaring the crap out of me. Only Stella, Spen, my bank and Home Depot had my number, so it didn't ring very often.

It took me a moment to find a rag to clean off my hands. The call was from a local number, but one that I didn't recognize.

"Hello?"

All I could hear at first was the sound of someone sniffing. I nearly hung up, but then a small, tearful voice spoke.

"Alex, will you come get me?"

"Katie? What's wrong? Where are you?"

There was more sniffing as I wrestled the keys from my jacket pocket.

"Honey, tell me where you are. Are you okay?"

"I'm at my dad's," came her quivering voice. "Well, I was at my dad's, but he had to tutor his student even though it's Thanksgiving and I wanted to watch my TV shows, but he said they were stupid and that this was more important, so we drove to an apartment building and I've been sitting in his car for a long time and I don't know where he is. I don't like it here and it's cold. I'm hungry and I need the bathroom."

She paused for breath, and I heard her sniffing back more tears. Rage boiled through me. I was appalled that her father would leave her alone like this. And what the hell was this garbage about tutoring a student on Thanksgiving? I knew he taught at Penn State Behrend in Erie, but surely not today. Even if it was some sort of emergency, he should have driven Katie home first. Asshole.

"What did your mom say? Did you call her?"

There was a hesitation before she spoke softly.

"No. She's working."

"I think she'd want you to call her."

"I called the office number and it transferred to Ashley's cell phone. She said Mom had to go out to do an urgent colic operation on Suki, Mrs. Kingston's Palomino. That means the stomach gets a strangulating obstruction and it really hurts, and Mom said I should only interrupt her if it's an emergency, and I didn't know if this was an emergency. So I called you."

I made my voice as soothing as possible, not wanting to let on that I was really worried, and fucking angry.

"Well, I think you should call Ashley back and tell her what you told me. And say that I'm coming to get you. Okay?"

"Promise?" she asked, her voice wobbling.

"I'm getting in my truck now. I'll be with you as soon as I can."

"Okay," she sniffed. "Are you mad at me?"

"No, honey. You did the right thing." *Even if your mom will hate it.*

"I'll come get you, honey. I'll be there real soon. Katie, this is important: how long have you been waiting in your dad's car now?"

I wasn't keen to get involved in their business if she'd only been there a few minutes, but she sounded really upset...

There was a short pause. "More than an hour?"

I swore under my breath and her voice trembled. "I was going to call Aunty Stella, but she's in Orlando with Grammy and Pops, and I thought Mom would be mad at me."

I couldn't tell the poor kid that Dawn would hate her calling me even more.

"Don't worry, honey. Do you know if the car doors are locked?"

I heard some scuffling, then she said, "I think so."

"Okay, that's good. Keep them locked and don't open the door for *anyone* except your dad. I'll be there as fast as I can. Call me if he comes back."

"'Kay," she said quietly. "I miss Stan."

My gut clenched. "I know. Me, too."

"And I miss you," she whispered. "So does Mom."

I didn't think it was the right time to respond to that, but it gave me a sudden small flash of hope.

It wasn't easy getting her to explain exactly where she was. She told me her father's address, and she knew that she was only a few minutes away from that. So I headed over there while I got her to describe what she could see from the window and what she remembered seeing on the way over. I think I could guess where she was, near some campus housing, but if all else failed, I'd knock on doors and try to find someone who could help.

157

A million thoughts flew through my brain on that short journey. It was getting late and I was worried that Katie was still all alone. I put my cell on hands-free in case she called again and said her dad had come back, but it didn't ring during the 12 mile journey.

When GPS told me I was nearing my destination, I called her.

"Alex! Where are you? I'm scared. Someone just banged on the window."

"I'm really close, honey. Can you tell me what kind of car you're in?"

"Um, a new one?" she said uncertainly.

"Okay, and what color is it?"

"Silver," she said, her voice more definite this time.

I immediately saw a silver Benz fifty yards in front of me.

"I can see you, Katie-kay. I'm flashing my headlights now. Can you see me?"

"Yes!" she shrieked. "Yes, I can see you!"

I parked behind the Benz and jumped out. Two seconds later, Katie had wrapped her arms around my waist and was hugging me tightly and crying almost hysterically into my shirt. I hugged her back, stroking her hair, telling her she was going to be okay.

"Did you call Ashley?"

She nodded, wiping her eyes with her fingers.

Suddenly Katie's phone rang.

"It's Mom!" she said shakily, sniffing hard. "Mommy," she said softly. "I waited and waited like Daddy told me, but it was getting dark and I was scared and cold and I really, really need to go to the bathroom."

She sounded very much like a little girl, and not the mini-adult she so often seemed to be.

"I'm okay." *Pause*. "I don't know." *Pause*. "It was a really long time. He said he had to tutor his student." *Pause*. "I didn't know what to do." *Pause*. "I called Alex and he came to get me. He's here now." *Pause*. "Yes. Yes. Okay." Katie listened intently, nodded several times then whispered, "I love you too, Mommy," then passed her phone to me. "She wants to talk to you."

"Alex?"

"Y-yes."

"Thank you so much for looking after my little girl."

Dawn's voice cracked, and I could hear the raw emotion. I wanted to reach through the phone to comfort her.

But then someone called Katie's name, and a tall, skinny man came running toward us.

"Katie! What are you doing out of the car?" he shouted.

I was pissed that his first reaction was to tell his daughter off, but I was going to give him a pass because I assumed he was worried that she was talking to some strange guy.

"My n-name is Alex Winters. I'm a friend of D-dawn's," I said, standing up straight and letting my free arm fall from Katie.

But Katie just hugged me harder and hid her face in my oil-stained shirt. Her father was scaring her.

He sneered at me. "You have five seconds to let go of my daughter before I call the police."

"Good idea," I said evenly. "Then you can tell them why you left your daughter by herself for nearly two hours while you were *tutoring* your student. On Thanksgiving."

His face flushed a dull red and he clenched his fists.

"While you're deciding to make the right choice, I have Dawn on the line."

I handed him Katie's cell and watched as his lips thinned. Whatever Dawn was throwing at him, her words were hitting the mark.

The call ended and he looked like he was about to toss Katie's phone on the floor. Instead he handed it back to me, then turned to leave.

"You can take her home."

"Don't you have anything to say to your daughter?" I asked, a quiet rage tightening my voice.

His eyes narrowed but he bit back whatever retort he'd been ready to spit at me.

"I'll call you, Katie," he said tersely, then opened the driver's door of his car, climbed in and sped away.

Katie was still clamped to my shirt, so I picked her up and carried her to the truck. She finally loosened her grip when I clipped her seatbelt into place.

"Let's go home now, okay?" I said, keeping my voice soft.

I was trying to sound calm and reassuring for her sake, even though I was burning with anger.

She nodded and wiped her eyes with her sleeve.

First stop was a diner so she could use the bathroom, and I offered to get her something to eat.

"You want a cheeseburger, Katie-kay?"

"No, I don't eat meat."

I raised my eyebrows.

"Okaaay. How about a veggie burger deluxe and fries?"

That got the seal of approval, and I ordered myself a milkshake.

I wasn't sure if Katie would want to talk, so I kept quiet at first while she ate. But once she was in my truck on her way home, licking her fingers that were covered in oil and salt, Katie seemed totally relaxed. Unlike me. I just hoped that Dawn would be able to smooth out any repercussions ... if she wasn't totally furious with me for messing things up with her ex.

I rubbed my temples with one hand and fought back the urge to find somewhere I could drink to forget. Without Stan to distract me, I found myself thinking about alcohol more frequently, an itch in the back of my brain —one I couldn't scratch. Only Stella's company kept me teetering on the edge without going over. Well, that wasn't the only reason, but it was a good one.

"Why are you and Mom fighting?" Katie asked suddenly.

How the hell did I start to answer a question like that?

"It's complicated, Katie."

She crossed her arms and frowned. She looked so much like Stella when she did that—it made me smile.

"Adults always say that to little kids when they don't want to tell them. But I'm not little and I'm not dumb! Mom says she's upset with you because you did something bad that she didn't like, but she won't tell me what it was, but it must have been really bad. Whatever you did, you just have to tell her you're sorry."

It sounded so simple when she said it like that. I liked her child's view of the world where one word could make everything better, put everything right, explain every mistake and fuck up.

"I don't think that's going to work," I replied carefully.

She shook her head impatiently. "You'll never know unless you try."

I had to smile. I didn't know that eight-year olds could tell you off like you were still in grade school. Maybe she'd be a teacher when she grew up. Or a shrink.

"Okay, I'll try," I said.

Her smile lit up her face. "She'll forgive you," she said confidently.

I didn't answer, concentrating on keeping my eyes on the road, and my hope locked down tight.

For the rest of the journey, Katie chatted about school and her friends, only becoming tearful when she mentioned Stan. I had a problem with that myself—I missed the stinky mutt. There was a hound-sized hole in my life.

When I pulled up outside Dawn's house, I felt the nervous tension that I'd been experiencing for the last ten minutes kick up a notch.

Katie bounced out of my truck as Dawn opened the front door and swept her daughter into her arms. I hesitated before climbing out of the truck, then waited in the background, not sure how welcome I'd be.

But when Dawn turned to me, she had tears in her eyes and a fierce look on her face.

"Thank you," she mouthed over Katie's shoulder, as she drew her toward the house.

I nodded and watched the two of them, dark heads bent together, arms around each other. I hated that it was possible to miss something you'd never really had. I went to climb back in the truck. But then Katie realized I was leaving.

"Mom!" she yelped, her feet grinding to a halt. "I want Alex to stay. He said he's lonely without Stan."

I hadn't said those words exactly, although that didn't mean she wasn't right. And I hadn't been looking forward to going home to an empty house, especially since Stella's absence was making me more twitchy than usual.

I also knew that I had to give Dawn the chance to get out of this without any flak from Katie.

"I'm good thanks, Katie-kay, so..."

Dawn interrupted.

"You'd be welcome to join us for supper," she said firmly. "So long as you don't mind vegetarian chili. It's leftovers from last night..." and her cheeks turned pink. "I thought I'd be by myself today. I know it's not really holiday food..."

I tried to read from her expression whether or not she really wanted me to stay. But her eyes were carefully blank, so in the end I gave up and decided to take her words at face value.

"Thank you. Chili sounds great."

I was wondering whether I should mention that I'd already taken Katie to a diner, but Katie grinned at me and wrinkled her nose, and in the end I decided to forget to mention it.

The conversation over dinner was light, with Katie doing most of the talking, but there was still a heavy tension between me and Dawn.

After we finished with chocolate chip ice cream, I watched some TV with Katie while Dawn cleaned up in the kitchen, refusing my help. Maybe she didn't want to be alone with me. The thought was painful.

Katie tried to put barrettes in my hair, but grumbled when they fell out because I still kept it short, although it had grown enough to curl slightly.

Dawn smiled when she saw Katie's efforts and shook her head.

"At least she didn't try and put makeup on you."

"I could," Katie said thoughtfully. "Alex has really long eyelashes so if he wore mascara..."

"Definitely time for bed," Dawn said firmly.

She ignored Katie's pleading to be allowed to stay up later because it was a holiday.

"Can Alex read to me tonight?"

"I'm sure Alex would like to get home now," Dawn suggested.

"I don't mind."

It was true. I'd enjoyed reading to Katie the one time I'd had the chance. I wanted to read to her about lions who talked, and sailing in magical ships—a world of childish wonder, a world where bad things didn't happen to good people, where fathers were responsible and loved their kids, and no one hurt innocent animals. And besides, there was nothing waiting for me at the cabin.

Katie fist-pumped the air, but Dawn gave me a weird look as if she'd rather I just went. I shrugged and followed Katie to her bedroom.

"What are you reading now, Katie-kay?"

She handed me a paperback with curling edges: 'The Last Battle'.

"It's the end of the series," she said sadly. "After this the story's over."

I turned to the page she showed me. I wasn't sure what a unicorn's voice sounded like, but I read the words anyway.

At first, she watched me, her eyes wide, her small hands gripping the sheets as if she was fighting sleep and willing herself to stay awake. But as I continued to read, her eyelids drooped, and soon she was breathing slowly and deeply.

"*I have come home at last!*" I read. "*I belong here. This is the land I have been looking for all my life, though I never knew it till now...*"

The words echoed something inside me, something too painful to explore.

I laid the book on her bedside table, pulled up the quilt so she wouldn't get cold, and crept out quietly.

Dawn was waiting in the living room, sitting in silence, her hands wrapped around a cup of coffee.

She looked as beautiful as ever, her short dark hair thick and glossy, her warm brown eyes hazy and lost in thought.

I stood in the doorway, and she looked up.

"Thank you for today, Alex. I'm glad Katie called you. It could have gotten ugly with her father."

I sighed. "It still might. He wasn't happy."

"Let him try," she bit out. "I've had enough of him treating Katie like garbage. Leaving her in the car while he screws some student. It's his business if he wants to mess around with co-eds, but not with Katie there. I won't put up with that. *My* lawyers will be in touch with him first."

"I'm sorry if I've made things worse," I said honestly.

She shook her head.

"No, I've let things go on long enough. It's time that asshole shaped up ... he's always cancelling at the last minute, saying something important came up ... as if Katie isn't important! And if he doesn't get his head on straight, then Katie doesn't need him in her life."

"That's not the only reason I'm sorry."

Dawn's lips pressed together.

"Can we *not* apologize to each other? I don't want to do the apology thing —who's the most sorry." She took a deep breath and met my eyes. "Can we just say that we'll try really hard not to be in a situation where we need to apologize again?"

My heart gave another small jolt of hope.

"You're making me have all these *feelings*," she forced out through gritted teeth. "I hate it—and I love it."

She said the word 'love', but yanked out of her like that, it sounded all wrong. Maybe today was a new low point in her life, when a recovering alcoholic was more reliable than her daughter's father.

The words rolled around in my head and I didn't know what to do. I knew what I *wanted* to do—I wanted to push her against the wall and wrap her legs around my waist. But what did Dawn want? A frown screwed her face into obvious doubt.

But when a man has been numb as long as I have, finally meets a woman who makes him want to live again, and then loses that woman...

It was time to throw my final hand on the table.

"Dawn, I can't ask you for a second chance, or even a third chance or a fourth chance, because I won't make promises I can't keep. I'll be fighting addiction every day for the rest of my life; it will always be one day at a time. But I can tell you that I've never wanted anything more than to make things work with you and Katie."

I was wearing my battered heart on my sleeve, waiting for her response.

She didn't answer immediately, and I felt the hope drain away again, drop by stinging drop.

"You say you've never wanted anything more than to make things work with me and Katie," she said at last, "but that's not true, is it? You want a drink more. Right now, you want a drink."

I nodded slowly. "I'll always want a drink, but it's not true that it's the only thing I want, or even the first thing that I want. Being an alcoholic is a disease, but it isn't everything that I am. I won't let it define me anymore. I want you and Katie in my life." *Otherwise, what's the point?*

I walked toward her and sat on the sofa, keeping a small distance between us. She took a deep breath, still seeming conflicted.

"What about your wife?"

My eyebrows shot up. "Charlotte?"

"Charlotte..." she rolled the word around, then looked away. "I never knew her name. I always wondered..."

"Why are you asking about her?" I snapped, too aggressively.

She flinched slightly, then straightened her shoulders and met my irritated gaze.

"I met her. In town. She was asking for directions to the cottage. I didn't like her very much."

I gave a hollow laugh.

"No, not many people do. My brother couldn't stand her. Turns out he was right. She was a complete bitch. I'm very glad she's not in my life anymore."

"But she is! She was here in town."

I shook my head, confused and annoyed.

"What exactly did she say to you, Dawn? Because I swear, it makes me want to hunt her down."

She gasped. "That's a terrible thing to say!"

"Jesus, I'm not saying I would! She ... damn it!" I stared at Dawn. "Why are we talking about her? She's been out of the picture for two years!"

"But she was here! In town!"

My hands folded into fists, the knuckles cracking.

"She wanted me to work for the business again. My business. I'm an architect—I design ... I used to design offices, corporate headquarters, that sort of thing. Go to Denver and you'll see half-a-dozen downtown buildings that are mine."

Dawn seemed stunned.

"I had no idea! I knew you worked in construction..."

"Yes, you could say that: *Winters & Carter*. That was my business. I started it with my ... best friend, Warren, right out of college. I was the Chief Architect, Warren was the CFO, and Charlotte was the office manager, but it was *my* business."

"What happened?"

I mulled that over. What *had* happened? I hadn't seen it coming. Somehow, I missed all the signs. Too damn trusting.

"The simple answer? Charlotte and Warren had an affair. I found out, and I left."

The longer answer was more complicated, but the result was the same.

"Oh, I'm so sorry. I know what that's like ... I mean, I..."

Dawn seemed flustered, and I remembered that I'd only heard about Katie's dad from Stella. Dawn didn't know I'd been clued in already.

"Don't worry," I said tiredly. "Stella told me what happened with Katie's father. She said he played you both—the way Charlotte and Warren played me."

Her eyes closed and her body slumped.

"I kind of hate that we have that in common. But Stella ... at first, I was just so angry with her. I thought she was jealous. It never occurred to me that she was serious about him. She used to bounce back from breakups quicker than hangovers. I had no idea that she was with him, let alone engaged to him. She always called him 'Matt'. I had no idea he was also Matthew—the same man that I was seeing. I felt sick when I found out."

Her expression changed again.

"Charlotte wants you back."

"Fuck what she wants!"

I was trying not to shout and wake Katie, but Dawn was making me crazy.

"I told her I wasn't interested. We're divorced. That's it. Done. Forever. And anyway," I said, frowning at Dawn, "Charlotte doesn't like animals. She hated Stan."

"Oh!"

"I told you she was a bitch. It wasn't until Carl sent Stan to me that I really understood it."

"Oh, I see."

"Do you, Dawn? Do you really? Because all of this ... this *bullshit*, it's ancient history as far as I'm concerned. We had something real, you and me. Don't you think so? Didn't it feel real to you?"

"Yes," she whispered.

"Thank God!"

She folded her hands in her lap and gave me a direct look.

"I want to take a chance on you, Alex, because I think if I don't, I'll always regret it, the road untaken. But if I take a chance and it goes wrong, I'll always regret that, too. I'm thirty-four and a mother—I can't be irresponsible. I have to do what's right for both of us, but Katie comes first. I can't screw up her life just because I've screwed up my own."

I wanted to reach out and touch her, to tell her to take a chance and that I'd never let her down again—but that would be a lie. Instead, I stared down at my hands, smudges of oil still staining my fingers.

"I can't make that decision for you, although God knows I want to. There are no certainties in life—we've both experienced that." Unwillingly, my eyes sought hers, searching for a sign. "I want you every way, Dawn. I ... I think I could be a good father to Katie. I want you: in my life, as part of my world. I want to spend a whole day with you, a whole night, then another, and another, and another. I want a life with you and Katie. Because I love you. I love both of you. The package deal. Everything."

She flinched as if she'd been scalded.

"That's not fair," she whispered.

My shoulders sagged.

"Maybe not, but if I don't take this chance to tell you how I feel right now, I may never get another. The last two months have been shit without you. There were times when I didn't know if there was any point in struggling so hard, and then I'd think of you." I laughed without humor. "Your silence made me want to keep fighting—I didn't think I was a masochist, but maybe I am."

She smiled sadly. "We're not very good at this, are we?"

"We could be," I said softly. "Take a chance on life and love. We could be great."

"There are still so many things I want to ask you, to know about you. What about your police record? Dan said..."

"I'll tell you everything! Everything you want to know. I promise. No more secrets."

His eyes blazed with belief.

"We could be a complete car crash," she whispered.

"Then let's be the best fucking car crash we can be," I begged, inching closer to her. "I can't make you love me, but I can't stop loving you either. So you choose: take me, all of me, broken and put back in pieces, or say to hell with me. And I'll sell the cabin and move away—you'll never have to see me again."

That was it. The final roll of the dice. I held my breath.

"All or nothing, huh?" she asked faintly.

"Yes. But I want you to choose all."

"Do I have to decide now?"

I laughed a little.

"If you don't, I'll probably have a stroke waiting for your answer."

She smiled at that, then shook her head.

"Okay."

"And 'okay' means...?"

"I choose all," she said simply.

My heart thumped painfully, leaping and lurching to a new rhythm inside my chest.

"Thank you," I said, and I pulled her toward me.

Her lips were as soft and warm as I remembered, but a thousand times sweeter. Her hands reached up to my neck, pulling my head down so she could kiss me harder, her short fingernails digging into my skin.

There was no holding back, from either of us.

I wanted her, I needed her, and she was finally admitting that she wanted the same.

A new determination hardened inside me.

I would be the kind of man she needed. Someone she could rely on, someone who would share the load. I wanted to show that she could trust me.

And I ignored the spiteful little voice in my head reminding me that she couldn't.

For her—for Katie—for both of them I would fight the twin demons of defeat and self-destruction, and this time I'd win.

I wanted to deserve Dawn's trust and commitment; to be a real father to Katie.

If she'd let me.

"Can you please just hold me now?" she whispered, her eyes still creased with concern.

"Yes," I said, my heart reeling and spinning. "Yes, I can do that."

And I pressed her to my chest, listening to her heart hammering against mine.

$$Chapter\ Fifteen$$

TRIALS

Alex

"How long were you with your wife?"

We were sitting on Dawn's sofa, my arms around her as she leaned against me. I hated talking about Charlotte, but if Dawn needed to hear it to move on, then I'd talk till sunrise.

"Thirteen years, if you include dating for two years. Married for ten, but that includes being separated for 18 months, give or take."

"That's a long time."

"We met in college and got married right after. Carl had already joined the Marines so ... I think I was looking for a replacement family. Although her parents didn't like me much ... and then I worked crazy long hours building up the business. For a long while, I didn't even notice that we'd grown apart. I think Stan's arrival woke me up to what she was really like. She used to put him outside if I wasn't there, even if it was below zero or snowing. She'd always say it was because he'd been barking or made a mess, but I had my doubts. Later, I realized she just didn't like animals." *Thank God we never had children.*

"How long have you been divorced?"

"Six months."

Dawn paused, toying with a strand of hair, frowning, deep in thought.

"What did Charlotte say to you? Because after you and I had talked that morning, I thought ... I thought we were okay."

She sighed.

"I know. I'm sorry about that. To be honest, she didn't say much. She wanted directions to *Tanglewood*. I was in the bakery with Katie, and Mavis knew that I'd treated Stan ... at least, I think that was all she knew. So she told

Charlotte that I could give her directions to the cottage. I explained I was Stan's vet, and ... and she told me she was your wife. I felt such a fool."

"I can imagine," I said wryly. "Divide and conquer: I think Charlotte was born saying that."

"I'm sorry I didn't ask you about it."

"I wish you had."

"I know. I'm s—"

"You don't have to apologize, Dawn. I get it. I do. You thought I'd lied to you. You thought I was like Matthew, playing two women."

"Yes," she said softly, and looked up at me with a pained expression on her face.

"I'm not like that."

"I know. I know that now."

We sat in silence for some time, and I enjoyed the feeling of Dawn's soft weight in my arms after too many long, dreary days apart. Had we finished talking? Because I hoped that she'd let me take her to bed, make love to her, because one night hadn't been enough. Not nearly enough.

"Can I ask you about Stella?" she said quietly.

I sighed. "Sure."

"She says you're not ... dating, or anything."

"No! Not then, not now, not ever!"

"I'm s—"

"Please don't say you're sorry! Dawn, I promise, there's nothing going on between me and your sister. But she's been a good friend to me. I'm not going to cut her out of my life now that you and I are..."

I wanted to say 'together', but suddenly that seemed too great a leap, too much of an assumption.

"I wouldn't ask you to," she said quickly. "In fact, well, Stella ... we've been having coffee together a couple of times a week for over a month now. We're trying to be sisters again. It's nice. I've missed her. I knew she was seeing you ... as friends," she added hurriedly. "I was glad about that. I didn't want you to be lonely." She laughed sadly. "I was horribly jealous though, but Stella kept saying nothing else was happening. I wanted to believe her—she seemed so sincere. Anyway, things have been better between us."

"Good. I'm glad."

"Me, too."

"Can I ask *you* something?"

"Of course! Anything."

"What's with the vegetarian chili?"

Dawn laughed.

"Oh my goodness, that's totally your fault! Because you're vegetarian, Katie decided that she is, as well. I'm sure she was showing some sort of solidarity with you—my daughter can be very stubborn. And please don't say she's like me!

But I think she's finding it quite hard because she loves bacon with pancakes and maple syrup, but she's been sticking to a vegetarian diet. So I do, too, mostly. It just makes it easier at dinner time not to cook two different meals."

"Should I apologize for that?"

"No, I'm fine with it. She really missed you, Alex."

"I missed her, too. Reading to her tonight ... that was special."

"You're getting good at doing all the voices," she smiled. "Thank you for ... everything."

"It was my pleasure."

I meant every word.

We relapsed into silence, but I reached out to pull her hand into my lap, playing with her fingers.

Dawn hid a yawn, and I realized how late it was.

"I'm sorry," she said, yawning again. "It's been a really long day and I didn't sleep well last night. But there are so many other things I want to ask you," and she smiled up at me, "now that you're really talking to me."

"There's always tomorrow," I said, hoping it was true.

"Yes, and it's a holiday and I'm not working, and..."

"And what?"

"I was going to ask if you'd like to stay the night."

Her cheeks flushed pink, but she didn't look away, her eyes meeting mine. I loved that about her.

I wanted to stay, more than anything. Hell, yeah! But I wanted to build something permanent this time, something that couldn't be swept away with a single misunderstanding. We both had a lot of baggage. But I'd let Dawn set the pace.

"Only if you're sure. I want to do it right this time. I want to say yes so badly, but ... and what about Katie?"

"Katie will be happy to see you," she smiled. "I can't guarantee that she won't say something totally embarrassing, because that seems to be her specialty, but she'll be happy. She adores you, Alex."

"Adores me, huh?" I grinned back.

"You know it!" she laughed. "Don't get big headed about it."

"I have to take what I can get."

"So will you?" She smiled shyly. "Will you stay?"

"I think the problem will be getting rid of me," I said seriously.

I lifted her onto my lap and kissed her the way I'd been wanting to since before she'd begun her long list of questions. I literally ached to touch her, and only when my hands were sliding over her body, did the constriction in my chest begin to loosen.

Her breathing hitched as I shifted underneath her, and then she boldly ran one hand along the front of my jeans. I groaned into her neck, the sound rolling up my throat as she grasped me more firmly.

"I think we'd better go upstairs," she gasped, the catch in her voice telling me that she wanted this as much as I did.

And because I had her permission now, I stood with her in my arms and carried her up the stairs, claiming her, claiming the right to do this.

She smothered a surprised laugh by pressing her lips against my neck, and that made me almost levitate to the top of the stairs.

"Left," she whispered.

I pushed her door open with the toe of my boot, but I'd forgotten I was wearing my work boots with the steel toecaps, and the sound echoed down the hallway. We both froze.

But there was no movement from Katie's room, and I breathed again.

I didn't get a chance to see if Dawn's room matched her daughter's because she locked the door behind us without turning on the light. Hunger and need and desire that felt as sharp as pain ricocheted through me, and as soon as I crashed down onto her bed, we were rolling on it together.

Her hands were greedy as she pulled at my belt, jerking the zipper down violently and releasing my shaft.

I exhaled hard, then pushed her skirt up and her panties down. Her eyes blazed and I kissed her again, our mouths slamming together, teeth and lips and tongues.

My body was shaking with the effort of maintaining some fraying control.

"Don't," she said, pressing her finger to my lips. "Don't hold back. Love me the way you want to."

Her every touch was a powerful reminder that I was still alive. That I'd survived all the shit, all the pain, the crippling anxiety, the demeaning loss of self.

You can lose everything and everyone, but when you lose yourself, you are truly one of the damned. But somehow, in a haze of meds and despair, Dawn had pulled me back.

I bucked into her and she hissed, her teeth sinking into my neck.

Neither of us lasted long. She cried out as I jerked and swore, and her legs clamped around me.

Sweating and cursing and laughing, we flopped onto our backs. I turned my head to stare at her, with a desire to freeze that perfect moment, when her mouth was open in a wide smile, her eyes tightly shut, her chest heaving. Something both old and new awoke inside me—a fierce need to protect and cherish and love her.

All the loneliness evaporated, and I thought about how an old, tired and ill dog had brought us together.

Thank you, Stan.

The world looked different, fresh and new, with love hovering so close.

I knew better than to say the words while we were both breathless after sex, after making love. When we were dressed, when we were calm, I'd say the words again, and hope that the block between my heart and my mouth was dissolved forever.

Dawn opened her eyes, and I watched them crinkle as her smile widened.

"That was ... jeez, Alex! What *was* that? I've never...!"

I laughed a little, because I was shaken, as well.

"I'm just getting warmed up," I said, tugging at the hem of her blouse. "And this needs to come off now."

I was ashamed that I'd mounted her and thrust until I saw stars while we were both fully dressed. She deserved so much more.

Last time was hard and fast because I was afraid my brain wouldn't let me finish before the disbelief and urgency that I was really here washed over me.

Now, with the freedom, the permission to explore, I wanted her slowly. I wanted her naked on the bed so I could kiss her warm skin, enjoy the journey, fall in love with the landscape of her again. I wanted to taste her, feel her, make her come on my tongue, in my arms, over and over. I wanted now and tomorrow and tomorrow and tomorrow.

Dawn

The high pitched whine of a motorcycle driving too fast woke me. I stared down at Alex who was still sleeping, his face turned toward me, his hands tucked under the pillow as he lay on his chest.

We'd been awake late. Awake and making love over and over. I shook my head, smiling to myself. Yesterday had been filled with a rush of highs and lows, of storm-tossed emotions and a hurricane of words.

Yesterday, I'd woken up miserable because it was Matthew's turn to have Katie on Thanksgiving, so I'd volunteered to work. I hadn't expected to do an emergency surgery on an obstruction of the small bowel for a seven year-old Palomino. Happily, Suki was making a good recovery.

And then, to receive Ashley's worried message that Alex, of all people, had gone to Katie's aid because her father was missing!

I'd never been so grateful in my life to hear his calm, reassuring voice over the phone. I definitely hadn't been feeling calm when I'd finally spoken to Matthew; murderous was probably a better description. He wouldn't be getting my daughter on Thanksgiving again—my lawyers would see to that. I doubted that he'd fight it very hard. Sometimes I thought he only saw Katie to retain some sort of control over me. But we'd see about that.

And then there was Alex.

How could I explain why this perplexing man was sleeping in my bed after loving me in every wonderful way I could ever have imagined?

I slipped out of bed as quietly as possible and tiptoed to the bathroom, pausing outside Katie's bedroom, satisfied that she was still sleeping deeply.

Seeing my face in the bathroom mirror, I scowled. My neck and chest were red from Alex's rough beard, and my breasts and thighs also felt tender. My hair was a disaster, but at least I hadn't worn makeup yesterday, so there was no day-old mascara stuck to my cheeks. Small mercies.

I brushed my teeth and tugged a comb through my ratty hair, then tiptoed back down the hallway to my bedroom.

Alex wasn't asleep anymore. Instead, I found him gazing out at the sky, his face catching the slanting rays of winter sunshine.

He turned to smile at me, his eyes darkening to teak as he scanned the thin, silky robe I'd thrown on.

I untied the belt and let it slip from my shoulders. He licked his lips and gave me a sly smile that promised my little striptease would be rewarded.

I'd seen him naked, bathed in the weak sunlight of early morning. I'd seen him aroused, taking pleasure in studying his body as he stood proudly before me, his dick dark and straining to reach me.

But now, in the full light of day, stripped of his clothes, unhindered by bedsheets, he was not embarrassed by his arousal. For a man who'd hidden so much of himself, who had struggled with the things that we take for granted—basic human communication—seeing him like this was shaking the scales from my eyes.

He wasn't someone I had to pity, to feel sorry for. He didn't need me to hold his hand to make his way in the world. He'd achieved and been successful, and he'd survived terrible losses. He was a man. A proud man. Life had tried to crush him, ruin him, but he was still here, still standing, still fighting. And still so very capable of loving.

I reached out to touch the thick rope of muscle over heavy bone, and felt his flat stomach flutter against my fingers, my caresses teasing him.

"I really need to shower," he whispered, pulling me toward him and dragging his forefinger down my spine, making me shiver. "Come with me?"

"But..."

I stared longingly at the rumpled quilt of my oh-so-comfortable bed.

"I'll make it worth your while," he said, as he ran his tongue up my neck, nipping my earlobe.

I grabbed my robe, and he smiled in triumph as he plucked a sheet from the bed and wrapped it around his waist.

Moving stealthily, hand-in-hand, we made our way to the bathroom.

He locked the door and turned on the shower.

He'd had his own way so far, but now I was taking control. So before the water was even lukewarm, I ripped the sheet from his body, slowly sinking to my knees as our eyes locked.

His hands tangled in my hair as I took him in my mouth, trying every trick I'd read about in magazines, hoping to please him.

When his body began to tremble, he gently eased himself out of my mouth, his eyes intense and burning. My knees hurt and my jaw ached, but I would have stayed there, for him.

Shaking his head and grinning, he pulled me under the hot stream of water, steam swirling around us as he spun me to face the cooler tiles, pressing me against them, his fingers working my body, until I felt the slow, thick glide of his shaft inside me.

He built up a steady, powerful rhythm, angling my hips to suit himself, then began moving faster. My legs started to shake and I rested my head against my hands, crying out softly.

He stiffened behind me, one large hand locked on my hip as his thrusts shuddered deeper, and I felt him pulse inside.

It was hot and thick and abundant, his seed. I could feel it beginning to leak out before he'd even finished, running down my inner thighs, washed away with the water. It was intense and arousing to think that this could create a child.

Not now. Not yet. But one day. Maybe.

Breakfast was the most fun I'd had in ages. Katie's face when she saw Alex sitting at the breakfast table ... well, for her, Christmas had come early.

"Alex, you're here!" Katie shrieked happily, then hesitated. "I wish Stan was here, too."

"I know, Katie-kay. So do I."

She jumped onto his lap, snuggling into his chest, forgetting that she was all grown up, and for now, happy to be an eight year-old little girl.

"I hoped you'd stay." Then she narrowed her eyes and gave me a hard stare. "He did stay, didn't he, Mom? You didn't send him home all alone last night?"

"He stayed," I answered simply.

Katie grinned, then slid into her own chair.

"We always have pancakes for holiday breakfasts," she announced to Alex. "But only with maple syrup and eggs. I don't eat bacon anymore."

Alex hid the smile that I was sure lurked at the corner of his lips.

"Your mom's pancakes are awesome."

"I help her. I stir the batter."

"That's the important part," Alex teased, making Katie giggle.

"We're going ice-skating after breakfast," she said. "Come with us, pleeeeease! It's going to be amazeballs!"

Alex glanced at me to see if he'd be welcome, and I beamed back.

"That sounds fun," he smiled. "I'd love to."

So, once the dishes were stacked away and Alex had made a quick run home to change his clothes, we all piled into my car and headed to the ice rink at New Castle, a 90 minute drive away.

Poor Alex.

He was initiated into the estrogen-filled map of our lives. Songs from 'Frozen', naturally, but also 'The Little Mermaid', 'The Lion King' and many more of the Disney oeuvre. And because he didn't know the lyrics to her favorites, Katie replayed them several times until he sang them correctly.

I think he loved every second of it, although I did see him wince a couple of times when she made him sing about 'feeling like the Queen'. But if he was going to be a part of our story, he'd better get used to the assault on his eardrums.

And then he turned out to be incredible at ice skating, and admitted that he'd played varsity hockey in high school.

We circled the rink slowly, the three of us hand-in-hand with Katie in the middle, her happiness spilling over. She talked and talked, her words tumbling over each other as she filled Alex in on everything he missed while he'd been 'away'. Stan was mentioned frequently, and then her little face would crumple, but Alex would tell her some story about Stan breaking wind inappropriately or chewing something he shouldn't, and Katie would be all giggles again.

They were so natural together. I don't know where it came from, but it was real and warm, and dangerously alluring.

When my stomach decided it was time for hot chocolate, I plodded across the bleachers to stand in line, and Alex whipped Katie around the ring at triple speed, dodging around other skaters, until my daughter was a sweaty, happy mess of tangled hair and rosy cheeks.

We looked like the perfect happy family.

A shiver of fear trickled down my spine. I started to think of all the ways this could be taken away from us. And once I started, I couldn't stop. Alex noticed my change in mood, but he didn't say anything in front of Katie.

"Mom got me the DVD of 'Minions'. Do you want to watch it with me later?"

I was about to remind Katie that she was going to her friend Holly's for the evening and that we'd save re-watching 'Minions' for another day, but to my surprise, Alex frowned.

"I'm busy tonight."

Katie pouted. "Doing what?"

Alex didn't answer and that wasn't like him—he was always so careful of Katie's feelings. I wondered where he could be going on Black Friday when it was crazy crowded out there—all things I knew he hated. Why wouldn't say what he was doing? I hated that I was being so needy and wanting to know.

His face softened. "It's important, or I wouldn't go."

I smiled weakly without meeting his eyes, and gently reminded Katie about her movie marathon sleepover with Holly. She pouted and sulked, but not too much.

As I drove, Katie talked enough for all three of us, so she didn't notice the murky undercurrents rolling between me and Alex.

But after I'd dropped her off at Holly's—with many promises extracted from Alex that she'd see him soon—we drove back to my house so he could pick up his truck.

I was surprised to see Dan's police cruiser parked next to it, and I threw a worried look at Alex. He shrugged, seeming unconcerned, and that surprised me, too. But all the terrible things Dan had told me about him came rushing back, along with the certainty that I was about to hear more.

Dan climbed out of the cruiser slowly and walked toward us.

"Dawn."

His voice was cool, nothing like his usual friendliness, and there was a long uncomfortable pause before he acknowledged Alex with a curt nod.

"Hey, Dan. Happy Thanksgiving?"

My voice rose, turning it into an anxious question.

"Everything okay here?" Dan asked, his hard gazed pinned on Alex.

"Of course, why wouldn't it be?"

Dan shot me a look, and I bit my lip.

"Where's Katie?"

"With Holly. Why?"

"Let's talk inside," he said, glancing at my neighbor's twitching drapes.

Alex leaned toward me, his warm breath tickling my neck. "G-gonna go. I'll c-c-call you."

"This concerns you, too," Dan said firmly, frowning at Alex before his angry gaze snapped back to me. "I had a phone call from Matthew Hamilton."

"Oh, this is too much!" I muttered, marching to the front door and flinging it open. "How dare he call you! Don't tell me he reported this as a police matter?"

Dan and Alex followed me into the living room, but then stood there like a pair of matching statues.

"Cool your jets, Dawn. Some nosey neighbor called it in as being suspicious because there was a child and two grown men yelling at each other. They gave both vehicles' license plates, and the Erie PA talked to Matthew about what happened, and he agreed to check out things on his end," said Dan, hitching his holster higher as he eyed Alex whose face was stony.

"Cool down! You want *me* to cool down? He abandoned Katie, left her in the car for close to *two hours*, while he was making *house calls* to a student, on Thanksgiving. Thank goodness she thought to call Alex or God knows how long she would have been there!"

Dan shifted uncomfortably but didn't back down.

"Where were you?"

"The fact is, Matthew had his scheduled visitation yesterday. It was his turn to have Katie for Thanksgiving, and for once he didn't cancel. But if you have to know, I was working!" I snapped. "Ask Amelia Kingston, if you don'tthink you can believe me."

"Dawn," he sighed, rubbing his head tiredly.

"W-what ... w-what am I b-b-being accused of?"

Alex's lips were pressed together, his face red, and his hands clenched into fists. I understood that this was from his frustration, his difficulty in forcing out words, but to Dan it seemed aggressive, and he stood up taller.

"Nothing. Yet," he said. "But I don't like you hanging around my goddaughter, Winters."

Alex's eyes flashed to mine. It was true that I'd omitted to inform him that Dan was Katie's godfather. But there were things Alex hadn't told me either. I'd been such an idiot—instead of asking him about his police record, I'd focused on his friendship with Stella. I hadn't wanted to make the same mistake twice. No, I'd just made a completely new mistake instead.

"It's not your call, Dan," I seethed quietly. "And Matthew will be hearing from my lawyers first thing on Monday morning."

"What the hell are you doing still seeing him?" Dan rapped out, jabbing a finger toward Alex, his own temper rising as he ignored my words and glared. "After everything I told you!"

Alex took a sudden breath, his eyes darting between us.

"You didn't tell me very much at all, Dan," I pointed out furiously. "Alex told me himself about his issues with alcohol."

"Is that what he told you? Is that *all* he told you?"

I swallowed, feeling on shaky ground. "I know about Charlotte, his ex-wife."

"Jesus, Dawn! I didn't want to do this, but I'll spell it out for you."

And he flipped open his notebook. My worried gaze turned to Alex, wondering how he was going to react, but there was a grim expression fixed to his face, something like determination, maybe even satisfaction. I couldn't read him at all, and I shivered.

"Public Indecency," Dan read out.

My mouth dropped open. That was *not* anything like what I'd expected to hear. I turned a startled face to Alex.

He was wearing a broad grin, which earned a furious glare from Dan.

"There was even an unconfirmed report that he owned a dangerous dog..."

"Stan?" I asked, bemused.

Alex laughed loudly, and I know I looked incredulous. Dan's face reddened and he moved on quickly.

"And Disorderly Conduct..."

Alex frowned and shook his head, but I didn't think he'd be capable of talking coherently again, not with Dan in the room. I wondered about finding Katie's iPad so he could type out some sort of rebuttal.

But then I stopped, my brain finding a new serenity that I wouldn't have thought possible under the present circumstances. It was so simple.

I realized that none of what Dan was saying had convinced me that Alex was a danger either to me or to Katie. I was still concerned, but not as gut-churningly scared as I had been.

"Come on, Dawn! Doesn't this paint a picture for you?"

"Yes, it does," I said calmly, despite my thundering heart. "And as soon as you've gone, Alex is going to tell me all about it. His words," And I turned to gaze at Alex. "Aren't you."

He nodded, a tiny smile curving his lips.

Dan's eyes bulged.

"I'm not leaving you here alone with ... with a crazy guy!"

"He's not crazy and this is my house, Dan," I reminded him gently. "Thank you for everything you've said, and for caring about me and Katie, but I'll call if I need you."

Dan wasn't happy, and we argued it back and forth for several minutes, but in the end I persuaded him to leave.

Alex was still standing, watching me carefully, his smile long gone when I returned to the living room, collapsed onto the sofa and closed my eyes.

He sat down next to me and took my hand, holding it between his warm palms.

"D-do you want me t-t-t-to go?"

I opened my eyes and tiredly peered up at him.

"No, but will you tell me the truth this time?"

His jaw clenched and his eyes darkened with anger.

"I didn't l-lie to you."

"Every time you had a chance to tell me the whole truth and didn't, that was a lie."

His nostrils flared, and he stood abruptly, pacing the small room.

"And you told me everything, Dawn?"

I flinched. He was right. I was the queen of hypocrisy.

"You want to know everything?" he said through gritted teeth.

I nodded, uncertain that I really wanted that, but feeling that I should.

He took a deep breath and stood with his hands on his hips, staring out the window. Then he turned around and glared at me.

"Fine. You want to know everything? Let's start with the day I learned that my brother had been killed by an IED in Afghanistan, and I came home from work to find my best friend fucking my wife. Would that be a good place to start, Dawn?"

I swallowed, blinked a couple of times, and nodded weakly.

Chapter Sixteen

INQUISITION

Alex

I was trying to control my anger, but it wasn't easy. Every time I hoped to put all the sadness, pain, humiliation and aching loss behind me, it got dragged out again.

Damn the fucking interfering asshole Police Officer!

I'd wanted a firmer bond between me and Dawn before I had to wade through this sea of shit with her.

Tough. I was out of time.

"Charlotte and Warren." I shook my head, a sneer on my face. "My wife and so-called best friend. We'd all been together since college, so it never occurred to me that I couldn't trust them. We were business partners for seven years. I don't know how long they'd been having an affair. Maybe years— I never did get a straight answer on that. Certainly months. The day I caught them, I'd been working late on an important new contract: municipal offices in downtown Denver. It was a huge break for a small firm like ours."

I closed my eyes, remembering that fucking awful evening.

"I'd been at my desk since 5AM finishing up some of the details, and I was still working 15 hours later, pretty much sitting in the same position, bloodshot eyes, pounding headache, and everyone else had left a couple of hours earlier. But then I looked up from my screen, surprised that anyone was still in the building. Walt, the security guard must have let them in. As soon as I saw the uniforms, two men in Dress Blues, I knew.

"I keep wondering if they went to the house first but didn't get an answer. It's a dumb thing to think about, but I can't get it out of my mind..."

I shook my head.

"I'd been dreading this happening since I was 15 years old, when Carl first

178

joined the Marines. I'll never forget their words ... 'Sir, on behalf of the Secretary of the Army, I regret to inform you that your brother Sergeant Carlton Winters was killed in action yesterday in Helmand province by an IED'."

I paused, feeling like it was just yesterday, the pain fresh, the aching loss.

"It didn't make sense. The war was supposed to be over and Carl was guarding the US Embassy in Kabul. Why the hell was he out on patrol? No one would tell me and I still don't know the answer to that. I asked if Carl suffered. I wanted him to say no, expected it, but he didn't. He said he didn't know the answer to that question."

Dawn had her hand over her mouth, an expression of horror frozen on her face.

"I guess he didn't want to lie to me, but I think about that, and I wish he had. Which is ironic, as lies almost destroyed me. Anyway, I didn't want to tell Charlotte over the phone. I wanted to tell her in person ... and you know how well that went. I left the house the same night and took Stan with me. I didn't have anywhere to go except the office. I couldn't go to my best friend's place...

"Walt found me the next morning. I'd picked up a bottle of vodka on the way over and drank the whole thing. And then puked it up on the carpet in reception. I don't remember much about that. I do remember that Stan had taken a shit on the floor because he hadn't been able to wake me up to let him out.

"I don't know what Charlotte expected. I think part of her assumed that I'd just be able to carry on and it would all be ... civilized."

I laughed bitterly.

"I didn't feel like cooperating. The Marines sent their Casualty Affairs Officer to help me plan the funeral. I was in no shape, so he pretty much did the whole thing. Even got me washed up and into a clean suit on the day. Stopped me falling in the grave because I was too drunk to stand.

"I went back to the office that afternoon and took out all of the petty cash from the safe—about $5,000. I gave it away to everyone on the street who had a dog, because I figured they were the only ones I could trust. Charlotte had already tossed all of my clothes into garbage bags but I didn't care. I was checking out. I'd lost everything— family, friends, wife, business ... maybe my sanity at some level, because things, objects, possessions ... none of them meant anything to me. I couldn't think about living until tomorrow, let alone the end of the week. So I gave away everything, and when I had nothing left, I started giving away what I was wearing. It felt incredibly freeing."

Dawn raised her eyebrows.

"Yeah, in December," I smiled. "It was fucking freezing. That's when I got arrested—all that shit your Police Officer friend just told you about. The arresting officer was a woman, and she got mad when I dropped my pants and told her ... uh ... I told her she wouldn't be needing them with me."

Dawn looked as if she didn't know whether to laugh or cry. I didn't blame her—it was a crazy story.

"But the worst part was that they took Stan away from me while I sat in jail. They sent him back to Charlotte and that bitch took him straight to a high-kill dog pound. She'd found another way to get back at me for the stunt with the money. Or for humiliating her, she said. She'd have found a reason—take your pick. Stan was released to me the next day, but I'll never forgive her for that.

"I smashed up the house and my office, and that gave her what she needed to get me kicked out of my own company because she had a restraining order put on me. I couldn't go within 250 yards of her or some shit. I didn't even want to, but it meant that I had nowhere to go, nowhere at all.

"I slept on the streets for a couple of weeks. I would have frozen to death if some of the other homeless people hadn't helped me. I had money in bank accounts, but Charlotte had emptied our personal ones and had me frozen out of the business accounts. I think ... I think I wanted to die."

I'd gotten so lost in the memories that I hadn't realized Dawn was crying.

I wanted to go to her, comfort her, but she needed to hear all of it. And now I'd started, I didn't want to stop.

"I was drinking every day and taking a lot of street drugs—half of it, I couldn't even tell you what it was. I started feeding any stray dog I came across, just two or three to start with, then a few more, and later, when the police became interested in me, there were nearly twenty.

"I began hearing word on the street about illegal dog fights, and when one of my pack didn't turn up at the usual time, I found that he'd been killed. King Rollo I called him. He was a big guy, part Alsatian, but a real softy. He had his throat ripped out."

"Oh no, that's horrible! What did you do?" Dawn whispered.

"I got revenge."

She swallowed, her face pale. I could see she wanted to ask me what I'd done. I hoped she didn't, because I didn't want to tell her the truth, that I'd burned down the building where the fight had happened. I'd felt bad after—it was wrong of me to have risked the lives of firefighters, and I'd decided I wouldn't make that mistake again, but I wasn't going to stop either.

She hesitated, wondering how much truth she dared to ask for. Her gaze dropped to her hands.

"Dan mentioned an ongoing investigation?

Somehow, I found the courage to continue.

"A few weeks after Rollo was killed, I saw this guy being dumped out of a limo—he'd had the crap beaten out of him. I didn't see the beating, just the aftermath. It wasn't enough to get a conviction ... and the guy had connections."

"You mean...?"

"Yeah, mob connections ... one of their top wise guys, I was told."

"Oh, God!"

"It sounds bad, but in the end, when I took the stand, I was more useful to the defense."

"But ... about what Dan said?"

"I warned the prosecution lawyer that I'd make a shitty witness. I'd been wasted when I saw the limo and I wasn't in a good place. I was drinking every day, Charlotte had the business and the house. I was living out of cheap motels, places that would take Stan ... they put me on the stand anyway, and I was ripped to pieces. I was stuttering badly, and the defense lawyer wouldn't let me finish a word, let alone a sentence. He was the one who started the St. Francis thing—making out like I was crazy, like I was on a mission. Maybe I was, maybe he was right, but he wanted me to sound completely nuts. The District Attorney and the police weren't happy that they didn't get their conviction—and I made a useful scapegoat."

She shivered and closed her eyes.

"Coming here was a fresh start, but bad luck seemed to follow me. From the day I moved in, dead animals started turning up at the cabin."

Her eyes popped open wide.

"Oh my God! The dead raccoon! Did the mob boss do that?"

I took her hand, holding it gently, and shook my head, hoping to calm her down.

"I considered that, but I don't think it's likely."

"Why not? How can you be sure?"

"Well, for one thing, guys like him prefer the more direct approach—that sort of 'warning' ... I don't see it."

Dawn looked terrified.

"But it could be him!"

"No, I'm more use to him alive and discredited, a joke, rather than dead and therefore interesting to the police."

"This isn't a game!" she snapped, tugging her hand free.

"I'm not playing any game," I said sharply. "You wanted the truth, Dawn. This is what it looks like."

She drew a sharp breath.

"That's not fair! You're twisting my words."

I sighed.

"I'm not trying to, but the mob is the least of my worries. After the court case, they lost interest in me. But it did change things."

"What do you mean?" she asked, slightly mollified.

"Afterwards, I thought the St. Francis gig might be a good idea, and I didn't have anything else to do. I fed any stray I found. I used to go to all the parks and feed the birds, stealing food out of dumpsters to do it. People started to use the saint tag—someone told me that there was even a newspaper article about 'The New St. Francis of Denver'. Most people thought I was just a crazy homeless guy—harmless, but a weirdo. It was just a coincidence that I found out that the same criminal I'd faced in court was the one organizing the dog fights. It was my extreme fucking pleasure to cause him maximum discomfort."

"I'm afraid to ask..."

"I found ways of stopping the fights. It wasn't entirely legal, so you're better off not knowing."

I relished the memories, smoking them out, taking them down one by one. I started small fires with damp rags—lots of smoke, very little heat.

"Didn't the police help? Did you even ask them to?"

"No. Who cares about a few stray dogs, right?"

"That's why we have animal shelters, Alex."

I shrugged.

"They're all full or high-kill shelters. The cute little dogs get picked first. The ones like Stan, no one ever wants them."

I could see the moment of awareness in her eyes.

"Stan was one of them? A fighting dog?"

"Yes, in Afghanistan. That's what Carl saved him from."

"I thought so ... when I saw his scars. But I can't imagine it. He's ... he was so gentle." She chewed her lip. "What about the other dog that you brought to me?"

I frowned. Remembering that failure hurt.

"Everything had gotten so crazy in Denver. I knew I'd end up dead if I carried on like that. Honestly, I wouldn't have cared, but I couldn't do that to Stan. So I checked myself into a rehab that accepted pets. When I was clean, I didn't want to stay in the city. Charlotte and Warren had shoved me out of the business—had me declared incompetent or something. It's all a bit hazy now. Basically, they bought me off for a fraction of what I should have got, but it was enough to pay for rehab and ultimately the cabin.

"It was strange being told that I'd had a breakdown. I thought I'd feel more, but I was numb. I literally had to be told to get out of bed in the mornings, had to be reminded to eat. My brain wasn't functioning on any level. But there was Stan: always there, always happy to see me, didn't judge me, didn't care if I hadn't washed or hadn't spoken for ten days. He was just there, with me. Yeah, you could say he saved my life."

"And that's when you stopped shaving?"

"No. It was before that. I didn't shave again after I was given the news about Carl. Besides, having a beard keeps you warm in winter," I said, unconsciously touching my jaw that was covered in two days of stubble. "But that wasn't the reason—I just didn't care about shaving, I wanted to hide, be someone else. I remember going to the dog park with Stan one day in April. One of the women who'd worked for my company for three years walked right past me and didn't even recognize me. I felt invisible—only animals could see me, and I liked that feeling."

I didn't realize that I was running my fingers over my tattoo until Dawn placed her hand over mine, and turned it palm upwards to study the words inked into my skin.

"Is that when you had this done: We are all creatures of one family?"

I nodded.

"I began to think that I'd been saved to live this life with purpose, helping animals. Coming here, a new start, I wanted to feel like myself again. *You* made me want to feel. So ... I stopped taking all the prescribed meds..."

"Just like that?"

"Yeah. I know it wasn't the smartest thing to do, but I was tired of taking pills, and I'd started to think that they weren't really helping, just making me ... numb. It took a couple of weeks before I'd gotten all the drugs out of my system."

I didn't tell her that going cold turkey had nearly killed me. Detoxing too fast had really screwed up my system.

"That's why I missed Stan's appointment. I was getting clean. I didn't even want prescription drugs anymore."

"Oh, Alex! I wish ... I wish I'd known!"

I looked away. At the time, it would have been the last thing I wanted— her pity. Dawn was the most compassionate person I'd ever met. But I'd never wanted to be just her charity case.

I nodded slowly, acknowledging her words, then continued speaking.

"When I felt ... better, I needed to do something more—something for more than just me and Stan. So I looked for animals to rescue."

"All the injured animals..."

"I spent a lot of hours just walking through the forest."

Many, many hours—most of them with Stan, before he got sick. I looked down.

"Can I ask you something?" she said tentatively.

"I think we're beyond keeping anything back," I answered cautiously.

She nodded slowly.

"Why did you ask for a male vet, you know, that first appointment?"

I sighed.

"Since ... everything that had happened, with Charlotte, I just found it easier to talk to men without stuttering. Men, kids, dogs—I could talk to them. Women ... not so great."

"I wondered if that was it. I'm glad you can talk to me now."

"So am I, Dawn. So damned glad."

I meant it. Every word.

She smiled with her mouth, but her eyes were still troubled.

"And the dog you brought to me?"

"I found him in Cleveland. I wasn't even looking for trouble," just a drink, but I wasn't going to tell Dawn that. "Trouble just kind of naturally found me."

I gave her a tired smile.

"I literally walked into a parking lot and saw this guy beating a dog. I lost my temper and ... well, he walked, or crawled away from that. But I was too late to save the dog. When I had time to think about it after, I thought that it was one hell of a coincidence, and maybe I was doing exactly what I was supposed to do. So, I started hanging out, asking questions, and that's when I found out about this new dog fighting ring that's set up, shuttling between Pittsburgh and Cleveland."

"How bad is it?"

"I could tell you ... or I could show you."

"Sh-show me?"

"Yes. Tonight. There's an illegal dog fight taking place in Cleveland. I'm going to stop it."

She stared at me like I'd lost all reason, sparking an anger buried deep inside me.

If she wanted crazy, well, bring it on. I'd call down the darkness and watch the sky burn. I'd show her how bad it could get. I'd show her every dark place inside me. I wouldn't hold back. She wanted to know the truth, I'd give it to her—in every black and bloody detail.

Her eyes widened and she licked her lips, glancing at her cell phone.

"Why don't you just call the police?"

I laughed.

"Yeah, right. Because you know how much they like doing favors for me. You saw your friend, Dudley Do-Right."

"Dan's a good guy!"

"Yeah, sure he is. But he won't help me."

"You don't know that! Dan's an animal lover, too!"

"Listen, Dawn, I'll tell you exactly what he'll do. He'll call it in to Cleveland PD and they'll tell him that they'll look into it. Then they'll put it at the bottom of long list of shitty jobs, starting with patrolling the shopping malls because it's the holidays and people are tearing each other apart over the latest PlayStation, and the next day, there'll be ten dead dogs stuffed in dumpsters."

"That might not..."

"That's exactly what would happen," I said remorselessly. "Except I won't let it, because I'll be there instead."

Dawn looked so shocked, I was afraid I'd already lost her. But she needed to understand that this drove me—helping these animals that no one else gave a shit about.

Because I knew how they felt.

Because I'd been where they were.

And it kept me from drinking.

"But there's no point in this, is there?" I said softly.

"What do you mean?" she asked nervously.

"Talking about it when I can show you. Show you why I do what I do. Cut through all the bullshit. That's what you want, isn't it? The truth?" I looked away from her. "I told you I had a prior engagement tonight."

"You can't go vigilante on them," she said, her voice trembling.

"Why not? The police won't stop them. They didn't last time."

"This is so crazy!"

"I'm not c-crazy. Not in the clinical sense." I gave a sarcastic smile. "I've had the cure, remember?"

She bit her lip, then shook her head.

"I can't go. It's too dangerous. I can't be that ... irresponsible. If something happened ... I can't rely on Katie's father. I want to understand, Alex, I do. But I can't go with you."

I felt sickened by my selfishness. Of course she couldn't come with me. I knew how dangerous it was. These guys were mob—and they carried guns.

"Okay," I said slowly. "Wait here for me?"

And I didn't know if that was a question, or whether I'd want to hear her answer.

"Alex, please! You're scaring me! I don't want you to go."

I paused and smiled sadly.

"I know you don't. But I have to."

Dawn didn't want me to go, but it was something that I needed to do. I knew she didn't really understand why it drove me, but she would.

She needed to know how bad it could get.

She had no idea...

But at the same time, I'd promised to be careful and that wasn't something I said lightly. So I abandoned my original plan to use smoke bombs to create as much mayhem as possible. Instead, I stopped at a mall in Cleveland and bought myself a state-of-the-art GoPro that could record at night, with a head cam mount so I could keep my hands free. The police needed hard evidence, so I'd give it to them. And this way, I'd honor my promise to Dawn.

Then I drove to a sleazy part of Cleveland navigating my way through the tangle of backstreets. I'd spent a lot of time here, watching, waiting.

It was also a red light district an area of drug dens, if the groups of heavy-looking guys hanging around outside empty shops or the women waiting under streetlights was anything to go by.

I circled the block before stopping a short distance from one of the bigger roads, but it was still secluded enough that the truck wouldn't look out of place.

I looked around carefully, then jumped out of the truck and walked deeper into the knot of shadowy streets.

I nodded at a couple of the working girls as I passed. Giselle had told them I was okay, but hands off. At least, I think that's what she told them, because they never gave me any hassle. They just watched.

I kept to the darkest parts of the street, then paused at the narrow entrance behind the derelict bowling alley. It smelled like something had died here.

Giselle saw me immediately and stepped out from under a streetlight, strutting along the sidewalk.

Her cheeks were sunken and her thin shoulders shook with a racking cough. It sounded bad, but she said that she didn't like doctors.

"Hey, lover," she grinned. "On the prowl again?"

I nodded and jerked my head at the backpack which held the GoPro.

"Looking for trouble?" she sniggered, which started the hacking cough again. "They're in the same place as before, lover," she said, speaking more quietly. "A bigger than usual crowd. Some out-of-towners, if you know what I mean."

I nodded, then passed her a fifty dollar bill. She paused, as if she was going to say something else, but then she just shrugged and tucked the note into her bra.

"See you around, lover."

She slunk back to the same section of the sidewalk, her gaze returning to the passing cars.

As traffic in the area slowly increased, I waited. The first dogs began arriving—some in crates, some on chains, their handlers using brutal methods to control them, if that's the word.

A large group of people, mostly men and a few women, made their way into the back of the abandoned bowling alley. They were laughing and drinking, openly discussing the fights they were going to see and the bets they'd place.

More people arrived, in groups or alone. It always amazed me how such large numbers could be involved in something illegal and the police didn't know. Or maybe no one cared. Except me.

When a guy dressed in a dark suit propped open the bowling alley door from the inside, I pulled up the hood of my sweatshirt, casting my face into deep shadows. I might not be the only one here with a video camera. And he had mob written all over him.

I waited, watching the fight crowd stream inside.

Finally, the door closed and the fights started. This was the hard part— waiting until the bastards were preoccupied.

As I inched toward the abandoned bowling alley, I saw two men leave the building by the back entrance, their faces hard, slashed with disappointment and disgust. And they were dragging something with them.

At their feet, lay a large dog, its eyes glazed and body limp. Some sort of Pitbull, I'd guess. Even in the deep shadows, I could see the glossy sheen of blood darkening its coat.

It looked dead.

But when one of the men kicked it in the ribs, it whimpered softly, its paws paddling as if it was trying to get away, but couldn't.

"Fuckin' useless," sneered the vicious-looking man. "Cost me $500 and won't even be able to fight next month."

"Or ever," laughed the other.

When they kicked the dog again, I saw red.

People say that all the time, but it's just words to them. If it ever really happens, you should be fucking scared.

My vision dipped, narrowing like I was in a tunnel, the scarlet rage a vise across my eyes. And I exploded with fury.

Adrenaline surged through me as I leapt forward, punching at exposed throats, noses and eyes—all the weak places and with the element of surprise, just like Carl had taught me. Blood streamed over my knuckles as a man's nose erupted, and he toppled backward, clutching his ruined face. My boot slammed into the other man's knee and he howled.

I was lost in a blaze of hatred and lust for revenge. I couldn't feel the punches and kicks aimed my way, couldn't feel my knuckles splitting and my mouth bleeding, until I was stamping down on a man's ribs, enjoying the satisfying crunch and the way his body flopped like a caught fish.

I heard the begging and pleading of the other man above my ragged breathing and hoarse, heaving gasps.

I hacked up a mouthful of phlegm, my spittle red and frothy like a rabid animal, and I spat at them.

The dog's eyes were closed, but I could see its chest moving with shallow breaths.

I ignored the crawling scum to crouch down beside the battered dog, swallowing bile when I saw blood bubble up from a deep wound in its throat, smelling the metallic scent of gore all over his fur, all over me.

The dog's eyes opened when I stroked him gently. Then they rolled up in his head and he died. Right there at my feet. He just died.

I stood up slowly, and the two men were backing away from me, one holding a hand to his broken nose.

Picking up a loose brick from the ground, I prowled toward them, but then they turned and ran. I stared after them, torn about whether to take them down, or head for the mother lode.

I spat on the ground. Evil fuckers.

Sometimes I really hated people. Loathed them. Despised them. Men and women were entertained by watching two animals tear each other apart? And I was the one they called crazy?

My head jerked up as a sudden roar rose from the building—humans cheering and shouting, jeering and calling for blood.

Seeing the dog kicked to death in front of me, I felt a dizzying rage alongside the fear. I pulled out the camera and zoomed in on the corpse. I hoped that if I showed what happened, showed the end result, other people would understand why I did what I did. Maybe Dawn would understand.

Keeping to the shadows, I walked further into the dark beside the old bowling alley. There was a metal fire escape swinging overhead, and I pulled it down, glancing around when it clanked into position, but no one came. The noise coming from passing cars cloaked any small sounds I was making.

From the fire escape, I climbed a nearby drainpipe, hauling myself up easily.

It was the screaming that I heard first. A chilling sound, and I knew that it was a dog. Shrieking with pain, its cries almost human—childlike. It was probably dying right now ... for people's sick pleasure.

Hurrying, I worked my way through the series of gutted rooms that had once been offices, until I was crouched at the top of the rotting staircase and could see the small crowd of people in the main arena. I was reminded of all the gladiator movies that I'd ever seen, with the crowd shouting and yelling. But movies don't smell so bad that your stomach climbs up through your throat. Movies don't make you gag with the scent of urine and feces, and the deeper smell of a moldy, decaying building.

My eyes were drawn back to the two snapping, snarling dogs.

I felt nauseated and burning with fury as they circled each other, saliva and blood dripping from their teeth. For sport. For entertainment.

I pulled out the camera, making sure I zoomed in on as many faces in the crowded room as possible before I filmed the sickening action in the fight pit.

The dogs looked like Staffordshire-Pitbull-crosses and were fighting in an enclosed space about the size of a boxing ring. One was on his back, being pushed around the floor as his paws scrabbled uselessly against the other dog, who held him in a death grip.

I could see the whites of the smaller dog's eyes, the terror clear. And no one, *no one* came to help him. For the briefest second, he managed to scratch and bite his way free from the other dog, blood pulsing from a deep wound in his neck. He clawed frantically at the wooden panels forming the walls of the arena, but was pushed back by men with clubs. I saw his panic, his desperation, but there was no escape.

And then the other dog was on him again.

The crowd jeered and yelled, and I saw money changing hands. And every time blood was smeared on the concrete floor, they screamed for more.

Red sheeted both animals, but there wasn't much fight left.

With a final shake, the bigger dog—the top dog—crushed the throat of the smaller one, ripping his teeth free, a piece of fur dangling from his jaws.

The crowd yelled and cheered and I felt ashamed of humanity.

Was this what we'd come to? Were we so hardened by life that entertainment came from causing suffering and pain?

The winning dog seemed exhausted, covered in blood, some its own, one ear all but torn off. It limped around the ring until its owner grabbed it and pulled it over the side, and the next two dogs were tossed in, growling and barking at each other.

I wanted to stop the sadistic spectacle personally. I wanted to release the rage inside me, but two things stopped me. Or, more truthfully, two people stopped me: thoughts of Dawn and of Katie. I wanted to be part of their lives even more than I wanted to taste the violence again. So instead, I'd go through with my new plan.

I edged backward slowly, until I was out of sight and well hidden. Then I crouched down by my backpack and pulled out a burner phone. I dialed 911 and played a pre-recorded message, giving the address of the bowling alley.

If the police were quick, they'd catch all the sick bastards who like to watch this shit, as well as the assholes who'd organized it.

I cringed at the sound of a dog screaming, but I had to wait.

It was the longest and most miserable two minutes of my entire life. I watched the horrific fight, keeping the head cam pointed at the ring, and listened to the gory sounds of another dog being torn to pieces—literally tortured to death. My stomach rolled and cold sweat made me shudder.

Frowning, I pointed my flashlight at my wristwatch, counting off another minute. The police needed to catch them in the act, but listening to the dog fight below was nauseating. I was itching to do something more than just wait and watch.

I promised Dawn. I promised her.

Police sirens sounded in the distance, and my eyes narrowed. It was time. I pressed my lips together in a cold smile, then headed out through the blackened rooms. I'd been here too many times to become disorientated.

When I finally reached the window, I clambered out onto the rickety fire escape, not sure if it was the metal that was shaking or me.

I landed silent and catlike, the way I'd practiced, then slipped away from the alley, finding a safe place to watch.

Soon I heard more shouts and yells, but the vicious tone of approval had turned to panic as the sound of the sirens grew closer.

Suddenly, the bowling alley doors slammed open, and two mob guys ran out, guns in their hands, as people began to pour from the building.

There was nothing more I could do. Now it was up to Cleveland's finest, so I jogged back to the truck and gunned the engine, speeding away as three squad cars slid to a halt behind us.

My work here was done.

I drove back to Dawn's house, aware that I was covered in blood and filth, and stinking of smoke.

As soon as I pulled up outside, the door was flung open and Dawn ran out. I just had time to climb from the truck's cab when she threw herself at me.

She hugged me tightly, her hands gripping my shoulders, her face pressed against my chest as heaving sobs wracked her body.

Guilt and disgust and despair filled me. I'd done this to her. Again.

It was several minutes before she could speak.

"I was so scared! I thought..."

I nodded, my expression stern.

"I'm sorry, Dawn ... but I have something to show you..."

Chapter Seventeen

OBSTACLES

Dawn

I watched Alex, my heart racing, as he linked his video camera to my TV.

I studied the blood on his clothes, the bruise on his cheek, his split lip and his bleeding knuckles that were starting to swell.

Silently, I went to the kitchen and filled a small bag with ice, handing it to him without a word being spoken.

He looked up at me, his eyes storm-filled and solemn.

"Thank you," he said softly.

Then he pressed *play*.

The sound was slightly muffled, but I could still hear distressed and angry barking, people shouting and cheering. Then the camera came into focus, and I gasped.

I watched for a horrifying 20 minutes as two sets of dogs fought each other, and even the grainy black-and-white film couldn't hide the gross depravity of what I was watching.

Finally, the recording ended, and I held my hands over my face.

"That was ... that was the vilest, most disgusting..." I couldn't finish.

Alex glanced at me, his gaze cautious, contemplative.

"I was shown some videos at veterinarian school," I went on, "but seeing this and knowing that you were there..."

He nodded, the angles of his cheekbones casting shadows across his face.

"What ... what will happen now?"

Alex sighed.

"It depends on whether they caught the organizers."

"I meant, what will happen to the dogs? There were other dogs there, right?"

He grimaced.

"Any dogs that the police find, they'll be euthanized."

"Oh!"

"Dawn, you know the shelters are over-flowing, and no one has the time or patience to retrain a fighting dog, although I've been thinking I could do something ... but no one wants to rehome them, so they're just killed."

"Then why?" I cried out. "What was all this for?"

He sighed and rubbed his eyes.

"Because it's a better death than them having their throats ripped out, or forced to fight again. You're a vet—you know this."

I did. And I hated it, but he was right. I knew from my contacts in local animal shelters that large dogs were difficult to rehome at the best of times, and could be kept in concrete cages for as long as three years, hopelessly waiting for someone to want them. I could never decide if high-kill shelters were a better option than keeping a dog imprisoned in a cage for years at a time.

But it helped me understand Alex's hatred a little more.

"And the organizers?"

"If they caught them, it will stop temporarily. I'll email the film footage to Cleveland PD anonymously, in case they need evidence. If they didn't catch them, the organizers will just move the action out of Cleveland for a while, so I plan on checking out Pittsburgh. With luck, I'd find another whore with a soft heart to help me. But the money behind it all, the mob money? That will seep back, eventually. More evil, more darkness, it never stops."

He laughed bitterly, without mirth, as if he didn't know what laughter was for.

"What does that say about the society that we live in, that a hard-as-nails prostitute cares more than the average man on the street?"

I didn't know who he was talking about, but I had to believe that people would care if they knew.

"That's not true, I'm sure of it. If you told people, if you showed them..."

He shook his head again.

"You think I'm c-c-crazy."

I remembered the look on his face when he'd brought in that other fighting dog. And I understood, I did, but I didn't want to be part of the violence. I *wanted* to leave it to the police. I *wanted* it be stopped legally.

"No, not crazy..."

"But...?"

"Surely you'll stop now?"

He was silent.

"Alex! Those people are dangerous! What if they saw you? What if they're waiting for you to go back? If they find out they were recorded ... you can't continue—it's too dangerous. You have to stop!"

Alex's face was as hard as granite, his jaw clenched.

"It never stops."

A sudden flash of insight halted the words that I would have said.

"Oh! The fighting, your crusade—it's just another addiction, isn't it?"

His eyes widened.

"No," he said, uncertainty in his voice, "that's not it."

"I think it is. You're addicted to it, Alex. I can see it in your eyes. The rush of adrenaline, taking the fight to these monsters."

"It's not the same as..."

"Isn't it? Isn't it just another addiction? Another way of blotting out the pain of ... of living?"

He looked surprised, but he seemed to be considering what I was saying.

"I care about you, Alex, so much! This scares me, I'm scared *for* you. And ... I *need* you! I need you to be in my life. For me, for Katie. Don't you realize how important you are to me?"

His eyes widened.

"I think what you're doing is too dangerous! God, Alex! There are other ways you can help! You could ... I don't know ... you could ... you could volunteer at a dog rescue center. Start your own. Build your own! You have the skills!"

He didn't answer, staring at his damaged hands and the bag of ice that I'd given him.

I thought about the stream of injured animals that he'd continued to bring to the office even when we weren't talking to each other. He seemed to have an affinity for the sick and hurt. I wondered how many hours he'd walked in the woods to find so many animals needing help.

And I thought about Stan. After Alex's ex-wife's betrayal, he had learned to speak again, but other than Stan, he'd had no one to talk to for a long time.

And in the end, was our love about *me* learning to speak *his* language?

I shook my head, but it didn't stop the sun from setting, the tide from turning, or walking away from Alex for the last time.

It would be the right thing to do, what I *should* do.

I should think about Katie and forget about Alex Winters.

Forget the gentle way he touched me, the passionate way he possessed me, forget that a good man with a streak of crazy wanted to be part of my world.

I can't do that.

And I wasn't scared of Alex. I was scared *for* him.

"I hate what happened tonight," I said in a low voice. "I hate that you were involved with it, and you scared me. I know I should walk away. I'd have to be crazy not to. And you were so ... but I can't stop loving you either."

The words spilled from my tongue before I could catch them.

Love meant accepting every part of him: the fun, the flaws, the damage, the baggage, just as it did for me.

His poor, bruised hands tightened in his lap.

"Do you mean that?" he whispered.

"God help me, but I think I do."

We sat in silence, not touching, just being. I didn't know what to do with all the new information I'd learned about Alex. I don't think he knew what to say to me either, but he seemed calm, as if having me see everything, experience it through him, lifted a burden he'd been carrying.

I also knew that I loved him and wanted him. But I also loved Rocky Road ice cream with hot fudge and chocolate sprinkles—it didn't mean that either were good for me. Or my daughter.

Oh God, Katie.

What if something had gone wrong tonight? What if Alex had gotten hurt —worse than a bruised face, split lip and cut knuckles? What if he'd been caught? What if he'd been arrested?

What if? What if? What if?

My heart pounded as delayed shock turned my blood to ice and my body started to shake. And then I felt Alex's warm hand close over mine.

"It's okay. I'm safe now. It's over."

"Is it?" I gasped. "Until the next time! There'll always be a next time, won't there?"

His face was serene as he answered.

"Yes. But if they get raided enough times, they'll move into other cities, or other areas of business."

He ran his thumb over my wrist, his rhythmic strokes soothing me, lessening the tremors that wracked my body.

"I don't understand it," I shivered, "The people who watch *that* for … for sport! You saw them, Alex. They didn't all look like gang members. Some were just ordinary people. People who'd probably spent Thanksgiving with their families having dinner. Just ordinary people who do something so despicable. I don't understand. At least when it's boxing or MMA, then people are choosing to take part, but those poor animals, they didn't have a choice. It's a felony offense in every state!"

He was silent, but his expression was grim.

"I don't even want to think about how they make those dogs so aggressive."

He scowled.

"Torture. They chain them up, make them hold onto baited meat then dangle them above the ground, inject them with steroids, sometimes even make them eat roach poison so their fur tastes bad to other dogs, cut off their ears and tail so there's less for another dog to latch onto. And … they use other animals as bait to train them to kill. Weaker animals … pet cats."

"Please don't tell me anymore," I begged, putting my hands over my ears.

I sat there, too tired and numb to move.

After a moment, he shifted to face me.

"Dawn, this doesn't change how I feel about you. Does it change how you feel about me?"

"Yes. No."

"Dawn, please. No head games. I'm fucking dying here."

"Of course it changes how I feel about you! I was so scared ... not just for me, but for you. I *hate* that you're involved in it. I hate that it exists in the first place."

"Do you still want me in your life?"

"Only if you promise, absolutely *promise* that Katie won't be dragged into it in any way."

He was silent for a long time.

"Alex?"

"She's going to ask questions, Dawn. She'll wonder why I have a bruised face, why my knuckles are cut and bruised, where I disappear to some nights. Do you want me to lie to her each time or ... or just stay away from her?"

"I'd rather you didn't get into a situation where either one is necessary."

He growled in frustration.

"Then no. I can't promise you. I can't promise her. All I can say is I'll be careful. I want to be here for you and Katie. I don't want to lose you."

I stared at his damaged hands.

"This is a deal-breaker, Alex. It has to be."

I looked up and met his eyes as he searched my face.

"You'd walk away from ... from what we have?"

I swallowed, but held his gaze.

"Yes, because I can't be a part of that ... violence. I can't be that selfish. Not for me, and definitely not for Katie."

He reared back like he'd been stung.

"Selfish? You think I'm being selfish?"

"I think you're being reckless with your life! And we *need* you! So yes, if you call that selfish."

He looked away.

"What if I promise to be really careful? More careful than I used to be. Remember what I said about Stan? About not wanting to leave him alone in the world, about having something to live for? Well, that's you and Katie for me now. *You* are my reason for living."

I felt the weight of his words and the awful responsibility of loving someone, of being loved by them.

"Alex..."

"What if I said that I won't get involved? I'll even work with the police. I'll just video the evidence. Please, Dawn. Don't ask me to stop doing what's right —stopping this cruelty."

He was trying so hard.

All relationships have problems. Ours were just a little ... different. Maybe I needed to try harder, too. Maybe.

Cold was seeping through me and I shivered again.

"It's late. You should go to bed," Alex said quietly.

I hesitated.

"Will you come with me?"

His eyes fluttered closed as a smile curved his poor, damaged lips.

"I was hoping you'd say that."

He leaned forward as if he was going to kiss me, then pulled back at the last moment.

"I'm kind of a mess," he said.

It was true. He stank of smoke and was covered in sweat, blood, grime and my tears. I shuddered at the reminder.

"I'll need to go back to my place and..."

"Alex, I'm so tired, I just want to sleep. Let's worry about your clothes tomorrow."

He gave me an apologetic smile tinged with immense sadness. Then he nodded.

I climbed upstairs as if my shoes were made of lead and I weighed a thousand pounds. But more than anything, I wanted to forget. I wanted to believe that the world was a wonderful place and that evil didn't exist. I wanted to believe that I could love and be loved and nothing would ever come between us. I wanted to believe that I could keep Katie safe from all the bad things in the world.

I fell into bed, and a minute later, he followed. I heard the soft whir of the washing machine from the utility room.

His skin felt warm as he slid into my bed and carefully curled himself around me. Then he pressed a kiss into my hair, and I felt his body relax with a long sigh.

Safe within his arms, I fell asleep immediately.

The slow pull of morning brought me to consciousness and I stretched out, smiling when I felt Alex's warm palm graze my hip.

"Morning," I said, my voice husky with sleep.

His hand slipped under my t-shirt, palming my breast, and I groaned with pleasure, arching my back, my breath quickening.

He kissed the back of my neck, running his chin along my spine, scratching my skin pleasurably.

More widely awake now, all the thoughts and hopes and fears of last night came racing back, and I tensed, my brain at war with my body.

Was I really going to ruin this?

I'd found the treasure I'd been looking for my whole life.

His hand moved back to my hip, his fingers dipping below the elastic of my panties, slow circles making me gasp and press against him.

I could feel his hard heat between the cheeks of my ass, and he groaned softly as I pushed my hips backward.

No, no more thinking. No more doubts. All or nothing. The best car crash we could be.

He pushed the material down further and I thrashed with my feet to kick them off, making him chuckle warmly into my hair.

Then he changed the angle of his body, shifting in the bed and lifting my leg, giving him room to push inside me.

Slow morning love; hot heated night times; lazy loving, furious thrusts— every part of my body responded to his touches. I didn't want our story to have an ending. I wanted it to go on and on.

Who needed perfect when I had someone loyal and kind?

Slight mental problems, of course, but he knew me inside and out and put up with all my own quirks, challenged and soothed my insecurities.

Alex synchronized his circling fingers with the thrusts of his hips, both speeding up, sweat gluing his chest to my back, the erotic slaps of skin on skin.

I came with a scream that poured out of me like my soul was tearing free, wild and wanton and unafraid. My silent lover jerked and clenched behind me, his words, as ever, swallowed by his passion.

And that was fine by me.

We lay side by side, panting and grinning inanely at each other.

"You can wake me every morning like that," I smiled.

"Don't say it if you don't mean it."

He was still grinning when he spoke, but I knew that he wasn't joking.

"I do mean it, but let's take it slowly anyway. I like being wooed by you."

He laughed quietly.

"I haven't done any wooing! We haven't even been to dinner or the movies yet."

I turned on my side to look at him, lovingly running the tips of my fingers over his rough beard.

"Silly man! You wooed me every time you did something kind for Katie, every time you made her smile, every laugh, every word you read to her. You wooed me with every injured bird, every crippled creature, every time your heart hurt for animals maimed and sick. Don't you know that?"

His smile slid away.

"I wasn't doing that to impress you."

"I know, and that's why it did."

He sighed and closed his eyes.

"I'm not going to give you a jet-set way of life, Dawn. I'm never going to be the life of the party. Hell, I can't even go in a bar right now or be around alcohol. I can't talk when I meet strangers, and I'll do things that you don't approve of."

"I know."

"And ... you're okay with that?"

"Yes."

He gripped my arms and pulled me on top of him, hugging me fiercely as he whispered into my hair.

"But I promise you this: I'll love you harder than anyone else ever could. I'll protect you and I'll give you everything I have. I'll be the man I need to be for you and for Katie."

"I know. Because I love you, too."

Tears glistened in his honey-colored eyes, his smile huge, and his lips when he pressed them to mine were full of intensity, full of passion, tasting of truth.

I felt loved. I felt needed. I felt rewarded.

We weren't perfect, but we didn't want to be. We were real and honest and probably going to make each other crazy. And stupidly happy.

An hour later, we were having a leisurely breakfast of eggs, toast and coffee. I tossed Alex's freshly washed clothes in the dryer, and he wore a towel while we were eating, but his naked chest was very distracting. I couldn't help imagining drizzling maple syrup over him then licking it off. And lots of other very wicked thoughts.

Alex kept catching me looking and would smile or wink.

I could get used to this.

Alex broke the tension by tugging my hand into his lap, then raising it to his mouth, kissing gently.

"What time will Katie be home?"

"In an hour or so. Why?"

"Because first, I want to take a shower with you, and second, I thought maybe I could fix you and Katie-kay lunch at my place today. It'll just be pizzas..."

I didn't even need him to finish speaking before I was nodding with enthusiasm.

"Yes, please, to both."

His smile was breathtaking.

Yes, I wanted to run my hands over his hard body while hot water swirled around us, and yes, I wanted to eat lunch with him today and every day. I wanted it all. With him.

Suddenly, there was a loud knock on the door, making me jump.

"Oh my God! What if it's Dan?" I yelped, starting to panic. "What should I say?"

I stared at Alex anxiously, but he didn't seem the least bit concerned.

"Depends on what Dudley Do-Right says."

"He must know something! Why aren't you worried?"

"Because I did the right thing."

"Alex! You broke a gazillion laws last night!"

"Such as?"

"Breaking and entering."

"Well, I entered ... but there was no breaking ... *this time*," he muttered under his breath.

The knocking started again, louder this time.

"What do I do?"

Alex didn't answer, instead he stood up impatiently, adjusting his towel as it threatened to slide from his hips, and walked to the front door, pulling it open.

"Hey, Dawny, I..."

Stella's voice broke off suddenly, her words stuttering to a halt as she started to laugh. "Jeez, I'm gone for a few days and this happens! Maybe I should go away more often."

Alex laughed, and I didn't hear what he said next, but then Stella was laughing too, when she followed him inside.

"Well, hello there, little sister. No need to ask how *your* Thanksgiving went."

I tugged my robe around me more tightly, my cheeks scarlet as I tried to sound less flustered than I felt.

"Stella! I thought you weren't flying home until tonight?"

"Mom and Dad made a last minute decision to go on a mini-cruise to the Bahamas—they send their love—so I took a taxi to the airport first thing and changed my flight. Where's Katie? Or did you send her away for the night to have some private mommy and daddy time?"

Alex grinned and winked at her.

"She's at Holly's," I said, rather stiffly. "But she'll be back shortly."

"Yeah, I'd better go shower," Alex said.

I watched him leave the room, my eyes reluctantly dragged back to Stella as she started to laugh again.

"By the way, you look like shit, sis," she chuckled, her eyes roving over my flushed face and birds-nest hair.

"Wow, thank you," I said, infusing my voice with every ounce of sarcasm at my disposal.

Stella had come back from her Florida vacation looking tanned and relaxed. And, of course, beautifully dressed and well groomed, even at this early hour. We were so unalike. Although we did seem to have similar taste in men.

She gazed at me with critical eyes.

"Seriously, you look like you haven't been sleeping—and not completely in a good way. So," and she paused. "So, are you going to tell me what's going on with you and Alex? I'm assuming it's serious since he was sitting at your breakfast table in a towel, which was a very nice welcome home, incidentally. Thank you for that visual."

My laugh was rather hysterical.

"God, Stel, I don't know where to start."

Her smile faded.

"He took you to a dog fight, didn't he?"

"You know about those?" I asked, shocked.

She nodded.

"Yes, he told me some of it."

"I didn't go—I couldn't. But he filmed it and I saw... well, what do think about them ... about what he's doing?"

"I think he's crazy but in a good way."

"What do you mean?"

"It drives him, gives him something to live for—a challenge. Although he gave it up for a while. Did you know that?"

"No, I didn't."

"Moving from Denver was deliberate. He wanted to get away from it all. It's just one of life's ironies that it found him again. But for the first few months he was here, he looked out for forest animals instead. It was his way of continuing the work."

I thought about that.

"So he really wasn't looking for fights to stop when he came here?"

"No. From what he says, he redirected his energies. I think it helped that there was a certain veterinarian he was interested in."

I sighed.

"Well, he's into it again now and I don't think there's anything I can do to stop him."

Stella huffed noisily.

"Is it bat-shit crazy day and no one told me?"

"What?"

"Of course you can't stop him, but you can ... redirect him, like I said. He's already thinking about building an animal shelter here in Girard."

"He is? I suggested that to him last night, but he didn't say anything."

Or maybe he'd been about to ... I tried to recall everything that he'd said, but I'd been in shock. Had he mentioned retraining fighting dogs? I wasn't sure if he'd said it or I'd just imagined it.

Stella lifted her eyebrows.

"Jeez, do you two ever talk to each other, or are you too busy getting frisky?"

My cheeks heated.

"Keep your voice down, Stella!"

She smirked at me.

"Well, at least one part of your relationship is functional."

I shook my head, tears pricking my eyes as I smiled at her.

"I didn't want to love him, for all sorts of reasons. It's so hard, trusting someone, letting them in. And Alex is so ... but every time he goes out, he'll be taking these insane risks, and just thinking about it terrifies me. I didn't want to love him. But I do. I've been falling in love for months, I was just too stubborn to realize it—or rather believe it. I don't have a great track record with men."

Stella raised her eyebrows, one corner of her mouth lifting in a mocking smile.

"Neither of us do. But I've never stopped believing that I'd find someone. I'm really glad that you've found Alex. He's one in a million. I'm jealous as hell, mind you. But ... and it's a big one ... because of him, I have my sister back."

She stood up and walked around the table to hug me.

"Just make sure that you don't let anything get in the way of that," she said fiercely.

I didn't know if she meant in the way of us being sisters, or of loving Alex. In either case, she was right.

"I've told him that I love him, and he loves me, too. But I know it's not going to be easy."

She took my hand and squeezed it.

I saw the sadness and regret in her eyes, and a new understanding was born between us.

"He's a good man, Dawn. You must know that?"

"I do. And he's wonderful with Katie. It would have just been nice if he was..."

"Normal? Honey, let me give you a tip. I've dated *a lot*—before and since Bob—and there is no normal, just varying kinds of craziness. Truthfully, Alex is a little higher on the totally-nuts scale than most people," she paused. "Okay, a lot higher, but that just makes him more special, don't you think?"

"You're right. He is special. Very special."

"Good call. Now, tell me, because I'm dying to know—what's he like in bed?"

"Stella! I'm not telling you that!"

"Uh-huh. That bad? Pity."

"No! He's amazing!"

"You're just saying that."

"I'm not!"

"It's okay, you can't have everything, since you've just finished agreeing with me."

"Shut up, Stel! He's amazing in bed!"

Stella started laughing and I whipped around to find Alex leaning against the door, a huge grin on his face.

"Am I interrupting, l-ladies?"

He was fully dressed now, his hair damp from the shower and beginning to curl.

Still grinning, he scooped me into a hug and threw an arm around Stella at the same time.

Just as I was beginning to think this day was going to be fine after all, another loud knock at the door made me jump.

"What's going on this morning? It's like Times Square in here!" I huffed.

Stella peered out of the window.

"It's Dan. He looks grumpy."

Horrified, I glanced at Alex but he just shook his head slightly. I didn't know what that meant.

"Go get dressed and I'll make Grumpy Boots some coffee," Stella suggested.

"I'll make him c-coffee," said Alex with a smile.

I almost laughed at Alex's nerve, and he strolled over to the coffee machine, a small smile on his face.

Stella opened the front door, and I heard Dan's voice, his tone sharp. Then he followed Stella into the kitchen.

"Dawn."

"Hello, Dan. This is a nice surprise."

He clenched his jaw, his glances volleying between us.

"I see you didn't take my advice," he said coldly.

"Dan, sit down and have some coffee with us. I'm just going to get a shower. I'll be five minutes."

Reluctantly, he sat as Stella filled a cup for him.

Throwing a final, panicked look at Alex, I ran out of the room, jumped in the shower and was out again 30 seconds later, then fought with my clothes as I struggled to pull them on over a still damp body.

My mind was racing, trying to decide what I needed to do and say, or not say, as well as how much lawyers cost on holiday weekends.

In the kitchen, Dan was leaning against the door, a cup of coffee in his hand while he glared at Alex, who stared back stonily.

The display of testosterone was balanced out by Stella who was painting her nails a pale peach, keeping up a cheerful monologue about 'the season's palette', whatever that was.

When she looked up, she gave me a tight smile and raised her eyebrows, her glance flipping between Dan and Alex.

Dan cleared his throat and looked pointedly at me.

"Well," I said to Dan, "two mornings in a row—I'm honored."

"It's no laughing matter," he scowled.

"Hence my lack of amusement," I said crisply.

He cut me a sharp look, then glowered at Alex again.

"Where were you last night, Winters?"

"He was here in my bed, Dan."

Alex grinned, and Stella hid a laugh by pretending to cough. Dan's face turned red, probably from anger.

"All night?"

"Way to go, sis!" Stella chuckled.

"Goddammit! This is serious." Then he turned to Alex again. "Where were you last night?

Alex screwed up his face, his chest heaving, then he spat out a single word. "D-d-d-disneyland!"

Stella laughed, but to me it was a painful reminder that his speech impediment wasn't going away. My mind rushed back to our first encounter— his inability to speak a sentence, his furious frustration at his own limitations. He was so easy with us now. And with a jolt I saw it all plainly, saw what everyone but me had already known: Katie, Stella and me—we were his family.

With us, he could speak. With us, he could be himself.

And it was my turn to protect him.

"He was with me."

Which wasn't untrue.

"He got you covering for him now, Dawny, lying for him?"

I stiffened at his dismissive tone, and Alex took a step toward him.

"I'm not lying—I'm doing what's right, that's all," I said, trying to sound calm as I stepped between them.

Dan sighed.

"Anyways, I didn't come over here about that." He looked at Alex again. "This morning, we got a call from, uh, a man who claimed to be out for a walk on your land. Looks like he'd gotten caught in a snare. Thing is, we found a whole bunch of them in a bag just a few yards away. We think he was carrying and tried to throw them away when he got caught. I'm pretty certain we'll find they're his and he'd been setting them, then went and broke his ankle tripping over one. The paramedics took him into hospital."

Alex looked furious and stood up straighter.

"Wh-wh-who?"

"Guy's a damn owl," Dan muttered.

I punched him in the arm at the same time Stella slapped his ass.

Alex's eyes had darkened and his fists were clenched.

"Okay, okay!" Dan yelped. "I'm sorry, that was a cheap shot. I apologize, Winters."

"*Mister* Winters," I said angrily.

"Ahem, *Mister* Winters, I apologize. It's been a busy weekend."

Alex nodded stiffly.

"Wh-wh-who?" he asked again.

Dan scratched his neck.

"Well, if that isn't the darndest thing—it was Bob. Your ex-husband."

Stella's eyebrows shot upward.

"Bob is the one laying traps? I wondered, but I didn't want to believe it."

I stared at both of them.

"You mean, like that day you found the dead raccoon?"

Alex nodded.

"You got any proof of that?" asked Dan, flipping open his notebook.

Alex shook his head, then shrugged.

"Well, if you can give me times and dates of any other incidents, I'll look into it."

I knew Dan was being sincere. It was his way of making up for being such an a-hole before.

"We were talking about it the other night," said Stella. "There was a real estate developer from Pittsburgh interested in buying properties along the lake. You know Bob has always wanted to be part of the big time."

She laughed bitterly.

"I'll look into it," Dan said again. "You got my word on that."

Alex nodded at him, his lips pressed together.

"Dawn, Stella ... I'll see myself out."

Dan tipped his hat then left the room. None of us spoke even when we heard Dan drive away. I hoped that we could mend our friendship one day. But he wasn't my priority. The angry, silent man in my kitchen was.

I turned to look at Alex. His face was grim and Stella was anxious. I don't know how I appeared to them: worried, angry, maybe even pleading.

I opened my mouth to speak, struggling to find the words that would be right.

"Mommy! I'm home!"

Suddenly, Katie came crashing into the kitchen, her mouth dropping open when she saw us all.

"Alex! Aunty Stella!"

Screeching like a banshee, she flung herself forwards, winding her thin arms around us in a spontaneous group hug. Her timing couldn't have been more perfect.

"I have the coolest family," she said, her happy voice muffled against Alex's shirt.

Family.

My family.

A warm feeling spread through my chest and my eyes watered. Alex's gaze softened and he placed a gentle kiss into my hair, winked at Stella, and tickled Katie's side, making her giggle.

Yes, I had a very cool family.

My daughter was very wise.

Chapter Eighteen

NEO

Eighteen months later...

Katie's Diary

June 5th—my 10th birthday!

Mom and Alex are being all lovey-dovey again. Well, all the time. Holly says it's cute.

I'm ten today and I still think boys are weird. And they smell funny.

I like living here, by the lake. Alex says I can call it my house now, too. Mom gave him a funny look when he said that, but then he gave her a big hug and that made her smile. He laughed at her because she didn't argue this time, and Mom *always* argues with Alex. Not in a mean way, but because he always wants to buy us treats and do stuff for us. I don't know why she gets so mad at him.

We spent our first Christmas here and it was awesome because Alex has a real log fire. I even helped him chop the logs. I did! He showed me how to stack the pieces of wood on top of a really big log so he could split them into kindling. He wouldn't let me touch the axe. But then he showed me how to set the twigs and logs and little scraps of paper so that the fire catches. Then Mom made us a feast! Wow!—and we had all our presents piled up around a real Christmas tree that Alex got out of the forest. Aunty Stella came, too, and gave me some really cute earrings. Yep, I got my ears pierced for my last birthday and I have a really great collection now.

It's great having Aunty Stella around. She's super fun and we do cool stuff like paint our nails ten different colors. She's going to go riding with me and Mom, and she says she's going to teach Alex. I've been on her horse, Beau

Brummell, but it's a bit scary being up so high. She says she's going to buy me a pony so I can ride on something smaller. Mom says she can't, but I think she will.

I got some more books for my birthday and Alex got a subscription to Netflix. He says it's for me, but I think it's for him, too. He loves watching movies as much as I do. The only ones he won't watch are anything to do with animals getting hurt. He turns those off or walks out of the room.

I really like having Alex around and Mom is sooooo happy—like a gazillion ooooo's on the end of soooooooo. That happy!

Oh, and Mom's going to have a baby. She was really nervous about telling me and I got so scared, I thought she was going to say she was sick or something. When she told me it was a baby, I burst into tears, so she thought I was upset. I was just glad that it was a baby and not something bad.

Alex looked really happy and started laughing when I said I couldn't wait to have a little sister. I guess it would be okay to have a brother, but I'd rather have a sister. As long as she doesn't borrow my makeup or clothes. Holly says that's what younger sisters do. I guess she'd know. I borrow Mom's makeup sometimes, but she makes me wash it off before I go out. That is so dumb! I think she should wear more makeup, but Alex says she's perfect as she is. Gag.

I wonder if Mom and Alex are going to get married? I could be their bridesmaid, as long as I get to choose my own dress. Alex could be my dad—that would be cool. I mean, I've already got a dad, and he said he was really sorry for leaving me on my own at Thanksgiving that one time and promised he wouldn't do it again. Mom was really mad at him and so was Alex.

I'm really excited to spend summer at the lake and school lets out next week. Alex got a sailboat and he's teaching me how to sail. He's good at loads of stuff. He can make campfires and he's really good at building things. He's making me a tree-house that's big enough to sleep in if I want to.

He says he's getting me something really amazing for my birthday but he won't tell me what it is.

I can't wait.

Dawn

I didn't know it could be like this. I swear Alex has turned me into a bowl of mush—either that or it's all the hormones going crazy inside my body.

We talked about having a baby together for a little while before we did anything about it. I could tell that Alex really wanted us to try, but he was nervous too, and that made *me* nervous. It took me forever to pry the reason out of him. What it boiled down to is that he was afraid that the stress would push him over the edge and that he'd start drinking again. It breaks my heart that he's so scared of failing us. I don't see it like that—instead I see that every day he chooses to be strong for us. I feel safe and protected with him, and when I'm in his arms, the world surrenders. See what I mean? Mush!

I ended up getting pregnant on pretty much our first attempt. Alex was *very* smug about that and said he must have super-strength swimmers.

Unfortunately, Katie overheard that particular comment, so now she thinks he was some sort of swimming champion. She's made him take her swimming in the lake every day, even when it's been quite chilly. Seeing them together is beautiful.

Matthew still has her one day a month and he doesn't cancel as often as he used to, but it's still really uncomfortable for all of us.

Having Stella back in our lives is wonderful. I missed my sister so badly. Mom and Dad were over the moon about it, too. They've met Alex, and although it was a slightly rocky start when Dad tried to bond with him over beer, and Alex had to tell him why he wouldn't, I think they've accepted him. Of course, they're my parents, so they're already waiting for the other shoe to drop. I suppose I am too, sometimes, and I know Alex is terrified of it. He's got it into his head that he's not 'worthy' of us, whatever that's supposed to mean. But if it takes a lifetime to convince him that he's the best thing that ever happened to me and Katie, then that's what I'll do.

He's not perfect, far from it. I think he's definitely OCD, and he gets upset having a mess around the house—which is inevitable when you've got a lively nine-year-old. Ten years old! When did Katie get so big?

Anyway, it's a losing battle trying to keep everything tidy. I'm afraid he's going to have a heart attack with a baby around the place—he really doesn't know what he's in for. Which is why I don't get too mad with Katie for leaving her toys lying around—it's good training for Alex.

Every couple of months, he disappears and twice has come home with split knuckles, one time with a black eye, and the last time, with three ex-fighting dogs. None of the shelters would take them, so he built the dogs a kennel each outside and a large run where he's working to retrain them. But he has bigger plans, too.

Katie was really upset, and it caused our first major argument. In the end, we decided she needed to know some of the truth, so he told her that mean men had hurt the dogs, and he'd saved them.

Of course after that, she hero-worshipped him even more. She always asks him to drive her to school, never boring old Mom. I'm fine with that. Seeing them together makes me smile.

It's been a rocky road, but one that we've chosen together, as a family.

We heard that *Winters & Carter* closed with the loss of 17 jobs. Alex ended up receiving $400,000 from the sale of the building, which was still in his name—something his ex-wife hadn't been able to get her claws into.

So, the big plan! We're going to start our own rescue shelter on Alex's land, focusing on ex-fighting dogs. That's where most of the money from *Winters & Carter* has gone. Officially it's going to be named 'The Sanctuary' but unofficially, we call it 'Stan's Place'.

The original three ex-fighting dogs are being retrained to be family friendly. It's fairly experimental and I'm not convinced it will work, but Alex is determined. He's doing most of the training himself, but since word got out, quite a few people from Girard have volunteered to help, too. Including Dan, which was a big surprise. I think he feels guilty about some of the things he said, trying to steer me away from Alex. He knows now that he's not a bad guy.

Alex is still a little wary of him, but if anything will work, it's Dan spending time with the dogs.

When the new shelter is up and running, we'll be able to do a lot more. Alex is working on some amazing designs. I'm so proud of him.

We talked about it and agreed that Stella would make the perfect person to help with fundraising to keep the shelter running once it's been built. She knows everyone, and will be fantastic at getting the money we'll need. Plus, she needs a job, so it will all work out great.

Stella loves helping out at the kennels, too. She was always good with animals—I guess that's something else we have in common. She says that when the new shelter is built, working there will be her dream job. She's still the world's biggest flirt, but she's my sister and I love her. It feels good to say that.

Alex didn't press charges against Bob, although he did visit him in person. Alex wouldn't tell me what he said, but I know that Dan spoke to him, as well, and after that Bob left Stella alone. The last I heard was that he'd left town and was working on some real estate deal in Pittsburgh.

Telling Katie about the baby was daunting. Luckily, she was really excited about it, although we haven't told her yet that the baby is going to be a boy, and honestly, I think she's more excited about Alex's birthday surprise.

Alex and I aren't married, so that's given the gossips in Girard something new to talk about, especially now that I'm four months and beginning to show. We're both rather gun-shy of marriage, me more so. Of course, my parents want us to marry before the baby comes, but I think one step at a time. Besides, I don't want to look fat in our wedding photographs.

Katie is pushing for it hard. She wants to be a bridesmaid and has already picked out a dress that she thinks would be "super awesome". I don't know. Maybe. But we're happy as we are right now.

There was one cloud that darkened our days. Alex's friend, Giselle, died of pneumonia. We only found that out several weeks after it had happened. Alex was really upset about that.

We're naming one of the new puppies after her in her memory. Oh, yes, we're getting two puppies. Alex says he wanted to do it as the big surprise for Katie's birthday, but I think they're just as much for him.

I hope we can give these little creatures a better life than Giselle ever had. I'd like to think that she'd approve. Alex says that she'd laugh her ass off at having a bitch named after her.

The male puppy is named Rocco. I understand why now,

I still get so scared when Alex disappears off on his crusades, but since he's much more willing to work with the police now, it's not so bad. I think Dan helping out with retraining the ex-fighting dogs has had a lot to do with that. And he has some useful contacts that he's been willing to share.

Alex has been taking on quite a lot of freelance architectural design work, although he says he won't work 24/7 like he used to. And the rest of the time his passion and conviction is focused on me and Katie. It isn't a bad trade off.

He was right, about his stutter. With family, it's almost absent, but with strangers it's as bad as ever. I mentioned once about him getting therapy, but Alex says that me and Katie are the best therapy in the world.

I'm loved more than I thought was possible. And I was wrong about only having enough love for my daughter. I love my sweet, silent man so much.

So much.

EPILOGUE

Alex

Dawn is waiting for me in bed—in *our* bed. Her dark eyes burn into me as I enter the room, and I get hard just looking at her lying back on the pillows.

It's not long before I'm stripped naked and showing her with my body how much she means to me.

She pushes on my shoulder, telling me she wants to be on top tonight. I roll onto my back, pulling her with me, then run my hands over her swollen belly. She's never looked sexier to me now that she's carrying our child. She starts to move and the words pour out of her, telling me my body is hers, that I'm wanted, that she's feeling possessive, and the thought comes to me, *How did I get to be so lucky?*

"Don't call me baby-momma! I'm not a teenager, Alex!"

Dawn has no idea how much it turns me on when she lays down the law. Our sex-life is off the charts at the moment, and a couple of times we've had a close call with Katie coming home early when she got a ride with Holly's mom. Seriously, three or four times a day: who needs a gym? She said I shouldn't get used to it, because after the baby's born, I'll need to get reacquainted with my right hand.

I know she's scared that I'll panic when the baby comes and start drinking, but there's no way I'd allow that to happen. I'd rather slit my own throat than let them down again. That doesn't mean it's not there, the elephant in the room, because it is. I wasn't lying to her when I said the urge to drink will always be there. But I'm coping.

I keep going to AA meetings, and sometimes Stella comes with me. She helped me when I hit rock bottom, so spending time with her feels good. It's a relief that they're sisters again.

I feel very protective of Stella. She's family. That word still makes my gut churn, but more in a good way now, I think. I have a family and I'm part of something wonderful. It's the most fulfilled I've ever felt.

Somehow, we weathered the Girard gossipmongers. The worst was when Katie came home from school crying because of shit some other kids had said —that I was crazy and a freak, that I couldn't talk properly—the usual. They were just copying what their parents said at home, so what could I do? It's not even completely untrue.

Dawn went ballistic and was all for marching up to the school and reading the riot act, but in the end, talking it through as a family, we figured it would be best to just let it run its course. It was a rough couple of weeks for everyone, but in the end, it was nothing more than old news.

I'm working on getting the designs for the shelter done so we can break ground as soon as possible; I'm just trying to get through as much as possible BTB—before the baby. Sometimes Dawn makes it sound like the world is going to end on that day. I suggested that we name the baby Damien, like in 'The Omen', but she didn't think that was funny.

Living together has been a learning curve, that's for sure. Katie is really a slob, and Dawn isn't much better. They drive me crazy, but I love it, too. I see their clutter around the place and I know that I'm not alone anymore.

I haven't heard from Charlotte again, not even when the business that I started was shut down for good. I'm happy not to hear from her—that door is closed as far as I'm concerned. I've got the future to look forward to now. God, that sounds good.

"Come on baby-momma," I say again, just to see Dawn's eyes flash when I call her that.

"Don't!" she hisses at me, but I just laugh.

Katie gives her a look. "Mom! Don't be mean to Alex."

Yep, Katie's got my back, and Dawn knows it. She's trying to give me her best 'I'm pissed' look, but she can't pull it off and her lips keep twitching like she's trying not to smile.

"Where are we going?" Katie asks for the hundredth time.

"I told you, Katie-kay, it's a surprise!"

"But it's my birthday," she whines. "You have to tell me!"

I just raise my eyebrows at her and she slumps in the back of the car. Dawn smiles: she knows exactly where we're going.

After half an hour of driving, Katie figures it out—some of it.

"We're going to Pittsburgh?"

"Sort of," I reply.

"Are we going to the Aquarium?"

"Nope."

"Are we going up in the cable car?"

"Nope."

"Well, are we going to Kennywood? They've got six rollercoasters!"

"Not even close."

"Al-ex!" she whines again.

"Trust me, Katie-kay, you'll love it when we get there. I'm not going to spoil the surprise."

"Fine," she huffs, muttering under her breath, "But it's *my* birthday!"

Finally, I pull up outside an austere concrete building, and I can see Katie frowning until she reads the large sign out front.

"It's an animal shelter?" she says, her voice rising with excitement.

"Yes," says Dawn. "Alex thought ... well, *we* thought ... that maybe you'd like to get a dog. I know no one can ever replace Stan, but these are all dogs who need a good home. And there are two puppies, brother and sister, who need someone to love them. What do you think?"

Katie's lip trembles and Dawn shoots me an anxious look.

"Two puppies?"

And then she squeals so loudly, I think my eardrums burst. Katie's smile is one of the best things in the world—second only to her mom's.

"Oh wow! That is the *most awesome* birthday present ever!"

We head inside and one of the volunteers at the shelter shakes our hands. I've gotten to know all the other shelters in the area. None of them work with ex-fighting dogs like we do, but they've been really helpful.

"Welcome, Mr. and Mrs. Winters. And you must be Katie."

I grin at Dawn and she gives me the stink-eye, but hey! I didn't tell the guy we were married. Maybe we just *look* married. I like that idea.

But once we're inside the kennel area, my grin fails. God, all of these dogs have a desperate air about them, a look that says they just want to be loved. Not so different from people, I guess. Humans pretend it's so complicated, but really it's simple. I feel bad that I'm not taking one of the older dogs, one like Stan. But I thought Katie should have dogs that she could grow up with. And right now, I'm not sure I could stand having an older dog and losing another friend.

Katie seems upset.

"They look so sad," she says, her voice small and worried.

The rescue worker steps in with expert timing.

"I have your little guys, right here. This is Giselle and this is Rocco."

He shows us to a cage where two of the oddest looking balls of fur are staring up at us.

They've got long bodies but their legs are stubby and short, with long tails from their Labrador mother, and their bodies from their Jack Russell father. I have no idea how the logistics of that worked, but obviously it did. Giselle is mostly white with a brown face, and Rocco has brown and black fur with white socks. Weird, definitely, but very cute, too.

"We think they're part Bichon Frise, part Jack Russell and part Labrador."

Interesting mix.

"They love chasing a ball and playing, and they're both really good swimmers, too. They've had all their shots and been neutered."

That makes me wince and Dawn smirks at me.

"Why did they end up in a pound?" Katie asks

"Their mom was living on the streets when she was found," the rescue worker explains. "She wasn't chipped and nobody came to claim her. They're seven months old now and they're looking for the right owner, someone to take care of them."

Katie squats down next to the cage and puts her fingers through the grill. I'm right by her side, ready to haul her back in case the dogs get over excited. But instead they crowd up to the front of the cage, and Giselle investigates Katie's fingers with a long pink tongue.

"They like me," giggles Katie.

"They've got good taste, Katie-kay," I tell her.

She cocks her head to one side, looking at Rocco. "Why does he have one ear up and one ear down?"

"Energy saving," I reply seriously.

Katie squints, giving me a look like she's not sure if I'm teasing her.

Half an hour later, we're bundling Rocco and Giselle into the car next to Katie, and my family has grown by two small, furry people.

A proud warmth fills my chest: *my family*.

The drive home is uneventful and the puppies are pretty damn near perfect. They're not Stan, but they're cute and adore Katie already.

Stan was special—he saved my life more than once, so no dog could ever take his place, but the puppies have their own charm. Giselle is busy playing with Katie, but Rocco looks up so I can see him in the rearview mirror, and I think he's asking the same thing I ask myself every day: *How the fuck did I get to be so lucky?*

THE END

ACKNOWLEDGMENTS

To Audrey Orielle whose wise words help more than she knows.

To Seth Clayton for lending his voice and talents to this story.

To Sheena Lumsden for her friendship, humour and support.

To Dina Farndon Eidinger—my wonderful, trusted and much-loved friend.

To Lisa, wielder of the sword of truth who fights pirates whenever she can.

To Crystal Ordex-Hernandez and Aime Metzner for the use of their names.

To all the bloggers who give up their time for their passion of reading and reviewing books—thank you for your support.

NOWZAD - THE WAR DOG

Stan is real, too. Except that he wasn't called Stan, but Nowzad. Now Zad is a small town in Helmand Province, Afghanistan, and Nowzad was a stray that had been taken to be trained as a fighting dog. His ears and tail had been cut off so other dogs wouldn't be able to latch onto him so easily in a fight.

He was rescued by Royal Marine Sergeant Pen Farthing.

Their friendship resulted in Pen making sure that Nowzad traveled back to the UK when his tour of duty was over. But he also knew that many other Soldiers and Marines were being forced to leave their furry friends behind—something that Pen was determined to change.

> These soldiers are not only a salvation for the animal; the dog or cat are often described as 'lifelines' to their soldier, providing a respite from war, a moment of peace, home and love.
>
> When the soldier's tour of duty comes to an end, it is unthinkable to leave their four legged comrade that they've bonded with, behind.

The charity now helps many animals and also funds an animal shelter in Kabul. Animals have been rescued from Afghanistan, Kuwait, Iraq, Libya and the Ukraine, and been sent to start new lives in the UK, US, Australia, Belgium, Canada, Germany, Holland, Italy, Spain, Jordan and South Africa.

www.nowzad.com

TANNER - THE CANINE COVER MODEL

Meet eight year-old Tanner!

He's from St. Petersburg, Florida and belongs to model, TV host and fitness enthusiast, Justin Maina.

Tanner is a Shepherd-Chow-Lab and Maybe Something Else ... a little bit of everything and a lot cute! His favorite food is ice cream. Rocky Road?

Tanner is just getting started in his modeling career.

"I'm very fortunate to have landed this book cover. I'm very grateful. My first job was earlier this year with my dad, Justin. I'm digging this industry so far and looking forward to the next opportunity. I'm a beachy kind of dog, my nickname's Salty Dog, so I'm very laid back and appreciative. I'm living the life here in Treasure Island!"

In a typical day, Tanner enjoys roaming around the house looking to please, play, kiss and make new friends. He also loves laying out on the dock, swimming in the pool, running with Justin and his personal favorite, going out on the boat.

And Tanner really loves his dad. Justin saved him from the dog pound? "I knew when I first saw him that he was the one!"

And I think that Justin was very lucky to have found a pup like Tanner.

REVIEWS

Reviews are love! Honestly, they are! But it also helps other people to make an informed decision before buying my book.

So I'd really appreciate if you took a few seconds to do that.

Thank you!

MORE BOOKS BY JHB

Series Titles
The Education Series
An epic love story spanning the years, through war zones and more...
*The Education of Sebastian (Education series #1)
*The Education of Caroline (Education series #2)
*The Education of Sebastian & Caroline (combined edition, books 1 & 2)
Semper Fi: The Education of Caroline (Education series #3)

The Traveling Series
All the fun of the fair ... and two worlds collide
*The Traveling Man (Traveling series #1)
*The Traveling Woman (Traveling series #2)
*Roustabout (Traveling series #3)
*Carnival (Traveling series #4)
*Gypsy (Traveling series #5)

The Justin Trainer Series
The bodyguard and the billionaire
Guarding the Billionaire (Justin Trainer series #1)
Saving the Billionaire (Justin Trainer series #2)

* *The EOD Series*
Blood, bombs and heartbreak
*Tick Tock (EOD series #1)
* Bombshell (EOD series #2)

The Rhythm Series
Blood, sweat, tears and dance
*Slave to the Rhythm (Rhythm series #1)
*Luka (Rhythm series #2)

Standalone Titles
Contemporary Romance
The Lilac Cadillac
Battle Scars
One Careful Owner
*Lifers
At Your Beck & Call
The New Samurai
Exposure

New Adult
*Dangerous to Know & Love
Dazzled
Summer of Seventeen

Paranormal
*The Dark Detective: Venator (Book #1)
*The Dark Detective: Paukúnnum (Book #2)

Novellas
Playing in the Rain
*Behind the Walls

Anthologies of Short Stories
*The Year Book Volume 1
*The Year Book Volume 2
*The Year Book Volume 3

Audio Books
One Careful Owner
(*narrated by Seth Clayton*)

On the Stage
Later, After: Playscript
Trailer

With Alana Albertson
Father Figure

* These titles are published in languages other than English.
Please check Jane's website for details—and receive **a free short story every
month** when you sign up for her newsletter :)

QR code for Jane's website

ROMANCE WITH STUART REARDON

Books written with my lovely co-author

Two book series - contemporary romance
*Undefeated
*Model Boyfriend

Three book series - romcom
*Gym Or Chocolate?
*The World According to Vince
*The Baby Game

Standalone
Survivor Love Island (*romcom*)
*Touch My Soul (*novella*)

WRITING AS BERRICK FORD

Police Thrillers, UK

Dead Water
Dead Man's Dive
Dead Reckoning
Dead Shore

www.berrickford.com